Viridis

Lauren Hemphill

Viridis

Copyright © 2018 by Lauren Hemphill

Cover art by Gabrielle Ragusi

ISBN 9781732586604 (paperback)

ISBN 9780692153895 (hardback)

*For those who believed in me. But most importantly, for you.
May you never forget that you are needed in this world.*

Chapter 1

"Jade, are you ready yet?" Aris' voice came from the other side of the door. Jade huffed and latched two sleek, metal bands around her wrists.

"Yeah, yeah, keep your pants on," Jade replied. She stood, her armor jingling against the scaled rye-mail underneath. She reached over to the wall where a small, spider-like robot was clinging. Within its jaws was a black helmet, and, as Jade smiled at her arachnid creation, she took the headgear. The little machine clicked its mandibles together happily.

"Are you making eyes at that robot of yours again?" Aris grumbled from outside the flat. Jade frowned.

"No." She tucked it under her thickly muscled arm, giving the helmet a quick glance before Jade moved through the small apartment towards the door. She had painted a crimson skull over the polished black finish of the helm, and her unskilled hand had accidentally allowed the paint to drool over the sides, making it appear as if the skull was melting. Despite the look not being exactly what she intended, Jade took pride in its appearance now. She pulled her red hair into a ponytail before tugging the helmet over her head. She rolled her shoulders back and opened the door.

The apartment building was made up of several open floors, which allowed for anyone to step out onto the walkway between rooms and glance across the complex to see someone else do the same. It stood at an unsatisfactory seven levels above the surface. However, on military pay, there wasn't much else the two women could afford and, luckily, this place had its perks. The open floor plan eased most of Jade's anxieties, and a nearby taxi stop allowed for Aris to escape Jade's constant mechanical tinkerings.

Aris leaned against the railing, peering down to the communal space a few floors below. At the sound of the door closing, she turned around, her long, white dress flaring out around her plump body in the process. The smile on her light-skinned face vanished the instant she saw Jade. Her jaw locked and she rubbed her brow.

"Jade," she grumbled as she eyed her taller roommate over. Jade chuckled, one hand on her hip.

"What?" Jade gestured to her blue-tinted set of armor, one she ensured had all the matching pieces. "You don't like this set? I thought the gold accents would be fancy enough for you."

Aris flashed a tight smile, shaking her head. "Jade, you realize we're going to a *party,* right?"

With a nod, Jade crossed her arms. "Exactly why I should wear armor. What about you?" Jade eyed her friend, whose blonde hair was tied away from her blue eyes. A small, heart-shaped patch of skin, lighter than the rest, sat upon her left collar bone. Jade's eyes lingered on it as her friend grumbled in agitation. Aris almost never let her vitiligo show.

"Couldn't you at least wear your goggles?" Aris smoothed out her dress and tugged at her sleeves. "It'd be more personal. And…that stupid thing doesn't even match." With one hand, she lazily motioned to Jade's helmet. Jade grinned widely, the tinted visor hiding her reaction from her friend.

"Ah, that's just rude, Aris. You should hear all the nice things Chloe has to say about you! You're just going to hurt her feelings."

Mistress, you are going to ruin my image, " the helmet replied, her voice only audible to Jade.

"Besides," Jade huffed, walking to Aris' side and looking out over the railing. It was surprising to see a few people mingling in the common area as most people wanted to be able to deny they lived in an apartment building so close to the ground. It was a direct demonstration of how little money they had, and not many wanted to admit such a thing. "Chloe matches everything." She tilted her head at Aris, who snickered in response, her agitation placated. Aris stared into the distance without a word. Then her eyes settled on Jade's visor.

"Listen, I know you're not incredibly eager about this," Aris said. Jade gazed back at the folks below. The human male looked furious, his arms flaring about as he shouted at someone just out of view. His voice carried up the building, though his words were lost. Maybe he forgot to bring milk home. Aris generally got just as angry when Jade forgot— "...And don't you dare shut down, Jade." Aris hissed, nudging Jade's arm and pulling her away from her thoughts. "*You're* getting a medal. This party is for *you,* okay? So you'd better take this seriously."

"Sure, mom," Jade teased, her voice dry. *Why are we throwing a party when we should be honoring the dead? So many people have lost their lives for me to get here. For me to survive.* She exhaled, looking at her gloved hand. From the corner of her eye, she could see Aris watching her, frowning. Her face was pulled into a hard, frustrated expression, one Jade saw only once before. When they were on Taotar, Jade was celebrated for her efforts in a recent skirmish, and she could see Aris' eyes narrowed from within the crowd. As Jade watched Aris now without the blue-eyed woman noticing, her brows furrowed with confusion. *Why is she looking at me like that?*

"What is it?" Aris' expression softened the moment Jade lifted her head a little. Jade reached back and scratched her neck, the black undersuit that was layered beneath her armor and rye-mail wrinkling beneath her fingers. *Maybe I'm just seeing things.*

"Did you tell Salene?" Jade's voice was barely above a whisper. She didn't really want Aris to hear her, and wasn't sure she even wanted to know the answer. Aris eyed Jade's impenetrable visor, her brows pressing together in thought.

"Did you want me to?" Aris asked.

"No."

With a sigh, Aris walked past her, her heels clicking neatly against the floor and sending echoes through the building. "Come on, we're going to be late."

Jade followed Aris to the main entrance, where they stepped out onto a circular platform, the rest of the city buzzing above them with lingering shadows sitting below. Sounds of ongoing ads, distant chatter, and the hum of hover-cars buzzed in the air. Aris looked Jade over as a taxi flew down to pick them up.

"You don't have a weapon on you, do you?"

Jade laughed. "I swear to Vix, you honestly think you're my mother!"

"Don't tell me it isn't something you'd do," Aris said, walking up to the hovering car and slipping inside. Jade joined her, and the vehicle ascended into the throngs of traffic that wove around the city, reminiscent of the spider nests that the planet was once known for. She glanced downwards, where distant flickering lights of the surface could be seen, the land long since rendered barren and lifeless.

That's overpopulation for you, I suppose.

Factories sat at the lowest tier of the towered buildings that scraped the sky, long pipes stretching high into the air to pump fumes away from populated areas. These stacks of smoke met up with the cloud of smog that dwelled silently in the atmosphere ever since Jade could remember, completely blocking out the small, secondary star that orbited the large planet.

"I bet you they'll have beer," Jade said, a smirk pulling at the corner of her lips.

"Seriously, where do you get your alcoholic tendencies from?" Aris spat back, humor in her voice. The taxi dipped under one of the many walkways that provided brown-eyed civilians a way to navigate the city without the use of a car.

Vendors crowded the walkway, and artificial trees bent their synthetic branches over lovers. Jade wrinkled her nose at the sight and averted her gaze. The higher the car travelled, the more of these paths they had to dodge. Eventually, golden-eyed citizens crowded these spaces, glancing out at the passing vehicles with wealth clinging from their clothes, dripping from them in forms of necklaces, earrings, and delicious desserts held between their thumbs and forefingers. They owned the highest levels of the city, though many argued Golds owned the entire planet itself. Blackmail, bribery, mysteriously missing persons—all of these were at the Golds' disposal.

Jade had never gotten along with any of the Golds she had met. For some reason, they hated the Opes without remorse. They hated their own soldiers. Aris' parents hated her.

"Okay, I've been thinking," Aris said, shifting in her seat to face Jade. Jade arched a brow, smiling back at the shorter woman.

"Yeah?"

"I propose," Aris said, her face serious, "we take as much food as we can and bring it home."

Jade grinned. "Right, and where are we hiding this smuggled food at?"

"We don't have to smuggle the food—you're the guest of honor. They should be *honored* you like the food enough to take it home!"

Jade laughed. "Sure, we could use all the food we can get. Believe it or not, I'm getting sick of ramen."

"I'm glad we're agreed."

"Does this mean I can—"

"You're not bringing any alcohol into our apartment, Jade."

Jade waved her off with a laugh. The taxi's pace slowed, and the two of them glanced out the front window, where traffic had dwindled to a crawl.

"Just take the lower levels," Jade said. Aris nodded.

"It'll be faster than just sitting here. We're already late as it is." She cast Jade a glare, who replied with a shrug.

"Gotta dress to impress." Jade placed her hand on her arm and flexed. Aris rolled her eyes.

"Ladies," the driver began, his words slow and deliberate. His brown eyes flickered to the rearview mirror. "The lower we get…" He trailed off as Aris' expression grew ever darker.

"Is there something wrong with the lower levels, sir? Didn't you pick *us* up from the lower levels?"

Jade smirked and eyed the driver. His features constricted with displeasure, but he nevertheless spun the wheel and dove into the lower city. Lights helped illuminate the path as shadows swallowed up the space around them, cracked pipes leaking plumes of black smoke from their bellies. The stench seeped inside, causing the driver to cough. Aris shot Jade a look, as if saying, "What a baby." Aris had long since gotten used to it.

Traffic in the lower levels was sparse. Within the dim spaces between the lights, dark shapes moved, and brown eyes glittered from the darkness, watching the passing taxi. On the walkway between the buildings, someone was running and, when he stepped out of the light, a gunshot rang out. The sound bounced around the cabin of the car and both Jade and Aris tensed instinctually. The shot was not at them, but the taxi careened up once again, slipping into the main flow of traffic before settling down on a large landing pad on the twentieth level in the middle of the city. Jade shifted awkwardly in her seat. The shots made her nervous, but sometimes they were drowned in the noise of the lower levels. There had been times Jade didn't even notice them at all. While no taxis had been shot down in years, she understood his hesitance now. It wasn't the smoke, it wasn't the fact it was filled with Blues, it was the fear of violence that all of them were so accustomed to.

"Sorry," Aris said to the driver. "It happens frequently enough I forget about it. My apologies."

The driver hissed something about bloodthirsty Blues as they approached their destination. Aris frowned but said nothing.

The building that housed the party was built of metal but painted to appear as if it were wood. It was ornately decorated, and well-kept stairs led up to the large double doors. Floating lanterns hovered alongside the path, adding more light to the already brightly gleaming cityscape. They were unnecessary, but Jade liked them.

Near these lanterns were more artificial trees which kept oxygen levels high enough for most sentient species. While still widely inaccurate as to what real trees looked like, these did a better job replicating the originals with black, curling trunks and purple leaves. Most artists took creative liberty when designing these synthetic creations, as most Browns hadn't seen a real tree on Nevar in hundreds of years. And the mass populace seemed to enjoy the exotic-looking trees with their neon yellow trunks and their flower-filled bark. Jade, however, preferred the real thing, with brown bark and seasonal leaves, like the ones she grew up around on Daoth. Despite the weariness in her bones from her mother's harsh morning training sessions, their shadows always offered some respite from the afternoon heat. With a disapproving huff, Jade shook her head and stepped out of the cab. Aris paid the driver and did the same.

"You know, I wonder what it'd be like to be so ignorant that I didn't know what trees looked like," Jade said, walking over to Aris as the car left. Aris chuckled.

"Don't be rude, Jade. If it weren't for the war, I doubt you'd know—"

"I doubt *you'd* know, Miss Raised-by-Golds." Jade grinned. "You're the one from Nevar. On Daoth, we *have* trees."

"How could I forget? You only remind me every day."

"Shame on—"

"Jade, look!" Aris nudged Jade with her elbow, pointing to two large flags hung over the walls of the party building. The gray-red base color was accented with a golden trim, and in the middle the insignia of the Exuro Empire's military branch, the Opes, was stamped. A gold circle around a blood-red handprint, with their motto written in the circle's band: "We Do Not Bow."

"Never would've thought the Golds would let the Opes flag be flown in the middle of the city," Aris said with laughter in her voice. Jade cast her a sideways glance, forgetting that Aris couldn't see her expression. "Guess this is a day to be remembered, huh?" Aris beamed at Jade. Jade smiled.

"Sure."

"Well, we'd better get your honored butt up there. Come on, Cavvar-kid." Aris started up the stairs, Jade trailing behind. Guests lingered by the front doors, two guards situated nearby, looking into some sort of device. Jade's heart clamored up into her throat.

"Chloe," Jade said, her voice quiet and not audible outside her helmet.

"Mistress, it appears that there is an eye scan up ahead."

"Shit." Jade slowed her pace. Aris glanced at her, then to the doors.

"You'll be fine," Aris muttered. They approached the doors, and Aris leaned towards the circular device situated on one of them. With a blue light, it scanned her eyes, then blinked a momentary green. Aris smiled, nodded to the guards, and slipped inside with a glance back at Jade. Jade tapped her shoulder guards to ensure they were in their proper place.

"I'm Corporal Jade Cavvar," Jade said. "I opt out of the eye scan."

The two guards looked at each other, and the one with the beard scratched his chin.

"Mistress, he seems to know you."

Jade looked at him.

Jade lay in the sand of Taotar, burns beginning to cover the scars on her back. Blood dripped from her flesh, drenching the desert beneath her and begging it to get stuck in her wounds. She could hear someone coming. Maybe they were coming to kill her. Maybe the Thrax had finally arrived to—

She forced the memory away, terrified of what it might bring with it. She blinked a few times and focused her eyes on the man.

"How could I not know who you are?" The man laughed, grinning wide. "You wear that damn thing everywhere!"

"*Her*, David," Jade shot back, saluting him with a smile. She bundled both her hands into fists and placed her left fist over her heart, and her right over her left. David and his companion returned the gesture.

"Sir?" muttered the stranger, his brown eyes clouded with confusion.

"Don't you know who this is?" David shot back, moving forward and slapping Jade on the back. Jade flinched, moving away from the touch, adrenaline instantly flooding her veins. David recoiled.

"Sorry, Corporal, I completely forgot." He bowed his head respectfully. Jade forced the distant lullaby away from her mind and hammered a smile onto her lips in an effort to calm her nerves.

"Mistress, your heart rate has increased."

"It's all right, David. Can I go in?" She ignored Chloe's remark.

"Of course, of course." He stepped aside. Jade nodded her thanks and moved past him. "And Corporal? Congratulations. You deserve a thousand medals for what you've done out there."

No, Jade thought to herself. *I don't.*

Chapter 2

The bright lights startled Jade for a moment, but her visor quickly compensated for the change. When she could finally see, she stood rooted in awe, gazing out over the hall. The main floor was large enough to fit hundreds of people inside, and chandeliers hung in great numbers from the high ceiling. Massive archways indicated entrances to different rooms, and chairs lined the walls, leaving plenty of room for guests to mingle and dance. Two circling staircases led to a shadowed second floor on either side of a large stage, which was backed by floor-to-ceiling windows. Jade knew the Golds were rich, but this? She couldn't imagine wasting so much kniri on a party like this, not when *children* were battling and dying on the field of war. Her fists clenched. It was all so *pointless.*

"Mistress, it would be wise to calm down."

Heeding Chloe's words, Jade took a slow breath and let her eyes wander the crowd. Leathery-skinned kodarian men stood in red military uniforms, speaking to human businessmen. The nostrils above their blue, serpentine eyes flared with annoyance and, when they turned their faces away to look over the crowd of various people talking, the jewelry hanging from their horns caught the light and sparkled. A few of the younger members of the crowd dressed in their military uniforms glanced over at these jewels, their expressions awed by the beauty. They couldn't be much older than sixteen, and several of them had visible scars across their bodies. Some of them were retired due to the loss of limbs, their blue eyes fading into hazel, and hadn't even reached twenty yet. One in particular, a boy that looked to be eighteen, was without a left leg and used a cane to walk. His left eye was closed, scar tissue keeping it shut, and with his right, he watched men in black tuxedos pass with trays of wine, beer, and hors-d'oeuvres. His form was swallowed up by the ever-surging crowd, his sorrow consumed by the laughter that erupted from the Golds within the crowd.

Jade hadn't even formally walked into the space and she could already feel her armor close in on her. She chewed the inside of her cheek, tension rising in her shoulders. *Fuck it, I'll drink in the bathroom if I have to.* She moved towards one of the servers with beer on their tray. A hand grabbed hers. Alarms rang and in the distance, she could hear a lullaby.

"There's this guy over here who wants to meet you," Aris said, helping Jade's mind yank itself back to reality. She pulled her hand from Aris' and steadied herself, frowning at the shorter woman.

"A guy?" she huffed. Aris crossed her arms.

"I will drag you there if I have to."

"There's beer right over—" Jade motioned towards the server when Aris grabbed hold of the metal armor piece on Jade's arm, dragging her away.

"What did I say about drinking?" Aris replied, Jade stumbling as she fought to regain her balance. Aris shoved through the crowd, pushing past guests without discrimination. Judgmental glances were shot at her, but most eyes fell on Jade's heavily protected appearance.

"Blues," someone grumbled in the crowd. "Lower beings, the lot of them."

Jade snarled, showing the Golds her teeth, despite having her face completely hidden by her helmet. *Sorry, am I intruding? You must be so wrapped up in your social schemes you completely forgot about the fact that this is an Opes party.*

Jade's eyes fell on the back of Aris' head. She wondered how Aris survived Gold politics before being recruited.

Aris led Jade into a small room closer to the stage. Only a handful of people lingered inside, most of whom hovered near a man who leaned against a heated wall panel. Jade could feel the increase of temperature the moment she stepped inside.

She yanked her arm from Aris' grasp and rolled her shoulders back, grateful to be out of the crowd.

"Congratulations, mistress. I believe you sweated off that .01 pounds you've been meaning to lose."

Jade rolled her eyes. "Ha-ha, Chloe." Her words were trapped inside the helmet.

The man most everyone seemed to have an interest in had naturally-spiked, raven-colored hair, a few locks falling in front of his blue eyes. His cheekbones were defined and long sideburns led to a goatee that sat under his lip. He wore a tight black suit, and the women around him couldn't stop touching it. Jade glanced at Aris, who seemed to be wearing the same sort of smile the other girls wore. Jade's eyes narrowed and she leaned closer to her roommate.

"Aris," she hissed. "If this is what I think it is, I swear to Vix—"

"Shut up." Aris turned towards her. "Even your mom agrees you need a boyfriend."

Jade blinked, recoiling. "When did you talk to my mom? I feel like you and my mom have this entire relationship I don't even know about." Aris smirked. Jade shook her head.

"That doesn't matter—I'm fighting a war, Aris. I don't need some useless man—"

"Jade, you're twenty-seven years old and you haven't dated *once*."

"I don't need to date!"

"Excuse me." The man stood a few feet away, hands behind his back and a smile on his face. He was a few inches taller than Jade and had an air of royalty about him. Jade scowled. The other women began to disperse back into the main hall.

"I hope I'm not interrupting anything," he said.

"Not at all," Aris replied before Jade had the chance to. She shot a look at Jade, her smile cruel.

No. Don't you dare, Aris. Don't you dare.

"I was just leaving." With a wink, Aris spun on her heel and slipped away. Outside, Jade could hear Aris loudly proclaim the room was for private parties only.

"I'm Thaddeous Malkov," the man said, offering his hand to her. "And you might be?"

"Leaving." She turned to walk away. He chuckled.

"You're Jade Cavvar, are you not?"

Jade sighed and scratched her neck. She glanced at him. "What do you want?"

"Well, simply to congratulate you! I mean, you *are* the hero that stopped the massacre on Sobek, are you not? The woman who sabotaged enemy forces with those mechanical beasts of yours? I even heard a rumor that you are responsible for keeping your Exuro unit alive when under attack by the Mad Queen." His smile was wolfish.

Hatred crawled in from the corners of Jade's mind. The Mad Queen. The legend. The monster. The woman who slaughtered her people. The woman who exploded Opes soldiers into chunks across the forest. The woman who was unmatched in her brutal forward march on Sobek. Jade's eyes narrowed.

"And not only that," he continued, "I heard you saved yourself and a private when you were attacked in an Air Void. Is that right?"

Jade's teeth ached from clenching her jaw. Her fingers curled into tight fists at her sides as she debated whether or not to break his nose. He was acting like he knew her, like he was there. Did he not care about all the people they had lost? Was he really just going to brush over all of it and pretend like she was some sort of Vix-sent angel?

"Mistress, please remember not to punch anyone," Chloe muttered.

Jade spat out a laugh and spun around towards him. "We don't know if it was the Thrax, Blue." Her words were little more than a growl. "And what on Nevar do you know about the Mad—wait." Jade's face fell. "Did you say 'Exuro'?"

A snipper walked in, brushing past a rather frantic Aris. Jade's confused gaze shifted to the newcomer.

Snippers were the native species of Nevar, and were among the first to allow humans to settle their planet. Though there had eventually been a war between the two, the relations between them had become rather friendly, and most animosity over events hundreds of years ago had passed. At least, as far as Jade could tell. The four-armed arachnoids weren't the easiest to understand.

This snipper wore a red dress over the thin hair that covered her body. Her large pincers snapped at the air as she frantically came to a stop by Jade, her eyes—each holding three pupils within them—running over Jade's attire.

"When they said you wore armor a lot, I didn't think you'd be so brash as to wear it to your own *party!*" The snipper's voice was high-pitched and squeaks filled the gaps between words. Her eyes narrowed. From over the snipper's shoulder, Aris gave Jade an apologetic smile.

"And who might you be, madame?" Thaddeous asked, stepping near Jade before she formulated some sort of response.

"Oh, like you haven't heard of me!" The snipper pressed one hand over her chest. "I am the great—" She continued to speak her name and title in a dialect Jade wasn't able to understand. In the corner of her visor, she saw Chloe quickly recording the information and running it through translators. The snipper flashed a proud smile when she finished. Aris arched a brow at Jade, seemingly bewildered despite her trilingual background.

"So," Jade stalled, hoping Chloe would figure out what the snipper had said.

"Mistress, I am unable to figure out a proper—"

"Squeaks," Jade said, an uncomfortable smile on her lips, hidden by her helmet. The snipper looked less than pleased with this name, and Aris shook her head with a hint of a smile on her lips. "Are you…here for a reason?"

"Oh, you fool!" Squeaks threw her hands into the air. "I am the *party manager!* And you were supposed to be in a *dress!* So that a medal may be *pinned* on you!"

Aris snickered. "I had one laid out for her. Told you that you should've worn it."

"Oh, shut up, Sell-out," Jade snapped back, humor in her voice. Aris chuckled, shrugging helplessly.

"I'm so pleased you both find this hilarious!" Squeaks crossed her arms, her pincers tapping against each other furiously.

"My lovely madame," Thaddeous said. He took one of the woman's hands and kissed it. Jade made a face. "I am sure you can excuse this folly. Surely, with your genius you can find another way to handle this."

Squeaks blinked a few times, moving one of her hands to her mouth to hide a faint smile. "Oh—oh, yes! Yes, of course!" She laughed dramatically. "Do not worry, I shall fix your *folly!*" She scurried out of the room. Jade huffed.

"*My* folly?" Jade whispered.

"Mistress, if you had worn the dress Madame Aris had given you, this whole situation would've been avoided."

"It's not my fault parties are the best places to be attacked. Just look at the creep next to me. Don't tell me he's not weird."

"I am in your company daily, mistress. I feel my judgement may be impaired by this."

"Okay, ouch."

"Well," Thaddeous said, turning to Jade with a smile. Jade frowned. "It was a pleasure to meet you. Until next time, Corporal. And congratulations." He gave a bow before slipping out of the room. Aris moved to stand next to her.

"He likes you," she said.

"He fucking *bowed.* That's weird, dude."

"Oh, he's trying to make a good impression." Aris shook her head with a grin, nudging Jade. "It's what people *do,* believe it or not. They try."

"Really? Wow," Jade crossed her arms. "Trying sounds like way too much work."

Aris laughed. "Says you. How many times have you *tried* to make an H-blade?"

Jade shoved her with a grin. "That's completely different! That's a matter of life and death!"

"Yeah," Aris said, pushing Jade's hand away. "Maybe for us if you keep causing them to explode."

"You know, I bet you like everything covered in ash. I've seen you—you think it smells nice!"

"I do not!"

"Bet you throw some under the bed to use later. I'm totally checking next time we get home," Jade teased.

"You come into my half of the apartment and I'm throwing you off the balcony." Aris fixed her with a joking gaze. "Don't tempt me."

"I have to cross through your side to get to my side, Sell-out."

"Don't tempt me!"

Jade snickered. The snipper rushed back in, nearly tripping over herself. She flung a red sash over Jade's shoulders and wove Jade's right arm through the circular opening in the fabric. She clapped once as she stepped back with a grin.

"Splendid!" she cried. "This will do perfectly! Don't you—oh." She looked around the room, frowning. "Where did that gentleman go?"

"Might I have your attention, please?" A female voice boomed from the main room, stopping all conversation. Squeaks grabbed Jade's arm and dragged her into the crowd. Jade yanked it away.

"Congratulations," Squeaks whispered before stepping aside. Jade dusted off her arm and turned her eyes to the stage. She moved to stand near the edge of the crowd, doing her best to keep her back from being vulnerable.

The woman speaking wore a red cloak with golden trim, the hood up. Most political leaders addressed the public this way, keeping their faces hidden to protect themselves from their enemies. It made it difficult to know who was leading the Exuro Empire at any given moment, however. Hovering before the woman was a small microphone, which she stuck close to.

"I am General Fain. You may not have heard of me, but I was there with the woman we honor today when she fought off the Thrax forces on Sobek. I was also first on the scene of the wreckage from the Thrax raid." Jade's brow furrowed. *She was? I don't recognize her voice.*

General Fain continued: "Her quick thinking saved her companions from certain death during the raid, just like she saved so many during that massacre." Fain's tone went sour. She cleared her throat and continued on, head turning to look over the crowd. Her shadowed face stopped in Jade's direction. Jade shifted on her feet, uncomfortable. "She was a worthy enemy for the Thrax, bold and commanding. She did not falter even after her armor was shattered and her arms were broken. The Thrax didn't know what hit them." There was no smile in her voice. "It is my honor today to award her with the medal of Indomitable Will. Please, if you would welcome our armored hero to the stage!"

The crowd burst into applause. Those that had given Jade strange looks before now smiled and clapped as she walked by. She scowled at them from under her helmet. They didn't understand what had happened. They didn't care. She didn't deserve this medal. She didn't want their praise. Many had died in the raid, on Sobek, on that ship. Their bodies were probably still out there, floating in space. Their bodies probably still littered the dirt on Sobek. The Mad Queen was likely busy planning her next homicidal attack to send more children to early graves. Jade's jaw grew tense. They should be spending this kniri on the war, not throwing parties. They should be spending kniri on giving injured soldiers their limbs back.

From the crowd, Jade noticed Thaddeous smile at her. He dipped his head in respect as she walked past.

"He is attempting to be kind, mistress."

Jade huffed. "He's still a creep." She climbed onto the stage, hoisting herself up onto the stair-less stage. General Fain offered her hand and Jade took it. The general pulled Jade up the rest of the way, and, awkwardly, the corporal waved at the crowd.

"What an honor," General Fain whispered, facing Jade. Jade turned back to the woman and saluted, right fist over left, pressed tightly to her heart.

"Thank you, General," Jade replied quietly.

"You're welcome, Jade," Fain hissed, returning the salute. Left over right.

Jade froze. She stared at the incorrectly placed hands and her eyes flickered up to the shadowed face. General Fain reached into her cloak.

"Chloe," Jade said, voice tinted with suspicion. Without further prompting, files with war-time information flashed across the left side of Jade's visor. Face after face, error after error. A red alert appeared in the middle of Jade's vision and flashed once, before both the documents and messages vanished.

"General Fain is MIA."

Jade's eyes went wide. *How did she get in?* Fain yanked out a Heated-Blade the size of a dagger, the edge of the silver metal a searing red. She swung for Jade's neck.

Jade jerked back. The blade narrowly missed her throat.

The imposter's hood fell back, revealing malicious red eyes. Several gasps came from the crowd and political leaders turned and ran. Those from the military either dashed for some sort of weapon or threw up their hands, trying to use whatever Helix they had. One of the few Atmo users generated a storm overhead, but the lightning did not strike Fain, and the rain only made the stage slippery. Fain grinned.

"No Helix for you," she cooed, falling into an offensive stance: right arm out with the dagger, left leg forward, both knees bent. Jade steadied herself and fell into a defensive pose: both fists up near her face, both knees bent, left leg forward. She could ponder how Fain was somehow disabling everyone's powers later.

"I don't need any powers to kill you," she spat.

"Don't you?" The imposter lunged forward, the heated edge of the blade evaporating whatever rain touched it. Jade jerked her arm forward to protect her face and the knife slammed against the armor on her forearm. Given the chance, the blade would burn through. Jade could only block like this for so long without a weapon.

Shit. I knew I should've worn something better.

Jade shoved the dagger back. Fain's fist smashed through an opening in Jade's armor, cracking against the rye-mail there. A buzzing pain rushed over her side and forced her to grit her teeth.

She pinned Fain's arm against her body and slammed her elbow against the woman's wrist. Fain screamed. The weapon clattered to the ground as Fain's knee jammed itself into Jade's side. Spots dotted Jade's vision and she hissed out a breath of pain. Warmth spread from the impact and her grip on Fain loosened. Fain noticed.

Jade's back crashed against the ground with Fain on top of her. She snatched the dagger from off the floor and stabbed it down towards Jade's face. Jade jerked to the side and the blade stuck into the ground next to her helmet.

"Mistress," Chloe warned.

The dagger came again, this time towards her throat. Jade threw her hands up, grabbing Fain's wrists and doing all she could to keep it from killing her. The blade wavered. Jade's arms weakened. The tip of the dagger cut into Jade's visor by her left eye. Her skin began to burn.

Shit! Jade sucked in a lungful of air and yelled. She bundled all her strength up and managed to force the weapon away. She pitched her hips to the side and the unbalanced Fain fell off her. Jade scrambled to her knees, glaring darkly at the red-eyed woman. Fain's eyes widened.

"You—"

A blur of white tackled Fain, the blade falling from the imposter's grasp. Jade glanced to where the two bodies stopped, and there Aris was, hair frizzy and long dress torn. She sat atop the woman, pinning her. Aris' arms bulged with her Helix, Charge, the ability to access the entirety of her muscle strength.

Thank Vix for that woman. Jade felt her shoulders lower as she relaxed, a soft smile crossing her lips. Three men got onto the stage and two rushed past her to take over for Aris, while the third helped Jade to her feet. Jade closed her left eye as she addressed the man until Aris reached Jade's side. Jade looked at her with a grin.

"If you say a single thing," Aris warned.

"You should've worn armor." Jade smirked and crossed her arms. "Told you parties are the best place for an ambush." Aris rolled her eyes and punched Jade's shoulder.

"Lot of good that did you. C'mon, let's get out of here. You've got a helmet to fix." Aris jumped off the stage.

A snapping sound came from behind Jade. Like jaws gnashing together. Like lightning. Jade's heart climbed into her throat and she whirled around, both eyes opened wide. Fain's hands gripped the men's faces, blue electricity racing off her arms and burning marks into the men's cheeks. They opened their mouths to scream and blood squirted past their lips. Their eyes rolled into the backs of their heads and they slumped to the ground.

Fuck.

Fain's eyes locked on Jade's and a sadistic grin split her face. Blue Lightning crackled over Fain's cloak-covered arms. Jade's eyes flickered to the dagger on the ground. The edge had grown cool without the blade being held. Fain lunged forward. So did Jade.

Jade grabbed the dagger first and moved to her knees. A lullaby dug through her skull. Fain narrowed the gap between them, a twisted smile on her face. A *knowing* smile.

Her hand reached for Jade. Soft fingers caressed Jade's flesh beneath her armor. Fain knew what she was doing.

Fain knew.

With a terror-filled snarl, Jade thrust the knife into Fain's sternum and tore it upwards through her chest. The lightning sputtered and died as Fain's momentum stabbed the blade further into her flesh. She tried for breath. She grabbed at Jade's hands as blood bubbled up into her mouth and poured from her torso. She coughed, crimson splattering against Chloe's visor, marring some of Jade's vision. The smell of burning meat filled the air as the H-Blade began to cook Fain's insides. She reached forward and hooked two fingers through the hole in Jade's helmet. A shaky smile stained her blood-covered lips.

"Green eyes."

Her body went limp.

Chapter 3

"She's waking up."

Mother? Jade's eyes cracked. The harsh yellow lights made them water. She caught the blurred figure of a woman standing near her. The thick stench of sweat clogged her nose. *No. That's not Mother. Mother's pretty. Where's Mother?*

The blur scoffed. "She's a fighter."

Yes. Mother is a fighter. Where is she?

"...under. He's not ready to see her yet."

Who's not? Is Father coming?

"Where...?" Jade's mouth moved without her consent. There was a clamor of motion and something shattered to Jade's right—or was it her left? People were shouting and figures rushed around her. One blur shook its fist in the air. Another blur grabbed the first blur and said something Jade couldn't understand. Why was everyone so excited?

Something stabbed her left arm and sleep started to creep in on her again.

"Ow." She tried to rub the feeling away but she couldn't move her arms.

"…too *close!* Next time…" The female voice droned on as Jade wondered where Mother might be. Her half-closed eyes flickered across the room, trying to find someone tall enough to be Mother.

The smell of sweat lingered a moment longer.

ϕϕϕ

"You must *think* before you act, Jade."

Jade frowned, tugging her too-big shirt over her small body and looking indignantly at her mother. The veteran's hazel eyes stared back at Jade and her red lips formed a grimace. She stood a few feet away, grip tight around the sword she held pressed into the ground. Mother wiped her hand across her face, pushing strands of red hair behind her ear, and put her free hand on her waist. Her stomach was exposed in an effort to combat the planet's humidity. Jade held her own sword, though it shook in her hand as she gasped for breath. She would have a new round of bruises in the morning.

"You're too big!" Jade let her sword fall so she could rid her brow of sweat. She looked up at the cerulean-colored sky that glittered with white diamonds, mocking her lack of freedom. Her eyes flickered to her left, longingly gazing at the bundle of trees that gathered at the bottom of the hill where they hugged a winding river. A jump into the chilled water would be nice.

Mother sighed. "Are you giving up already? Are you a fighter or a coward, Jade?" Her eyes held lingering impatience and her voice was balanced on an edge. Jade frowned and turned back to her mother, images of splashing in the blue current disappearing.

"I'm no coward!" Her voice cracked as she lifted her blade again.

"Prove it."

Jade's green eyes narrowed. "Fine, I will!"

φφφ

"Tests came back negative…"

Negative? No, sir. I passed all my exams. I always pass all my exams.

"…isn't Helix testing your specialty?! Test her again! This time—" The words were harsh and commanding. He must be angry she failed her tests. She was sorry she failed him.

Forgive me, sir. I don't know what happened.

"She's waking up!" The woman's voice was high-pitched and loud, as if she had leaned down next to Jade's ears just to scream. Jade wanted to tell her to shut up, but she thought it might be rude.

"It might be the hunger. Her body stopped accepting…"

Jade did feel really hungry. It felt as if someone had filled her gut with air and it was getting close to bursting inside her. An empty vacuum, getting ready to consume her if she didn't fill it. She wondered when she had eaten last. She could almost smell the cheap noodles her and Aris made in their apartment. Sizzled butter and salt, they advertised, but the taste was more like wood mixed with wet dirt. Her stomach growled with anticipation. Noodles were better than starving.

"…*cannot* have her awake yet!" the voice boomed.

It's just noodles. They aren't that *bad.*

"When is the prince coming? We can't…"

There's a prince coming for noodles? No wonder everyone is so excitable. Do princes even like noodles? The scuff of feet echoed near her, bringing with it the acidic stench of cleaning supplies. Jade started to choke on the smell.

Did someone bathe in cleaning products?

"…come when he's ready."

Jade groaned. *Is Aris cleaning again?* She wanted to shove the person who bathed in bleach away, but the pinch of leather straps pinned her wrists.

A presence moved closer and smelled of wet cut grass. A hand touched her arm. The fingers were soft and uncalloused. Those weren't the hands of a soldier, or even a field medic. Aris' hands weren't even that soft. Her heart rate spiked. She knew those hands.

I know those—

A needle pressed into her vein. Consciousness started to slip from her grasp.

ϕϕϕ

"The Mad Queen is reported to be moving east," Salene said as she ducked into the tent she shared with Jade and Aris. Salene's blue eyes glanced to Aris' before settling on Jade's face with a look of concern. Her brows pulled upwards, tugging at the burn scar that covered a large portion of her face. The black hair that survived was combed to one side and fell a little past her jaw, revealing her dark scalp and her mangled right ear.

"How's your leg?" Salene inquired.

"Getting there," Jade muttered, glancing down at her bandaged calf. Each heartbeat a new wave of superheated needles pressed against her nerves until they punctured the skin and travelled up to her hip. It hurt like hell, but she did her best to keep her expression from showing it. She reached up and adjusted the goggles on her face as Aris shifted on her cot.

"Did the general say anything about our orders?" Aris asked. Jade looked at her, the woman's head wrapped in gauze. Some of her hair had been burned off from the Mad Queen's recent attack. They were lucky to be alive.

"We're to stay here." Salene sat down at the end of Jade's cot.

"Stay here?" Aris pressed. "But we're all injured—we're easy targets!"

"I'm just telling you what he said," Salene growled, her eyes flicking to Jade for backup.

Jade rubbed the back of her neck. "I'm sure the general knows what he's doing, Sell-out. We're just going to have to stay here."

Aris' face twisted with agitation. The calculating look in her eyes worried Jade.

"We'll be fine," Jade ventured, hoping to calm Aris down. "We've been fine so far."

"You're barely able to walk, at least ten people are out of commission due to burns, fifteen of us died—that we know of—and the rest either have broken hands or shrapnel stuck in their arms. And that's from the blast alone! We had to have lost at *least* twenty or so when the Thrax came down on us—"

"Can I see your leg?" Salene cut in. Aris scowled and rolled her eyes. With a hard swallow and a thankful look cast to Salene, Jade swung her leg onto the cot and pulled it near her.

"It's fine, Salene. Don't worry about it." She flashed a smile as a shard of pain dug into her nerves. Salene arched a brow.

"You're a terrible liar."

Aris laughed, the sound bitter. "I don't even know why you try! Everyone can see right through you."

Jade shuddered at the phrase, hiding the reaction with a nervous grin. "Yeah, well..."

Salene reached her hands for Jade's unarmored leg. "I've patched you up before. Let me just see it, okay?"

Chewing the inside of her cheek, Jade tentatively nodded. She hoped the memories wouldn't return. She hoped she could keep her mind focused.

Salene gingerly pulled Jade's leg onto her lap and began to unwrap the bandage. Jade grimaced as it pulled at her skin, her fingers curling against the sheets as she grabbed hold of them for support. Tears bit at the corners of her eyes. Each centimeter the fabric moved, it felt as if a layer of flesh was flayed with a dull knife, slowly, over and over again.

"Almost there," Salene said, sparing a quick look in Jade's direction. She peeled the final layer back and revealed a partially burned puncture wound, where a large section of shattered rock had lodged itself before Jade had pulled it out. The gaping hole had been cauterized while they were on the run, further adding to the already severe burn there. Aris peered at it from her cot, but remained where she was with one hand on her temple.

"That looks pretty bad," Aris murmured.

"Thanks," Jade grumbled back.

"It looks like it should be okay," Salene said. "I'm going to need to touch it, okay?"

"What?" Jade blinked at her. "Why on Nevar would you need to touch it?"

"I need to make sure the nerves aren't gone," Salene explained. Jade chewed her lip. Salene was the most knowledgeable person on the subject of field doctoring that they had available. It would be foolish not to let her do what she needed to. Jade's eyes shifted to Aris, who gave a shrug. Jade nodded.

"Okay."

Salene brushed her fingertips over the rough flesh near the wound, and frowned when Jade did not react. She then moved her thumb to the fringes, where the burn looked less severe. The moment she did, daggers stabbed Jade's nerves all at once. She jerked her leg away, hissing a breath through her clenched teeth.

"Sorry. I just had to be sure," Salene breathed. "Are you okay?"

"Yeah," Jade said, calming the rising pain. "Yeah, I'll be fine."

"We can reapply the bandage in a bit," Salene said, standing and moving to her cot at the back of the tent. "And if it starts to itch, let me know."

Jade lay back against her pillow, chuckling through her agony. "I'm not letting you anywhere near my leg."

Salene rolled her eyes as she flopped down on her cot, her brown hair billowing up around her face. A smile played at her lips. "Get an infection, then. I'd love to see you try to walk as bacteria eats away at you."

With another chuckle, Jade let her eyes close, exhaustion from a day of near-death finally taking its toll. As sleep steadily approached, the wind outside picked up. Pitter-patters of rain danced against their tent.

"Like we need more rain," Aris said. "It's going to make it hard to keep wounds clean if we have to fight."

A flash of lightning lit up their tent. Jade's eyes flew open and her heart climbed into her throat.

Where are your friends, Private?

Thunder crashed a few minutes later. Aris scowled.

"Thunder will hide enemy activity."

"Don't worry so much," Salene said, her voice shaking. "The patrols will keep us safe. Right, Jade?" She looked to Jade for some sort of comfort. Thunder crashed again in the distance.

You're not holding out on me, are you?

Jade reached up and grabbed her hair. *No. Nonono. Calm down. You're not back there. She's not here. Calm down.* Her heartbeat filled her throat, making it hard to breathe. *It's just a storm. It's just a storm. Calm down. Jade, calm down.*

A flash of white lit up the tent and there, atop her, was the woman. Her crimson eyes burned holes into Jade's mind. She pressed her hand over Jade's mouth as her brown hair fell around her jawline. She smiled, her other hand caressing Jade's cheek.

"Hello, Private," she purred.

Jade screamed, biting at the hand and kicking the woman off her. She threw herself onto the ground and scrambled away, dragging her injured leg through the dirt. The woman sat on Jade's cot, chewing on her fingertips as she watched Jade with twisted glee.

"What's wrong, sweetie? I thought you'd be pleased to see me."

Jade's ears rang as thunder filled her mind. She shoved herself farther away, pressing her body against the fabric of the tent. She pulled her knees to her and pressed her head into them, her hands over her ears as she tried to block the woman out.

Not real. Not real. She's not real, Jade, she's not real.

"Jade! Jade!" Aris yelled. Jade looked up, her breathing shallow and quick. Aris knelt in front of her, Salene by her side. Jade swallowed. Relief washed over Aris' face.

"Vix, Jade, are you okay?"

Thunder. The woman lingered on Jade's cot. She smirked. Jade hid her face again.

"Shit," Salene hissed. "Jade, listen to me, you're okay. You're going to be just fine."

Jade sensed someone sit next to her. She hoped it was Salene. She hoped it wasn't the woman with the wicked smile.

"I'm right here," Salene whispered. "Me and Aris are right here."

"And so am I, love," purred the other woman. Jade felt soft hands on her spine, running over the scars that lay there. "I'm always right here."

ϕϕϕ

"Look at these scars," someone wondered, fingers tracing lines on Jade's back. Jade didn't have the energy to see who, or to tell them to keep their hands to themselves.

"There's no way we can inject it into her spine. These are too thick." The finger followed the arch of Jade's scar.

Stop. Your hands feel like ice.

"…beautiful. What do you think caused them?"

Awe. Why are they in awe? Scars aren't beautiful. They're failures etched into my flesh. Stop touching me.

The person moved closer, filling Jade's nose with the smell of food. Of meat. She could smell it as they breathed her air. The peppery spices native to Sobek. Her and Aris could never afford meat on their own, but after the victory on the battle-torn planet, the generals purchased a feast in Jade's honor. And the spices were fresh and new and exotic. Jade's mouth began to water and the air in her stomach tightened with hopeful anticipation.

Aris, buy us some meat. We're having a feast tonight.

"…Lichtenberg design. But they usually go away after…"

No, the feast will last all night.

The fingertip rubbed a spot where the tree-like design of the scars branched away from the main trunk. "They're not usually upraised like this." The finger followed the branch up near her shoulders, sending a chill across Jade's spine. With horror, she suddenly realized she was naked.

The hand jerked away. "She's awake!"

A beeping sound echoed somewhere in the room at the rate of Jade's heart.

Why am I naked? What's going on? Open your eyes, Jade! Open them!

"…into that vein! It might collapse!"

Open them, Jade!

"…choice! Do it!"

A thousand needles stabbed into a single nerve in Jade's arm, finding her veins, and flooding her body. She flinched, eyes snapping open.

White. All she saw was white.

Chapter 4

Jade was shoved to her knees, her cracked scouting armor allowing the dimly lit sand to find its way to her flesh. She ground her teeth and tugged against the restraints that kept her wrists bound behind her back. A light breeze slipped through the tent's open flap. She spat on the ground, her saliva mixing with blood and sand. The bruises on her jaw ached.

Fuck. This is bad. Her green eyes flashed as she looked around in the darkness. She could make out a bed to her left and a blue chest at its foot—which was oddly vibrant in such an orange-saturated planet. Movement caught her attention and she focused on a figure in the darkness.

A woman?

"Ah. You're the foolish scout we captured, aren't you?" The woman's voice eased Jade into a sense of calm despite her better judgement. The woman stepped closer, the singular lantern at the entrance casting light across her face. Short brown hair fell straight against the sides of the woman's slim, pale face. She didn't look up when she motioned with her gloved hands for the soldiers to leave. Soundlessly, the entrance to the tent closed and the breeze faded away.

"Do you know what happens to prisoners of war?" the woman hummed, the shadows making her red eyes ever more vibrant. A smile crossed her red lips. She knelt down against the desert planet's sand and her ankle-length skirt bundled up by her black military boots. "We torture them."

Jade sprayed a mist of blood and saliva against the woman's upper lip. Jade smirked.

"I'm not telling you anything," she said.

The woman's eyes flashed. She wiped the spit from her face and grabbed Jade with her other hand, her fingers digging another bruise into Jade's jawline.

"Won't you, love?" Jade's captor reached up and brushed away the strands of hair stuck to Jade's face by blood and sweat. "Where are your Exuro friends, hm? We'd like to remind them who's in charge." The hand trailed across Jade's jaw and down her neck, stopping at her throat. Her thumb fingered Jade's jugular. "Surely you understand."

Jade swallowed, feeling her throat press against the woman's thumb. "What?" She shakily began. "Don't want to brave the Taotar day cycle? Afraid you might get a sunburn?" Her voice didn't pick up confidence as she continued, instead it grew more strained and uneasy. She shifted in the woman's grip. "Stop touching me."

"Do you know who I am?" The woman murmured quietly, as if to a lover. Her left hand fondled Jade's neck while the other tightened around Jade's jaw.

"A perv?" Jade replied, arching away from the woman's hands. Alarm bells sounded in her head. She needed to get free of this woman's hold, *then* she could think. If she could just—

Her captor laughed, the sound like the wind chimes Jade's father would hang around the house. A sense of odd comfort rose up in her. Then the woman's thumb thrust into Jade's throat. Jade's eyes widened. Her pulse pounded in her ears. She tried to jerk away, but the woman held her firmly in one place. The world blurred.

Shit.

"My name, dear," she started, her voice like a mother wishing her child good night, "is A'doxia Calavar, Second in Command of the Thrax army, General of Branch Twelve."

The words meant nothing to Jade. Her eyes fluttered. Her lungs burned. She needed to breathe. And, as if granting the wish of a starving child, A'doxia mercifully released pressure on Jade's jugular and air flooded her lungs again. She doubled over, coughing, and closed her eyes against the glass shards that poured into her lungs. She grimaced.

This is really fuckin' bad.

A'doxia's finger found the edge of Jade's armor by her collarbone and wedged her thumb between flesh and metal. Burning lungs forgotten, Jade threw herself back, but the fingers followed. Her face contorted in a violated snarl.

"Don't touch me," she hissed between coughs. She wanted to sound strong, but only desperation rang in her words.

A'doxia flashed a sweet smile as she found Jade's dog tag and yanked. The chain shattered on the back of Jade's neck and pinched her nerves, causing a grimace to contort her face as the broken item was stolen from her.

"All right, love." A'doxia stood, still smiling, and eyed the words engraved in the small metal tag. "Private Jade Cavvar, is it? Oh, you poor dear."

Jade half expected A'doxia to lean down and kiss her forehead good night. She winced at the thought and tried to prepare herself for whatever the woman might do next.

"Your metal isn't even scratched yet. What, is this your first day?" A'doxia hummed. Jade swallowed, eyes narrowing.

"Just good at killing Thrax without taking a single blow," Jade sneered. A'doxia arched a brow, a humored smile on her lips. Jade shrunk beneath the gaze and suppressed any further coughs. A'doxia giggled and flicked her wrist in Jade's direction, launching the dog tag into Jade's face. After making impact with her nose, it fell to the sand and Jade's furious eyes locked with her captor's.

"If you're going to torture me, get on with it. I've got places to be."

A'doxia chuckled and turned away from her, moving into the dark where Jade couldn't see. Instantaneous relief spread through her body with A'doxia gone and Jade exhaled slowly through her mouth, allowing herself a second to recoup. She used her hands to feel around the back of her shattered armor, fingers searching for something to use. She had been stupid to get caught, but at least she was going to make one kick-ass escape.

A'doxia strode back into Jade's range of sight, holding a small dagger. She touched the tip of the blade to her gloved finger and watched as a small trickle of blood spilled out from the hole in the leather.

"How about," she purred, licking the blood from her finger, "you tell me about those green eyes of yours, hm?"

Jade flashed a cruel grin as she wedged her thumb beneath a loose piece of her armor. It came free and hit the sand not far from her bound hands. All she had to do was get it.

Then she opened her mouth.

"So, are you a slave to the *real* Thrax general? I heard they love women who beg—"

A'doxia's fist connected with Jade's cheek. Spots cluttered Jade's vision. She smashed into the sand and inhaled a lungful. The room spun. Her entire jaw screeched with agony. She hacked up blood—when did she bite her tongue? She tried to locate A'doxia in the dark, spotted, spinning room as her hands searched the floor for her improvised weapon. *Where the hell is it?*

The Thrax was there, kneeling in front of her. She tilted her face, watching Jade's eyes try to focus. A lullaby floated from A'doxia's lips.

Beautiful art, how lovely you will be.

A'doxia twirled the dagger. Jade watched in growing horror. Where was that piece of armor? Where had it gone?

Beautiful art, how pretty you will be.

"How do you like your kennock?" A'doxia whispered as she lifted her weapon-less hand. "Roasted?" Blue Lightning consumed it as the question left her lips, tendrils of electricity dancing over her glove. They curled and bounced, occasionally reaching past the leather and raising the hairs on her arm. The blue strips of electricity snapped at the air and lit the eager expression on A'doxia's face. "Or fried?"

ɸɸɸ

Jade's eyes flew open, heart pounding. Her head swam and hunger tugged at her stomach like crows on a corpse. She needed food, and she needed it soon.

"Aris?" Her voice came out strained and hoarse. She cleared her throat and grimaced against the stinging light, like that of the first Daoth sunrise. She moved to stand but something pulled at the flesh on her arm. Startled, she spun towards the aggressor, her other hand up, ready for a fight. Except the only thing there was an IV pressed into her inner elbow, dripping green liquid into her veins. Holes dotted the skin from her hand to her shoulder, following her veins. She touched the scabs, frowning when she discovered that most of them were still tender. *What is going on? How long have I been here?* Her brows furrowed, but she didn't have time to think about it. She needed a way out first. She wrapped her fingers around the IV and took a deep breath.

She ripped it out.

Blood started bubbling to the surface immediately. Jade bit her tongue against the pain and pressed her hand against the wound while she took inventory of the rest of her body.

54

Needle-points lay over her weary flesh with nothing but a thin patient gown draped over her, already covered with droplets of red. Her heart beat against her ribs. This didn't look good. She needed to move. Her lethargic muscles begged against it, insisting instead that they rest. She took a deep breath and closed her eyes, recollecting herself.

This is bad.

She rolled her shoulders back and opened her eyes. Everything looked blurred, distant, surreal. She blinked a few times.

Focus, Jade. Focus.

She ran her hand over the cloth that covered her, frowning. She couldn't fight in this. She needed something more.

All right, food and armor. Focus. Find food and armor.

Jade swung her legs over the side of the surgical table, lifting her hand gingerly to look at her wound. Blood still seeped from the hole. She would need something to help stop the bleeding before too long. A trail of blood could give her away. The corporal touched her gown but decided against tearing it up. Maybe she could find something else before resorting to running around naked. With an exhausted sigh, she moved to stand.

Or at least, she tried.

Her legs gave out under her the instant they carried her weight. Her ankles pitched to the sides, then her knees buckled and took her body with them. She threw out her arms to grab hold of something, anything, but only managed to grab a tray full of medical supplies and bring it toppling on top of her. Spare needles clattered to the floor and vials burst open upon impact with her, soaking her gown. Jade gasped for breath, her body lacking the strength she once had. She cursed and closed her eyes as the room spun and her ears rang.

Chloe could figure out what they did to me. I need to find her.

Jade took a deep breath and opened her eyes, settling them on a piece of used gauze. She reached for it, the fabric stiff from dried blood. She sucked air in through her teeth.

"Sure hope this is my blood," she muttered to no one as she wrapped it around her arm. Hopefully old blood didn't carry diseases.

The soldier pushed herself back to her feet, using the bed as support. Shards of glass fell off her gown and cluttered the floor around her feet. She grimaced.

Fucking fantastic.

She looked around the room, which was painted in a sterile white with lights hidden in corners and crevices, making the room almost shadowless. Other than that, the only items of interest were the bed she had been previously lying on, the medical tray now discarded on the floor, and a disconnected heart rate monitor in the opposite corner of the room.

Across from her, there was a large one-way window with a door stationed beside it. She pushed off from the bed, wavered, and staggered her away around the main glass shards and towards the door.

Food first. You really need some food. Then find Chloe and some armor. Vix, I hope Aris isn't here.

The door slid open before she could reach it. Three human men stood there in white lab coats, irises all red as they chatted and laughed. Jade froze. They froze.

"Shit," Jade muttered. How in hell was she supposed to fight three well-fed men in her condition? "Don't suppose I could have a meal before we get started?" Her words were ragged and she wondered if the men even understood her.

"Get her back on the bed!" the tallest man ordered. All three charged forward. Odds were against her.

She took a deep breath. Well, at least it'd be more fun this way.

A man with sunset eyes reached for her left arm, fingers curling towards the gauze. Jade sidestepped and slammed a hook into his jaw. He staggered into the wall, eyes distant. Clearly, he wasn't trained to fight. Hopefully a single punch was all it took on the rest of the Thrax.

Jade whirled around as the shortest of the trio, a man with more beard than neck, slammed his shoulder into her ribs. He rammed her into the wall, spit flying from her mouth from the impact. Her feet hurt and she hoped glass hadn't found its way into her flesh. Everyone else had shoes on. She wondered if anyone was her size.

"Get the serum, sir!" the bearded one shouted to the tallest human, who nodded and rushed for one of the needles on the floor. Jade bared her teeth and jerked her knee into his gut. He gasped, doubling over. Jade kneed his nose and felt liquid splatter against her flesh. He staggered back and fell into the pile of shattered glass, howling in pain.

The tall man had the syringe full with the green liquid she was once hooked up to and faced her. He dashed over his fallen comrade, needle out, and swung wildly. Jade's legs shook as she ducked, threatening to throw her to the floor. *I know you're hungry, but just hang in there.* With the man's arm over her, Jade grabbed his wrist and used his own momentum to turn the needle back at him. She shoved it into his chest and pressed the plunger. As he tried to back away, he tripped over his friend and landed on the floor. Jade sucked in oxygen and, body full of adrenaline, she made a dash for the door, slipping by the first attacker on her way out.

She made it through. Her pace slowed as three different directions spread out before her: left, right, and ahead. Jade pushed herself towards the hallway directly in front of her.

A flash of movement caught her eye.

She tried to throw her arms up, but she was too slow. She felt a needle carve its way into her neck.

Shit. Her green eyes spun on the attacker. *Shit!* The syringe pressed deeper into her flesh. Jade's hands reached for it. A'doxia smirked.

"Miss me, Private?"

Chapter 5

"What do you *mean* the serum doesn't work?" the woman's voice hissed with venom.

Serum? Oh, is that the new sort of ale?

"…trained against it," the male said with little concern.

Heh. I am a good drinker, aren't I?

"…don't do that." Bitterness crept into her words.

You can't tell me what to do.

"…up collapsing all her veins like this. Or starving her."

Ha! Like I would be beaten by ale. Just give it to me already!

"…not sure that'd be a bad thing."

She knows what I'm talking about.

"The prince—"

"I know what the prince wants," the woman growled.

The prince likes ale? Oh. Does he like it with his noodles?

"…the morning. Keep her alive until then."

φφφ

"Oh, come on, Jade. All he wants to do is meet you." Aris grinned at the message on the receiver attached to her wrist. She stood beside Jade, waiting for her to open the door to their apartment.

"He *already* met me. Besides, if he really wants to meet, why did he send the message to *you?*" Jade growled. She pushed the door to their apartment room open and let Aris in first.

"Well, *probably* because he doesn't have your number."

"And how does he have yours?" Jade closed the door behind them and flipped the lock. She walked into the single room where two beds were placed at opposite ends. She tugged Chloe off her head and tossed her onto the bed nearer to the bathroom. Jade had repaired Chloe after the incident at the party, and the new visor gleamed proudly back at her.

"Wouldn't you like to know," Aris hummed, walking into the bathroom with a wink in Jade's direction. Jade rolled her eyes and flopped onto her pillows face-first, exhausted from a day of walking the city, only for her nose to smash against something underneath. She grimaced and rolled onto her side, one hand covering her nose, and pulled her pillow off the box of chocolates hidden underneath. Her brows furrowed.

"What the fuck?" she grumbled behind her hand.

"What?" Aris peeked out from the bathroom, her hair undone from her usual ponytail and falling around her face. Her jacket and scarf were discarded on the floor, and she was moving onto her shirt, yanking the white fabric off her body. She stood in her bra and black jeans, her vitiligo displayed in a spotted mess on her abdomen. It covered the majority of her chest, stomach, and leg region, though was often hidden from sight. Jade was the only person Aris had ever shown it to, and even then, it had been an accident. Jade had walked in while Aris was changing one day, and Aris had been horrified.

Jade lifted the box of chocolates with a look of suspicion. "From you?"

Aris snickered. "Like I'd buy *you* chocolates."

Jade sneered at her, then turned to the box. The heart shaped container was tied with a red ribbon and she pulled it off, a note coming loose in the process. She opened it, brows stitched together.

Dearest Corporal Cavvar,

I apologize for being of no use to you during the attack the other night. I could not get to the stage quick enough. I hope you are all right. Someone of your stature surely had no issue fending her off. However, I would like to meet you in order to formally apologize, if you would be willing. Perhaps lunch?

Thaddeous Malkov

"It's from that fuckin' creep," Jade hissed.

"Kajel? I thought you broke his nose."

"No, not *that* one. Thaddeous. Mister Fuzz-Face." She held up the note, the stench of flowers smacking her nose. She scowled. "He even wrote it with fuckin' flower-scented ink. How rich is this asshole?"

"He did have a lot of hair on his face, didn't he?" Aris walked over, pulling her hair to the side and leaning over Jade's bed to look at the note. "Aw, he's concerned about you. He must have sent this after what happened last night."

"That doesn't explain how he got in here."

"Oh, I'm sure the landlord did it, Jade. Relax." Aris returned to the bathroom and the sound of running water indicated she was washing her face.

Jade squinted at the letter. "The *landlord?* That anti-social kodarian wouldn't hide it under my pillow. That's almost a…"

"Romantic thing to do?" Aris called, humor in her voice. "So you're not as oblivious as I thought."

Jade yanked the box open, taking a look at the neatly decorated chocolates inside. *Would the landlord really have let someone in to do this?* Her nerves bristled with the idea of someone else poking around their home. Were these drugged? Was this a cruel joke on some Blues the landlord wished would leave? Would they eat these and die?

She took note of her thundering heart and took a few calming breaths. *No. The landlord wouldn't do that to us. And the box was unopened. I have to believe these are safe. And that Mr. Fuzzface doesn't want me dead.* She exhaled slowly.

"These aren't poisoned, right?"

"No, Jade, they wouldn't be poisoned. A Blue hasn't been poisoned in years."

"Okay. Do you want to get not poisoned with me?"

"Sure." Aris returned, the water off and a towel in her hand as she patted her face dry. Jade tilted the box so Aris could choose, and after a moment of silence, Aris snatched a caramel-filled dark chocolate square topped with salt. She plopped it in her mouth with a smile.

"I haven't had chocolate in years," she said around her mouthful. "Back when I lived with my parents."

Jade picked a chocolate-covered wafer and bit into it. "Yeah?" she replied, closing the box. "I bet you guys had stores of this totally not poisoned stuff in the kitchen." She rolled onto her back, looking at Aris upside-down. Aris snickered.

"It's not poisoned, Jade. The landlord probably just let him in so he could do something nice."

"It's super creepy."

"We're Blues, Jade," Aris reminded her. "It'd be different if we were Golds. Or even Browns. We were probably asking to get our privacy violated by living so close to the surface."

Jade sighed. She closed her eyes and let herself tentatively enjoy the taste of the smooth chocolate in her mouth.

"You *sure* your parents are still mad at you? Can't we pay a quick visit and snag some of their chocolate? I'm sure the cook would let us in."

Aris snorted and a smirk flickered across Jade's face. *At least Aris seems unbothered by all this. That's a good sign, right? Things are normal. I just have to breathe.*

"Very funny," Aris said. She walked around Jade's bed to her own near the door and opened a small closet that was situated on the bed's right. She rifled through the tightly hung articles of clothing and pulled out a baggy knee-length shirt. She threw it on and promptly slipped out of her bra the moment she could.

"So do you want to hear Thaddeous' message or not?" Aris pressed.

Jade closed her eyes and groaned, her hand falling over her face. "Will you leave me alone if I do?"

"Not likely." A small beep filled the irritated silence and Thaddeous' voice rang through the speaker on Aris' wrist. Jade opened her eyes and stared at the ceiling.

"Hello, Corporal Jade Cavvar." There was a pause. "We met last night, I'm not sure if you remember me. My name is Thaddeous Malkov. I'm sending this message in light of recent events in hopes you are well and unharmed. I'm sorry I wasn't of more help last night, I wish I could've done something more but I simply could not get to the stage." He sighed. "I'd like to express my concern in person, perhaps buy you lunch? Getting your mind off things might help you to relax. Please, contact me if you'd like to meet again." With that, the message ended. The silence spread out around Jade until it was too much and she glanced at Aris, who wiggled her eyebrows with a massive grin on her face. Jade picked up the chocolates.

"I will eat all these myself, Sell-out. And die of not poison."

Aris laughed. "Oh, come on! He's trying! Besides, it *would* be good for you to go do something other than train and drink. Maybe *he* could pay for something."

Jade rubbed her eyes. "I'm not meeting him, Aris. I have more important things to worry about."

"Oh yeah? Like what?" She held up her finger before Jade could respond. "And it only counts if it doesn't have to do with the war."

Jade pointed to the ceiling where Spidey, her small spider-bot, sat. "Have to give him an upgrade." She looked at the robot with a smile. "You'd like that, wouldn't you, little guy?"

Spidey clicked his fangs happily and dropped onto Jade's lap. He made the closest sound he could to a purr by lifting two of his six legs at a time in quick succession, making the motor in his body rumble. Jade laughed.

"And he's so excited, too. You can't deny him that." She looked up at Aris, who furrowed her brows.

"Jade, you need to have a life outside the war. It's not healthy for that to be the only thing on your mind."

"I have plenty in my life, Aris." She frowned. "I don't need a man to make my life better."

"Someone looked past all…*this*," she gestured at Jade's armored body. "He looked past your less than accommodating attitude and still wants to buy you lunch. And that's all it is—okay? Listen," Aris walked over to Jade and sat on her bed. "You don't have to commit to anything with him. I just want you to do something different. Try something new for once."

Jade looked at her, making a face. Aris nudged her and Jade dramatically fell over.

"Ugh, fine!" Jade said, grabbing her shoulder. "You're so abusive."

Aris snickered. "Oh sure, *I'm* the abusive one." She stood with a stretch. "I was thinking ramen tonight for dinner?"

"Ramen?" Jade gasped, hand over her mouth. "We *never* have ramen. I haven't tasted its delicious cardboard flavors since this afternoon!"

Aris grinned. "Well, wait no longer! I'll get it set up. You want the veggie flavor or the cardboard veggie flavor?"

"Is that even a question?"

Chapter 6

"Jade! Jade, come *on*, wake up already!" Two hands shook Jade's armored body, and she grimaced with the sudden movement.

"Ugh, leave me alone, woman. Go bother someone else."

"Like who, you big baby?" Aris snapped back. "You're going to be late. You're meeting Thaddeous today, remember?"

Jade pulled the blankets over her face, groaning louder. "That's today? Reschedule. I want to sleep."

"Did you stay up drinking last night?"

Jade huffed. "Yes, *mother*."

"You're going to kill your liver, Jade. What good will you be to the army if you're puking up blood?"

"Is that what happens? Vix, I thought you just straight-up died." Jade sat up, rubbing her eyes as the blankets fell off her. "To think, I've been playing it safe all this time." She snickered when she heard Aris sigh in defeat.

"We talked about this, Jade. You said you'd give him a chance. Nothing more than that." Aris, who was wrapping her only scarf around her neck, stood in the area between the two beds, looking at Jade. Jade rubbed her eyes once again, this time with more irritation.

"Okay, okay." She lifted her hands in surrender. "I know what I said. Let me get dressed." Jade stood and sleepily meandered to her closet, situated near the bathroom door. Inside was a secondary set of rye-mail and a variety of different pieces of armor, most of them dismantled to be better stored in the small space. She pulled out a large chest piece with access to a secondary oxygen supply stored as a tank between her shoulder blades, two matching arm guards, shoulder plates, and a leg set. The armor wasn't exactly cohesive, and most of them had been repainted by Jade's hand which made them less of a joy to look at. Nevertheless, she tossed them into the bathroom and closed the door to change.

"I swear you have some sort of mechanical limb or something," Aris teased from the other side of the door as Jade peeled off her sleepwear—a suit of armor rigged to send electrical pulses into her body the moment someone other than Aris opened the door. Jade looked in the mirror, her hand falling on her hip where one of the many scars could be felt beneath the rye-mail. She took a deep breath.

"If I told you, I'd have to kill you," she replied, turning her attention away.

Aris snorted. "Just hurry up, would you?"

φφφ

They took a taxi to a higher section of the city, the Market District. As they stepped out of the vehicle, a nearby air vendor electronically displayed the going rate for fresh oxygen. Aris coughed and grimaced as smog rolled around her feet, but Jade was free to breathe easy with Chloe strapped over her head and connected to her chest piece. Aris peered at the rounded rectangular shape of the vendor and frowned at the cost. She strode further into the market district and Jade kept pace with her.

"You should've worn that nice set—the silver and gold," Aris said, glancing at Jade's mismatched armor. "It would've been more…presentable."

Jade grinned behind Chloe's tinted visor. "What? You bashing my fashion sense now?"

Aris snickered and shook her head. "You're hopeless," she said as the two walked under one of the many archways built in the market. They were, as usual, crafted from metal but painted to look like marble.

The duo continued forward and strode around a fountain placed on grass. The walkway was paralleled by statues of great political leaders, and their wealth was prominently displayed by what expensive material was used: the poorest chose metal and tried to hide it by having an intricate paint job to make it look like something else, others had stone or marble, and the wealthiest chose wood, which contrasted with the inorganic buildings around it.

Jade didn't pay much attention to political life, though she figured she ought to. But gazing up at the different faces—kodarian, snipper, human—they all had the eyes of those who would send children to a war they barely even funded. Jade was thirteen when she was drafted. Most were sent to the front lines two years later, but she skipped a year. She watched as fellow children froze when the first battle broke out. Some of them begged for their lives. Others cried for their mothers. Jade watched as one kodarian child, faced with the impossibility of fighting, threw herself onto her H-blade.

"How do I look?"

Aris' question pulled Jade out of her thoughts, and she felt a moment of relief. She wasn't sure if Aris noticed her slip down memory lane, but Jade was thankful for the interruption. She looked over at her roommate.

Aris wore comfortable shoes and black jeans. A white shirt was layered beneath a black one, and a black jacket was pulled over her shoulders, the cuffs rolled up around her wrists to reveal white fur. Around her neck hung her only scarf: yellow and black checkered fabric with small tassels hanging from the ends. Her hair was pulled into her usual pony-tail and she wore a little blush on her cheeks. In short, Aris was well-dressed, as always.

"Are you meeting someone?" Jade gestured to Aris' blush. Aris didn't own a lot of makeup as it wasn't a necessary expense. Aris grinned.

"Well, of *course*, Jade. I wouldn't want to be the third wheel on *your* date."

Jade frowned. "Why would I ever have thought otherwise?"

Aris chuckled. "He seems really nice. When you're done with Thaddeous—or when you bail on Thaddeous," she muttered, "you should come meet him."

"How'd you two meet, anyway?"

"Online," Aris said with a shrug. "Can't really meet them anyway else unless I want to date another soldier. And you know what they say about dating soldiers." She grinned and nudged Jade, who snorted out a laugh.

"They're pretty unreliable, from what I hear."

A few half-hearted chuckles were exchanged before dying on their lips. They had seen a lot of fellows die in the war, never to return to their families.

"I'd better go meet him." Aris stopped near another archway and motioned to a café not far away. "I'll just be in there. Try to have fun today, okay?"

Jade shrugged. "No problem, Mom."

Aris rolled her eyes and patted Jade's arm. "See you later." She turned and walked away. Jade glanced around before moving to lean against one of the many archways. After some time, she eventually sat down, ignoring the glares from people as they walked past, annoyed that someone was blocking the walkway.

"Chloe, how much time has passed?"

"Fifteen minutes since Madame Aris left, mistress."

"Fuck this." Jade climbed back to her feet and rolled her shoulders back. She turned and strode further through the buildings that rose up beside her, passing where Aris was meeting someone and entering an area with less foot traffic. There, she spotted the distant neon sign of a blacksmith shop and ducked inside.

"I'll be right with you!" someone called from the back room. Jade looked around, finding the place to be messy and unkempt, per usual. Sections of half-finished armor sets were scattered across the small space, and broken weapons were placed in a pile. She strode up to the counter, dodging the random bits of metal on her way, and leaned against it. Through a curtain, and man walked into the room, smoke following him on his way in. Soot covered his olive-colored human face, and his black hair was partially burnt off in sections. His brown eyes settled on her helmet and a smile broke across the retired soldier's face.

"Jade! It's wonderful to see you again. Or, well," he gestured to her heavily armored appearance, "sort of see you. You know, I heard a rumor that you have red hair? I told them that was bullshit, because you're clearly just an android with no fleshy form." He smirked at her. Jade chuckled.

"You got me, Tiber."

"What can I get for you?"

"Well, I was hoping for some more parts to make an H-blade."

Tiber stopped behind the counter and his smile dropped from his face. He sighed and wiped his forehead with his arm, smearing the soot there.

"Jade, how many times are you going to blow up your apartment before you realize you simply cannot make weapons? It's a science, and if you don't get it just right—"

"Listen, I was really close last time." Jade put her hands on the counter.

"Mistress, I believe that's called a lie."

"*Really* close," Jade continued, ignoring Chloe's vote of confidence. "It took five whole minutes before it…fell apart."

"You mean exploded?" Tiber sighed again, shaking his head. "Does Aris know you're here?"

"C'mon, Tiber, she's not my mom."

"How many times are you going to cover that poor woman's bed with grease and oil?"

"I clean it up!" Jade protested. "Tiber, I've got the kniri, I can pay."

"Why don't you just stick with making armor? You're an expert at that. In fact, I'd purchase any sets you have no use for—"

"I need to understand how my weapons work. How am I supposed to repair what I've got out on the field if I don't even understand how it's supposed to go together?"

Tiber gave her a stern look. "You carry around tools with you in war?"

Jade shifted uncomfortably. "Totally."

Tiber snorted out a laugh. "Sorry, Jade. For the well-being of your roommate, I'm not selling you any of those parts. At least for now. Give her some time to recover."

Jade groaned. "How much? Two kniri? Will that cover it?"

"No, Jade. Find something else. I've got some good new sets of metal in. That special shit from Sypher—what's it called?"

"Three kniri? How about three?"

"Nigferra! That's it! Same shit that makes the weapons you're so obsessed with. I bet it'd make killer armor."

"C'mon, Tiber, three is all I can afford to pay."

Tiber turned towards her fully and stared at her visor hard. "No, Jade. I appreciate your business, but I'll turn you out if you keep pushing me like this. You put yourself and Aris in danger each time you fuck up making an H-blade. You simply can't do it. Get over it and move on."

"Tiber—"

"Corporal Cavvar!" Thaddeous' voice broke through Jade's attempted persuasion and she whirled around, scowling at the man standing at the door. He wore a suit, but his face was bruised and a newly formed cut across his nose was starting to bleed. Jade's brows knitted together.

"Vix!" Tiber cursed behind her.

"What the fuck?" Jade spat. "Did you get into some alley brawl?"

"Yes—I mean, no—I mean—" he shook his head, trying to collect his words. "It's Aris!"

Immediately, without Jade having to say anything, Chloe began to call Aris. Jade lurched forward, grabbing Thaddeous by the sleeve.

"What about her," she hissed.

"She's in danger! Some men with guns cornered her in an alley! I tried to stop them, but—"

"Where is *she*?"

"F-follow me." He spun around and dashed out the door. Jade followed. They sprinted back towards where Aris had gone to eat. The call continued to ring. Thaddeous steered them into an alley. They burst out on the other side. A tall railing closed off the walkway's edge, and the path was thin behind the buildings. Constricting. Suffocating. Jade grabbed the railing and looked around. No one. She glanced below, down the thousands of feet to Nevar's surface. The buildings were swallowed up by darkness and vehicles that flew down there vanished from sight.

She can't have fallen. She can't have been pushed. Jade grabbed at her helmet. *Vix, she can't have—*

"Jade?" Aris' icon popped up in the lower left corner of Jade's visor. "I'm in the middle of my date. What's wrong?"

Jade's gut filled with rocks.

"Fuck!" Jade spun around to Thaddeous just as he shoved her, his arms rippling with Charge, the same Helix Aris had. Jade's middle back caught the railing, but his strength forced her over it. She flipped off the pathway.

Jade scrambled, grabbing at nothing as she spiraled down through the open air. Her entire body buzzed, the sensation of falling and dizziness beginning to overwhelm her. Visions and blurs of cars and flashing lights and dark shapes and buildings and neon signs crowded into Jade's mind until she shut her eyes. Her stomach lurched. Vomit filled her mouth.

"Mistress, stay with me! Mistress!"

Chapter 7

Jade woke up.

Her nerves screamed, fangs of a thousand demons tearing at her flesh. She grimaced against the pain and the light, squinting until her eyes adjusted.

She was in the same room, the same bed, the same space she had been when she had woken up before. Needles were jammed into both her arms. In the corner, near the door, was a sleeping kodarian, slumped to one side and his mouth wide open as he snored. His tusks curled an inch past his upper lip, the tips pointing partially towards his skin.

High-pitched beeping resonated in the room and the heart monitor opposite of the kodarian showed a cascade of straight-edged waves. She glanced to the man, who continued to sleep through it. *Right then. Time to get out for real this time.*

She went to roll over but her wrists refused to budge. She scowled and glared at them, where leather binds kept her tied down. *Apparently these Thrax kidnappers learned from their mistakes. Maybe if I—*

The door slid open and a woman walked inside. Military boots peered out from under her long skirt. She wore something smaller than a half-top, fabric strapped solely around her chest. Black gloves covered her hands and her crimson eyes lit up when she saw Jade helpless on the table. Jade blanched.

A rigid snore cut the tense gaze of A'doxia Calavar, and her joy vanished as she looked to the sleeping guard. She swept her hand up her skirt, lifting one side and producing an H-blade that was strapped to her leg. The blade unfolded from itself, extending into a small dagger with a gleaming red edge. A'doxia stepped closer to the man.

"Darling?" Her fingers brushed the side of his face. The man's eyes flickered and a small smile crossed his face. "Time to wake up." She slammed the blade into his leg, just above his knee, and twisted it. He screamed, jerking his leg back and causing for the wound to grow larger. His eyes, wide open now, looked for his attacker as he grabbed at the blade. He froze, tears burning at the corners of his eyes.

"Ma'am," he stammered, looking at her with desperation. A'doxia's face lit up with pleasure and a twisted giggle slipped from her lips. Blood sizzled from around the blade.

"Were you sleeping on the job, love?"

"I—I was ma'am. Please forgive me."

A'doxia's other hand pressed against the bleeding wound, the smell of burning flesh starting to taint the air. The kodarian's face twisted with pain.

"Just this once," she hummed, sweetly, her nose inches from his. "But if I catch you sleeping on the job again, you're going to end up worse than her." She pointed to Jade and smiled. Jade squirmed in her bindings.

Shit!

"Yes, ma'am. Of course."

"Leave this in there until you get to the medical wing." She tapped the blade, pushing it further into his leg, then released the hilt. The blade cooled, and she stepped back so that he could hobble out of the room. When he was gone, A'doxia sighed and looked to Jade.

"I never thought I'd see your pretty little face again, Private," she chimed, sauntering closer. Jade wanted to dissolve into the table.

"It's corporal now," Jade muttered in reply, her words weak and heavy with fear.

Fear? You think showing your fear is going to make things any easier? Shit! Focus, Jade! You need to relax!

But how could she? A'doxia stood at her side, her fingers dancing against Jade's arm, a hum slipping from her lips. And Jade was strapped down. She couldn't do anything. She couldn't fight back, she couldn't run. Her heart drummed in her ears. It was happening all over again. She was captured. She was caught because she was being a fool. And now she was restrained in this woman's presence once again.

She could feel the sand pressing against her flesh already. She could feel the lick of electricity burning lines into her back that a blade would cut open and let bleed. She was there, now, lying in the sand, naked. Blood gushed from her back and her mind filled with fog. The first sun of Taotar was rising and it wouldn't be long until the second sun caught her body aflame.

"Corporal?" A'doxia repeated, her brows lifting with surprise as her fingers traced the veins in Jade's arms. "What an honor!" Her fingertips danced against Jade's wrist. "Congratulations, love."

Don't show fear. Don't show fear. Focus, Jade, focus.

"Thanks," she said. "My goal is to impress you."

Don't show fear and don't fucking taunt her for fuck's sake!

A'doxia, however, seemed mildly amused. A smile played at her lips.

"How sweet. I didn't realize you cared so much. Well," she leaned closer to Jade's face. Jade strained her neck to try to move away. "Maybe I can show how much I care about *you* sometime, hm?" Pressure increased on Jade's wrist. Discomfort distorted her face. "A little private time, just you and me. We can even visit a sandy beach to make it feel more authentic. How's that?"

The door behind A'doxia opened and she pulled away. Jade sighed with relief.

"Prince!" A'doxia's voice brimmed with surprise.

Jade peered at the door and, there, dressed in a dark blue suit, was the Prince of the Thrax.

Thaddeous Malkov.

"You," Jade hissed, eyes narrowed. Thaddeous glanced up from a small tablet in his hands. His eyes were green. Shock washed through her. Green? Another *Green?* How could there be another one? Only one was alive at any given time in the galaxy. How was he a Green? Hadn't he used a Helix before? How was he a prince with the eyes of a demon? How was

A'doxia treating him with respect? Her mind reeled. *What the fuck is going on?*

"…sure if she's ready," A'doxia said.

"I'm sure she's fine, thank you." Thaddeous walked around to Jade's right, opposite of A'doxia. "Good to see you again, Corporal Jade," he said, unsmiling. He looked down at her.

"Why the *fuck* are your eyes green?" Jade snapped. "Weren't they blue before? What the fuck is going on?" Thaddeous lifted one hand as if it had the power to calm her down. It didn't. "What?" she pressed. "You think because you're some sort of prince that I'll just do what you say the moment—"

A'doxia's fingers danced against the top of Jade's hand. Jade scowled and held her tongue. Thaddeous chuckled and leaned closer to her. Jade moved her face so that their noses wouldn't touch.

"You're right, Corporal," he whispered. Anger began to etch itself into Jade's features. "They were blue before. But now they're green. I wonder what that could mean?"

Jade jerked forward, clamping her teeth around his lower lip. She held steady as he yanked back, his flesh tearing and getting caught in the caps between her incisors. Blood gushed and iron stained her taste buds. She spat skin on the ground.

Thaddeous staggered back until the wall touched his spine and his hand pressed against his lip, eyes wide. A'doxia rushed around the table to him, but he stopped her with a single flick of his wrist. Her crimson eyes flickered to Jade's. The corporal winced.

Yeah. Smart move.

Thaddeous caught her eye. She expected hatred, perhaps vengeance to fill them, but instead, the lunatic wore a bloody smile. A short laugh exploded from his throat.

"You're smart, Corporal. I didn't expect someone like you to get that close to me. Especially after our date."

Revulsion consumed Jade's expression. "*Date?*" she hissed. "You're joking, right? You pushed me off the fucking *building*. How did I even survive that? Did you have a fucking posse with you?"

He looked down at his tablet, spitting blood onto the floor as it filled his mouth. He didn't respond, as if he hadn't heard her. Then:

"Are you hungry, Corporal?"

Jade locked her jaw. The empty pit that served as her stomach was deepening, wallowing in want. Her body was wasting away. Her stubbornness, however, kept her mouth shut. He glanced at her and chuckled.

"I'm going to say yes. I'll make the arrangements. Jade, A'doxia." He nodded to them both, tucked the tablet under his arm, and exited the room.

The instant the door closed, A'doxia was atop Jade.

"Go ahead," she whispered, her face a fraction of an inch from Jade's. "*Bite me.*"

Jade swallowed and tilted her head to look at the wall. A'doxia laughed, wind chimes filling the room.

"What? Don't like women the same way?" She brushed Jade's cheek with her hand. "You're going to make me jealous if you keep showing Thaddeous so much interest," she murmured. "And, well, sometimes I just can't control myself when I get jealous."

Jade, despite herself, closed her eyes. She could hear her mother's words: *What are you doing? Fight back! Do something! Don't let your fear control you!* But her mother had never been captured by enemy soldiers. Not like this. Not by this woman. All she wanted was to block A'doxia out.

"I can do this all night, Private. Tell me where your friends are."

Blood everywhere. The darkness banished with the flickering glow of lightning.

"F-fuck you." How long had it been? Days? Weeks? Maybe years had passed. Was anyone even looking for her?

"Aww," A'doxia cooed, "is the little private scared after all? I do love it when you have that pathetic little look on your face, love. You're almost irresistible." The weight on Jade's body lifted and Jade peered out of one eye. A'doxia stood at the end of the bed. Her eyes were filled with wicked delight. "*Almost.* Alas, I have more important things to attend to. Another time, love." She turned and slipped out of the room, just as Thaddeous walked in.

Thaddeous looked up from his tablet when he entered, his other hand holding a cloth pressed against his bleeding lip.

"What's your favorite food?" he asked.

Jade blinked. Her body sang a wretched song of violation from A'doxia's touch and her mind was still back there, on Taotar, in the sand and in the blood.

"What?"

"Your favorite food." He smiled at her. "Everyone has one. What's yours, Corporal?"

Jade couldn't think but her body reacted, answering out of desperation for something to eat. Before she could stop herself, the words came tumbling out of her mouth. "I really like fried kennock."

Chapter 8

"Very good," Thaddeous said, inputting commands onto his handheld device. Then he set it down on the empty chair and strode closer. "And why don't we let you walk around the room?" Jade stared at him quizzically.

"What?" he asked as he put his hands near the IV's in her left arm. "It's not a trap, if that's what you're thinking." Thaddeous grabbed a small bandage and prepared it by applying light green foam to the underside. "These have been keeping you alive for the last week," he said as he set the bandage aside and smiled at her.

Week? His mouth was moving. *I've been here for a week?* Her mind spun in circles, chasing its own tail until she realized it: *I've been here for a week, meaning that Aris will be getting a party together to search for me. All I need to do is last until then.* Her eyes narrowed on Thaddeous' green pair. *Or, I can take out the Prince of the Thrax as soon as he—*

"—three." Thaddeous yanked out a thick needle from Jade's arm and her eyes shot wide, fingers of pain sprouting through her nerves. She gritted her teeth. Thaddeous applied the bandage and the bleeding subsided a moment later. He arched a brow at her.

"I did warn you. I even counted down. You...were listening, weren't you?"

Jade scowled. "Come a little closer so I can bite off your nose, too."

Thaddeous sighed and offered her a shrug. "Of course, if you don't *want* to be able to move, I can keep you there."

Jade locked her jaw. "Do whatever the fuck you want, Thrax. I can take it either way."

"Don't be so tense, Corporal! I'm not here to hurt you."

"Vix, wonder why I would've thought otherwise," she replied dryly. Thaddeous shook his head and bent down near her skull, peering at something Jade couldn't see.

"After you woke up and harmed a few of our researchers, we couldn't just let you run around. And the needles are to keep you alive. For the most part."

"What are you looking at?" She arched her neck to try to see what he saw. "And what does 'for the most part' mean?"

"Calm down, Corporal Cavvar," he murmured, his fingers touching bare skin on Jade's head. "You're perfectly safe here. Now, let me just take these out of you." With one quick movement—and a spike of agony that faded into a background buzz—he tugged three needles from Jade's head and set them on the medical tray beside him. He applied the foam and placed a bandage over the wounds. Jade's eyes filled with fire.

"What the *fuck* were those? Why were they in my head?"

"Please," he said, stepping back, "calm down. They were to monitor some extra vitals. As a Green, you're very interesting to us."

"Then throw yourself on the operation table and leave me out of it."

"I wish I could, truly. But I'm not a true Green." He smiled. "You, on the other hand, are perfect. You're exactly like all the stories."

The condemnation made Jade recoil. "I'm not like the stories."

"You are! Strong and powerful, able to change the course of entire lives just by existing." Thaddeous' eyes gleamed. "It's inspiring, really."

"I'm not like the stories," Jade insisted. She wasn't. She wasn't like them. She couldn't be like them. For Aris' sake. For her own sake. Thaddeous raised his hands in surrender.

"Fine, fine. You're you, not like any stories. But that's impressive enough for me. Here." He moved to her ankles and untied the restraints. Jade rotated her feet, enjoying the ability to move again. He moved to her right, pulled out the needle that lay buried in the crook of her arm, and covered the small hole with the same materials he had used before. He untied her right wrist and she went about untying her left.

Jade sat up and rubbed the rawness from her flesh, watching as Thaddeous strode back to the empty chair and fetched his device.

"Take your time standing up," he said. "You haven't walked in a while, and your muscles aren't in the same condition as they were before. And A'doxia will return soon with some clothing that you can wear." He diverted his eyes for a moment. "I assume that's something you'll want, correct?"

Jade glanced down at the white sheet that covered her body. "You don't have a suit of armor I can wear?"

"Armor?" he asked, brows upraised. "We're not going to attack you, Corporal Cavvar. You have my word."

Jade swung her legs over the edge of the bed and felt the exposure of her sides burn hot. Thaddeous kept his eyes either on her face, or not on her at all.

"If you're trying to butter me up, the least you can do is get me a set of armor." The corporal rubbed her shoulder, trying to pull the tension out of her muscles. Jade would need to be ready if the time came, not rigid. "And my helmet."

He sighed. "Very well. I'll inform A'doxia. You must understand for safety reasons we cannot give you your helmet, as its communication features could prove detrimental to us. Once we are able to successfully jam the signals, then we can return it."

"You want me to trust you, but not the other way around?" Jade's toes brushed the floor.

"I trust you, but others may not be as willing to do the same." He tapped the screen of his tablet. "There. Is there anything else you need?"

"A ship off this rock." She put a small amount of weight on her left leg, testing its strength.

"I understand your desire to leave, Corporal Cavvar, but that isn't possible in your state."

"The only reason I'm like this is *because* of you," she snapped. "So, I'd say we cut out the middleman and I just go home to recover. Where I'm not *surrounded* by hundreds of enemies."

The door opened and, before Thaddeous could offer a rebuttal, A'doxia strode in, arms laden with blankets, clothes, and on top, a simple set of armor. She smiled at Thaddeous, then set her pile down next to Jade. Their eyes met, A'doxia's hand lingering a moment longer than it needed to on the armor. Her gaze flickered over Jade's exposed side. Jade covered herself.

"Hopefully all the sand has been cleaned out of this," A'doxia said, tapping the armor. "It was last used on a desert planet, Taotar. Have you ever been there?"

"Oh, that's right," Thaddeous interjected. "You two haven't formally met. A'doxia, this is our guest, Corporal Jade Cavvar. Corporal, this is General A'doxia Calavar. Now, I know you two stand on opposing sides in the war, but please, put that aside for now until our business together is finished." Naively, he flashed a smile. "Agreed?"

Jade pulled the clothes closer to her, frowning. A'doxia smirked.

"Of course, my prince. Agreed."

"Jade?" Thaddeous prompted.

Jade's eyes narrowed. Her body hummed with the desire to attack, to smash his head against the floor and find a way off this shithole. Her gaze flickered to A'doxia's. She'd never make it.

"Get out so I can change," Jade said at last.

Both of them left and Jade fumbled to pull off her gown and tug on new clothes before she paused, half-undressed. She stared at the large one-way window and stood, frozen. Who was watching her right now? Was A'doxia standing on the other side of the glass, waiting to see the scars on Jade's back? She gritted her teeth. She needed the armor. She needed protection. Even if it risked violation now, at least she'd have something to fight in later. With a steadying breath, she tore her eyes away from the window and shifted to glancing over the provided materials, ensuring nothing in them would harm her. When she was satisfied, she pulled off the rest of her gown and stepped into her pants. She pulled her shirt on and layered large-gapped rye-mail over it, the easiest and cheapest to construct due to the large openings between each link. She strapped the chest piece on over her torso and did the same for the arm and leg guards.

It was light. Her stomach was rather exposed, and without her specialized modifications, it wouldn't protect her from A'doxia's electrical touch. She grimaced as she lay back on her bed, the movement having exhausted her. The armor was terribly uncomfortable. And there was no way it'd keep her safe for too long if she wasn't in peak condition.

What have I gotten myself into?

A knock at her door caused her to glance towards it.

"Corporal Cavvar?" Thaddeous called from the other side. "I have your kennock for you. Can I come in?"

Jade sat up again, her body remembering her hunger with a momentary weakness of her muscles. She was going to need to get her strength back up. And if a knife was provided to help cut her meat, then all the better.

"Yeah," she responded, and the door slid open. He smiled when he saw her.

"You look more comfortable in that."

"Just give me the damn food."

With a laugh, he brought the plate to her and rested it on the bed. Kennock meat stripped from a domesticated, six winged, five-foot tall bird lay shredded and fried on her plate, the light brown meat tinted with a distinct bluish color. It rested atop potatoes, a food carried on board the first human ship discovered, and the whole meal was covered in thick gravy. A plastic fork was provided. She glanced at Thaddeous, who pulled up the chair to sit beside her.

"Enjoy," he said, nodding to the plate. "The chefs had it specially made."

The smell of Sobek spices filled the room. Her stomach ached. She poked at the food with her fork. *Is it poisoned? Filled with something that could kill me in an instant?* She chewed the inside of her cheek. *If they wanted me dead they would've killed me already.*

The thoughts stung. She had gotten herself captured. She had been an idiot. And she could've died. She *should have* died. With an inhale of breath, she accepted as best she could this horrific fact. He had thrown her off a building. If she was supposed to be dead, she probably would be.

She pressed her fork into the meat and took the first bite.

"Do you like it?" Thaddeous inquired. She shrugged, the taste incredible. It wasn't hard to beat the cardboard-flavored noodles, but she was amazed that such flavors existed nonetheless. The crunch of the outer crust encased with a spicy heat paired perfectly with the moist, sweet meat beneath. It made her mouth water.

"It's fine," she answered, restraining her movements so she wouldn't devour the plate whole. He beamed.

"I'm glad. Well, I will leave you to it, then." He stood and moved towards the door.

"What did you do to Aris?" Jade asked. Thaddeous peered at her. Jade met his gaze. In this moment, as her body tensed, she realized there were a million other questions she should've asked. *Why am I here? How did I survive that fall? Are they going to torture me—and if so, why are they feeding me? What on Nevar is going on?*

With a hint of a pitying smile, Thaddeous replied, "I did not touch a hair on Aris' head, Corporal. As far as I know, she is safe."

Relief consumed her and Jade's shoulders relaxed as she looked down at her food. She exhaled.

"I'm going to kill you."

"It's worth the risk," he said.

She looked at him. "Why am I here?"

"Quite simply, you're here because you're a Green. And you have the potential to end the war."

"I'm not joining your cult," Jade hissed. "You're a Green, do it yourself."

He smiled. "Be ready in the morning. I'll show you around then." He turned and slipped out of the room. Jade scowled, making a fist as a wave of familiar anger suppressed her thoughts. She closed her eyes, and in an attempt to calm herself, sharpened her anger into a guidable force. The one thing she lacked right now was her strength.

Time to get it back.

Chapter 9

Private Jade Cavvar entered the Taotar base's community bathroom, the facility dark and abandoned. Long shadows stretched across the floor, her flesh vulnerable without her armor. A shiver ran down her spine. Her bare feet pressed against the moist ground and she peered down the aisle of showers.

"Hello?" Her voice echoed against the empty walls, empty floors. She turned and closed the main door, latching it shut so no one else would enter. Then, she let her towel fall to the ground.

She looked over her naked skin, her hands running along its curves as she tried to become comfortable with it once again. How easily her armor had been torn away. How easily she had been torn apart and mutilated. Her fingers found her hair and curled tightly around the strands, eyes shut. *Never again. Never again.*

She pushed her way into the first stall in the large, echoing room. She closed the door and latched it before turning the water on. It was already scalding when it burst through the pipes, the Taotar suns undoubtedly heating them. It took a few minutes to cool, and as Jade waited, steam spun around her ankles. When she could bear the heat, she stepped under the water and streams spread like fingers across her freckled body. It curled over her front and bubbled up against the upraised scar tissue that covered her back. She lifted her face and let it cover her ears and destroy her senses.

Try to forget. That's what the doctor had told her. But how could she forget? The lightning had followed the path her veins made beneath the skin and A'doxia's blade followed shortly after. And that wretched song. Jade could hear it when anyone lifted their voice to sing. It didn't matter what it was about—victory, love, death—it was all the same to her. A'doxia's voice was all Jade could hear.

A hand touched her shoulder and lips neared her ear. Someone pressed their body to the curve of her spine.

"What beautiful skin, Private," A'doxia whispered.

Jade threw herself forward, away from the hands, and spun around. Her foot slipped on the water. Her head cracked against the wall and Jade fell to the floor. She grimaced and blinked through the pain, peering at the empty space before her.

She's not here.

Jade curled into a ball, the water hitting the floor just past her feet. She wrapped her arms around her head and pressed her forehead to her knees. Tears burned at the sides of her eyes.

"What's wrong, Private?" A'doxia whispered, crouching in the water by Jade's feet. Jade looked up, her face white. A'doxia placed a hand on Jade's knee with a smile. "Here, love, let me wipe those tears from your eyes."

"You're not real," Jade said, her voice low. Then, again, with more conviction: "You're not real!"

A'doxia laughed. Jade shut her eyes and pressed her face into her knees.

"You're not real," she repeated to herself. A'doxia's hands ran down Jade's spine before they wrapped around her in an embrace. A'doxia's chin was on Jade's head.

"I'll sing you a song to calm you down," she murmured.

Chapter 10

Jade screamed, throwing herself into a sitting position as her heart pounded in her ears and behind her eyes. She wrapped her arms around herself, her back arching against the wall behind the operation table. Her flesh was slick with sweat. She took a few deep breaths and grabbed a bundle of her hair.

Breathe. Breathe, Jade. In and out. In and out. You're okay.

Her mind replayed the wretched image of A'doxia in the shower and burned her touch into Jade's flesh. She could feel A'doxia's hot breath against her neck. Jade's fingers gripped her hair tighter. In a desperate attempt to ground herself back in reality, she cast her eyes to her left. Aris' bed would've been there had Jade been back in their apartment, but instead of her friend's usual sleeping form nearby, Jade was greeted with the white walls of the medical room. Her heart rate increased. She opened her mouth to cry out, but the words died on her tongue.

Prisoner. I'm a prisoner.

She unclenched her hands and ran them over her face, taking a few steadying breaths. At least the momentary terror allowed her to focus on her surroundings, not on her memories.

Jade looked over herself, making sure she knew how she was doing. Her arms and legs felt sore, but manageable. Her armor was still clinging to her frame, which likely contributed to her restless night. She opened and closed her fist.

All right. Let's get out of here.

"Good morning, love." A soft, seductive voice sauntered through the room. Jade's head snapped up to the door to the left of her bed, where A'doxia stood. She smiled. Jade threw herself back against the wall and pulled her knees to her chest. A'doxia giggled.

"Aw, not excited to see me?" A'doxia strode to the right of the medical table. Jade launched herself off the left. Her head clipped the wall and her ears began to ring. Spots dotted her vision. A'doxia ran her gloved fingers over the sheets of Jade's bed.

"They're wet, love," she murmured. A coy smile caressed her lips. Her red gaze remained on Jade. "Thinking of me?"

"Get out," Jade whispered. A'doxia arched a brow. Swallowing, Jade tried again: "Get out!"

A'doxia put a hand to her chest, feigning offense. "How *rude*. After I came all this way to see you." A'doxia started to make her way around the bed, towards Jade. Jade scampered to her feet and pressed herself into the corner. She grabbed for something to defend herself with while keeping her eyes on the approaching Thrax. Her fingers wrapped around something small. She yanked it in front of her, holding it threateningly.

It was her plastic fork.

A'doxia stopped a few feet away and laughed. "Are you going to eat me? Or are you just being a tease?"

"G-get out," Jade stammered. "Leave me alone."

A'doxia stepped closer. "Oh, but you're so *enticing,* love. I simply can't stay away."

Jade's mind reeled, fear blistering her throat. Her hand shook as A'doxia inched closer, relishing in every moment. Jade had to do something. She had to fight back. She couldn't just wait to see what A'doxia would do, but how was she supposed to fight the woman? How could she hope to beat her after everything she'd done to Jade? A'doxia stopped less than a foot away and reached for Jade's face. Jade sucked in a sharp inhale. When she was on Taotar, she didn't even have a chance. She had a chance here. She couldn't waste it.

With a locked jaw, Jade swung for the Thrax. A'doxia stepped back and snickered, the grin on her face growing. Jade swung again, and missed. And again. And again. A'doxia's eyes were alight with glee. Terror built in Jade's throat and climbed into the back of her head. Her hands grew sweaty. Her swings grew wild.

Why aren't I hitting her? Why can't I hit her?

A'doxia swept Jade's foot out from under her. Jade collapsed to the floor hard on her back. Her teeth smashed together and her entire jaw filled with a ringing, gnashing pain. A'doxia rested her hands on her hips, smirking down at the fallen soldier.

"You know, it's a pity. You simply do not please me as much as I hoped. Maybe I need to look elsewhere for my entertainment." She tapped her lower lip, eyeing Jade. The corporal dragged herself back a few steps, trying to get her head to stop spinning—but mostly trying to flee the woman who had broken her years before.

"How about Aris?" A'doxia mused. Jade froze. "I heard she's still got some fight. I wonder if she'll cry when I cut her open."

Jade's vision darkened around the corners. Her knuckles grew white as she clutched the fork tighter. Corporal Jade Cavvar got to her feet.

"You screamed for over an hour when I had you. Do you think she'll go longer?" The room disappeared. Only A'doxia stood in the darkness. "Do you think she'll call for *you?*"

A guttural wail escaped Jade's lips as she lunged forward, her fury making her assault televised and easily blocked. A'doxia caught Jade's downward swing with the fork and grasped Jade's other wrist with her free hand. Jade seethed.

"Stop, corporal! Calm down! It's just me!" A'doxia said. Jade yanked her head back and smashed her forehead into A'doxia's. A'doxia grimaced. "Corporal, it's me! Calm down! It's just me! Thaddeous!"

Jade blinked. *What?* The room returned around her. A'doxia's image faltered as Jade staggered back. She grabbed her head and dropped the fork on the floor as she sunk to her knees. No. It had been so long since her last episode. It had been *months*. She had been free of the hallucinations for *seventeen weeks*. She gripped her hair with both hands. She stared at the floor. Her fingernails dug into her scalp and her labored breath drowned out the sounds around her. She had almost forgotten what it was like not to trust her own mind.

"Corporal?" Thaddeous knelt down in front of her, his eyes filled with concern. Jade met his gaze for a moment. The prince of her sworn enemies was taking pity on her. This man, who sat next to the king that had ordered her people to be killed, was looking at her as if she were some abandoned animal. He saw her own mind play tricks on her. He knew her mental state was frayed. And yet, he had pulled her out of her fit.

Jade's brows knitted together. No one other than Aris had been able to do that. No number of water buckets, or shakings, or gentle words had ever pulled Jade from her episodes. And yet this…this *Thrax* had? She looked at him again, her heart settling down.

How?

Light spilled into the room from the open door and framed Thaddeous' face. There was nothing special about him. Had his immense normalcy somehow calmed her? Had he somehow said the magic words, or somehow held her just right to wake her? Only Aris had been able to do this. Some enemy combatant shouldn't have the power to save her from herself, let alone the prince of them. Jade wouldn't accept it.

"Jade, what happened?" He stared at her hard, his face slowly twisting with surprise. "Jade…your eyes, they're—" He rested a hand on her knee. A'doxia sat before Jade, smiling. Adrenaline spiked into Jade's veins and she snatched the fork off the ground and stabbed it into A'doxia's hand. Blood squirted from the holes as she—no, as *he*—jerked back. Thaddeous howled in pain. Jade leapt to her feet and sped out the door.

"Jade, wait!" Thaddeous called. "You're not well! You need your rest!"

Jade threw herself down the left hallway, dashing through it as she let her gut guide her path. *I've rested long enough.* The hallways were bright, the lights by her feet vibrant. Was it morning? She would have to be prepared to run into Reds. She chewed her lip. That would be a problem. Jade looked over her shoulder, where she caught a glimpse of Thaddeous as he turned a corner. Even from her quick glance, she could see his left hand was bleeding badly. *Who knew a fork could be so dangerous.*

Her body didn't take long to react to her swift movements. A cold sweat broke out on her back and forehead. Her muscles grew stiffer with each step, sore from last night's workout. She grimaced.

Fuck.

Running off into the enemy base while not at her full strength was on the list of 'Jade's most idiotic plans,' but she hardly had an alternative. She only wished she had taken the fork with her. At least she'd have something sharp to stab people with.

"Jade, please! You must stop! I'm not going to hurt you!" Thaddeous' words chased after her. Jade pressed on, pushing past bewildered civilians. When Thaddeous called for them to stop her, they did nothing. They only watched her dash by. She focused on making sure her body wouldn't give out on her instead of thinking about why they weren't all trying to kill her and pretending Thaddeous hadn't just yanked her out of her waking nightmares. She gritted her teeth. She could ponder that when she wasn't trying to escape.

Except, of course, she wasn't the only one that needed that freedom. Chloe was somewhere hidden as well, likely stored away with the rest of Jade's belongings—wherever those were. Her breathing grew labored. All Jade needed to do was find out where Chloe was being kept. And she could think of one person that would know.

"...yes," Thaddeous said. Jade looked over her shoulder, where Thaddeous was sprinting after her and speaking into his wrist holo—a small device allowing him to make voice and visual calls. His green eyes flickered to hers. "We're headed down corridor D-45. I'm going to need your help restraining her." There was another voice that Jade couldn't make out. He scowled down at his wrist. "No, I can't. Just cut her off. That's an order."

Jade snarled and pushed herself harder, increasing her pace. She didn't know where she was going, but she would figure it out on the way. She was good at thinking on her feet. It had gotten her this far, hadn't it?

Trapped in a Thrax base without weapons, Chloe, or Aris. Yeah. Got me real far.

She shook the pessimism out of her head and spun a corner. She just had to get Thaddeous into some empty corridor and make him tell her where Chloe was. With Chloe's help, she'd be able to easily leave—

Someone stuck their arm out to clothesline her, and Jade narrowly dropped to her knees and slid under it. She staggered back to her feet and turned her gaze to the person who had attempted to stop her. Blood fled her face. Her vision narrowed and all she could see was the smirking woman with a long skirt and a bikini top. A'doxia giggled.

"Good evening, love. Running off, are we?"

"Chloe, real?"

The moment the words left her mouth, Jade stepped back. A'doxia's face filled with confusion, before understanding consumed the expression. She laughed. Sweat broke out on Jade's brow. Thaddeous turned the corner and came to a stop, gasping for breath. He glanced at the laughing A'doxia before looking to Jade. He smiled tentatively.

"I'm glad you stopped. Listen, running around the halls isn't safe. You already look pale and you're covered with sweat. We need to get you to—"

"Did you just ask if I was *real?*" A'doxia squealed, her face filled with twisted glee. "Oh, sweetheart, I really fucked you up, didn't I?"

"What?" Thaddeous' brows furrowed. "You two know each other—?"

Jade dashed farther down the hall.

"Jade! No, wait!" Thaddeous cried.

Two pairs of footsteps followed her. A'doxia's soft cackle spread into Jade's skull. *Nononono! Shit, this is bad. She knows. Now she* knows!

"Jade!" Thaddeous called. "Stop running! What's going on? How do you two know each other?"

She knows she knows she knows she...

"Oh, we were intimate at one time," A'doxia purred from behind. "Isn't that right, Private?"

Jade slammed her hands over her ears and veered down a path to her left. She didn't want to hear it. She wouldn't hear it. She would escape this hellhole and she wouldn't have to hear it.

A force clocked her side, shunting air from her lungs as she slammed to the floor. A'doxia's arms wrapped around Jade's middle. Jade's head reeled. Her vision doubled as her heart raged inside her ribs. A'doxia was on her. A'doxia's fingers touched her body. Electricity buzzed over Jade's armor, causing her hair to stand on end. A'doxia pinned her to the floor and pressed her gloved hand onto Jade's face.

"No more running, okay?" she purred. Jade stared at her. The smell of rain and cut grass clogged her airways. All she could see was A'doxia. The world around them vanished. What could she do? Fighting back would only make it worse. She had tried before, in the sand. She had tried to escape. She had resisted.

"A'doxia, that's enough! Get off her!" Thaddeous grabbed A'doxia by the shoulders and pulled her away. The moment the pressure left Jade's body, she scrambled to her feet and stepped back. She leaned against the wall to steady her head, to collect herself. She glanced to her left, where the 'T' in the hallway continued on. Her eyes moved back to Thaddeous as he gave A'doxia a firm look. He rested his eyes on Jade and his expression softened. Jade did her best to wipe the terror from her face.

"Please stop running away, Jade. There really isn't any point in it."

"Where's Chloe?" Jade said, forcing herself to keep her hands to her side instead of reaching up to feel if she had a fever. She was certain her body was much warmer than it should be, despite her chill. But she wasn't about to show weakness with A'doxia's eyes following her every move.

"Chloe?" Thaddeous arched a brow. "I don't know who that is. I didn't take anyone with me when I..." He trailed off.

"Kidnapped me. Chloe's my helmet." Jade grimaced as her head grew lighter than it should. She tried to steady her breathing. *Fuck.* She wouldn't be this out of breath had she been well. She wouldn't have been tackled, either. Without thinking, she cast an angry glare to A'doxia, who winked. Jade immediately looked away. She heard A'doxia giggle.

"Your helmet? Is that what you're after?" Thaddeous sighed and shook his head. "All this trouble… A'doxia, go fetch Jade's helmet. I'm sure the jamming signal is up by now. It's in the lower floors."

"I know where it is," A'doxia replied, her tone making it seem like she had visited Jade's things on more than one occasion. Jade shivered. "Ta-ta, love." She wiggled her fingers goodbye before striding away. The moment she left Jade's field of view, the corporal's shoulders slumped and breathing became easier. Thaddeous eyed her.

"How do you know A'doxia?"

"I don't." Jade pressed a hand to her forehead. She didn't have a fever. That was a relief.

"She said you two met," Thaddeous replied. He pressed his thumb against the wounds in his hand. "And you were…?"

Jade pushed away from the wall and rolled her shoulders. *Chloe is being fetched by a crazy woman I can't fight. I don't know where I am. I don't know how to get home.* She grimaced. *Okay. Let's start with one thing at a time.*

"Where are we?" Jade asked. Thaddeous' brows furrowed.

"I would've shown you around today if you hadn't stabbed me."

"Sure." Jade eyed him. *He's too relaxed. I could sweep his foot and smash his head into the floor in an instant. But that still leaves Chloe…I need him until she's in my hands.*

Thaddeous sighed. "I don't know why—"

"You could show me around after I get Chloe," Jade suggested.

Thaddeous peered at her, then down at his hand. He tentatively lifted his thumb to see if he was still bleeding. "Only if you promise not to try to run again. You're not in the best physical shape right now."

Jade scoffed. "I outran you."

Satisfied his hand was no longer bleeding, he returned his full attention to her. "I have no doubts about your abilities being greater than mine, Corporal Cavvar, but it's obvious that you're not well when you get covered in sweat from mild activity."

She shot him a glare and wiped her brow. To her annoyance, it was coated with perspiration.

"Maybe because someone kept me drugged up for weeks and unable to move," she growled. Thaddeous shook his head.

"I was not on—I was not here at the time. I was tending to other issues."

"So you kidnapped me then didn't even have the common courtesy to make sure I was all right?" Jade ran a hand through her knotted mess of red hair. "Appreciate it."

Thaddeous blinked, clearly taken off guard. "No!" he said. "No, I just—the travel to get here was pretty long, and I couldn't have you waking up then and trying to throw yourself off the ship, and then we needed to run some tests before we let you wake up, so I went to tend to things on the other side of the city, and from what I heard, you *kept* burning through the drugs much faster than they could test anything, so it was a constant battle to keep you under, and…" He looked uncomfortable and looked down at the floor. "By the time they had finished the tests and let me know, it had been a while since your original procurement."

Jade wrinkled her nose. *Procurement? Fuck. Fuck, what does that mean?* Her mind moved back to when her general used the word on Taotar ages ago. Her unit was ordered to fetch an item of importance and bring it back to the Opes base. *Does it mean…does it mean to get something?*

"Don't you mean 'capture?'" Jade hissed, hoping she had remembered the definition of the word properly. Thaddeous frowned. *Shit, I got it wrong, didn't I?*

"If I believed you would have gone with us willingly, I never would have employed such measures."

Oh shit! I got it right! Jade stifled a smile.

"I wouldn't have gone with you because you're a *Thrax*," Jade replied, hiding her excitement over remembering a word's definition properly. *If only Aris could see this right now…*

Thaddeous scowled. "Corporal, it is not that simple. Just because we're—"

The device around his wrist began beeping and it stole his attention. He tapped a button and answered the call he was receiving.

"Thaddeous," the woman on the other line said. Her voice was deep, rich, and filled with a hint of self-satisfaction.

"Voshell," Thaddeous grumbled in return.

Voshell? Where have I heard that name before?

"Is the Green with you?"

Thaddeous looked at Jade, who stiffened a little. "Yes, she's here."

"Can she hear me?"

The prince paused, then walked past Jade and down the hallway. Jade could hear him answer the woman, but as soon as he turned the corner, their voices died out. She stood awkwardly alone in the middle of a Thrax base with no true sense of direction. Either she should head back the way that she had come, follow after Thaddeous, or follow after A'doxia.

Or I stay here, like he probably wants me to.

She wanted to laugh at the idea, but instead, begrudgingly, she gave it more thought. *If I stay here, Chloe is going to be returned to me. If I stay here, Thaddeous isn't that far away and A'doxia doesn't seem overly keen on attacking me in front of him.* She ran her hands through her mess of tangled red hair.

"Shit," she hissed. She paced a small line back and forth. "*Shit.*"

Do I just stand here? Do I just wait? What do I do? What do I want her to see when she returns? A small part of her wanted to go find Thaddeous, to wait by him so A'doxia would leave her be. He had already seen her hallucinate and get tackled. Curling up in a ball near him as she tried to ignore the existence of an entire person surely wouldn't be much worse.

So what? I just sit and wait? Like a good little captive? She scowled. *I just have to go find her. I just have to intercept her, take Chloe from her hands, and run out of here.*

She turned around and stopped abruptly. Inches from her, wearing a smirk, was A'doxia. This close, A'doxia's slightly shorter height was evident, but Jade somehow felt like the other woman was looking down at her.

"Did he leave you all alone, love?" she purred. Jade swallowed hard. She took a step back.

Chloe. I need to get Chloe. Her eyes quickly lowered and ran over A'doxia's body. Casually tucked under the Thrax's arm was the black helmet. A'doxia stepped forward and placed her hand on the side of Jade's cheek. Rigidness threatened to consume the corporal's muscles. She could feel sand between her toes. Her scars ached.

"Are you going to ask if I'm real?" A'doxia murmured, leaning closer.

"Mistress, now!" Chloe's coded voice of mangled words and letters broke through the outer speakers. A'doxia blinked, surprised by the sound. Jade jerked her hands out, grabbed Chloe, and shoved away from the other woman with the helmet now in her possession. A'doxia stumbled back, her brows raised with shock. Jade clutched Chloe close to her body and watched A'doxia's face for a moment.

"We need to leave! Mistress, now!"

Anger rusted over A'doxia's surprise. Her crimson eyes filled with fury and she slowly met Jade's gaze. A twisted, malicious grin crossed her red lips.

"Okay," she said with a soft chuckle on her tongue. "Let's go for a round two."

"Mistress!"

The moment A'doxia lunged forward, Jade stumbled back and ran. She rushed around a corner and yanked Chloe over her head. She sprinted a few steps completely blind for a moment as the black screen inside the visor booted up. Then her vision was filled with light and a small heart rate monitor appeared on the lower right side of her sight.

"I know the path she took me down, mistress. Follow the arrows."

On cue, a small, transparent red arrow appeared on screen, pointing her towards her next turn. A'doxia's footsteps were not far behind. Jade's heart thundered in her ears.

No...wait.

She looked over her shoulder. A'doxia was reaching for her, electricity dancing on her fingers. They curled around a piece of Jade's armor.

"Chloe, shut down!"

"Mistress—"

"Now!"

Jade's screen went black. Lightning poured into her body. Her knees impacted with the floor. Splinters rushed up through her bones, mixing with the daggers that tore into her nerves. A'doxia's other hand grabbed Jade's wrist and bent it back. Jade struggled, trying to tear herself away.

"Is this real enough for you, darling?" A'doxia murmured.

A larger wave of torment consumed her. Her eyes clamped shut. She writhed, trying to fight the urge to scream. She knew that was what A'doxia was waiting for. She knew that was what A'doxia wanted. She clamped her teeth down on her tongue, blood filling her mouth. She wouldn't scream. She wouldn't scream. She wouldn't—

It was too much. Jade bent her neck back and wailed. She kicked and clawed, hoping against hope that she would somehow find an escape from A'doxia's touch. She howled for hours. For days. Her throat grew raw. Her body boiled. Consciousness began to mercifully abandon her.

And suddenly, numbness.

A'doxia screamed and let go. Jade slumped back. Her head smashed against the floor. Darkness found her and took her from reality.

Chapter 11

Aris burst into General Kasaar's office building, cracking the door as she stormed inside, hysteria clinging to her body. The receptionist, a Brown, stammered out a few meaningless attempts to get Aris to wait to be served. Aris shoved past the man at the desk and sprinted down the hall, throwing open the door. Fissures formed in its frame.

Kasaar was a kodarian, and at the opposite end of the room he looked up from his desk, the light from the massive floor-to-ceiling window silhouetting his form. He was one of the few kodarian born with small horns and tusks, traits that made him desirable by his kind. His horns each held a single piece of dangling jewelry, and his tusks looked like nothing more than enlarged lower canines. He stood as Aris dashed to his desk. She slammed her hands on his glass-covered table, creating hairline splinters. Her Charge was out of control. She didn't care.

"Jade sent a distress!" she shouted. Aris pressed the receiver on her wrist and played back the coordinates of the distress. She had already searched the area. It was out in open air. Jade had been thrown off the side of the Nevar building, but no one had reported a suicide. There were no remains anywhere, and there had been no car accidents in that area at the time of the distress. The corporal had disappeared into thin air.

Which was impossible. Jade never would've gone down without a fight, so how had she been pushed off the side without so much as spilled blood indicating her existence? She would've fought and bled before she allowed herself to get killed on her own planet.

How *had* she been attacked here, anyway? She was home—who would've dared attack a fully armored soldier? What had happened? Where was she? The only logical conclusion was that after she fell she was picked up by a waiting vehicle of some sort, meaning she had been kidnapped. If Jade fell a good distance—especially if she was spun into the air—she would've lost consciousness at some point. She would've been unable to defend herself. Still, why was she there? Why had she been near the edge of the balcony? If someone came up on her, she would've noticed them, so why had she not resisted? How had she been bested?

The general was slow to process Aris' words. He looked at her quizzically and opened his mouth to say something. Aris slammed her fist on the table again, making the fractures grow.

"Taken, General! She's been kidnapped on our own planet! I don't know who did it, I don't know why, but she's gone!"

"Calm down, Aris," Kasaar said, raising his hands and motioning as if trying to calm a wild animal. Aris snarled.

"General, with all due respect, Jade wouldn't send a distress for no reason! Something has happened! She's missing and she's not answering any of my calls!"

Kasaar considered this and scratched his leathery chin. "Where was she and who was she with?"

"She was on the upper levels with me, she went with a man—Thaddeous Malkov. She was going to meet with him while I was on a date."

"A date?" Kasaar smiled. "How did it go?"

"Poorly, General!" Aris snapped. "Considering she's missing!"

He waved her off. "I'm sure she's perfectly fine. She probably just sent the distress on accident. If she's with a man, then, well, all sorts of accidents can happen."

Aris felt something within her break. She wanted to grab him by the horns and launch him out the window. She wanted to smash his smiling face into the glass and watch him bleed. It wasn't often these violent feelings rose up in her. She always played the part of the calm one, Jade was the reckless, aggressive fool. But without her here, Aris found it difficult to control herself. With a grimace, she did her best to bite back the rage that bubbled in her chest.

"General Kasaar, I understand nothing like this has happened before but—"

"Close the door, would you, Aris?" the general asked, his gaze darkening. Aris frowned. She sensed the change in his mood more than she heard it. And as she walked back to close the door, she realized something: Thaddeous' eyes were blue.

He was one of them. One of us.

Aris closed the damaged door. She took a breath and calmed the growing rage inside her. She turned on her heel and strode back to the general, who now gazed out the window at the cityscape that expanded behind it.

Her eyes found their way up to the decapitated head of a victer in the small space between the window and the ceiling. Once upon a time, she and Jade had fought one of the barbaric beasts. All of them were half-mad, but the most intelligent of the species usually worked as guns for hire. When Jade helped Aris take one down that was hired to kill Aris' family, the beast split open the chest piece Jade was wearing with its bare hands. And its beak tore off Aris' mother's hand as if it were plucking a flower.

Seeing the hooked beak gleam menacingly from above was supposed to intimidate her, she supposed. She figured the general would appear strong for having taken down such a beast. Aris' eyes settled on the back of the general's head. Did he already know of Jade's disappearance? Was he the one who had ordered it?

Would she have to kill him?

She had thrown a man out a window before. She had watched him scream on his way down. The general was no simple civilian, but she was sure she could do it. The window was big enough. She stopped in front of his desk.

Would Jade do that for me? Aris pushed the thought away.

"Did you ever notice?" he asked without turning towards her.

"Sir?" Aris replied, calm, collected.

"I suspect it is the type of thing you notice after a while. Unless she never took off that helmet around you?"

Aris didn't reply. She narrowed her eyes at the back of his head. And, when he turned around to face her, her face seamlessly shifted to confusion.

Oh, what ever could you be talking about, General? I do wonder.

"But that would strike you as odd, too, wouldn't it?" Kasaar smiled. "You are quite bright, after all." He linked his hands behind his back. "But as bright as you are, you've never gotten nearly the amount of attention she has, isn't that right?"

Aris shrugged. "All I did was help, sir." He was trying to hit a nerve. He succeeded, but Aris wouldn't let him know that.

He waved her formality out of the air. "You seem rather calm all of a sudden. Have I upset you?"

"Not at all, sir. I only realized how rude I was being a moment ago." She dipped her head respectfully before looking him in the eyes again. "My apologies."

His small, blue eyes watched her, revealing nothing. But—*there!* The look in his eyes shifted. He was going to ask her.

"Did you know she was a Green, Private Sell?"

Aris had to suppress a smile. *Knew it.*

"I did, sir. I discovered it a few months ago when I came home earlier than she expected. I assured her that I would not tell a soul."

"Private—"

"Forgive me for interrupting, sir, but I did it in the best interest of the Exuro. I figured keeping her happy while I gathered information about how she functioned would be useful to us." The general blinked, surprise washing over his features. Aris pressed on: "I have learned a great deal, sir, and was hoping to get her away for enough time that I might come report my findings. But you see, she checks up on me often, and I would not want her to grow suspicious of what I was doing. As you may now understand, this is why I was so frantic when I discovered she had gone missing."

Kasaar considered this. "If that's true, Private, you kept important information from us for quite a long time. This is cause enough to be considered traitorous to the Opes and the Exuro."

"I understand, sir. I will accept whatever punishment, but please let me help find her. I know how she thinks, and she knows me. She'd be leaving hints for me to find wherever she could."

Kasaar's eyes narrowed into slits. "You wish to help find her?" Suspicion was laced into every syllable. Aris was unaffected by his concern.

"I will report every step and every finding directly to you, sir. I can understand if you do not trust me. After all, I'm sure I convinced you I was her best friend." She flashed him a smile, and he looked uneasy. "But that was the goal. If everyone else believed it, she would, too."

"You are a skilled actress, Private Sell." The general regarded her with respect. "I am proud of your dedication. Therefore, I shall go easy on you: you are grounded to Nevar for the time being. Understood, Private?"

Aris saluted him. "Sir, you are most generous."

He waved her off. "Go. I will give you access to everything you need as you search for her—*it*." He frowned as if tasting something bad. "I want a report every day, Private."

Aris nodded. "Understood, sir."

"Dismissed."

What a fool.

Chapter 12

Aris was certain Jade was no longer on Nevar. After a thorough search through what few cameras were set up around the massive city, along with looking through records of any accidents or reported deaths, it was unlikely Jade was somehow still on the planet. She would've woken and made some noise. Not to mention the general grounded Aris, increasing the odds of Jade being off-planet. Thaddeous was a Blue, and he was the last person Aris saw with Jade. Meaning somehow, the Blues, her people, had a hand in Jade's disappearance. Keeping Aris from leaving would be the best way to hide their tracks.

Still, that didn't explain why Kasaar was allowing her to search for Jade in the first place. It was a thought that constantly plagued Aris, despite her attempts to ignore it. She had found no solution to such an inquiry, and only had her gut to guide her. And her gut told her Jade wasn't on Nevar.

Upon request, she received shipping manifests and outbound ship logs. She reviewed them on a computer in the library, hidden away in a private, closed room. She scanned the documents, discovering that at least twenty ships had departed shortly following Jade's distress. Aris chewed on her fingernails. This was something akin to a lead, but it wasn't enough. The ships sailed to different planets, all of which would be impossible to escape to and search without the notice of her general.

The private leaned back in her chair, stretching out her tense muscles, a yawn slipping past her lips. She had hardly slept in the week Jade had been gone, and showering was out of the question. All of Jade's things were there, and Aris couldn't stand the sight of them. She stood and paced around the small, enclosed room.

So, what did she have, exactly? She had enough money to buy her way to another planet, but not enough to return. And if she bought a ticket, she wouldn't be able to buy food. She'd need to barter. She had a few of Jade's things, gadgets Jade was working on before she left. None of her armor would fit, but she could take one of Jade's prototype blades and bring Spidey along. Spidey would be invaluable in hacking, and the weapon, well…Jade never could figure out how to make an H-blade. As the generator was incorrectly wired to the blade, Aris was better off considering it a bomb. She chewed the tip of her finger.

Aris also had three different planet names of potential places Jade could be. Aris had already searched Nevar as thoroughly as possible and, with the Opes forces backing her, she was certain Jade was not here. She had to be on either Ferges, Daoth, or Sypher. Ferges was the home of the victer, and a rather neutral planet—if the home of barbarian cultists could be called that. Daoth was Jade's home planet, a place Aris doubted Jade's captors would risk taking her to. And Sypher was the powerhouse of the war. It supplied weapons and armor to the highest bidder, regardless of who they were fighting for. It was home to the sypher people, with their many limbs and small bodies, all scampering around and plotting how to swindle some passing fool. Sypher would be a likely place for a Green to be hidden on, as with enough bribe money, no one would spill the secret of her existence. The kidnappers would also have access to the best equipment around—be that for torturous means, or otherwise.

Teeth tore through Aris' flesh and she grimaced, yanking her thumb away from her mouth. A spot of blood bubbled up from the puncture, and Aris let out an agitated hiss.

But why would the Blues take one of their strongest and recently celebrated soldiers away from the frontlines? Jade was the daughter of a war hero, and her disappearance could only be hidden for so long. Eventually Jennifer, Jade's mother, and other loyal companions would start to ask questions. Why risk it? Even if she was a Green, why not keep her on the field of war? Greens were commonly regarded as demons, but if the Opes were so concerned about Jade's potential demonic nature, why not let her die in the war?

The only thing she knew about Greens was common knowledge: eventually, Greens snapped. They would turn on their own people and kill their loved ones. But why not send her out on a suicide mission? Jade's arrogance and aggression had faded over the years, but she would still surely accept such a task. And she would get killed, without the Opes having to dirty their hands. They were at war. People died.

Aris' blue eyes flickered to the door. Perhaps the general's computer had some answers. And perhaps that would be enough of a clue to solidify a lead. It would certainly be risky, and she would have to scope out the office building frequently while still keeping up the appearance of her desperate search for Jade. She gnawed on the tip of her thumb.

I'd better get started.

Chapter 13

The screams of those long dead echoed in Jade's Dark Place, coming to keep her company in the solitude of her mind. In the form of a child, she sat curled up in the darkness, her small arms wrapped around her knees. She listened to everyone scream, cry, ask why Jade hadn't done more. Jade pressed her face into her knees and shut her eyes.

"Why didn't you save me?" said Jason, the new recruit who had been cut in two on Sobek.

"Why did you put her life above mine?" asked Ryne, a fifteen-year-old girl who had suffocated in the Air Void.

"Why did you let go?" accused General Tyrn, who died because of Jade's fear.

"Why did you leave?"

Jade lifted her eyes to find Salene standing before her. Jade's face fell.

"I didn't leave," Jade muttered, reaching for Salene's hand. "I never left."

"You never visit me." Salene pulled her hand away, her blue eyes full of hurt. "Why don't you ever visit me?"

Jade looked up at her friend and in an instant they were on Sobek, trees rising up around them and grass covering every part of the floating island. They were by a river, the rushing waters spreading out wide. Moss and water made the nearby rocks slick. Salene stood atop one. Jade buried her face in her knees, shut her eyes, and covered her ears. *No. I won't remember. I won't remember.*

"Why didn't you save her?" A'doxia's voice sang through her defenses and chilled Jade to the bone. She curled tighter into herself and the wind chimes of laughter danced in Jade's Dark Place. A'doxia wrapped Jade in a hug from behind.

"It's your fault she fell, isn't it? If you had just stuck to the plan, she would've never broken her back."

"I…I was just doing what I thought was right," Jade murmured into her flesh. "I was just trying to keep everyone alive."

"And look where that got you, hm?" A'doxia giggled. "You can't even go visit her. Because you know it's your fault, don't you? You know that if you had just listened, if you hadn't been reckless, the Mad Queen's plan never would've—"

Someone was shaking her awake, pulling her from her sleep. If it could be called sleep. Her eyes cracked open and she shoved the hands away, growling her protest.

"Corporal Jade," Thaddeous whispered. "Wake up, I have something to show you."

Jade scowled and sat up, the bed beneath her shaking. She wrapped her fingers around the edge, finding rope instead of a mattress.

A hammock? Why am I on a hammock?

"Come, Corporal." Thaddeous took her hand. "Before they're gone." He pulled her out of bed, Jade stumbling as her body jolted awake. Confusion swam through her as he pulled her from the unfamiliar room and up a set of stairs. *What happened? Why am I here?* Her mind grabbed hold of a single, horrifying memory: A'doxia's touch. Her face paled. A'doxia got her. A'doxia touched her. *Where am I?*

"Let go of—" Jade started, yanking her hand from Thaddeous' grasp as they stepped onto a ship's main deck. Stars glistened around them as their sails caught the wind and carried them through the expanse. The deck had only a handful of crewmembers out, with several glancing to the port side of the ship. Jade's eyes settled on the lights just past the railing on her left. She froze.

The wind stream that pushed against the ship's sails carried them past a series of floating Air Islands, where trees grew atop small sections of land. Their thick limbs branched out into space, their leaves rustling from the passing wind, and their roots protruded out from underneath the isles and wound around themselves. The Dark Lights were the lanterns hung on the trees' branches, flickering with black fire and dancing within their glass cages. Jade found herself at a railing, leaning over the edge as she watched the islands rush past, the lanterns swaying in the breeze. Momentarily, she had nothing to be afraid of. Momentarily, she was wrapped up in the beauty before her.

"Stunning, aren't they?" Thaddeous asked as he strode up next to her. She glanced his direction, a brow arched. *Biggest understatement of the year.* He smiled at her and they both turned back to the islands. Only the lanterns were gone. The swirl of distant galaxies spread across the backdrop of space, no longer concealed by the lights. Jade frowned. She knew Dark Lights appeared and disappeared quickly, but was it truly only a matter of looking away?

"Tricky little things, huh?" Thaddeous mused, a soft chuckle rolling from his lips. "I had a few of the crew watch them while I fetched you, but they must have fallen asleep." He rested his arms against the railing. Jade stared at the darkness where the lights once were, leaving the Air Islands and their trees unadorned.

"The Thrax have a saying, you know," Thaddeous continued, Jade's silence apparently encouraging him to speak again. "That the Dark Lights only appear to those with dark futures."

Jade looked across the ship. She had seen the Dark Lights once before, when she was serving as part of a team to reinforce the soldiers on Sobek. Those trees held the lights by their roots, however. Perhaps she should've seen that as a sign. She rubbed her eyes.

"Where am I?" *Wait.* Her hands ran over her face again. *Where's Chloe?*

"We're on our way to Hallow—"

Jade grabbed the jacket of his tux and yanked him towards her, her eyes aflame and her jaw set.

"Where's my helmet?"

Thaddeous arched a brow. "It's in safe hands, Corporal. Don't worry."

"I'm going to ask again," Jade said, each word slow and deliberate. "Think about what your answer is this time, or we'll see how long a human body holds up in the Stream before it gets torn apart." She pushed him towards the railing. Thaddeous' face grew grave. Various Streams filled the Known Galaxy and allowed for quick travel between worlds, but its winds were deadly without a ship's shields. "Where is my helmet?"

"I shall have it returned to your bunk by morning."

"Not good enough." She pushed him farther, his body arching over the railing and the wind snapping at his hair. Someone placed a hand on her shoulder. Jade ignored it. "I want her back *now*."

Thaddeous' eyes narrowed. He stared her down for a few moments then spread out his arms. "As you wish, Corporal. You," he said, referring to someone behind her, "return Jade's helmet."

The hand on Jade's shoulder lifted. Jade released Thaddeous, leaving him to scramble to regain his balance to keep from falling off the ship. She rolled her shoulders back and a kodarian returned with Chloe in hand. Jade's eyes shot a glare at Thaddeous as she snatched Chloe back.

"What were you doing to her?"

"Since we are leaving the range of the previous signal that scrambled all Exuro communications, we needed to ensure the mobile signal worked."

Jade tucked Chloe under her arm. Her eyes scanned the crew of the small ship, all of whom had stopped what they were doing to watch them. There were about seven in total, not including Thaddeous. Poor odds. Not to mention she hadn't flown a ship alone before. Attempting to kill them all would leave her to figure that out by herself, and while she was certain Chloe could help, she wasn't so sure about how to get home. And whatever injuries she sustained from murdering all of them would be problematic to deal with. Her eyes settled on Thaddeous.

"You said you want to keep me alive, right?" she asked.

"Mistress, what are you doing?" Chloe asked, her coded words spilling from her external speakers.

Thaddeous peered at Jade, smoothing out his jacket. "Of course, Corporal. We did not bring you here to harm you."

"Then why did a Red try to assassinate me the day we met?"

He stopped and stared. Jade arched a brow and waited, her eyes never leaving his face. He looked away.

"Alas, that was out of my control. I am pleased you—"

"How did a Red even get on my planet? How did *you* get on my planet? She's a Red and you're a *Green*. My people would've killed you the instant you stepped foot near them."

"Mistress, his eyes were originally blue."

"That's right," Jade hissed. "Your eyes were blue before. How did you do that?"

Thaddeous sighed and raised his hands in defeat. "Please, allow me to clarify some things for you. My sister, Voshell, was the one who sent the assassin. Her name was Hisa, and she was with the group that followed me to Nevar."

"You had a *group?*" Jade seethed. How had this happened? How did Reds stroll onto Exuro's capital planet?

"I did not think it possible for me to capture you alone, Corporal," Thaddeous explained. "And I was correct—had I been alone, it is likely you would've either been killed or killed me."

"A vehicle caught you during your fall, mistress. He is telling the truth."

This didn't soothe Jade's nerves. She had almost died on her own planet. Her hands curled into fists.

"Hisa was the third member in my group, but I was unaware she had orders from my sister to kill you."

Jade's eyes narrowed. "She had lightning. Why did you bring a lightning user with you?"

Thaddeous blinked and watched her quizzically. "I…I had no reason, Corporal. She was someone who I trusted and…?"

"It is unlikely that Thaddeous knows of your past with A'doxia, mistress. Voshell may be the culprit here."

Wonderful. More mentally unstable women to torment me. With a tense inhale, Jade nodded for him to continue. Still clearly confused, Thaddeous proceeded.

"As to how the four of us got onto your planet, that is simple: there is a—"

"Your Majesty," interrupted someone to Jade's right. Jade glanced at the woman who shifted uncomfortably. "Is this…I trust the Green, but…" Her eyes fell to Chloe.

"You got a problem, asshole?" Jade said.

"Corporal, please," Thaddeous said, frowning at her. He turned to the woman. "It will be all right, Haldis. You are right to trust the Green, and her helmet is currently unable to relay any information to our enemies. Please, be at ease."

Jade frowned. *Trust the Green? Why would they trust me?* Scampering bugs crowded her nerves. She didn't like this.

Seemingly calmed, Haldis nodded and stepped away. Thaddeous addressed Jade once more.

"The Thrax have developed an experimental eye droplet to change the color of one's eyes temporarily."

The corporal stepped back, surprise quieting the bugs inside her. "What?"

She had tried everything—*everything* to get her eyes to change color. The droplets she found in the undercity were thick and she stood in the bathroom of some seedy store a mile from the surface of Nevar. The instant the liquid hit her eye, it felt as if she had stuck a hot rod into it. She let the droplet fall to the ground and gripped the sink as waves of agony rushed through her, flushing her face. She managed to peer into the mirror. Her eye was blue. But the pain and the color lasted only an hour.

And now, with something as long-lasting as these Thrax had, they could infiltrate the Exuro Empire. They could kill Opes on the field of war, they could hide as spies, they could—

Wait.

"What color are your eyes?"

"I am a Green, Corporal. I may not be a true Green, gifted with the ability you no doubt possess, but I do have the eyes." He gestured to her. "They were aided by the droplets, but as you know, Greens are able to change their eye colors naturally."

"That's ridiculous. I can't change my eye color," Jade shot back.

Thaddeous arched a brow. "You don't know?"

"Mistress…"

"Know *what?*" Jade hissed, her nerves prickling. "What are you saying? You think that on top of being a Green I'm…*disloyal* to being a Green?"

Thaddeous looked unsure of what to say. Jade's tension rose to her shoulders.

"That's not possible—that's simply *not possible.*" She stepped back, shaking her head, laughing. "You can't change your eye color. You can't. You *can't*, Thaddeous."

"It's—it's not a disloyal thing," he stammered. "It's like—like self-defense! The records say—"

"Self-defense?" Jade spat out the word as if it were poison. She grabbed Chloe from her hip and held the helmet at eye-level, scowling. "When has it happened, Chloe? Why didn't you tell me?"

"Times of stress, mistress, when it was unwise to tell you such a thing."

"And you never thought to tell me outside of those times of so-called stress? Are you fucking *kidding* me?"

"I...wished to protect you, mistress." Chloe's voice was small. Jade locked her jaw, agitation and fear mixing into a volatile concoction. Even when Blues retired and their eyes turned hazel, it was seen in a negative light. They were no longer loyal to what once mattered to them; they weren't loyal to themselves.

But what did that mean for a Green? A monster created by Ghawor to destroy all of Vix's creations? Did it mean she didn't want to be a Green? That she could somehow escape this fate? Or was it simply because, at the heart of all things, she was just as traitorous as all the stories said? Jade ran a shaky hand through her long, tangled hair. She never wanted to be this—to be a demon. But being a traitor to her own eye color was worse. She wasn't loyal to anyone, not even herself.

She looked at Thaddeous. "Did you see them change?"

Thaddeous didn't meet her gaze. "Once."

"Mistress, your eyes have been blue before," Chloe said, her voice rushed, as if hoping to cut off Jade's next question. Jade ignored her.

"What color?"

"Mistress, they've been blue."

"What color, Thaddeous?" Jade pushed. Thaddeous exhaled slowly.

"Red."

Jade could feel herself closing off, running somewhere deep into her mind where she could hide. She already saw herself locking away this information, doing her best to forget it existed. She couldn't handle this. Not while she was on a Thrax ship. Not when she needed to get home. Not when Aris was waiting for her.

She would forget. She had to forget.

Jade walked away. Thaddeous did not try to stop her.

Chapter 14

"Aris?" Jade called up to the crow's nest, the breeze spinning her red hair in front of her goggles. The galleon was set for Sobek and Aris was tasked with spotting any issues in their path. She momentarily shirked her duties and glanced down at Jade, distaste etching lines into her face.

"What *are* you wearing?" she huffed. Jade grinned.

"Heavy armor suits me, I think." She knocked her knuckles against the large, metal armor which wrapped around her body and created an air-tight seal—save for where it opened up around her neck, awaiting a helmet.

"You look like a moose," Aris grumbled.

"Like you've seen a moose," Jade shot back.

"I saw one in a children's book once," Aris replied with a sneer. She crossed her arms over the nest's railing. "What do you want, anyway?"

Jade held up a breathing helmet, capable of suctioning against the wearer's neck to create a seal.

"Brought you something," Jade said.

"You do realize we're not stopping to take a picnic in the Air Void, right? We're flying right through. The captain says we won't even notice it."

Jade made a face. "So what? Better safe than sorry, right?"

Aris rubbed her eyes. "Is this about those lanterns? Look, I know they were different but—"

"Private!" boomed General Tyrn, startling Jade into attention. The snipper strode up to Jade, her gaze cold. "Are you pestering our lookout *again?*" Standing before her, Jade was reminded of how oddly large Tyrn was for a snipper. Not only was her size intimidating, but her ability to wield a weapon in each of her four hands made her unstoppable on the field of war. Jade tried not to shrink away.

Tyrn grabbed Jade's face with one hand, the rest of her arms behind her back. She moved Jade's jaw left to right as her mandibles clicked, her eyes scrutinizing.

"You're not injured, Private. So what is it? Are you just that terribly dim to not realize you were given direct orders?"

The grip was tight, familiar. Jade grimaced as A'doxia flickered into view where Tyrn should be. A cold shiver ran down her spine and she bit the inside of her cheek. *She's not there. She's not there.*

"Well, Private?" A'doxia purred. She moved closer, grip still on Jade's chin. "Anything you want to say?"

"Just worried about the Air Void," Jade hissed between her teeth. *She's not real. She's not real.*

"Give me some respect, Private."

"Just worried about the Air Void," Jade repeated, her jaw tightening. "Ma'am." *You're talking to your general, not A'doxia. That's who's in front of you.*

A'doxia laughed. "Oh, sweetheart. Don't you trust your fellow comrades?" She released Jade's jaw. "Scurry off then, love. I have business with Aris, anyway."

It's General Tyrn, not A'doxia. It's General Tyrn, Jade. It's your general. Aris will be fine. Turn around and leave. Jade turned on her heel. *Now leave, Jade. Walk forward. Leave.* Jade couldn't. Her feet were planted. She couldn't leave Aris alone with A'doxia.

No, that's not A'doxia, Jade. That's Tyrn! Now move!

When Jade was alone with A'doxia she was tortured for hours. Would the same happen to Aris?

"What are you doing dawdling, love?" A hand touched Jade's back. Her vision narrowed, black fog filling in her peripheral. Her body grew rigid for a moment, then loose as her fists rose. She spun on A'doxia.

"What's the matter, hm?" A'doxia crooned. "You're not really going to fight me, are you?"

Jade lunged as Aris screamed something from above. Jade's fist smashed into the side of A'doxia's face, blood pumping in her knuckles and thunder in her ears. She swung again but A'doxia struck first, her knee smashing against Jade's armored body with enough strength to form a dent. Needles dug into Jade's lungs. Spit flew from her mouth and splattered against A'doxia's leg. Jade used her hand to keep herself from falling to the ground. Coughs tore at her throat.

"Oh, is that all?" whispered A'doxia, an audible smile in her voice. She leaned down and caressed the side of Jade's face. "Well, if that's all you're going to do, might we get started? I have a new song I've been wanting to sing you."

A yell spilled from Jade's throat as she spun, eyes wild beneath her goggles, and threw herself against A'doxia, hurling them both to the ground. Jade struggled to stay atop the woman who slammed Jade's stomach with punches. Jade raised her fist, ready to rid the world of A'doxia's wicked grin.

An explosion shattered the side of the ship, throwing her to the opposite railing. All the breath in her lungs abandoned her and another blast hit somewhere below deck. The galleon rocked and was shoved out of the Air Stream and forced to float with its momentum directly towards the Air Void. Another blow broke the mainmast in two, sending it toppling over and crashing into the deck before its weight forced it overboard. Jade scrambled to her feet as the ship slowed, the air growing colder from the approaching Void. Helmets. Everyone needed helmets.

She dashed towards where her scuffle with Tyrn had been, her ribs aching as she looked for the helmet. Aris was there, having climbed down from the crow's nest, and was scrambling to tear off the light, basic armor that had no ability to keep her flesh and organs safe without air pressure. The rye-mail and armored plates attached by leather bands fell to the floor within seconds and the instant she was free she sprinted to the middle of the main deck, where a small cubby was hidden beneath hinged floor panels. She yanked it open, seven skin-tight suits inside that would protect her from the lack of air. As she pulled one blue suit out, Jade found the helmet wedged between railing beams. She tore it out and rushed for Aris, who had her feet in the suit just as the ship shook from another blow somewhere below deck.

And then they were in it. The Air Void. Aris pulled the suit over her body and it sealed, but without a helmet it was useless. Every troop floated upwards without gravity, and Jade managed to throw herself through the air and hand Aris the helmet. Her momentum kept her flying towards the stairs to the lower deck where the new recruit, Ryne, was dashing up the stairs. She wore one of the suits, one that any helmet was able to seal with. But over her head was Chloe. Chloe accepted no one else besides Jade. And because of that, Ryne's suit wasn't sealed. Jade rammed into Ryne, her body allowing Jade's to slow. Jade yanked Chloe from Ryne's cranium, tore off her goggles, and donned the black helmet, not yet painted with a red skull. It sealed with her armor immediately and pumped oxygen into Jade's lungs. Ryne's young blue eyes stared at Jade in horror, grasping for the helmet. Jade grabbed Ryne's hand.

"Chloe, you will accept Ryne as co-owner. You will provide her with oxygen."

"Negative."

"Chloe!"

Their momentum pulled the two of them to the edge of the ship and Jade grabbed the railing, keeping them from flying into open space. Ryne grew limp.

"Chloe, please!" Jade pleaded. Ryne was no older than sixteen. She had a life to live.

"Cannot provide oxygen to the dead," Chloe replied coldly, voice without inflection. Jade looked at the young girl. Bubbles formed in the child's skin. Jade's heart sank.

"I'm so sorry."

And Jade let her go.

Chapter 15

It took Jade a few minutes to realize she was screaming. Her voice echoed off the walls of the Thrax engine room. A cold sweat covered her body and she tore Chloe from her head and proceeded to try to wrench her sweatshirt from her body. When she couldn't manage to take it off with shaking hands, she grabbed at her ears, a low ringing consuming her mind.

"It was only a nightmare, mistress! It was only a nightmare." Chloe's voice was supposed to calm her down. Jade tore at her hair. Everyone had died. The images of floating bodies hung in her mind, condemning her. *Everyone died.* No one got to burn their dead. No one lifted their bodies up to Vix. Not even little Ryne's family. Had they even gotten closure? Had they even moved on?

Jade shut her eyes. Her nerves were on fire. She should've done more. Her jaw clenched. The flesh of her cheek burst blood onto her tongue. She should've tried harder. Had the bodies even been recovered? Had anyone even seen what happened? Surely, someone had. They had to have checked the wreckage. Right? *Right?* Jade curled into herself, the hammock beneath her swaying. The smell of desperation clung to her. When had she last showered? Did it even matter? Did *she* even matter, after everything she had done? Everything she had seen? Her fingers brushed the scabbed surface of her scalp, where wires had once been jammed into her skull.

"Mistress, please, breathe! Please! Calm down, mistress!"

Calm down? Jade opened her eyes, her heart still pounding her ribs with a hammer. She could feel them cracking, splintering from the force. Blood spilled into her lungs. She was going to drown in the lost lives of everyone she had doomed. Ryne, Tyrn, Salene. Countless more. Everyone else. Her chest constricted, refusing to fill with oxygen. Everyone. She was going to end up killing everyone. The pastors were right. Greens were a blight. She was *already* a blight. She hadn't even snapped yet—or had she? Had she undergone the 'snap' which signified the lost sanity of a Green? Where the Green went about and killed everyone they were supposed to be loyal to? Her eyes already changed colors, so no doubt she was already disloyal. No wonder everyone was so afraid of Greens. No wonder. *No wonder.*

A slam came from her left, but she didn't bother to open her eyes. She tried for breath but couldn't find any. Her body panicked, demanding she try again and again. She couldn't breathe. She really was suffocating.

Hands grabbed her shoulders and pushed her head against a chest. Her hands were torn from her ears and her eyes flew open, startled. She could hear the pounding of someone's heart. The low, quick thud. The smell of vanilla swallowed her whole. Filled her senses, spilled into her chest cavity. It provided support for her breaking ribs, it stole away the blood drowning her. Her mind wavered at the edge before it, too, was tugged from the cliff and brought back to sanity. The rope of the hammock beneath her dug into her flesh. She balanced precariously on it, most of her weight against whoever held her close.

"Breathe, Jade. Deep breaths. Okay? Breathe with me. In—one, two, three—out—one, two, three. Okay? Do it with me." Thaddeous' voice was calm and caring. Jade's eyes flickered as she did as he instructed. Her heart calmed. Her breathing slowly returned to normal.

"Good," he said. With gentle movements, he pushed her away and she sat upright on the hammock, looking at him. He kneeled down next to her, his brows pulled upwards over his green eyes. His smile was empathetic. "You'll be okay now."

Jade curled her hand against her chest, peering at him. "How did you do that?"

"I've had practice. Did something happen?"

Jade opened her mouth, wanting to explain her thoughts to him as if he were her friend. She clamped her mouth shut and looked into her lap. She was supposed to hate him. Supposed to want him dead. She curled her hands into fists. She could probably do it. She could probably smash his head into the ground. She'd be a hero.

Until someone saw her eyes.

"What…what do your people think of Greens?" Jade murmured.

"They're angels," Thaddeous said. He sat down and crossed his legs before looking up at her again. "They're seen as beings meant to save people."

Jade spat out a laugh. *Save people. Yeah, right.* "That sounds like wishful thinking."

Thaddeous frowned. "I am not a religious man, Jade. But my people are desperate, and even those who aren't religious are putting their faith in you."

Jade's brows furrowed. "What?"

"How many of us do you think there are?"

Jade tilted her head, her hair falling around her face. Chloe spoke up from her spot on the floor.

"What an odd question, mistress."

"I don't know. How would I ever be able to guess that?"

"There's less than a million of us. We're dying, Jade. We're not going to survive the war."

Jade blinked. Why was he telling her this? They were enemies, they were—

Her eyes settled on his. Her bewilderment faltered. They were the same. They were Green. He trusted her because they were the same.

"You…you're doing well on the battlefield," Jade stammered. "How are you so low in numbers?"

Thaddeous shook his head. "Because we don't have a planet, Jade. We don't have a home."

"But our scouts—we were told—"

"Two moons, medium size, right?" He chuckled. "A diversion. While your people went searching for our home, we were able to focus all our efforts in winning the war." He exhaled, the sound sad. "But we won't. We'll have to surrender before that happens."

"Then why don't you?" Jade pressed. "Why don't you surrender?"

"We've tried to come to an agreement, but each time a representative is sent, they don't return." His eyes met hers. For once, the calm, caring expression was replaced with rage. Jade scowled.

"So have we. We got word that they were ambushed."

"Why would we kill when we're already dying, Jade?"

"I don't know!" Jade threw one hand in the air. "How am I supposed to know? I don't even know if what you're telling me is the truth! I don't even know why the fuck I'm here! I don't even know what it means to be a Green! How am I supposed to know what you're doing and why you're doing it?"

Thaddeous held her gaze for a moment while she let her hand drop back into her lap. He smiled.

"I guess you'll just have to trust me."

Jade recoiled at the suggestion. But he was right. If she believed him in this, she'd be trusting his word. She'd be trusting *him*. She cast her gaze away. He'd had plenty of chances to kill her when she was out cold. He could've let her die when she fell off the building on Nevar, he could've killed her while she was sleeping, he could've let her have her panic attack and could've waited for her to pass out before slitting her throat. And even if she wasn't wanted dead, as he frequently insisted, he could've kept her as a hostage, as someone who was unable to leave the confines of her cell. They could've tried to break her, turn her against her own people.

But they didn't. *He* didn't. She was here, in a hammock, breathing normally because he helped calm her down. She gritted her teeth. How was she supposed to do this? How was she supposed to trust a Thrax?

She looked at him. Maybe she couldn't trust a Thrax. But she could trust a fellow Green.

"So," she muttered. "How exactly are two Greens alive at one time?"

Thaddeous' smile grew wide. "It is rather curious, isn't it? That you and I are both living, when everything I've read says that such a thing isn't possible. Perhaps it's some kind of omen? Perhaps it has something to do with the fact that, while you're a true Green, I am not?"

"What does that even mean?"

"I imagine you're aware of your own...Helix limitations," he said.

Jade nodded. "I don't have one."

"Mistress."

The instant the words left her mouth, the blood drained from her face. It was the first time she had ever admitted to not having a Vix-given power out loud. Aris knew, but Jade never said those words to her. Aris just figured it out. Her parents knew, but they gave birth to her. They saw her grow up without any powers. Jade tried to run a hand through her hair, but her fingers got caught in tangles. She was admitting something grave to Thaddeous, but he smiled with understanding.

"I know. I, however, do. I have Charge."

Just like Aris.

"Then what do green eyes mean? I always thought it had something to do with not having a Helix," Jade said.

"Who knows?" Thaddeous shrugged. "I need to do a lot more research on that to be able to give you any kind of answer. And with us being alive at the same time, I'm not sure I'll really get too much data. I need more than one subject, and since one Green is alive at a time, usually, it'll only work if you di—" His face fell. "I mean—I'm saying because, you know—"

"I'll die in war," Jade said. She looked at the red skull on Chloe's frame. "You'll probably meet another Green sooner or later."

Silence spread between them. Thaddeous broke it.

"Is that what you dreamt about?"

Jade shook her head. "Just had some nightmares."

"I get them, too." Thaddeous flashed a heavy smile. "I used to have two older brothers."

Jade frowned. "Had?"

Thaddeous' gaze grew distant. He looked at his palms. "One day, an assassin came into our home. No one knows how he got past security. He found us all bunked in the same room. We were close, all of us brothers. We often slept together. Adrian was the second oldest, Lionel was the third, I was the fourth. My sister was first." His tone grew sour. He snarled at the floor.

"Voshell had the audacity to claim that the whole thing was planned, that it was all meant as an attack against her. She told me that our very father let the victer in, that he was trying to kill her, that—she wasn't even there! She wasn't even—!" He cut himself off and took a deep breath. "We were all playing a game when the victer came in through the door. I had heard stories of them, you know. Barbaric beasts, blood sacrifices, rituals to their gods. Most of them couldn't even speak the common language." He shrugged. "That's what I heard, at least.

"But when that avian beast opened the door, he could speak. He could speak *well*. Sometimes I can still hear him talking to us, telling us we're all going to be torn apart and sacrificed, limb-by-limb, to his god. My brothers jumped to defend me and cried out for our father when they were..." He closed his eyes. "With his talons, he just..." He tried to steady himself with an unsteady inhale.

"I hid under the bed. My father and a series of guards shot him when they finally came. I watched his body slump over Lionel's intestines." He glanced up at Jade, then back at his hands. "I slept under the bed for days, terrified he might return. My sister lost her mind. She screamed at my father, blamed him for everything. She tried to kill him one night, and was sent to an institution. They say she's better now, but..." He shook his head. "I don't know."

They were silent. Jade listened to her own breathing for a few minutes, unable to find words to say. Chloe helped her:

"That's terrible."

"That's…that's terrible," Jade said. "I'm sorry. What color eyes did he have?"

Thaddeous chuckled and shrugged his shoulders. "I have no idea. But does it really matter? He killed my brothers. And I didn't do anything."

"You were a child," Jade said. "What could you have done?"

"I don't know. I won't ever know."

Jade rubbed the inside of her hand with her thumb. Her eyes fell on her bare feet, and she curled her toes.

"Thaddeous…where are we going?"

"Oh." Thaddeous looked up at her. "I'm sorry, I thought I told you. We're headed to Hallow."

"Hallow?" Jade blinked. *The ice planet? The planet completely dominated by Thrax troops, forced to be loyal?* She peered at him. "Why?"

"I heard the rumors on Nevar while I was there. Your people believe we force planets to serve us, but not only do we not have the manpower to do such a thing, we wouldn't impose our will anyway. Hallow is in our ranks willingly. And I want to show you that."

Jade pondered this. She glanced at Chloe. Chloe said nothing.

"Okay," Jade began. "Then how did I get on this ship?"

"I was able to carry you. Sorry, I wasn't sure when you'd wake up." She peered at him quizzically. He looked equally perplexed. With a start, he realized why she was confused.

"You don't know what happened, do you?" She shook her head. "I found you unconscious on the floor. We had some crazy electrical surge, so I couldn't get to you right away. You were alone when I found you."

Electrical surge? I bet I can guess what that was. Still...why do I seem to remember hearing A'doxia scream?

"The cameras are still being sorted, but once they're up and running again, we'll figure out what happened. Which reminds me," he murmured. "Do you know A'doxia?"

Jade didn't answer. He stared at her for what felt like years. At last, Thaddeous stood.

"Fine," he said, displeased. "Are you going to be all right if I go back to bed?"

Jade nodded, her mind elsewhere. An entirely new planet, potentially alone with Thaddeous, could open up opportunities to escape. She knew the information about his people dying out would be useful. Her heart twisted and she grimaced. But did she want to relay that to the Opes? To the Exuro? Did she want to condemn his people to a potentially sour deal, or outright death? She scratched her neck hesitantly.

"If you need anything," Thaddeous said by the door, "I'm in the captain's quarters upstairs."

Alarmed, Jade turned her full attention to him. "Upstairs? How did you hear me?"

Thaddeous smiled, but it was full of pain. "I had a nightmare."

Chapter 16

Aris pulled two all-nighters in a row, sending General Kasaar bogus updates nearly every hour. She told him tonight she would be catching up on much needed sleep, and he gave her the go-ahead—she was certain her constant stream of messages had kept him awake. And if she played this right, she *would* actually catch up on some rest, but she could never be too sure.

Dressed in a hooded sweatshirt and baggy pants, she strode through the dim cityscape. A flash of red caught her eye and she spun towards it. A woman with long, red hair strode up a set of stairs that led to the level above. Aris, heart thundering, started towards the stranger before she stopped herself. It wasn't Jade. She knew it wasn't Jade. Jade was gone. Jade was the reason she was out at this hour. Quietly, she watched the woman walk up the stairs and out of sight, pulled back to the day when she and Jade had taken those very stairs. After a dreadful break-up, Jade had taken Aris' hand and lead them away from the route to the grocery store.

"Jade," Aris had said, her tone full of exhaustion. "I don't want to do this. Not right now." The morning light filtered through the smog cloud and danced against the reflective surfaces of the city. Their breath formed white dancers that waltzed in the cold air. Aris pulled her hand from Jade's, stumbling to a stop after Jade was no longer pulling her. Jade spun on Aris, her black-lensed goggles snug around her eyes. A grin grew across her face and she seemed incapable of containing her excitement.

"Oh, c'mon, Sell-out," she begged, reaching for Aris' hand again. Aris let her have it but refused to move, squinting at her overly excited friend. Jade wasn't known for grand displays of emotion besides anger. She was oftentimes reserved, hidden behind her helmet with her arms crossed over her chest. And yet she looked ready to jump out of her skin and dance.

"Just trust me," Jade had insisted, tugging at Aris' hand. "Please. There's something I want to show you, and once you see it you can go home and mope in our room." She flashed a playful smile and Aris blinked at her. For a moment, her sorrow was swept away by curiosity and surprise.

What has Jade so ecstatic, she had wondered.

"I'm moping after this, though," Aris replied, the hint of a smile on her lips. Jade's grin grew wider.

"Deal."

Jade guided Aris through the city, stopping at statues and vendors for breakfast and lunch along the way. Aris frequently asked if the newest sightseeing spot was what Jade wanted to show her, but Jade laughed and shook her head every time. Jade brought Aris onto sidewalk fountains designed for children and kicked water back at her and dragged her to a bridge's railing to look over the edge and make up lives for those passing by below. Aris followed Jade to a park where they sat on swings and Jade dared Aris to go higher than her. They competed until Jade flew off her seat at the peak of her swing, landed, rolled across the grassy earth, and sprang to her feet. The entire day had just about passed, and when Jade looked back at Aris, her face was alight with joy.

"Okay, it's time."

Aris was led into a dark alley with a large trash bin hugging the wall. They squeezed past and Aris gripped Jade's hand tighter.

"Where are we going, exactly?" she asked, peering through the darkness. Jade paused next to a black, unmarked door. She flashed a grin and gestured to it.

"You're going to love this. Go ahead, see what's inside."

Aris arched a brow and released Jade's hand as she reached for the doorknob. As soon as she began to pull the door open, light spilled out and the sound of music and low speaking voices stumbled into the alley. When she could see inside, her eyes grew wide and her jaw went slack.

Aris stood in the corner of a fancy restaurant with dark red hardwood floors and black cushioned seats around reclaimed metal tables. Above them were hanging chandeliers, a dim light setting the mood. To her left was an upraised stage where a band played jazz and a kodarian woman's thick, throaty song cloaked the entire room. Jade touched Aris' shoulder with a smile and pointed.

"Our table is right over there. Next to the kitchen doors."

"How did you…?" Aris started, eyes on Jade's goggles. Jade offered an innocent shrug and took Aris' hand, pulling her to the table. She tugged Aris' chair out and gave a half-bow.

"After you, miss." Jade's voice badly imitated that of a gentleman and her grin never faded. Aris laughed and sat down. Jade sat down across from her and put her napkin on her lap before leaning over the table.

"Got a secret for you."

"Another one?" Aris arched a brow, smirking.

"We can only afford an appetizer. You like lemon-glazed shredded kennock, don't you?"

Aris laughed. "What's with you and kennock?"

Jade chuckled. "Hey, it's good. And it so happens to be the only meat we can afford." She grabbed Aris' menu and set it atop hers. Aris shook her head with an amused look.

"So you take me out to a fancy restaurant—one I'm not even *dressed* for—and now you won't even let me look at the other menu options? What a tyrant you are."

Jade snickered. "You won't be missing anything."

Their food arrived shortly after, the long white plate set down between the two of them. Five rice balls encircled hidden spiced meat and a lemon glaze was drizzled over the top. Jade pulled two rice balls towards herself.

"Oh, no, you can have three, Jade," Aris stammered, insecurity snaking into her voice. Jade scoffed and bit into one of the rice balls.

"Don't let what that asshole said bother you, Aris. You're fine the way you are." She swallowed and pointed her fork at her roommate. "Now shut up and eat. These are really good."

Jade had never been one for kind words, even to Aris. Her love and admiration was usually cloaked behind layers of insults and sarcastic remarks. It had put Aris off at first, but in time she grew to understand Jade's language and her mild revulsion to anything sentimental or loving. And despite how short the sentences had been, Jade's statements filled Aris with sudden strength.

Aris blinked, washing away the stinging at the corners of her eyes. She took a breath and steadied her emotions, returning to the present, where Jade was nowhere to be found. She had a plan. And that required getting to the office.

Spidey clicked from the depths of Aris' purse as she strode to the large doors of the blue Opes office building. She hesitated for a moment as she gazed at the offensive color and curled her hand around her purse, forcing herself to continue forward. Jade was a Green. She knew this. The general knew this. She was lucky she wasn't exiled for hiding the information; she was lucky she wasn't killed. Everything she had ever longed for was about to be jeopardized by going through with what she was about to do. From a young age, she knew she was destined to be a soldier. She knew she was meant to fight in a cause greater than herself. She knew all of that. And yet, here she was, putting it all in the line of fire simply so she could find her friend. Her friend the Green. The supposed demon.

Perhaps if she were religious, this thought might bother her more. Most of the populace held a cult-like mentality, the possibility of helping a demon urging them to be suspicious of one another. Everyone was willing to kill someone suspected of being a Green. And though such a murder hadn't happened in years, Aris could see it in everyone's eyes. They were ready. They'd do it, if they thought they had to.

No, what bothered her most was how hard she had fought to be drafted into the Opes. With her parents being staunch Golds, and doing their best not to let Aris' true eye color shine through, they bombarded her with political jargon in hopes of being able to sway her natural disposition towards Blue. The first few years of a child's life are the only time the eye color can be swayed—though Blues go through another change upon death or retirement, when their eyes turn hazel— and Aris' parents intended to make the most out of those years. But when they could not sway her, and her true colors revealed themselves, she was locked away inside and declared as a Gold on all official documents. They would not have some dirty Blue taint their record. It wasn't until she killed a man that she was hurriedly drafted to avoid the death penalty. Facing public humiliation, her parents disowned her. And she was cut off from everything. She didn't even realize she had a brother until recently.

Yet after all that trouble, she was going to dare the galaxy to take it from her. All for a chance to find her friend. It was reckless. It was just what Jade would do. With a deep breath, she steeled herself. She would always be a Blue at her core.

She tried the handle, knowing she was in full view of whatever security cameras were around. She pulled off her hood, set her purse down, and peered through the windows. A long, exaggerated yawn escaped her mouth and she stretched, grumbling as she slunk away to a nearby bench, one that, she was also certain, was in the view of the security cameras. There, she curled up and fell asleep.

ϕϕϕ

"Private Sell! Private Sell!" Hands shook Aris' shoulders and she wearily blinked at the blurry figure before her. His dark skin and horns came into focus. General Kasaar.

"There's been a break-in at the office," the general hissed. "It was Jade."

Aris, seeming surprised, furrowed her brows and sat up, rubbing sleep from her eyes.

"*What?*" she muttered.

Kasaar nodded. "I don't know how she did it. One second the cameras are working, and the next the video all goes down. The audio, though, she couldn't turn off. We heard her voice. I don't know who she was talking to, but she was here." He looked at Aris hard. "I thought you said she wasn't on this planet."

"Me and fifteen of the men you sent to check my facts," Aris growled, standing. "Did she take anything?"

General Kasaar shook his head and looked at the office building. "Nothing. Not a single lock broken, not a single thing stolen. But she came here for a reason."

"General, I—"

He handed her the purse she had left in front of the building. "You left this inside last time you visited."

Aris took her purse, looking through it frantically. She exhaled, obviously appearing relieved that nothing was taken. And that Spidey was back, safe and sound in her purse.

"Go back home, Aris. Contact us if she comes for you." He started towards the office, then paused, looking back at her. Concern washed over his face. "Aris, when Greens…you know they snap. At a certain time. And…and just…" He rubbed his jaw and looked down. "Be careful, all right? She may not be who you remember her to be."

φφφ

Aris sat down at a library computer, the door closed to keep prying eyes at bay. Spidey crawled out of her purse, the small robotic creature clicking its mandibles together as he peered at Aris excitedly. He hopped from one leg to another, and Aris couldn't help but smile as she tried to shake exhaustion off of her body.

"I take it you got some good information?"

Spidey chirped. Aris chuckled.

"All right then, you little pest. Plug it in."

Spidey transferred what he had gathered to the computer, documents and folders filling the desktop. They ranged from texts that had the word 'green' in it, to files with actual information on what Greens were. Aris skimmed everything before she had a handful of documents to properly read, a few containing videos.

"Keep these," she said to Spidey as she gestured to the screen without looking at him. His small clicks indicated he heard her as Aris read the most recent document containing several mentions of 'Green.'

Transfer of the Green is complete. The reports were right—it's crazy powerful. I lost a few of my men trying to keep it contained. If something like this is spotted by the public, there's no telling what might happen. We'd probably have to execute it in front of everyone so that their fears are quenched. The thing is, I don't think we could kill this thing even if we tried.

It has no Helix to speak of, but it doesn't seem to be a disadvantage. If anything, it seems more like a fear tactic. Ghawor really had his hands full creating a demon such as this, General. I think he poured every ounce of malice and ill will into this beast. Do you really think it's on our side? I know a few Golds have your ear, General, but please understand. This thing is a Green, and more powerful than the ones we've encountered prior. I don't even truly know what it is. It's nothing that I've ever seen before.

I heard you had a run-in with a private of yours, sir. Please keep her away from the operations here, as we cannot be disturbed. We have the situation under control for now, but I feel like that's because this thing is letting us. If we make any wrong moves, I suspect you'll find nothing but a bloodstain left of me. If that Blue comes here and stirs things up, this Green might very well make its move.

I sent what we've gathered thus far on a shipment due to arrive any day now. Look for our number. You know the one. The cargo is fragile, so please handle it with care. This Green didn't let us get those samples easily, either. I'll need a few more men sent here if you want us to continue our research. I'm also in dire need of more restraints—enough to hold Vix himself. There are some available for bidding tomorrow, but the Thrax representatives have the highest bid. I'll need at least 7,000 kniri more if we want to ensure the purchase—and trust me, we need those restraints. This thing has already broken H-blades with its bare hands and tore off the arms of my second as if he were some child's doll. We cannot let this thing onto the streets.

One other thing, General: I heard you purchased a ticket to visit. Do not visit. We don't need you dying and your disappearance to be questioned and investigated. Continue to communicate through other means. I'll be sending a video of the Green soon enough. You'll be able to see the beast with your own two eyes and you'll understand why you're safer behind that screen of yours.

Sincerely,

Aris chewed her thumb, contemplating the words. They had a Green. Was it Jade? Did the Blues truly kidnap her right under Aris' nose? The words of the Church of Vix preacher came back to haunt her now:

"Only one Green can exist at a time, and that is time enough to destroy our entire way of life."

Only one Green at a time.

The general knew where Jade was. Why was he letting her continue her search? To keep her occupied, to keep her from investigating on her own and discovering his hand in the whole situation? Aris nibbled on her fingernails, squinting at the screen. The email had been received a little over a week ago—enough time for Jade to have escaped and come back. It would cover her tracks for now. And even if it didn't, no one but her knew Spidey existed. The general would have no reason to stop her investigation.

He had played the game wrong. Aris knew now. And all she needed was information on where that shipment was coming from, or where the general bought a ticket to. Two leads that would be difficult to cover up. Two chances Aris had to get this right. She grinned.

This was too easy.

ɸɸɸ

Aris gathered her things at her apartment: a change of clothes, Jade's likely failed attempt at making an H-blade, all the silver kniri they had—even Jade's share—and, of course, Spidey. She still had the rest of the documents and videos to look through, and there was no telling if she would need him to hack into camera systems and fool everyone with a recording of Jade's voice again. She bit her pinkie finger, anxious. She was sure she had everything she needed. All that was left was to—

There was a knock at her door. She froze. Did they find out? No, how could they? She had sent them an update only a few hours ago, telling them she believed Jade to be back on Nevar somehow and was searching for any eye-witnesses. The excuse would cover her if she were to be found wandering around with a large backpack, as well. So who…?

She set the backpack down and strode to the entrance, peering through the peephole. A package waited on the other side. She tentatively opened the door and pulled the small box inside. It was addressed to Jade.

Aris closed the door and strode back to her bed. She sat on the edge. Spidey chirped and clamored out of her pack, peering at the package. Aris glanced at him.

"Well, I'm sure she wouldn't mind," Aris muttered. Jade most definitely *would* mind. She hated when her packages were opened by someone other than her.

"They're like birthday gifts someone else unwrapped," she'd huff, arms crossed as she glared at Aris.

Aris chuckled at the thought and tore open the box. Inside there was a smaller, more decorated black box, which she gingerly unlatched and opened. Situated on a miniature pillow was a deep blue star with blood-red tips. The Indomitable Will medal. A stand-in had been used at the ceremony, and now the real one arrived, over a week later, with no one but Aris to see its glory.

She lifted it from the box and ran her fingers over its front. Her face twisted, her lips tugging down and her brows furrowing, vain attempts to keep the tears at bay. They bubbled at the corners of her eyes, spilling down her cheeks. She pulled the star into her chest and curled around it, choking on the sound of sorrow that rose from her throat. She clenched her eyes shut. And for the first time since Jade's disappearance, Aris broke down.

Chapter 17

Aris woke up, heart pounding and head ringing. Pinpricks of pain made her look down at her hand, where Jade's medal was still clutched tightly. She stuffed it in her bag and checked the time. Aris scowled. She had slept for nearly seven hours. If the shipment had already come in, she'd have to figure out another way to get into the general's office to gather the information she needed, or steal the data from one of the shipping offices—that is, if he didn't purchase a ticket offworld through a third party. She snatched her backpack and slung it over her shoulder, holding her hand out to Spidey who scurried up her arm and down into her sweatshirt's pocket. There, he clung for dear life as Aris sprinted from their room. But Aris paused as she was closing the door. She probably wouldn't see it for a while, if ever again. Maybe she should've grabbed more of Jade's things, so that when Aris found her the woman had something to change into.

But there wasn't time. Aris closed the door.

ϕϕϕ

The harbor was a massive space on the upper levels, semi-enclosed save for the entryway that was large enough to consume the space of three levels. Aris always felt small in such a large place, but she assumed she wasn't the only one.

Aris walked down to the designated area for shipments and cargo, where she found twelve different ships anchored. She hoped she wasn't too late and went about asking after a shipment for General Kasaar. Some of the Browns ignored her existence altogether, others told her to get lost. And, when she reached the end of the ships, she was empty-handed. Either the shipment hadn't come, or it had come and gone. She chewed her nails, her mind running circles around the next series of steps she would have to undergo. It would be difficult, and she would most likely get caught. Aris would have mere minutes to get off planet and escape to another.

She scowled. *Not good.*

"Private Sell?"

Aris' heart leapt into her throat and she spun towards the voice. General Kasaar glared down at her, his eyes dark.

"I thought I told you that you're grounded, soldier," he growled.

Aris smiled. "I know, sir, and I have no intentions of leaving the planet. But I wasn't having much luck finding any information on…our mutual friend, so I decided to see if maybe anyone in this crowd had seen her. I also thought it was a good place for someone like her to get lost." She looked over the crowd, the mass of bodies blurring together. "Still haven't had much luck."

Kasaar looked over his shoulder and shrugged when his eyes settled back on her. "We can't always be lucky, Private. Have you slept at all?"

"More than intended, sir." Aris chuckled. "Fell asleep against my will last night, so I'm trying to do some catch-up work."

"Don't push yourself too hard, Private Sell, else you'll be exhausted when we need you the most."

"I'll keep that in mind, sir." She looked around. "What are you doing here, anyway?"

"Came for a shipment." He smiled at her. "It's due to arrive any minute."

"Oh?" Aris looked out past the ships, eyes scanning the new arrivals. "A personal shipment, sir? Should I let you be?"

He moved to stand beside her. "No, I could actually use your help carrying the cargo off, if you wouldn't mind lending a hand."

Aris smiled. "Of course, sir."

ϕϕϕ

The ship that arrived was a small privateer, built for speed and little else. Its captain jumped off its stern and landed soundly on the dock a little to Aris' left, where he stood at nearly eight feet tall and flashed a toothy grin. Aris stared at him with blatant wonder. Never before had she seen a creature quite like him.

His mud-colored fur was spotted with blue and orange and laced with scars. Around his furred neck was a necklace of teeth, or perhaps they were talons, and his wrists were adorned with orange bracelets. He wore no shirt, but clinging to his waist were baggy sweats that stopped above the knee. A bushy tail swung from his spine and his feline gaze settled on Aris with vibrant blue eyes mixed with yellow. Aris' mind swam. *How can he have both blue* and *yellow eyes? What does that mean? Where are his loyalties? What faction are Yellows?*

His cat-like appearance wasn't just for show, as he walked without making a sound. He extended one clawed hand to the general and the other to Aris. She noticed his left hand was missing his pointer finger.

"Name's Ossi," he said, his voice energetic. "I'm guessin' you're the ones here to pick up the shipment?"

The general took Ossi's hand and shook it, and Aris did the same. Ossi's eyes swiveled towards the ship and he looked up at the deck.

"They're pretty heavy. Think you can handle 'em?" he asked. Aris arched a brow and he caught her eye, chuckling. "I wasn't talkin' to you, short-stuff."

The general stiffened beside Aris and she suppressed a grin. Ossi howled with laughter and slapped the general's back.

"Relax, leather-skin! I'm teasin' you. I'm sure you can handle yourself." He winked at Aris. "I had to haul ass all the way from Sypher to get this shipment here on time. Even if you couldn't carry it off, I'd sell it to the highest bidder."

"You would be committing an illegal act, Ossi," General Kasaar growled, burrowing holes into Ossi's head with his gaze. "And you would be thrown into jail for treason."

Ossi snorted out a laugh, flashing his pointed teeth as he smirked. "Maybe. But I'm guessin' you wouldn't be able to catch me." He crossed his arms. "I'm also guessin' that this loot is pretty important to your cause, and as me and my sorry crew had to take out a few pirates on the way in, I feel like it's only right you compensate me for my trouble."

"Is that so." Kasaar wasn't asking a question. He glared hard into Ossi's unflinching gaze.

"That is." Ossi raised his fingers to his lips and whistled. A moment later, another sentient being Aris had never laid eyes on jumped from the deck. The creature was akin to the dragons depicted in human mythology, though it was covered in fur and, instead of arms, it had wings with opposable finger joints at its bend. Its nose was formed after a canine's, and its tail swung gently behind it as it folded its wings against its body. It stood at about five feet tall, though Aris imagined if it stretched out its long neck, it'd stand at least seven. Its pointed ears were fixed in the general's direction and its pink eyes were centered on the general's face.

Pink? Who has pink eyes? Aris' mind reeled.

"This is my Second," Ossi explained, gesturing to the creature. "His name is Zahmur, and he will be dealing with you on the terms of our payment." Ossi put his hands on his hips and beamed. "He's better with money."

Zahmur sighed and looked up at the general. "If you would, sir." He gestured a few feet away where they could speak and not be heard by Ossi and Aris. The general stiffly followed. When they were out of range of hearing, Ossi turned and gazed at his ship.

"I've got a feeling you're not fond of that man," he said, his smile cemented on his face. Aris looked at the crowd, opposite of Ossi.

"What makes you say that?"

"Just a gut feelin' I got." Ossi stretched. "It's five hundred kniri round trip. We'll be here until midnight."

Aris arched a brow. "You think I want on your sorry excuse for a ship?"

"You wound me, short-stuff." Ossi chuckled. "I saw how your eyes gleamed when I mentioned Sypher. My guess is you'd like to get there, and get there fast." He glanced at Zahmur and the general. They seemed to be in a heated debate.

"Are you a Blue or not?" Aris pressed.

"I'm nothin', shorty. In truth, no one on my ship knows what they are." He snickered. "We're a cobbled together family."

"That's impossible. Everyone's eyes indicate what they're loyal to."

"Is that so, Blue? Seems pretty restrictive to me." He put his hands behind his head and gazed up at the ceiling. "Midnight. No later."

Zahmur and the general returned from their negotiations, Zahmur holding a small bag of kniri with his tail. He tossed it to Ossi, and Ossi caught it and tipped his head to the General.

"Good doing business with you, sir. Hope to see you again soon."

"Just let me get my cargo," the general hissed.

Aris helped him haul the large containers out of the deck of the ship and onto the dock, all the while running through scenarios of where Jade might be on Sypher. But she knew that answer already, didn't she? All she had to do was pay Ossi to take her to the place he had picked up the shipment, and she'd be close enough to start searching. And Jade wasn't known to keep quiet. She was sure to make some noise, and Aris had gotten good at following that sound.

By tomorrow I'll be a traitor.

But that didn't explain why the boxes supposedly carrying samples of the Green were heavy. Could they be padded, or disguised as something else with other various materials, in case someone decided to peer inside? That would make a decent amount of sense. Unless, of course, 'samples' of a Green meant hacked off limbs of—

Aris bottled up the thoughts and threw them aside as she hauled the last of the crates from the ship and onto the harbor. She excused herself from General Kasaar's presence and found cheap food from a grocery store to eat in an alley as she waited for nightfall. The soldier pondered the strange animalistic creature, Ossi. Aris had never met someone like him, let alone someone that held more than one color in their eyes. She found her way to a bathroom and stared in the mirror, analyzing her own gaze. The azure color was speckled with a few variations of blue—some like ice, and many like the blue nebula that she, Salene, and Jade all gazed at in the sands of Taotar.

She smiled at the memory. The three of them staring at the sky, before the events that took Salene's face from her and, later, her legs; before the severity that consumed Jade; before the war had truly taken its toll. The aquamarine color spilled out into the ebony, crimson, and purple sky, filled with a million dancing stars. Salene's eyes were half-open, a yawn on her lips, while Jade stared with ever growing fascination with her goggles strapped firmly in place.

"Do you guys think there are people like us out there? Someone lying in the sand, staring at our glittering star right now?"

Aris' smile faltered. Jade's wonder for the galaxy had been immensely subdued by whatever happened to her when she went missing on Taotar. And with Jade's hardness came a drive to be stronger and better than ever before. This led her to act rashly on Sobek. This led Salene to fall into the river.

She exhaled. Salene. She would probably like to know what was going on. Aris kept the woman up to date on important events because Jade refused to do so herself. Jade's guilt forced her to believe the events were caused entirely by her. She insisted she wouldn't speak to Salene until she was able to return her legs.

In some ways, Jade was responsible, but Salene's eagerness to please would've doomed her eventually.

Dusk fell and Aris purchased a small, cheap onigiri from one of the local vendors—a surviving recipe from human history. As she chewed on the rice ball, she let her mind wander back to Ossi.

If he isn't a Blue, what is he? Where do his loyalties lie? How does he have more than one color in his eyes? Everyone in the Known Galaxy displays their fealties through the pigment of their gaze. That makes Ossi a wildcard. That makes him dangerous.

She strode through the streets in silence, taking the stairs two at a time as she climbed back to the docks. She kept her head low and grabbed the straps of her backpack as if worried she might lose it. She watched her feet take her towards the end of everything she knew. A bridge stretched before her and she paused by its railing, gazing out over the city. Vehicles flew through the sky, other walkers waved from distant pathways, and lights gleamed from the many windows cut into the sides of buildings.

Concern crept into her skull. How much sleep had she gotten since Jade went missing? Was her mind frantic and muddled from the lack of rest? Perhaps she was jumping to conclusions, making problems where there weren't any.

Maybe that was the case before, but that document about a Green? There's no denying something serious is happening. Aris took a breath and returned to her walking. She found her way to the harbor, she offered Ossi the money, and in the quiet they slipped away.

There was no big hurrah, no intense moment of life or death. Aris was there, and then, quite simply, she wasn't.

ϕϕϕ

The crew of the ship was a small, rag-tag bunch of sentient species Aris had never encountered before. Besides the captain and his second, there was a massive insectoid being with a shell, pincer-like hands, and a small head. Her name was Katsu and had a soft voice and silver eyes.

Gull was a fiery bull creature that stood—at best—four feet tall. Her horns jutted upwards and a few spikes ran down her forearms. Her hooved feet made it impossible for her to be stealthy, and her aggression reminded Aris of Jade. Her eyes shone like blue flames.

Me didn't speak, and she stood as some sort of cross between humanoid and otherworldly. Two pincers the size of Aris' pointer fingers sat on Me's chest, guarding the gem embedded there. Tusks tore through the flesh around Me's lips, and a pair of miniature horns sat on her temples. She had four arms total, all of which seemed to always be crossed over her flesh-colored scales. With no apparent genitalia, all she wore was a red scarf around her neck. Her dual-pupiled, crimson-hazel eyes held no emotion when she gazed at Aris.

None of them had families. They told her this without pause, and Aris got the feeling they had lived their whole lives without knowing who they were or where they came from. It had to be lonely.

Aris busied herself by tending to the sails when needed and keeping an eye out for pirates or stray asteroids. When she went down for bed in the hammocks strung below deck, she pulled out her wrist holo. Spidey had transferred documents there, and when she clicked a button a screen appeared just above the device.

Battlefield Encounter: General Fier Una's Final Report

Format: Video

Bodies crowded the floor, soldiers shoving their guts back into their open wounds, some holding their severed limbs, others shaking from the shock of bleeding out from the neck. General Fier rushed past, ignoring those reaching out to him. He gripped a Balus in his hands, the only weapon besides an H-blade that could cut through a soldier's armor. Its ammunition was the tangled knots of intestines from a Rye-dragon's belly. It was more expensive than a top level flat on Nevar, and rightfully so. It was near impossible to make without killing ten workers in the process.

"This is a fucking massacre," the general hissed, glancing over his shoulder and down the hall he had rushed through. He spoke to the camera mounted on his helmet and grimaced when he saw a woman at the far end of the hall battling with two Blues. One of the woman's arms was missing, but somehow, suspended in the air where her hand should be, was an H-blade. Her blazing green eyes were narrowed and almost seemed to glow. The general cursed as the woman ducked beneath the Blues' attacks and split open their stomachs, freeing their trapped guts. They collapsed, screaming, pulling their small intestines back into their bellies the best they could with shaking hands.

The general spun around and kept sprinting through the base. "She's ripped apart half my unit—half *her own unit! Fuck!*" Lead bullets smashed into pieces of his armor, making small dents. He hissed another curse and veered around a corner. His pace was growing slower and his breath became more labored. Slowly, he stopped and turned to face whoever was following him, his weapon raised.

"The snippers were on us," he growled. "The damn bugs were demanding we surrender, but we had a secret weapon. We were going to eradicate them all when she fell to her knees and started screaming. She turned on all of us. Blue and snipper alike. Those spider freaks ran off but did she run after them? No. She came after *us*."

Footsteps echoed down the hall. His hands grew sweaty.

"Her best friend came up and tried to calm her down. He was trying to get her to remember who we all were, what we were fighting for. She cut off his head." He gritted his teeth, the steps growing closer. "I cut off her arm but her Invisible Hand is monstrous. It acts like the arm she used to have, and holds her weapon for her. I've never seen anything like it." Sweat dripped from his forehead. "She's stronger now than she was before."

The Green turned the corner and stared the general in the eye. She wore basic Opes armor, the bare minimum defense given to recruits and those who couldn't afford any better. It was completely covered in blood. Her H-blade swung gracefully in a circle like it was nothing more than a child's plaything. Her green eyes held fury and hatred. The general sighted his weapon's scope on her.

"Don't move, Efa!" He shouted. His voice shook. "Put your hand up! And drop your weapon!"

Efa moved towards him. The general scowled. "I said stop!"

She glared at him through the blood smeared like war paint over her face. "I'm done following orders. This all ends today."

The general pulled the trigger.

The mess of purple Rye-dragon intestines launched from his gun but froze in midair before Efa's face, the blood dripping from the guts and onto the ground, burning small holes with each droplet. Her weapon was discarded, and now the Invisible Hand protected her from the projectile more deadly than an H-blade. General Fier staggered back and fired a second time, then a third. Efa kept walking forward, dropping one bundle of entrails only to catch another. The splattered blood from each consecutive hit began to define the arm's ghastly form.

A clawed hand extended from the massive arm that attached to the cauterized wound at Efa's shoulder and was nearly twice the size of the woman herself. The general fired faster, but the Balus only had room to safely store so much ammunition. And before long, it ran out. Once that click informed the Green that he had nothing left, she sprang across the room and her massive hand gripped him around the chest and lifted him from the floor.

"Please," the general begged, tears streaming down his face. "I don't want to die. I don't want to—"

Efa squeezed. His ribs cracked and punctured his lungs, while his spine bent and burst holes into his bowels. He choked on blood, trying for breath he wouldn't find. His last moments were undoubtedly agonizing. Efa dropped his crumpled body to the floor and regarded him with distaste. She knelt down beside his limp form.

"You should've thought about that before, General." She turned to the camera and yanked it off the general's body, lifting it to her face with her fleshy arm. She smiled. Her eyes were bloodshot, her body shaking. Despair was starting to consume her features.

"Maybe now you'll stop. Maybe you'll see it now. Everything you've done, everything you've taken. Maybe you'll see it." Her Invisible Hand lifted a pistol to her head. "But I don't want to be here to find out. Hope you're proud, mom."

Her brains splattered against the nearby wall.

Chapter 18

There was a knock at the door while Jade was shadow boxing. Reluctantly, she lowered her hands and paused the simulation that Chloe had been playing through the visor. Jade answered the door. Thaddeous stood at the other side.

"I received a message that you might find interesting," Thaddeous said, buttoning his tuxedo's jacket. He straightened his tie and smiled at her. "Did I interrupt something?"

Jade shrugged and pulled Chloe off her head. She wiped the sweat off her brow and eyed him.

"Depends on the message."

"I'll show you. Come." Thaddeous turned and walked down the hallway until he reached the stairs that led to the main deck. Jade glanced at the helmet tucked under her arm, arching a brow.

"Wonder what it could be," she murmured.

"Likely something unimportant, mistress. The Thrax concerns are not your concerns."

Jade nodded, looking back at where Thaddeous was waiting. "I suppose that's true." She pulled Chloe over her head, rolled her shoulders and stretched her arms. She accompanied Thaddeous upstairs.

The deck was a bustle of activity in the lantern light. People were tending to sails, others mopping the deck, some cleaning the large cannons situated near the sides of the ship. She noticed a few people playing cards near the stern, with others watching Jade with sharp, scrutinizing eyes. They were heavily armed with weapons strapped to their hips and backs. Jade laughed, unimpressed.

"Bet they haven't even seen any action," Jade grumbled. "What a bunch of morons."

"With your intellect, you would fit right in, mistress."

"Oh, very nice. Thanks, Chloe."

She approached Thaddeous, who stood beside a biped, four-foot tall canine beast with fur the color of ice in the moonlight. His right hand was missing and his muzzle was mangled with scars. Crimson eyes pierced the air with malice as he watched her approach. Jade's brows furrowed.

"Chloe?"

"Mistress, this is one of the Thrax-aligned sentient creatures, a halo, from the ice planet Hallow. Not many are seen in Exuro-controlled space. Rumor is they are an

incredibly honor- and tradition-ruled society, mistress. This one is rather large for their kind."

"This is Ariar," Thaddeous began, nodding at the wolfish person beside him. "He's a messenger from a friend on Hallow. Seems the king found something that you might find interesting."

Jade crossed her arms. "Oh?"

Thaddeous nodded at Ariar, who stuck his only hand into the satchel strapped over his body. He handed her a small iron rod. Jade took it, pressed the button, and the screen extended from the rod like a scroll. There, a message in Os, the common trade language, was hand-written on the digital screen.

Mal,

Found a thing. Not far. Big E. Follow? Many storms. New freeze. Lost map. Interested?

Boy anxious. See you.

X

"Um," Jade said.

"I don't follow this line of...information, mistress," Chloe muttered, her synthesized voice taking a rather impatient tone. Jade handed the note to Thaddeous.

"Yeah, what the fuck is this?" Her voice carried through her helmet. Thaddeous took the note and glanced over it, chuckling.

"His Os isn't that good. Here." He moved closer to her and pointed to each sentence. "It says, basically, that he found a base not far from his home that isn't a Thrax base. Probably Exuro. Said his maps got lost during the frequent storms because of the new freeze and," he trailed off as he re-read the last bit. A smile played on his lips. Jade glanced at him from the corner of her eye. "That last bit about his son is for me." He handed the message back to Ariar, and dipped his head in thanks.

"So, what, there's supposedly an Opes base on Hallow?" Jade crossed her arms and dismissed the idea without further thought. Another piece of information locked away and forgotten in the darkness of her skull. "That's ridiculous. We've never taken Hallow."

"Opes?" Thaddeous inquired, his attention turned back to Jade as the halo jumped into a small, single-pilot ship. The sails unfurled and the jets activated as soon as he took the wheel. He steered himself down the Air Stream and out of sight.

"That's what the army branch is called," Jade admitted. "Exuro controls the Opes, but they're separate. In a way."

"Mistress, this information could be used against us."

"What, the correction of terms? I doubt it," Jade grumbled in reply.

"They're separated?" Thaddeous interrupted, not realizing Chloe and Jade were having a hidden conversation. "That's odd." He scratched his chin, gaze growing distant. "Anyway," he murmured, "when we arrive on Hallow, we can visit the place. After, of course, you see that we're not bad people."

Jade frowned. It was possible they weren't all terrible, but she wasn't sure she truly wanted to know one way or the other. Would her loyalties change? Would her eyes turn Red? They had before. They had shifted in her fear. Would—

Chloe interrupted her thoughts: *"Mistress, why would he wish to travel to an Opes base without desiring something from them? Documents, perhaps?"*

"Speaking of which," Jade muttered, rolling her shoulders, "why do *you* want to go to this so-called Opes base? Would it be because you want to steal the documents there?"

Thaddeous' eyes grew tired and he rubbed them with his thumb and forefinger. "Why must you always assume I wish to harm you and your kind in some way?"

Jade looked at him. Because he was Thrax? Because she was supposed to hate him? Because he just told her a base existed on a planet none of her people had ever been to? Because she should want him dead, but didn't? Because they were supposed to be at each other's throats, yet he helped her calm down, helped her breathe, helped her out of her waking nightmares? She bit the inside of her cheek. She didn't have an answer for him.

She turned and walked away.

Chapter 19

Jade lay on the hammock in the engine room, Chloe on her chest. A blanket was pulled over her body as she stared at the ceiling. She should hate him. She didn't.

The entire notion of this churned her stomach twice over, making her want to vomit the turmoil out of her system. She would be labeled a traitor for these thoughts. Just for hesitating, she'd be a traitor. She closed her eyes. Of course, she'd be killed if she even showed her people her eyes. And here? Here she was their only hope. She didn't want to be that for them, but it was better than being murdered by those she fought to protect.

"Knock, knock," Thaddeous' voice came from her left, and he peered in from the partially opened door. He smiled at her.

"What do you want?" she huffed.

"Thought I'd bring you something to help you relax." Thaddeous stepped inside and closed the door after him. He held up two bottles of wine with two glasses pressed between his arms and his chest. "This is a good year," he said as he strode closer. He set everything down on the floor and lay out a blanket with a few pillows to sit on. He motioned for her to join him as he opened the first bottle.

"What are you doing?"

"Pouring you a drink—isn't that obvious?" He set one glass aside and poured another.

"Why are you offering me wine? Aren't we supposed to be enemies?"

"Seems like you have something you need to talk about," Thaddeous continued, lifting his glass to her. "You keep shifting from seeming to be okay with me, to hating my very existence."

"I don't have anything to tell a Thrax," Jade hissed. He arched a brow at her. She flushed and glared at the wall.

"This is what I'm talking about," Thaddeous said, taking a drink from his glass. "So let's talk."

Jade rubbed her eyes. She was good at punching things, not navigating politics. She glanced at Thaddeous, who was watching in silence, and exhaled.

"Fine." Jade set Chloe on the hammock and strode over to where Thaddeous was sitting. She took her place on the pillow across from him and lifted the glass to her nose, smelling the wine before tasting it.

He was right. The wine was a good year. The mixture of the different races' fermented fruits created a layered flavor of sweet and savory before kicking her throat with the alcoholic burn. She couldn't help herself—a smile graced her lips, and she chuckled.

"Good wine," she said. Thaddeous grinned.

"Thought you might like it. It's my personal favorite."

"The prince's wine? My, I must be special." She quirked a brow, her words dry. He laughed.

"Does nothing humor you?" He took another sip from his wine and coughed after he swallowed. "It's a bit strong, though."

"Too much for your princey palate?" Jade teased, snickering. She grimaced. *He's the enemy, so why am I acting like this around him? Just because his eyes are Green?* She stared at him. She pushed the feelings aside and let herself relax. She'd enjoy the wine, at the very least. "Thought it was your personal favorite. You weren't lying, were you?" She took another sip. He laughed, rubbing the back of his neck.

"No, no, I wasn't lying. It's good wine—I just don't drink enough to be able to handle it as well."

Jade nodded, drinking from her glass. He drank his. She looked at the wall. He looked at his hands. She took another sip. He coughed after swallowing the last of his.

"You know A'doxia, don't you?"

"Don't ask, Thaddeous."

"Does it have something to do with those scars on your back?"

Jade fixed him with a glare. "Stop asking."

"I'm sorry," he whispered. "For whatever happened to you. I'm sorry."

Jade scrutinized his eyes. He was being sincere. She snorted out a sarcastic laugh.

"Yeah, well, fuck you."

He smiled. "Always such a charmer. I met someone once who responded like that to almost everything I said to her, you know." He started. "My father made me work a lot of jobs to make sure I knew what everyone else had to do to keep the city running. Sewer work, lawyering, even tried police work!" He chuckled. "I'm not a fighter, though. That didn't work out very well for me. But when I was working as a military scouting advisor, there was this woman…”

He droned on. Jade listened half-heartedly, only to find herself smiling more and more as he spoke. She forced her lips into a neutral frown and kept herself busy with drinking. He matched her until the second bottle had to be opened. Thaddeous' cheeks flushed as he continued, laughing about half-completed stories that didn't make any sense. Jade chuckled.

He spoke for what felt like hours, filling in the silence that Jade left. Perhaps it was the wine, but she found herself relaxing as he spoke, and more willing to laugh at his extravagant stories. Eventually, he staggered to his feet and lifted his glass. Jade smirked over the rim of her own cup.

“I propose,” he hiccupped, shuffling to the wall to lean against it, “a toast.”

“Oh?” Jade raised her glass in return. “What for?”

“For meeting the only woman in the universe worth meeting.” He tossed back his wine, lost his balance, and collapsed on the floor. Jade laughed until he showed no signs of getting up. She rushed to his side, pressing two fingers to his neck to check for a pulse as she lifted his head.

"Thaddeous?"

"Mistress, why check him? Would it not be more beneficial if he died here?"

Jade frowned. Chloe was right, of course. If Thaddeous wasn't dead, she should find a way to kill him without leaving much evidence that she did. And if she did leave evidence? It wasn't like she couldn't handle herself. She even had a glass bottle she could break for a weapon. Thaddeous' heartbeat pressed against her fingers and she felt the back of his skull for any signs of blood.

"If I killed him, it would make getting back to Aris a little difficult. I don't even know the way," Jade murmured. Chloe was silent. Jade dragged Thaddeous near the door, cleared off the blanket, and lay it over him. She stood, looking down at the Thrax prince. Softly, Chloe replied:

"Okay, mistress."

Chapter 20

"Hey, Blue!" Gull called Aris over from where she was sitting cross-legged near the main mast, reading more logs on her holo. Aris looked up, closing the text displayed on her wrist. Gull flashed a grin. She stood beside Katsu and Me, miniature compared to the tall creatures beside her.

"We're having a friendly contest. Care to join?"

Aris glanced at her holo and rubbed her eyes. It would be good to do something else for a change. She pushed herself to her feet, stretched, and strode over to where the others were sitting on the deck. Gull beamed.

"Told you she'd want to come!" she chimed as Aris sat cross-legged next to the others. Me was on her right, who said nothing and only stared, while Katsu rolled her small, silver eyes.

"No one said she wouldn't, Gull," she muttered with a grin. Gull huffed.

"You thought it!"

Aris' smile tightened.

"I did not, you little termite," Katsu retorted.

"Hey, Sell-out!"

"Little? Listen here, where I'm from, I'm the tallest one around!"

"Aren't you a little short to reach that?"

"And where's that, hm? Are you from a lifeless planet?" Katsu teased with a chuckle. "Are you the smartest around, too, without any competition?"

"Here, I'll give you a boost. Woah, chill! Don't flail around, or I'll drop you!"

Gull flushed and punched Katsu's arm. "Shut up!"

"This is actually a good work out—ow! I wasn't calling you fat—ow! Fuck, stop that!"

Katsu laughed and ruffled the fur atop Gull's head. "Explain the game already, twerp."

Aris frowned, wishing for Katsu and Gull to be silent. With a grunt, Gull turned to Me and Aris, laying down a deck of cards.

"The game's simple: each round you're given an amount of troops to use depending on the card you get, and you have to fend off attacking armies based on what you have and any sneaky tricks you've got. It's all about luck and tactics. At the end of the round, those defeated will have a chance to pledge their loyalty to another, and everyone will get more soldiers to add to their unit. Before you make your move, you also pick up one trap card and one offensive card. Each will have various uses depending on how you use them." Gull set down two pairs of dice. "And victory depends on the dice. Make sense?"

Aris tilted her head with a smile. "Sounds like a slightly tweaked version of Ossian Traitor."

Gull nodded. "Yeah, it's kind of our version of the game. Katsu and I came up with it."

Katsu smiled at Gull. Aris felt her smile falter.

"C'mon, Aris! Just one round, please? I'm sure you'll be great at it. Salene and I really want to make it up to you. Here, I even got you a drink—and no, it's not alcohol. It's just milk, since you're a baby. Hey! Don't hit me! Fuck, man, that's going to bruise. I'm going to report you for roommate abuse. It's a real thing, you know."

"All right," Katsu said, clapping her hands together. "Who wants to start?"

Aris blinked and looked down in front of her. There, a lone card sat. She flipped it over. 100 units. She wasn't sure if that was a lot or not in this game, but she wasn't about to look confused. She arched her brows and allowed a hint of a smile to cross her lips. Gull glanced at her and frowned down at her own card. Me tilted her head in confusion at her own, and Katsu laughed.

"Aris, would you like to start off? First you draw one card from each deck, and then you can choose whether or not you want to attack someone," Katsu said.

Aris nodded and took a card from each pile. Her traps were bear traps, guaranteed to take out fifteen soldiers, with a die throw that would calculate any others that would be caught. Her offensive card was a series of battle horns that would scare a certain number of enemy troops back into the opponent's hand, also calculated by a die roll.

"There are Thrax to the East, West, and North. Reinforcements are delayed and there's no telling when they'll arrive." Aris tapped the map laid out on the dirt ground. Her eyes flicked to Jade and Salene. *"The enemy doesn't know we're just a scouting group. They believe us to be a fighting force of at least fifty. It's possible they'll attack tonight, so we need to prepare."*

Jade slammed one fist into her palm, a wild grin across her face. "All right, then. What's the plan, Sell-out?"

She set her soldiers face-down in front of her along with her trap.

"I won't attack for now."

Gull followed suit, as did Katsu, but Me set her units in front of Katsu and attacked with an offensive card at her back: a forest fire. *It started slowly at first, a small bush caught on fire that Jade kept alive according to Aris' orders. Salene camped not far away on an outcropping of rocks separated from the forest by a river. Her sniper was set up and she peered through her sights. Aris tried to communicate with the rest of the unit by a small handheld device, but received no response.*

"Can't get through," Aris told the two with her.

Jade gritted her teeth from where she sat on the rocks. "Then we go through with it," she said, gesturing to the flames. "We set the whole place ablaze."

Katsu lost two-hundred of her three-hundred soldiers to the fire, and despite the drastic blow to her fighting force, managed to claim victory when red tongues devoured Me's entire army. Begrudgingly, Me swore loyalty to Katsu.

"So why are you wanting to go to Sypher, anyway?" Katsu asked with a soft smile. Aris drew her cards.

"Seeing an old friend."

"Oh, that's nice!" Katsu chimed. "I'm sure they'll love to see you."

Gull frowned. "Oh, that's weird. We're taking the exact route we took for our last customer."

Aris set her troops in front of Gull face-down, and displayed her offensive card that allowed her to hide the amount of soldiers she had on the field. She kept her other offense card in hand, ready, and didn't answer Gull's comment.

"Salene, you have them in your sights?" Aris knelt beside Salene, who lay on the rocks untouched by the raging fire. Jade sat nearby, her goggles dark, a wet scarf tied around her nose and mouth to help her breathing. Aris and Salene had similar wet cloths, though the smoke was growing thick enough to seep through.

"Yeah," Salene muttered.

Gull flipped her troop card face-up.

"Looks like at least a hundred of them."

Aris looked to Jade. "You ready?"

Jade glanced back and, despite being unable to see her lips, Aris could tell she was grinning. "Always."

"Is your friend in some sort of trouble?" Katsu pressed.

Aris shrugged. "She's always in trouble."

"Is she a Blue like you?" Zahmur strode up beside the group, his slender frame curling around itself somewhat like a snake as he sat down. The dragon-like creature held no smile on his muzzle. Aris didn't raise her gaze.

"She is, actually."

"What's her name?" Zahmur's eyes flickered to the playing field. Aris rolled the die.

"Now, Jade!" Aris hollered. Jade dashed into the forest, opening her H-blade and dragging it across the trunks of weakened trees. They cracked and splintered, then dropped to the earth and shattered upon impact. Several of the Thrax were pinned beneath them, others screamed and ran.

Aris leapt into the river, using her Helix to help her sprint up the stream, making as much noise as possible. She pounded her fist into the waves, hollered, and launched rocks through the air, which collided against branches, trees, and Thrax soldiers. Salene open fired, and the Thrax camp was consumed with disarray.

"No offense, but I don't think you've heard of her."

"Oh? We frequent Exuro-controlled planets all the time."

The Thrax camp was a mess. Those that didn't flee into the flames were shot down by Salene's precise aim or cut apart by Jade. Their terror made them useless in a fight, and, just like that, Aris won. Gull threw her hands in the air, huffing out an angry breath before pledging loyalty to the victorious Blue.

"Well, she's part of the Opes. Exuro and the Opes aren't exactly the same thing."

Zahmur tapped his chin with his tail, his keen eyes considering this with a hint of mockery. "I always thought that was strange." He watched her as Katsu gathered her forces defensively. "So she's a soldier, hmm?"

"Yes, she's a soldier. All Blues are soldiers." *Why is he pressing? Why is he asking?* Aris flicked her eyes to his. *Maybe he's working for the general.*

"The captain's not a soldier," Zahmur replied, gesturing back to the feline captain at the wheel of the ship. "He's not any good at it."

Aris frowned. "Is that so? Every Blue where I come from has loyalties to the Opes."

"Yes, but remember? We're not from here."

Aris attacked Me and Gull added troops to the fight. They crushed Me without losing much. Katsu gritted her teeth.

"I do remember you saying that, yes." Aris hissed. "So what does that make you, then? Loyal-less?"

"Oh, I wouldn't say that," Zahmur purred, watching with a scrutinizing gaze. "I'm loyal to my crew, my captain. Are you?"

"Of course."

Katsu retaliated, and the last battle of the fast game commenced.

"I'm guessing your general isn't part of that group, then?" Zahmur said.

"What makes you say that?" Aris muttered.

Aris' soldiers stayed behind a group of ditches with spikes, hidden beneath leaves. A quarter of the enemy force perished before they rushed straight into Aris' secondary defensive card: wild lions released from their cages decimated Katsu's forces.

"It seems like you're going behind his back for something. *Someone*, by the sounds of it." Zahmur's gaze was fixed on Aris' face. Her eyes were on the game. Katsu's offensive card had her units riding horses, which trampled Aris' frontlines.

"I don't see why you care. I paid you, didn't I?"

"I'm just trying to know more about you, Blue. No need to be so bitter about it." He smiled, the thin line crooked on his face.

"My friend is a Blue and I'm going to see her," Aris snarled. "I don't know what more there is to tell."

Two bad rolls got her units in a tight spot. She grimaced at the cards in front of her.

"I just want to know her name, is all. I don't see what the big deal is."

"I don't see why you need to know what my friend's name is."

"I'm being friendly, Blue. By Vix, you're a tight one, aren't you?"

Aris pushed Katsu's forces back with a good roll. Both armies were on death's door. The next roll would decide it.

"I just like my privacy," Aris hissed through a clenched jaw. She rolled her dice. They tumbled and bounced over the deck.

"So she must be a fugitive."

Sixes. Aris won.

The soldiers cheered, admiring from a distance.

She forced a grin on her face and a laugh from her throat, arching a brow at Zahmur. "That's the conclusion you came up with?"

Gull stood up and cheered, raising her fists above her head. "I won!" she cried. Katsu laughed.

Jade stood on a pedestal, smiling at her peers. Aris stood in the crowd.

"It's the only one that makes sense," Zahmur mused. "She's a known fugitive, and that's why you don't want me to know her name. I bet there's even a bounty out, isn't there? And you're worried I'll try to make a quick kniri."

"That's not at all what's going on."

"I won!" Gull struck a pose, beaming. Aris scowled.

Jade stood tall as the lieutenant celebrated Jade's victory. Aris shrunk in the crowd.

"I think it is, though." Zahmur looked smug. "I think you're worried your friend will be in some trouble if I find out who she is. You see, the thing is though: I always find out."

"I won!" Gull jumped up and down. *Aris stood and grabbed Jade's wrist, snarling at her.*

"I did all the work, Jade. You know I planned the whole thing! I worked out every little detail, and you acted according to what I told you! Why didn't you tell them I was who did it all? Why didn't you tell them it was me all along? That you were just the muscle? That you didn't think of a single point of the plan? Without me, you would be dead! Without me, we never would've gotten this far! You've done nothing but throw your weight around where I tell you to, so why? Why are you the only one who gets medals? Why are you the only one who gets to stand in the limelight?"

"Aris?" Gull's startled expression filled Aris' vision, the words atop her tongue but never spoken. Not even once. She released the minotaur's wrist and stepped back.

"You should've been up there," Jade murmured.

"No, you deserved it," Aris said, smiling.

"Jade. Her name is Jade." She turned and walked away, down to the bunks.

Chapter 21

Final Log by Green Researcher Melody Denise

Format: Video

"Look into the camera, dear," Melody said, her gold eyes gleaming from behind her glasses. She gazed at the woman hooked up to IV's and strapped to a table. The restrained woman stared at the floating camera bot hovering to Melody's right, her green eyes filled with panic.

"This'll be the last test. We just need to check your tolerance for Wall."

"I don't have a Helix!" the Green shouted, yanking against her restraints without any luck. "I don't have an immunity to any of them! Wall won't be any different!"

"Well, there's no way to know that for sure," Melody chimed. She looked to the camera. "Wall genetics aren't easy to come by but I was able to purchase a sample from researcher friends of mine. When I press this button, the injection will begin." She moved to where a nondescript button was flush with the wall. Melody turned her gaze to the struggling Green.

"Roshni has shown no signs of having a proficiency in any Helix she is introduced to. Blue and Red lightning both burn her, Telepathy gave her a headache, Atmo caused her to fall into seizures, et cetera—it's been a mess. Wall is the last thing we have to try. Are you ready, Roshni?"

"Fuck you!"

Melody smiled. "One…two…" She pressed the button. The camera focused on Roshni's reaction as the sample entered her bloodstream. A scream burst from her throat and filled the room. Melody rushed to the side of the camera.

"A normal reaction. She has a strangely low tolerance to all He—wait a second." Melody's eyes widened at the readings from her wrist holo. "She's not going to—shut it down!" She spun around, rushing off screen. "Turn it off!"

From the tips of Roshni's fingers, black, semi-transparent flames grew, covering her body and splitting the restraints around her wrists and ankles. She grabbed her head, her screams fading into whimpers.

"Roshni?" Melody murmured, walking back into the camera's view. "Roshni, it looks like you lied to me. You have a Helix. Though I've never seen Wall look like this before. And it's never covered someone's body completely. Oh, this is so exciting!"

Roshni's burning green eyes turned to Melody. She sat up on the table and yanked the IV's from her body. Melody stepped back.

"Now Roshni, please relax. We have to look over your vitals. Don't you see how exciting this is? You're the first person to ever have such mastery over Wall!"

Roshni put her feet on the ground, her eyes not moving from Melody's. Melody started shaking.

"If you don't sit back down, we will be forced to restrain you, Roshni. Please cooperate. We wouldn't want—"

"To what? Hurt me?" Roshni let out a bitter laugh. "You've done enough of that over the last two months, haven't you? Even when I told you everything I knew."

"N-now, Roshni, we had some g-good times, didn't we?" Melody stammered. Roshni scowled.

"Yes, I particularly liked that time you woke me up at midnight to stick needles in my neck so you could see how I reacted to violence. I remember that night with fondness, because my eyes changed color then, didn't they? They turned gold, just like yours. And when you marveled at them, I realized I would never get to see my kids again. I would die in this shithole." She strode towards Melody. "But I won't die here. I'm going to see my children one last time if it kills me."

"Fire!" Melody screamed. Gunshots rang from out of view and the lead bullets smashed against the black flames before falling to the ground. Roshni laughed, looking herself over.

"Well, not bad if I do say so myself. I'm guessing being the most masterful wielder of Wall is a bad thing for you now, isn't it?" She smirked at Melody. "I'm going to enjoy this."

Follow-up report: Roshni escaped the research facility after murdering all inhabitants. From there, she climbed up several levels, her apparent destination being her home. Along the way she killed anyone who dared approach or attack her, only to find her family had been taken into protective custody. Hearing this news, she turned her attention to those who were attempting to keep her family safe and killed them as well. Eventually, her Helix died out and her protective layer faded away. Rather than be taken for research purposes, she committed suicide by jumping off a bridge.

Chapter 22

Aris leaned against the ship's railing, reading the text displayed on her wrist by her holo. She scrolled through the document with her other hand, eyes dark as she soaked it in. Footsteps caused her to swipe her finger to the right, making the screen go dark and locking the device. She turned towards the noise. Zahmur stood with his wings folded against his sides and his head held high. His eyes stared at her. Aris arched a brow.

"Listen," Zahmur began, glancing back at the captain's quarters. "I'm here to apologize for my actions yesterday. I…do not approve of my captain's decision to allow you on board. I feel like you are hiding important details from us and that those details will get us all killed."

"I made a deal with your captain. That should be enough for you."

Zahmur gritted his teeth, his nostrils flaring. "You *are* hiding something, aren't you?"

Aris entwined her fingers together behind her back and watched him. "Do you want me to tell you my life story, or something? We all keep things from each other. I don't see how I'm any different than your crew members."

"We're open with each other!" Zahmur stepped forward, his wings jerking open in his aggression and his eyes narrowing. "We talk to each other—we're like a family! And you—you're not even that! You're just a bag of money my captain took pity on."

"I'm hurt. Here I thought we were best friends."

His ears lowered and his hair stood on end. "Your arrogance is detestable. You even attacked one of my own crew and Ossi said nothing! Yet *I* have to be the one apologizing." He flashed his teeth, his talons scraping across the floor as they curled. "What was that about, anyway? Do you just get off by causing strife?"

Aris didn't respond. She watched him without emotion.

Zahmur snorted. "Fine. I said my apology. At least I'm not some pitied fool." He whirled around and stormed towards the captain's quarters. Aris watched him leave before turning to look at the stars behind her.

"Tonight, we celebrate another brilliant victory dealt to us by the amazing Jade Cavvar! You're truly living up to your mother's image, Jade. You've impressed everyone! Cheers!"

I did all the work. I always *did all the work,* she thought.

Aris rubbed her eyes. This wasn't the time to muse about the past. She turned her wrist holo back on and scrolled through the text.

"Are you enjoying yourself, Aris? I'm only here because of you, you know."

"Oh, don't be modest, Jade! You deserve every bit of this celebration. You were the muscle, after all!"

And you weren't anything else.

Chapter 23

The ship landed on the Taotar surface, dust rising up around the new recruits as the anchor was dropped and the bridge was lowered. At the age of fifteen, Aris rushed to the railing, staring out across the vastness of the planet. The suns were just a sliver in the horizon, setting for the night. She had never been off Nevar before. She barely even got to experience the planet for what it was worth, either, since her parents kept her mostly locked away in the house. And now here she was, her blue eyes blazing brightly behind the goggles and a smile broadly displayed across her lips. She pulled her scarf up around her nose and mouth to limit the amount of sand she breathed in.

Vix, I'm even wearing customary Opes armor! Her heart thundered in her chest. All her life she knew she was born to be a soldier. At last, she was able to be one.

Recruits funneled off the ship to her left, collecting a few feet away, forming a circle on the sandy surface of the planet. They weren't allowed to take anything off the ship with them except what they wore. Aris went to merge with the line when a tall recruit shoved her out of the way. Aris stumbled back a few steps and fell, her spine smashing against the armor when she hit the ground. A hiss of pain escaped her. She shot a scowl up at whoever hit her and was greeted with a smug look plastered across the face of a light-skinned human, her freckles dancing across her cheeks beneath her tinted goggles. Her red hair was pulled up into a ponytail and one hand sat on her hip.

"Watch where you're going, fat-ass," the girl said. She sauntered off the ship and stood off from the rest of the group, arms crossed as she gazed out over the sand. Aris dusted herself off, scowling. *Who does that chick think she is? Some sort of goddess?* With a second glance, Aris realized she didn't recognize the older girl from their basic training. *Did she somehow finish early?* Aris' scowl grew deeper. *So, what, is she some sort of war machine?*

As she pondered this with anger in her veins, Aris got to her feet and disembarked. A tall man, around the age of thirty, followed her down. He stood in front of the recruits and hollered for attention. Everyone turned to salute him. The man's blue eyes shone against his dark skin as he paced the line the recruits had shoddily made.

"So these are the best they can give me?" he growled, looking over the group of twenty. "Two years of training and they give me this mess of *children?*" He spat into the sand. "The only one that could even make me look twice is Jennifer's child." He gestured to the red-head. "The rest of you morons look terrified of *sand.*"

Aris glanced down the line where she stood at attention. *That was Jennifer Cavvar's child? The legendary Opes war hero?* Aris frowned. *There is no way she was good enough to skip basic. The only reason she's here is because of her name.* Her eyes flickered back to the officer before her, who seemed to be beaming at the young Jade Cavvar. Aris' fists clenched from where they were pressed in the constant salute against her heart.

"But one girl cannot win the war alone. So." He stopped his pacing and looked the entire group over. "We will be holding a contest so I may assess your skills as soldiers. After this, I will be assigning you to stations around the underground base, where you will practice eliminate your weaknesses."

"We were already tested, sir!" said a kodarian boy near the middle of the line. The officer glanced over him.

"What is your name, recruit?"

"Jami, sir!"

"Lamie, you will be sparring against our war hero's daughter first. Any other stupid remarks? No? Then we shall move to the combat arena. Anyone who cannot keep up will be immediately disqualified from the tournament and will be on cleanup duty for a week. Once we get there, I will go about pairing up fighters and the battles will commence. The winner will be instantly promoted to private and be given the respect that comes with that title. The rest of you will have to wait several months to test your mettle before being promoted. Understand?" Before anyone could answer, he gave a stiff nod. "Good. Now, keep up."

The officer turned and kicked off from the sand, dashing to Aris' right and over one of the large dunes. The recruits hesitated, then leapt after him. Aris pressed herself to keep up, but as everyone sprinted through the desert, sand covered the air and clogged her throat. She coughed, pausing at the first dune despite most everyone else already making it over the third. Aris cleared her lungs and grimaced. She couldn't be last. She had to at least beat *someone*. With a deep breath, the young Blue sent her Helix rumbling through her body and strengthening her legs. Aris felt the muscles bulge. She lowered herself into a runner's stance, then used her added strength to rush forward, each stride growing longer as she picked up speed. At the top of the second dune, she threw herself forward, Aris' momentum taking her to the bottom, splashing sand up in the faces of those unfortunate enough to be too slow.

After seeing what she was doing, a few others began to use their Helixes as well—some had Charge, like her, and began making long strides, while others called about small storms at the top of hills, the miniature rain clouds hovering just above six feet, making the sand more difficult to trek through. Aris avoided most of the conflict and found herself on the heels of the officer himself. And the red-head.

The red-head glanced over her shoulder and smirked. She reached out her hand, ready to use whatever Helix she had at her disposal against Aris. Aris leapt to the side, her momentum abruptly stopped as she raised her arms to protect herself. But nothing came. She could hear the girl laugh as the fastest of the recruits passed Aris. She scowled.

What a bitch.

ϕϕϕ

Aris arrived with the middle of the pack to a hole in a large dune. The circular area was sheltered from outside winds rather well, despite the whole place being made of sand. The recruits sat down on the slopes, gasping for breath as the stragglers found their way to the arena. The officer that lead them made good on his word, and the first matches were set up. The red-headed girl's fight was delayed, as her opponent had not shown up. So she lay in the sand, paying no attention to the sparring below her.

Aris scoffed. *What an arrogant idiot.*

The first fights proceeded and Aris took in everyone's moves and tendencies during battle. When her name was called, she strode into the relatively flat arena at the bottom of the hole and faced off against her opponent: a black haired girl with Blue Lightning spiraling over her arms in anticipation. Aris readied herself, moving her Helix up to her arms.

"Ready? Start!" called the officer. Aris' fellow recruit lunged forward but Aris smashed her fists into the ground, throwing up sand. Aris closed her eyes and dipped her head low to keep her vision clear. *One. Two.* She lunged forward, connecting with her opponent. *Three.* The two of them fell to the sand, Aris on top. The girl raised her hands blindly, rubbing sand from her eyes, lightning licking out towards Aris. Aris smashed her fist into the sand next to the girl's head and exhaled. She would've won had it been a real fight. She stood up and dusted herself off, holding out a hand to her opponent.

Then she glanced towards Jade, to see if the girl was watching. She wished she hadn't.

Jennifer Cavvar, the famed war hero of a generation past, apparently passed on none of her good traits to her daughter, who now sat up, flashing a pitying smile at Aris. As if Jade *hadn't* just seen how quickly Aris had taken down her foe. As if she thought it was somehow pathetic.

Aris scowled and stormed away, taking her place on the opposite hill. She had wanted to finish the fight fast so her skills were not shown off, but now she wished she had done more. Somehow proven to that spoiled brat that Aris was better than Jade could ever be. Aris gritted her teeth, trying to push the feelings away but failing. She wanted to fight the war hero's daughter. And she wanted to win.

Chapter 24

"Mistress, movement."

Jade's eyes fluttered open. She shoved herself upright and her hammock swayed. Her blurry gaze searched the room and a shape appeared at the door. Jade rubbed her eyes, frowning.

"Thaddeous?"

The shape stepped closer. Female. Short. *Aris? No, that can't be right...* She blinked and peered at the shape again. The young woman was dressed in basic military armor, the leather straps that held the metal pieces to her frayed, burnt, and soaked. A large gash cut across the woman's nose, one that would later heal. But the burn mark that consumed half her face would not. Her black hair fell flat on her shoulders, and water dripped onto the floor beneath her. All the blood drained from Jade's face. Salene, the soaking, forgotten friend, reached out to her.

"Why?" Salene whispered, her pleading eyes the color of blue morning fog. "*Why?*" She stumbled closer, her legs buckling and launching her towards Jade. The redhead threw herself back, Jade's hammock swinging out from under her. She smashed her head into the ground and grimaced against the pain. She touched the moist section of her skull and, when her eyes flickered open, she was on Sobek.

A sheathed weapon was in her hand and a pistol on her hip—the gun a precaution in case she came across someone without armor. The smell of coming rain lingered around the camp, where broken remains of a house lay, burnt and unstable. She figured what they sat in now used to be a master bedroom, but there really was no way of telling. The roof was missing, and only the walls to her right and left still stood. There was a broken picture frame on the floor not far away. No one went to look at it.

"Salene, go look at Jade's wound," Aris ordered, her voice quiet. The three of them had been sent as a small, effective strike force to disorganize the enemy troops and serve as scouts for the bulk of the Opes troops. They sat in the stillness of a massacred town around a portable heater. The Thrax had wiped the place out a few weeks ago with fire.

At least, that's what they were told.

Salene put her sniper rifle down and set aside the supplies she had been using to clean it. She shifted to sit behind Jade and lifted the redhead's hair to glance at the source of the blood. She swatted Jade's hand away and sighed.

"Jade, put that sword down," she muttered. "I don't need you flinching and taking off my arm."

With a begrudging huff, Jade set the H-blade down and reached her now-empty hand to the heater. Aris rubbed her palms together across from them and pulled out a paper map. She analyzed it silently as Salene pulled out a small spray bottle filled with foamy green liquid. Jade glanced at it and arched a brow.

"How much of that do we have left?" she asked.

"Not much after your last injury," Salene said. "Can you handle stitches?"

"Is it that bad?"

Salene chuckled and put the bottle away in her pack. She produced a needle and wire, along with a small bandage. "It's really bleeding, Jade."

"I just don't really feel anything."

"You never do."

Jade frowned at the comment. Salene dabbed the wound clean the best she could with field supplies and proceeded to stitch it closed. Jade's discomfort grew and she focused on the sound of wind through the hollows of homes. Aris pointed to a spot on her incoherent map.

"We're here. From the scouting patrols we've done, it looks like we've got a group of four encamped here and a group of eight here, along the riverbank. Base is back here," she slid her hand over the river and a few more inches past. "That's where the commander is. He'll wait for us for another week as more troops arrive, but our rations won't last much longer than two days—including tonight." She glanced up at Jade with a smirk. "And since *someone* can't sneak up on a deaf animal to save her life, hunting isn't all that viable."

Jade snorted out false offense. "Hey, sidekicks need to be useful for something." She grinned. Salene jabbed a needle into Jade's flesh and pulled the string tight. Jade bit back a yelp, swallowing the pain.

"You mean for things *other* than patching you up all the time?" Salene moved away, patting Jade's shoulder. "You're good now, Jade."

"Thanks." She adjusted the goggles on her face and peered over at Aris' map. "So, what? I'm sure with Salene out of sight and you and I on the frontlines, we could take that many."

"If we all had your stupidity, we'd all be dead," Aris said.

"That hurt," Jade grumbled, grabbing her chest. "Really. Truly."

Salene bit back a giggle. Jade beamed at her. Aris rolled her eyes.

"*Anyway*, the plan is to go around." She traced a line around one edge of the river. "There should be a shallow part around here this time of year. We go around quietly—okay, Jade? *Quietly*—and we should be able to get back to base ahead of schedule. We can report where the troops are after that and take them by surprise when we're all together."

Jade frowned. "That sounds like a cowardly plan." She looked over at Salene. "Doesn't it? We should go take out one group at a time. We could do it." She waved her hand in the air. "Besides, didn't you just say I suck at sneaking? Why would it work now?"

Salene opened her mouth, but Aris cut her off.

"No, Jade, that's stupid. We'd get killed. I, for one, would like to get back to base *alive*. Now, we follow my plan." She rolled up the map. "We'll be a good distance away from the enemy so your poor sneaking skills should do just fine. I'm the one with the directions, anyway. So we go where I tell us to go. You can get your fight once we report back to base. *Then* you can run off and get killed."

Jade scoffed. "You worry too much, Aris. We've taken on more than this before. We could do it again."

Aris shook her head. "We stick to my plan and we all get out alive. Okay?"

Why?

Jade groaned dramatically. "Okay." She drawled. Salene chuckled and nodded in agreement.

Why didn't I listen?

Aris situated her backpack under her head and curled up against it. "I suggest we all get some sleep then."

If I had just listened…

Jade moved closer to the heater and curled up on her side, closing her eyes.

If I had just used my head for once…

She heard Salene sit down not far away. As usual, Salene's shift was the first. It sounded like she was cleaning her sniper.

Then Salene…

Jade felt herself drifting off. After a day of rigorous hiking, and the previous day full of small skirmishes with the enemy, exhaustion had finally caught up to her.

Salene would still be…

Salene reached out, her wet and bloody body pulling Jade back to the ship sailing towards Hallow. Her cold hand touched Jade's.

"This is your fault," Salene condemned. Her blue eyes pierced Jade's skull. "And you know it is."

Jade bit her lower lip and looked away, shutting her eyes. "I'm sorry, Salene. I'm so sorry."

"Mistress!"

Jade's eyes flew open, Chloe tightly around her head and her body sprawled out over the floor.

"Mistress, are you all right? You were tossing and turning and flipped yourself out of the hammock."

Jade pushed herself to her knees, grimacing. "Yeah," she grumbled. "I'm…I'm awake now, right?"

"Yes, mistress. You're awake."

Jade sighed and looked around the room. Thaddeous was gone, along with the bottles of wine.

"Nightmares again, mistress?"

"Yeah." Jade pulled her knees to her body and rested her arms on them, yawning.

"What was it this time, mistress?"

"It was about Salene."

"I see, mistress. I'm sure Aris is looking after her."

"It's not Aris' responsibility." Jade exhaled. "Besides. Aris hardly ever goes to Sypher."

"Perhaps she will go there now, to let Salene know what's happened to you, mistress?"

"She'd just call. Not that Aris would worry Salene about this, anyway." She stretched and fell onto her back, staring at the ceiling.

"You really should visit her more, mistress."

Jade closed her eyes. "So she can see the person who crippled her?" she scoffed. "No. I think I'm good."

"Mistress—"

"Is the hammock really that terrible to sleep in?" Thaddeous asked from the door, arching a brow at Jade. Jade shrugged.

"The floor has its perks."

Thaddeous chuckled and gestured behind him. "We should reach Hallow later tonight. You can see it now, if you want."

Jade pushed herself to her feet and rolled her shoulders back. "Yeah, all right. Got any more of that wine from last night?"

"Drinking after you wake up?" Thaddeous looked genuinely confused as she pushed past him. "Doesn't that give people headaches?"

Jade waved the question from the air. "Is that a yes or a no?"

"I have a few bottles left. Follow me."

They strode up to the main deck and as Thaddeous turned to the captain's quarters, Jade found herself rooted to the floor, staring at the blue and white planet that now consumed half the sky. A ring of frozen asteroids circled it, reflecting the sun's distant light and causing them to shine. Fractures ran around edges of the planet, with entire sections of the landscape torn from the surface and held nearby by gravitational pull. She raised her hand to shield her eyes a little, as the entire planet glowed with what little light it received so deep in space. She didn't know how long she stood there, staring at the extraordinary sight, but eventually Thaddeous walked up beside her with a smile.

"Breathtaking, isn't it? No one's quite sure why the planet tore apart like that, but it makes for some amazing views on the ride in." He raised a bottle of wine. "Got you this."

She nodded. They moved to a small collapsible table that had been set up previously by some of the crew and he poured her a glass. She pulled Chloe off her head and sat down. With Chloe in her lap, she drank and gazed out at Hallow.

"Is it always so blinding?" she inquired.

He chuckled. "No, this only happens once a rotation. It's the signifying of a new year for the people of Hallow, actually. They'll probably be celebrating for the next day or two." He leaned back in his chair as he gazed upon the planet. "We'll be there for their 'coming of age' tradition. They send out their young into the frozen wasteland to see who can survive. It's pretty intense."

"Sounds like fun." Jade took another sip from her wine, regret slowly creeping up on her. She needed food, not more alcohol.

Vix, I sound just like Aris. 'Don't drink in the morning, you idiot. Go get some real food.' Jade frowned. I hope she's doing okay.

"I think you'll like the halo people. Honor and fighting all the time." Thaddeous chuckled. "Always brawling to show who's best. You'd fit right in."

Jade spun her glass around, watching the wine swirl within. "Yeah."

I can't do this. I can't stay here. He may be a Green, maybe he's even trustworthy but...I have to get back to Aris. And I know I won't be able to do that with him around—I know they're going to try to keep me. I have to come up with a plan. It's impossible to always be watching me. Maybe I can smuggle myself away. Maybe I can...find a small ship to pilot alone? She looked back up at Hallow. *A ship without any Thrax markings so I don't get shot out of the sky.*

"Are you okay?" Thaddeous asked, watching her with concern as she glanced up. "You seem distant."

"I'm sharing wine with you," she replied sharply. He frowned. She looked away.

"You miss your friend," he concluded. Jade refused to answer. Thaddeous sighed. "We would've brought her with you, but…some things you need to do alone." He paused, then opened his mouth to say something more. "Jade—"

"Got any breakfast?"

"You really—what?" He blinked. She arched a brow.

"Like, food? And if that's an ice planet, don't I need something thicker to wear?"

"Something extra thick would be good, mistress. Say you run cold."

"I run cold," Jade continued. "Maybe two jackets?" She sat her wine down and stood up, Chloe in one hand. "In fact, I'm sort of freezing right now. Did the temperature drop since we got closer?"

Thaddeous nodded and got up, calling for one of the nearby crew. "A few jackets, a scarf, and some snow pants for Jade, please." He looked at her feet. "And maybe some appropriate boots." The crewmate rushed below deck. Jade turned to the main mast and grabbed hold of the ropes that lead up to the crow's nest. Thaddeous' brows furrowed.

"I thought you were hungry. I can't really feed you if you're up in the ratlines."

Jade laughed with forced humor. "Don't worry, I'll come back down." She wrapped one arm around the ropes and stuck Chloe back over her head. "Thanks for the wine." She pulled herself upwards, climbing to about mid-point—high enough to ignore those below her, but not so high as to make getting down too much effort. She linked her arms in the rope and relaxed, letting her head lull to one side.

This is where she'd spend her days on the ship with Aris and Salene. Salene usually hung from her legs a few knots away while Aris was on duty in the nest, whining about how distracting the two of them were being. A smile played on Jade's lips. As she stared out at Hallow, she felt a sense of familiarity wash over her. She could almost hear the two of them bickering. She let her eyes close.

"I assume you have a plan, mistress?"

"We're going home," Jade whispered in response. She looked down at where Thaddeous was speaking to someone dressed in an apron. "The wine's been good but I've got better."

"No you don't, mistress."

Breakfast was nice—and so was lunch, and the same with dinner. Jade layered the jackets and scarf over herself, and switched out her shoes for the thick, fur-covered boots they provided her. The air began to drop drastically in degrees as they entered Hallow's atmosphere, passing through layers of clouds on their way in. Ice clung to her jacket and she quickly brushed it off with her bare hands. Thaddeous strode up beside her and offered her a pair of gloves and a pair of snow pants, which she put on. She'd need all the warmth she could get. She'd also love a weapon, but she had no idea how she'd manage that.

They swooped low over the planet as the sails were tied down and the engines began to whir to life below Jade's feet. The jets strapped to the bottom of the ship took over the flying as they drifted over the frozen wastes. Snow covered every inch of land, though there were signs of a recent thaw. A breeze tickled the trees free of snow in some areas, revealing their vibrant flowers beneath. Rivers, though stiff with an upper layer of ice, still flowed where the water was the deepest. In the distance, city lights bounced off a fog bank rolling in, revealing the first signs of life on the Vix-forsaken planet.

As the ship steadily grew closer to the ground, Jade noticed fishermen in thick fur coats sitting in the middle of mostly-frozen lakes and waving as they glided by. Ahead, a harbor came into view. It was uncovered and allowed for only three ships to dock at a time, the frozen walkways looking anything but safe. As they dropped anchor, Jade peered over the edge, staring down at the slim twenty-foot fall. Larger ships must have to dock elsewhere. As soon as the ship steadied, Jade flung herself over the side and onto the dock, which was level with the ship's deck. It was slippery, and without railings she wondered how no one had ever fallen to their death. Or maybe someone had. She didn't know.

"How's it feel?" Thaddeous disembarked behind her, dressed in a heavy jacket and thick boots. It was strange seeing him without a suit on.

"What?" Jade threw out her arms for balance as she made her way to the ladder rungs at the far end, where she would have to climb down. It was a good thing heights didn't scare her.

"You're the first Opes on Hallow," he replied with a grin.

"Isn't there a base here?" she asked.

"You've got a point." He smiled at her. She smiled back.

Fuck. Stay focused, Jade. I'm getting off this planet and away from these Thrax. Then I'll tell the Opes everything I know and—and—

And be murdered for being a Green before Thaddeous' entire people are massacred. She grimaced at the thought. She didn't know why it bothered her now, after so many years in the war, after killing so many Reds. But it did. Now that she met Thaddeous, a fellow Green, she somehow didn't believe this war was as justified as it was made out to be. Not that it ever sat well with her. The hatred of an entire group of beings made little sense, especially if the first spark of the war, the reason they were all fighting, had been lost to time and erased from history. There was no point in fighting each other. There was no point in it at all.

But they kept killing nonetheless.

Thaddeous strode up to her and offered his arm with a smile. "You ready?"

Chapter 25

Jade didn't take Thaddeous' arm. Her mind continued to spiral with the new realization that she didn't want Thaddeous or his people to die. They were killing each other, killing children and parents and lovers, all for what?

Slowly, a title came to her mind: The Mad Queen. Jade stuffed her hands into her pockets as a rising hatred boiled up in her throat. The woman who helped steal Salene's legs, the woman who burned Salene's face. The Mad Queen butchered innocent civilians by strapping bombs on them, detonating them whenever an Opes soldier ran over to help. She set explosives in the trees and caught entire forests aflame. She placed landmines behind her rear line, making it impossible for the Thrax to flee, and for the Opes to make any ground. She sacrificed her own to ensure the Opes were caught in traps and massacred alongside the Thrax.

Thaddeous said they were less than a million strong, didn't he? So why is that lunatic killing them along with us?

She nodded for Thaddeous to lead the way. If such barbaric practices weren't being used on the field of war, if limbs weren't being blown off and getting stuck in trees and rivers and in the hair of comrades, maybe the desire for vengeance wouldn't be so strong. Aris hated the Mad Queen,

Salene likely did, and Jade knew several generals felt the same way.

But would it really be as simple as bringing down one woman?

Thaddeous headed towards the ladder on the opposite end of the precariously high harbor and climbed down the heated rungs. She followed after him, resolved to kill the woman should their paths ever cross. At the bottom was a carriage tied to a quartet of four-legged, three-foot-tall, furred beasts with massive snouts and fat feet. He gestured to the sled-like carriage.

"Our ride," he said.

Jade climbed inside, and he sat next to her and closed the door. The carriage lurched into motion, the beasts apparently trained. The ride was quiet and still, the smell of Thaddeous' sweat filling the space and battling against Jade's un-showered stench. She leaned her head against the window and watched the white landscape go by. Hills of snow extended into the sky and meshed with the clouds waiting in the distance, prepared to spill their contents upon the awaiting land. Jade momentarily closed her eyes. She was surprised at how peaceful she felt. For a moment, the war didn't exist. She wasn't a soldier. She was traveling through the snowy mountains to an encampment where she would meet Aris, and the two of them would explore the new world together. For once, the threat of torture and death did not hang over her head. For once, she forgot about how many she had killed.

"We're here," Thaddeous said, breaking the silence. He turned back to her with a smile. "Just don't be an ass and you'll be fine."

Jade couldn't help it—a single-note laugh burst from her mouth. His face lit up at the sound and she bit back the rest of her laughter. He opened the carriage door and stepped outside. Jade followed, her shoes crunching against the snow as she approached the fringes of a town. The smell of rotting eggs bombarded her senses before Chloe had a chance to filter it out, and she grimaced beneath her helm. Even behind the visor, each breath felt as if it were loaded with icicles that stabbed her lungs. Thaddeous lifted his scarf to his face, his nose wrinkling at the smell.

"You get used to it eventually," he muttered.

"Don't know if I *want* to get used to it," Jade grumbled in response, sticking her hands in her bulky jacket pockets. She saw the edges of his eyes crinkle as he undoubtedly smiled at her remark.

"C'mon, they're probably waiting for us by the hot spring."

"This place has hot springs?" She trudged through the snow alongside him. He nodded.

"They're the only places that don't freeze. Almost all the towns and cities on this planet are built beside one, otherwise it would be too cold to do anything. Give it a little bit and you'll start to feel it heat up."

They strode past the first set of homes made of ice, though as they travelled further, more of them were created from mud and stone. The earth beneath Jade's feet began to thaw, grass sticking towards the sky. She unzipped her jacket, the heat growing to be too much. Thaddeous smiled.

"Told you."

As they neared the center of the village, the noise of a crowd reached her ears. Eventually, the two of them came to the massive hot spring itself, where it seemed the entire village's occupants were standing on one side, talking excitedly with one another. Near the perimeter stood a three-foot tall halo with an ice-blue coat stood, looking over the crowd. On his left ear several small bones and blood-red feathers were tied to a piercing. The feathers that covered his feet and paws were of the same red color, and whisked away some of the moisture from his fur. His ear twitched and he turned towards Thaddeous, his muzzle instantly consumed by a grin.

"Thaddeous!" The halo spread out his arms. "I am glad you made it. We're about ready to begin."

Thaddeous clasped the halo's paw and returned the grin with a laugh. "I'm glad we made it on time. Is your son here?"

"He is! He's going to be running with everyone else today."

"He's strong," Thaddeous said with a nod. "I'm sure he'll do fine."

"If he keeps his wits about him, he will. The ice can be fragile this part of the year." The halo glanced towards the sky. "I believe it's time. I'll talk to you afterwards, Thaddeous." The halo slipped away into the crowd. Jade glanced at Thaddeous.

"You two seem like buddies. Is this your friend who sent us that well-written letter?"

Thaddeous smirked and gave her a sideways glance. "Don't be rude. That's the chief of this tribe. His name is Keme, and yes, he's a good friend."

"Surprised you didn't embrace him. You probably could've put him on your shoulders and ran around."

Thaddeous shook his head, his grin never leaving. "He's not a toddler, Jade."

Jade smirked. "Could've fooled me."

What am I doing?

Keme stood on top of a rock in front of the crowd and spread out his arms. Within a few short moments the crowd quieted and the chief began:

"Today we celebrate the end of a thaw and the beginning of adulthood for our young warriors." He gestured to four halo standing with just their feet in the hot spring beside him. "As the season of warmth comes to an end, we must prepare ourselves for the hardships of a new frost. These children will begin here, like every child before them, and will wade through the spring and out the other side. From there, they will flee into the wasteland beyond our village and survive the wilderness alone for four days. When they return, they shall be welcomed into our tribes as full adults, prepared for their new responsibilities!" His red eyes scanned the crowd. "My own son will be partaking in this ritual today." He glanced to a figure around four feet tall with a silver coat and white feathers on his paws. His ear was pierced with a red quill. "Now,"

Keme continued, tearing his eyes away from his child. "The ceremony shall begin!"

Cheers rose from the crowd as the four halos dashed into the water. They swam through the super-heated water, the smell of burning flesh and howls of pain filling the air as they threw themselves through the center of the spring. The spectators roared out encouragement, throwing their fists into the air and screaming for the swimmers to keep going strong. When those partaking in the ceremony reached the other side, howls rose up from the crowd as the youths ran past the homes and into the snow beyond. In a few minutes, the howling faded.

Jade arched a brow. "After getting soaked they're going into the icy wastes? Isn't that going to cripple their chances of survival?" Her voice was a low mutter and Chloe was the only one who heard.

"Perhaps it is supposed to be difficult to prove they are worthy of adulthood, mistress?"

"Damn, just stay a kid." Jade rolled her shoulders back. "That's what I would've done."

"Mistress, you would not have been able to pass up the opportunity to show you were the best in your youth."

Jade frowned. "Yeah, well, who asked you, anyway?"

"Incredible, isn't it?" Thaddeous said, gazing at where the last two youths dashed away. "To think that despite their advancements, they still cherish this tradition." He smiled over at Jade. "Culture is intriguing, isn't it?"

His eyes danced with joy and curiosity. Jade forced herself to look away as his bliss seemed contagious.

"I'm more of a…nature kind of gal," she heard herself respond.

"Oh? So you're probably intrigued by how such a planet works, right?"

Jade kept her eyes away from him. She wasn't here to make friends. *Remember that, Jade. He may be a Green, but I still have to get home.* "Yeah, sure. I mean, I like looking at trees and stuff more than I like *studying* trees, but yeah."

"You should see the trees here," Thaddeous continued, his voice energetic. "Incredible. It's astounding how they survive the winter months."

Jade glanced at his feet. "I saw a few trees on the way in. There are more?"

"There are entire forests, actually. They're beautiful during the warm months—maybe we could go out and see them before the frost starts to take their colors away."

Jade chewed her lip. She was the first Opes on Hallow, she should see what the planet was like—or at least, she was the first Opes *back* on Hallow, if that hidden base proved to be true. She doubted it was anything more than a misunderstanding, seeing as, if her people truly had been on Hallow at one point, she would know about it. Still, it would be good to know how her enemy's planet functioned. And trees were important to that function. Totally. She rolled her shoulders back and exhaled, shoving out the feeling of dancing bugs from her chest.

"Yeah, maybe," she said. Thaddeous arched a brow, looking disappointed for a moment before a knowing smile edged the points of his lips upwards.

"All right," he hummed in response. "*Maybe* is good enough for me."

From the lingering crowd, Keme nudged his way through with a large smile on his muzzle.

"So why are you here, my friend? Your message did not say," he bellowed, his voice surprisingly deep for such a small creature. Thaddeous peered down at him.

"My friend here is an Opes," Thaddeous admitted. A knot formed in Jade's throat and chest, so tight she found it difficult to breathe. Knowing Jade's request without her saying it, Chloe began to scan the crowd for any who might look like threats.

"An Opes?" Keme's brows shot up and he looked at Jade with surprise. "How strange! I didn't realize you were going to go through with it, Thaddeous." His smile turned sly. "Is this the one you talked about?"

Thaddeous tried and failed to hide his discomfort. "Yes."

"I can tell you, she does look rather impressive!" Keme put his feathered hands on his hips. "Miss, can I see your eyes?"

"I have a—" Jade began, the words 'I have a condition' beginning to fall from her lips without realizing it. How many times had she said those words to her own people? When asked to take off her goggles, or her helmet, during medical procedures, how many times had she pointed them to her records and told them her eyes were too sensitive to be out in normal light? When scrutinized for what her loyalties might be, how many times had she stood there and taken it, because she couldn't even be herself around people she was risking her life to keep safe and comfortable? And now, after all that, how was it that here, surrounded by those who were supposed to be her enemies—how was she taking off her helmet and displaying her eyes for all to see?

Jade's fingers curled around Chloe and pulled, lifting the helmet from her head. Her hair fell around her cheeks in a tangled mess.

Keme whistled. "What an amazing sight. Never thought I'd see a Green in my lifetime." Jade frowned and glanced at Thaddeous.

"No offense, Prince," Keme continued, "but I do mean a *real* Green. Well, I suppose you're going to show her around Hallow, then? Can I assume you won't be staying with us for long before touring other villages?"

"We'll be moving around, yes," Thaddeous confirmed. "But we'll stay here tonight, if that's all right, Chief."

Keme swatted the inquiry from the air. "Thaddeous, how often have I told you to just call me 'Keme?'" He chuckled. "Besides, we have four rooms open, so of course we can house you." Keme glanced between Jade and Thaddeous. "Separate, or together?"

"Separate," Thaddeous said before Jade could reply. "She needs her own space."

Jade glanced at Thaddeous from the corner of her eye. She, a prisoner of war, was allowed to have her own space? Being on the ship was one thing—there wasn't anywhere she could go. But on a planet like this? One without guards? Could she not slip away into the night and escape them all?

Keme didn't seem to have these questions as he nodded, accepting the verdict immediately. "We'll get your rooms ready. In the meantime, we're celebrating the New Year tonight. You'll be joining, I assume?"

"Oh, well," Thaddeous began, an expression of displeasure contorting his face. Jade arched a brow at him.

Keme began to laugh, nudging Thaddeous' leg. "Come on, you loved it last time! As I remember, you even tried to swim into the middle of the hot spring naked before we could convince you otherwise."

Thaddeous blushed, horrified. He looked to Jade, visibly searching for words to defend himself. Jade tried to hold her laughter back, but without Chloe over her head she couldn't hide the soft snicker and the grin splitting her face. She put one hand over her mouth, looking away, but all she could think about was him, spewing random stories about his life as he stripped off his clothes and dashed to the water. Laughter broke through and she pressed her hand to her forehead, her shoulders shaking as she howled.

"You?" Jade gasped. "*You* were so plastered you stripped *naked?*" She looked at Thaddeous, only able to hold the laughter back long enough to hear his ashamed 'yes' before she was laughing once more. "I can just see it!" Jade used the hand not holding Chloe to gesture broadly. "You, shouting stories about your life that make absolutely *no* sense, and becoming convinced you had to go for a swim!"

"We tried to tell him it was too hot!" Keme added with equal humor, snickering at Thaddeous' growing discomfort. "That's when he stripped naked, saying it would help him keep cool!"

Jade spat out laughter, doubling over. "You're the best drunk I've met!" At seeing her humor, a small smile had eased its way onto his features. "*Please,* we have to stay so I can see this."

"Only if you keep up with me," Thaddeous challenged.

Keep pace with you? Jade snorted. *I couldn't ask for a better way to get you out of the game.*

"You'll be passed out before you'll see me drunk, Prince." She straightened and put one hand on her hip. "But you're on."

Keme beamed and turned to the mingling halos. "Let the New Year celebration begin!" Cheers rose out. "Bring the ale!"

The halo people split up, some pulling out tables and setting food atop them, others rolling out barrels of alcohol and uncorking them. Keme ushered Jade and Thaddeous to a table and declared the competition to everyone:

"Green against our Prince! A contest that will go down in the history books! Who will win? Place your bets and keep the drinks coming!"

Jade laughed. "Are we really doing this?" The first mug was set down in front of her.

"I had meant it as a joke, but I guess it's too late to back out now." Thaddeous winked at her. She set Chloe down on the table and smirked.

"You're going down, Prince."

"Mistress, you have other things to worry about."

I know, Chloe. I know. for the first time in my life, I have a plan.

Chapter 26

Thaddeous couldn't last against Jade for long, as she expected. She was certain the ale was pure alcohol, considering the intense burning sensation, and they had only finished their fourth glass when Thaddeous' voice raised and he spoke about things that made no sense. The group that surrounded them laughed, the noise ringing in Jade's ears. She grimaced. Yeah, that was strong shit to make her feel tipsy so fast.

"Keme?" she hollered. The chief came to her side. "Where's Thaddeous' room? I don't think he can handle much more."

"No nude show?" Keme teased with a grin. "What a shame! But I agree, he won't last much longer. Here, I'll show you."

Jade picked Chloe up and strode next to Thaddeous. "All right, big guy. Let's go."

"Did I win?" he slurred, looking up at Jade with hazy green eyes. She chuckled.

"Sure, you won." She wrapped her arm around him and helped him stand. He leaned against her, staggering as he walked. And it was…nice to feel him near her. Just like it was nice to have Aris around, to have her sleep alongside Jade when her nightmares got too terrible to handle alone. Jade grimaced. *That's just the ale talking...right?* She needed to get out of here.

Jade followed Keme through the crowd and to a house near the hot spring. It was a single-room home, and two beds were pushed together so Thaddeous could fit comfortably. Jade helped him to the mattresses while Keme slipped back out. When Thaddeous was laid down, she pulled the blanket over him. After a few minutes, his breathing slowed. Jade lingered.

"Mistress, we should get going."

She sighed. "Yeah." She gathered Chloe and stood, just as a laughter danced into the room. Ice chilled her spine, stiffening her muscles.

Not real. She's not real.

She took a deep breath and turned towards the figure in the doorway. A'doxia stood there, smiling, arms crossed. She wore a thick jacket and long pants, with a small hat pulled over her ears. Her hallucinations never wore different clothes.

"Real, mistress!"

Jade's face paled as confidence left her body.

"Tucking him in goodnight?" A'doxia sung. "Are you going to read him a bedtime story, too?"

"Mistress, we must find a way to distract her."

Jade's mind moved sluggishly. Distraction. *Distraction.*

"Why are you here?" Jade managed, attempting to relax. A'doxia flashed a smug smile.

"Oh, well, I figured I should keep tabs on you and the prince. I mean, you *did* threaten his life and all," A'doxia cooed. "But more than that, I wanted to ask you a question." A'doxia strode forward. Jade held her ground, gritting her teeth. From her pocket, A'doxia produced a small tablet, opened it, and pulled up a video. She turned, pressing her spine against Jade's chest.

"Move, mistress," Chloe prompted. *"Do not let her do this to you."*

She couldn't, though. If she moved, she showed weakness. If she stayed, she at least proved she wasn't going to back down.

That, or she was too paralyzed by fear to move. *Fuck.*

The video on the screen flickered to life. It showed A'doxia and Jade in the hallway, where she had been tackled to the ground. Blue Lightning ran over Jade's body, completely covering her as she screamed. *Why is A'doxia showing me this? Just to taunt me? I was there. I felt everything.*

Jade gritted her teeth as A'doxia's scent filled her head. Then the corporal saw something new. The lightning that cloaked her body grew tainted with a black color, spreading across every blue tendril. It spiraled back up A'doxia's hands and arms, spreading over her body as A'doxia threw herself backwards, swatting at the electricity. She screamed, eyes wide with horror as the black lightning continued to pour from Jade's body, spreading across the metal floor of the hallway and up the walls. The camera sizzled and crackled before it overloaded and filled with static.

Jade grew stiff. *What was that?* Her mind reeled. *How did I do that? How did I hurt A'doxia? Helix users are immune to their own Helix. So how...?* She glanced at the floor. A'doxia peered up at her.

"Oh?" She reached up and touched Jade's cheek, her black gloves cold. "You look surprised."

Jade swatted the hand away and stepped back, brows furrowed. She looked at her hand. *How is any of this possible? I don't even have a Helix, let alone some sort of Black*

Lightning Helix. I haven't even heard of such a thing. It doesn't exist!

"I'm guessing you won't be able to answer my question then," A'doxia chimed, turning to look at Jade fully. "What a pity. Well, I suppose you and I can find the answer together, hm? I mean, this seems like it's the first time you've ever seen it yourself." Her fingers walked up Jade's arm. "Let's find out where it comes from."

Jade grabbed at her head with one hand, paying little attention to the nightmare before her. *I've gone years without a Helix—years! I've fought in a war without one, and now, all of a sudden, I get one? One that doesn't even exist? What sort of sick joke is this? Why would I ever want power over lightning—where the fuck is the return box?*

"Mistress! We need a plan!"

"My, your little helmet is chatty today." A'doxia smiled at the helmet in Jade's hands. Jade blinked, returning to reality. She would worry about her new powers later. A'doxia reached for Chloe.

"Mistress!"

Jade smashed her elbow into the side of A'doxia's cranium and dashed past. She pulled Chloe over her head as she darted into the crowd of drinking halos. All of them looked like nothing more than children compared to her. If she wasn't smart, A'doxia would find her in an instant. Jade gritted her teeth. Intelligence wasn't her strong suit. But would A'doxia be fast enough to catch her in a crowd? She sucked in a lungful of air and sprinted ahead, shoving past halos, overthrowing tables, her eyes set on the way the halo children had gone before her. She was sure their footsteps would still be in the snow. And if she caught up to one of them, perhaps they'd show her the way off this Vix-forsaken wasteland.

"Stop!" A'doxia's voice carried over the noise, unusually harsh. Jade let her fear of being caught fuel her speed. She shoved past Keme, who reached out and tried to grab her right arm, his claws tearing open a hole in her jacket.

"No, Green!" he cried. "The storms are coming!"

Storms? Jade scowled. She wasn't stopping now. *Storms will have to move out of the way.* Her feet beat into the ground until it turned to snow, the distant sound of lightning crackling behind her.

"You can't run!" A'doxia called. "That storm will force you back!"

Jade glanced up to the sky, noticing the thick black clouds rolling steadily towards her. It didn't matter. She was leaving.

"You think you can survive on this planet alone, Private? You think you'll find your way onto a ship and escape? I'll call for a lockdown the minute you leave!" Her voice was growing distant. She was falling behind. "You're in Thrax controlled space, you idiot!" A'doxia screamed. Her voice cracked with intensity. "You can't do this!"

Snow fell and a wind pushed the flakes horizontal. Jade was grateful for thick clothing.

"Stop, Private!" A'doxia said. "You'll die out there!"

Jade sneered. *That's what you think.*

The wind picked up until it was bombarding her body and visor. Chloe did her best to keep Jade's face warm, but she wasn't equipped with anything but basic air-circulation vents. With the rip in Jade's jacket, it was even worse. She swore every snowflake possible found its way in to melt against her skin. Gray clouds gathered around her, restricting her visibility. Each breath sent needles into her lungs. She brushed off the snow gathering on Chloe's visor. On the plus side, she didn't hear A'doxia following her anymore. Jade spared a glance over her shoulder. She couldn't even see the lights of the town, or smell rotting eggs. Her tracks vanished as quickly as she made them.

She stumbled and smashed her knees into the freezing layer of snow. With a grunt, she pushed herself back to her feet and pushed onwards. How long had she been walking? It didn't seem like all that long ago she had escaped A'doxia, yet the chill creeping in on her bones suggested otherwise. She'd need to find safety. There were caves to sleep in, weren't there? Maybe she could even find that Opes base on a Thrax controlled planet? A giggle ruptured her throat. *Like that actually exists.*

"Mistress, your core temperature is dropping. You need to find sanctuary."

"Where do you suggest I go?" Jade said.

"Perhaps build a shelter from snow, so that you are at least hidden from the wind, mistress."

"I should put more space between me and the village," Jade said. "I have to keep going a little longer." *I just need to go until I find someplace to hide. There's got to be something out here.*

"Mistress, that would be unwise. Please, stop and make shelter."

"I'll be fine." She fixed her eyes on the invisible horizon. "Hang on, Aris. I'm coming home."

282

Chapter 27

The storm only grew worse. Snowfall increased, piling halfway up Jade's calf. The chill grew more severe and her lips felt as if they were frozen. Hail crashed down from the heavens and bombarded Jade's arms and chest. Eventually, breathing grew difficult. She could feel bruises starting to form.

The wind made it difficult for her to walk in a straight line, and her right arm grew numb from being exposed to the elements. *Where are the forests? Where are the mountains and the caves?* She staggered through the snow. Jade's mind felt sluggish.

"Mistress, stay with me. Mistress, can you hear me?"

Jade nodded. She opened and closed her right hand, hoping to bring life back to her fingers. She could hardly feel her feet, either. It almost felt like they were wet. That wasn't possible though, right? They were clad in boots. Weren't they clad in boots?

"Tell me about that Black Lightning, mistress. What do you think about that?"

"Dunno," Jade murmured. Her foot pressed against the snow and hail, the crunch a dull noise to her chilled ears. *This was a stupid idea. So stupid. Stupid stupid stupid. Aris wouldn't have done something as stupid as this. She would've figured out a foolproof plan.* Jade stumbled, flaring her arms out to keep herself from falling. *Aris the Brains. That's a good nickname for her. I'll have to see how she likes it when I get back home.*

If I get back home.

"It's odd, isn't it, mistress? How a Helix would show up after all this time?" Chloe prompted. Jade shrugged and wrapped her arms around herself, moving onward.

"Dunno. Hey, you think Aris would be this stupid?" Exhaustion seeped into her voice, making each word slow. "She's a pretty cool girl, don't you think?"

"Yes, mistress."

"You know, I think she's the coolest girl. Like, she's always so nice to me. Why is she so nice to me, Chloe? You're not that nice to me." Jade swayed. "She's probably the best person in the galaxy. You know? She's probably the best one out there. Don't think I could have a better friend." She stopped. "I'm really sleepy."

"Keep moving, mistress. Tell me more about Madame Aris."

"She's cool." Jade's legs started to move again. "She's like, super, *super* smart. Like I think she's the smartest person in the world. Like, in this world and in Nevar. I dunno about Daoth though. There's some pretty smart people there."

"You don't think Aris could outsmart them, mistress?"

"I dunno, maybe."

"Where did you two meet again, mistress?"

They had met on a desert planet. Right? Jade frowned. What was the name of it, again? A nice place. It was a nice place, wherever it was. She met some nice people. Like Jennifer. *No. Wait*... Jennifer was her mom's name. Wasn't it? She couldn't meet her mom on a desert planet. Her eyes closed then opened. Where was she again? She looked up at the sky. Somewhere really hot. She was burning up.

"Mistress!"

Beneath her feet, the sound of shattering ice. She looked down, cracks forming around her foot.

"Mistress, move!"

The ground vanished.

Chapter 28

Format: Text

I've noticed Jade's startling lack of Helix abilities. Occasionally she will wear gloves and fool others into believing she has BL. However, she is masterful with electronics and I have my suspicions that her BL is nothing more than electrical discharges rigged up to give the illusion of being like everyone else.

When she isn't wearing her goggles, she wears a tinted helmet, both of which impair scrutiny of her eyes. I understand the condition she is claimed to have, and I have met those who indeed suffer from it, but my gut questions the authenticity of this doctor's judgement. Only a sixth of the population is diagnosed with it. And somehow the untainted genes of Jennifer Cavvar gave birth to such a defect? I am not convinced.

I am keeping an eye on her until ordered otherwise. Tomorrow we will be conducting a raid on an enemy base, and she will be beside me the whole way. I will get to the bottom of this and report back what I can. I understand you are fond of her, Kasaar, but if she is a Green, this could easily play out like Edith. Don't forget that.

General Yurn: Deceased at age 47 after a Thrax base raid went awry.

Chapter 29

"Most of those that have questioned Jade Cavvar's eye color have died or gone missing. This raises the question: does she somehow know when people are doubting her loyalties? Is she perhaps picking off those that are looking into her? We cannot act unless we are certain."

Aris listened to the audio while she watched the horizon swell with Sypher's distant light. They would be there within the next day, as the ship would need to leave the Air Stream and travel by external thrusters. It would be much slower, but the Stream didn't get close enough to Sypher for the ship to use its momentum to enter the atmosphere. Aris exhaled. It was her shift to watch for pirates while the rest of the crew slept. It had thus far been uneventful, and she was grateful Katsu allowed Aris to borrow a pair of headphones to listen to her Green audio in privacy. They were tweaked to fit Katsu's ears better, but they still did the job just fine.

"After some thorough research, there are no links with Greens in the Cavvar family line, so genetics must not pass down such traits—if Jade Cavvar is indeed a Green, that is. I have pushed for General Kasaar to allow me to meet the woman and do a physical exam, but he won't have it. I believe he wishes to live in denial about his top soldier's possible Green traits."

Top soldier?

"She is indeed a valiant fighter—the way she has executed pre-conceived plans is phenomenal. It's almost as if she's a different person on the battlefield, both strong and intelligent." Aris rubbed her eyes. "Perhaps that's the Green blood that makes her so excellent at all that she does."

Aris stopped the audio and pulled out the headphones, exhaling as she ran her hands over her face, trying to expel the feeling growing inside her chest.

I planned everything. Every little thing. And she followed along with it. I'm the one who made the calls, and she was just the weapon to enact them. Yet she's the one who is praised, the one who is spoken of so highly. I'm just a private *because she never mentions it was me.*

"Somethin' wrong, Blue?" Ossi whispered, his voice full of concern as he sat down beside her. Aris glanced at him and offered a smile.

"No, nothing. Just tired is all."

Ossi grinned back. "Right. I imagine this whole experience has been a little exhaustin' for you. I talked to

Zahmur, by the way. He's concerned for the crew's wellbein', but that doesn't excuse the way he's been actin' towards you. I want to formally apologize on his behalf. He doesn't speak for me." He put his hand over his scarred chest and dipped his head respectfully.

Aris let out a nervous laugh. "Please, it's all right. I understand his skepticism. I'd be the same way if I were in his shoes."

Ossi breathed a sigh of relief. "I'm glad you're not too upset. I hate strife on the ship. It's too small for that."

Aris chuckled. "Yeah, it is."

"He told me you were goin' after a friend?" Ossi asked. Aris began to build a wall. He waved his hands. "I won't press for details, Blue. I just want to commend your dedication. He told me that a bounty was recently placed on your head and that of a woman named Jade Cavvar. I imagine she's the friend you're after." He looked ahead. "The bounty on her is an impressive sum. It…" He scratched his chin. "It also says she's a suspected Green."

Aris honed her Helix into her left arm, the one hidden from his view. She felt her muscles ripple and double in size. She would throw him overboard if need be. She'd throw them all overboard.

"I'm not sure what a Green is, and why that eye color is special, but I know your people fear them." Ossi looked up at the sails. "I'm not interested in fear-mongerin', however. My job is to get you to Sypher safely, and that's what I'm goin' to do. What you do after that is your business." He looked at her and flashed his teeth in a grin. "I don't get what's goin' on with you and your life, Blue. But please trust that no one here is goin' to try to collect that bounty on your head, or that of your friend's."

Aris arched a brow. "Zahmur?"

Ossi laughed. "Not even that stick in the mud. He may be reckless in his words, but he won't go against my direct orders. If he did, I'm guessin' you could take him, though." He pointed to her left arm. "You were ready to kill me, after all. I doubt Zahmur would have much of a fightin' chance."

Aris let her Helix fade and her arm returned to a normal size. Soreness clung to her muscles after the expansion, which would only persist if she used her Charge again.

"I can't be too careful," she said.

The feline nodded. "I understand. Your own people are after you and your friend. It must be hard." He patted her shoulder. "I have a feelin' you'll make it, Blue, despite the obstacles." He stood and walked towards his quarters. "G'night!"

Aris watched him go. She offered a slight smile to his back. "Goodnight."

Untitled Audio File Continued

"…Regardless, she *is* someone to keep an eye on, whether or not the general accepts that. End."

The next file began to play automatically.

"There was a ship discovered caught in Sypher's gravitational pull, and I went to investigate it with a small party of guards. When we arrived, the ship was shattered and half destroyed, and seemed to be modeled after a ship I've never seen. The material beneath our feet was foreign, a sort of purple metal that looked more like wood than anything else and had grooves in its surface. We found a single creature alive on the ship. And it was a Green.

"Its rage was nothing like I've ever seen, and it lashed out with violence and fear, tearing us apart. Its prowess on the field of battle was unmatched, and one by one my party was destroyed. I fell to my knees and begged the Green to have mercy. It knelt down to my level and stared at my terrified face. Then it laughed. It told me I was pathetic and it had met smaller men with more courage in the war. Is this the Green I was told about? This monstrosity? Can they change that much after snapping?

"I asked it what its name was. It laughed again. It patted my head and gave me a twisted smile before picking me off the ground. It pointed to the surface of Sypher and threw me at my ship. I scrambled inside and piloted it alone all the way back to Sypher where I recorded the events here. If something were to happen to me, this audio shall catalog what transpired. I never knew Greens were so powerful.

"The Green put up no fight as we brought it to Sypher and carried it in a darkened vessel through the city. We had it enter a warehouse owned by the nearby factory. After moving the spare parts aside, we allowed it to exit the vehicle, where we attempted to speak with it. Its green eyes watched us as we spoke, but it said nothing. We tried to ask if we could take a sample, to which it didn't respond. When we proceeded to try to take some blood, it freaked out, ripping the limbs off the nearest doctor and throwing them at the rest of us. It screamed, its voice like searing metal. We kept trying and managed to get a saliva sample instead after losing most everyone to the beast. We fled the warehouse, locking it inside as it screamed.

"What have we brought to Sypher?"

Chapter 30

The ship Aris stood upon entered Sypher's atmosphere, the thick cloud of smog breaking as they made their arrival. They docked and Aris said her goodbyes, thanking the crew for carrying her so far. While Ossi told her where they had picked up the shipment, he handed her something and patted her hand with a smile.

"Good luck, Blue. We'll be rootin' for you."

When Aris disembarked, she found he had handed her every kniri she had paid him. She chuckled. *What a soft-hearted fool.*

Aris descended to the street level, where the city was bustling with civilians and foreigners alike. Humans, halos, kodarians, snippers, and syphers—three-foot tall fleshy creatures with four legs, two arms, a beak, and a brilliant mind—pressed past her on their way to their daily activities. The factory Ossi and his crew had taken the packages from was about a mile hike away from the port, so she started to make her way through the city. Three-story buildings and manufacturing plants rose up around her. With the planet not yet overpopulated, the grid-based tower system of Nevar wasn't necessary.

Aris' heart pounded in her chest. Jade was here, somewhere, among the bright lights advertising breakfast foods, the newest fashions, and employment opportunities. Her roommate—no, her *friend*—was somewhere stashed away. She glanced at the display windows of shops as she passed, idly noticing the signs that said "Browns Only." With Sypher being a neutral planet, Reds and Blues had attempted before to try to blend in to get information about each other. This practice was frowned upon by the government.

Whatever the case, Aris wasn't there to stare in windows and twiddle her thumbs. She was there to find Jade. To find a Green. And with only one Green ever being alive at a time, that meant the one reported to be here *had* to be Jade.

She didn't know what to make of the strange circumstances surrounding each Green, however. The deaths, the madness, the extensive Helix abilities when Jade had none. *Does that mean Jade will never fall victim to the madness like those who came before her? Or does she have some sort of ability she has hidden from me?* She shook off this thought. Jade, despite her guarded disposition, hardly kept secrets from Aris. At least, she didn't think so.

Of course, she had never thought Jade would be stupid enough to cause Salene to lose her legs.

No. Now is not the time.

Every Green with documented history in the logs had, at one point, snapped. This confirmed that such an occurrence was actually real, instead of just being one of the rumors that spread across the Exuro Empire. And if that was the case, could Jade snap? Had she *already* snapped? Is that why she was found in space on a ruined ship, is that why she saw things, why she had nightmares? Was it her slow decline? Aris chewed her lip in thought, her frown growing ever deeper. It would explain a lot. Every other Green file she had read included a moment where the Green lost control. Where they killed friends and family before ending their own lives. Her mind wandered back to what General Kaasar had said.

"She may not be who you remember her to be."

If Jade was arrogant and never bothered to acknowledge Aris for everything she did, then that would be exactly as Aris remembered.

Halfway through her journey she stopped at a street vendor—one of the many that crowded the walking space—and purchased a bowl of ramen. The snipper smiled at Aris and took her money before handing her a bowl. She turned to walk and eat when she bumped into a hover-chair. She spilled a little of the broth on the woman sitting in it and quickly apologized.

"Aris?"

Aris froze. She knew that voice. Her eyes focused on the person speaking.

The woman had dark hair that fell in thick curls around her face, framing the massive burn scar that split her head in two, mangling her right ear and stretching down her neck and onto her shoulder. Of course, the woman's hair was combed over to hide the damaged ear, and she wore a sweatshirt to keep the neck and shoulder sections from showing.

"It *is* you!" she cried, her hazel eyes alight. She raised her hands off the sides of her chair and opened them to hug Aris. "It's been so long!"

"Salene," Aris breathed. She didn't account for running into Salene. She hadn't even told Salene what was happening. *Salene isn't supposed to be here, Salene* can't *be here.* "I...I thought you were on the other side of Sypher." Aris tentatively gave the woman a hug. Salene's arms were still lean with muscle and her embrace was firm.

"I recently moved to live with my parents." Salene smiled. "Can't get a job without...well." She gestured to her legs, which were covered with a small, green blanket. "Did you bring Jade with you?" She looked around, her face hopeful.

"No, I…I didn't." Aris' mind raced. Salene had no idea what was going on. And she couldn't know. She would just get in the way. She would ask questions. If a fight broke out, would she even be able to defend herself? If Salene found out what Jade was, would she panic? If Salene was the first person Jade saw, would Salene take all the credit for what Aris had fought to achieve?

"Damn," Salene muttered. "Was hoping to see her. Haven't seen her since I turned Hazel." Salene's smile was weighed down by sadness. "Does she…does she still blame herself?"

Aris glanced around. She was wasting time.

"Oh, you're busy," Salene said. "Here, I'll walk—or, *float*, with you." She smiled and gestured for Aris to lead the way.

"No, no, it's um…you see it's…" Aris' mind was blank. She didn't plan for this. She looked down the street. Somewhere down there, Jade was being held. Aris needed a new plan.

"Let me run this errand real quick, Salene," Aris said with a smile, turning back to the hazel-eyed woman. "And I'll be right back, so we can catch up." A soft laugh slipped from her lips. "Actually, this was supposed to be a surprise for you. I'm picking Jade up so we can see you together."

Salene's eyes lit up. "Jade? She's here?" She looked down the street, her grin big. "That's silly that she didn't just stay at the port! Well, I'll go with you then!"

"No, no, we have to pick a few things up first," Aris insisted. "You hang out here, okay? I'll be back." She handed Salene her ramen. "Sorry for spilling this on you, but why don't you eat it for me? I'll just be slowed down if I have it."

Salene frowned. "Are you sure? The kniri Blues get is hardly enough to live on."

Aris swatted Salene's concern from the air. "It'll be fine! We're going back to active duty soon, anyway. We'll live off the rations until we get paid." She touched Salene's shoulder. "See you in a bit."

Aris turned and sprinted down the street before Salene could protest. She shoved through the crowds. Salene didn't deserve being lied to, not by the only people she knew. Not by Aris. Aris gritted her teeth. She was hoping it was only a half-lie, though. She was hoping she'd actually find Jade in the warehouse. She was hoping that red-headed fool would still be alive.

Chapter 31

Water spilled into Jade's lungs and crashed against the exposed skin beneath the tear in the jacket's sleeve. Her arms flared out, desperately fighting the current to reach the surface, to breathe again. *Please, Vix, let me breathe.* Chloe tried to create a seal, but the cold was slowing her processors. In a few minutes, she would shut down.

Jade shoved herself to oxygen, sputtering and panting, and air returned to her lungs. She coughed the water from her throat, adrenaline waking her from her delirious state. But the river would not grant her peace. It grabbed her legs and pulled her under once more, towards the bed where rocks jutted out and tore through her clothes, exposing more of her skin to the elements. Chloe's screen flickered on and off. She wouldn't last much longer.

A rock caught Jade's hip and spun her, causing her to spiral beneath the waves. She forced her eyes closed, trying to keep herself from growing sick. Which way was up? She felt as if icicles were forming on her skin, sapping her body of strength. She cursed inwardly.

Stupid fucking ice planet.

The trapped air in her chest started to swell, pressing against her ribs, demanding to be replaced. *Even water will do,* it seemed to say. She pushed air out from her nose, hoping it would help. It didn't. The strong arms of suffocation began crushing her ribs. She could almost feel them breaking and the splinters stabbing her lungs.

Nausea began to form from her nonstop spinning, bile rising up in her throat. She pulled herself into a tight ball. *Focus. I need to focus. All I need to do is get back to the surface. Then I can get to shore.*

Her frozen body didn't like that idea. It was steadily being consumed by stiffness and when she opened her eyes and reached for a rock, it was that stiffness that kept her from being fast enough. The rock slipped past her fingers, brushing her icy skin, and vanished in the sudden, consuming darkness that wrapped around her.

A massive tunnel surrounded Jade, cutting out all the light and offering her little hope of finding breathable air. She clawed to the surface anyway, reaching for freedom. Her fingers brushed against the smooth metal of the tunnel. Then she was pushed outwards and the tunnel disappeared. Jade was flung through the air and out of desperation, she took a deep breath. She launched into the still water below, and it quickly filled her airways. Her head throbbed from the lack of oxygen and quickly found the surface, tore Chloe from her head, and coughed until her lungs were free of liquid. Her chest ached. Spots dotted her vision. She dragged herself to shore and clambered onto a metal platform, water drenching her to the core. Blood barely managed to squeeze through her torn flesh, her fingers and toes hardly heeding her movements. She shivered, pulling Chloe to her chest as she curled up. Cold. She was cold. *So fucking cold.* She pulled her arms around her face, entire body shivering as water pooled around her. Each pound of her heart sent a wave of agony through her nerves, stabbing them repeatedly with a thousand needles.

"Are you just going to sit there and die?"

Jade's head jerked up, instantly alert from the sound of A'doxia's voice. The Thrax stood a few feet away in the outfit she wore on Taotar. She smirked at Jade.

"That's not like you, is it, Private? Just giving up." She strode closer, Jade's face growing harder with each step she took. "Maybe I should warm you up?" She knelt down beside Jade, electricity dancing in her hand. "Shall we cuddle?"

Jade pushed herself to her knees, grimacing at her complaining muscles and bones. The movement pulled at the flesh around her wounds, stretching the skin until they began to bleed again. *Shit. This isn't good.*

"You're going to die, you know. If you're not careful," A'doxia hummed, watching Jade stand. "You'll freeze to death if you stay in those clothes." A'doxia's face twisted into a sadistic grin. "Shall I help you out of them?"

Jade scowled, moving around the hallucination and walking farther onto the small metal island in the middle of the water tank. The river spilled in from the tunnel thirty feet up the wall, filling up the massive container about halfway. Her island was one of many, each outfitted with several panels with buttons and knobs. Water treatment, perhaps? A bridge extended towards a platform in front of a closed door. Jade started towards it. A'doxia appeared in front of her.

"Don't you think you're forgetting something?" A'doxia cooed, striding closer. She reached for Jade's face with a smile. "Don't you need to shed a few layers?"

Jade grimaced. *Not real. She's not real.* She exhaled and tested her luck, swatting A'doxia's hand away. Terror and exhilaration rushed through Jade. A'doxia's face changed slowly, hatred engraving itself into her features. Her eyes flashed to Jade's. Jade regretted her actions immediately.

A'doxia grabbed at Jade's clothes and tore off the jacket, throwing it in the water. Jade stumbled back, her hands—or were they A'doxia's hands?—tearing her shirt in two. Jade screamed out, thrashing and kicking, trying to get away. She fought against herself—or was she fighting against A'doxia?—but it was to no avail. A'doxia easily overpowered Jade, pushing her to the ground and ripping all the clothes from her body and tossing them all into the depths of the water around them. And when Jade was naked, A'doxia stood and stepped back, a cold, satisfied smile on her lips. Jade shivered on the floor, covering herself with her hands the best she could.

"Aren't you just the cutest thing?"

Chapter 32

Jade was freezing.

The little she knew about survival told her that wasn't the best thing in the world. And since A'doxia had thrown her clothes into the water and left her naked, she had nothing to warm herself up with—except maybe Chloe, but Chloe wasn't responding. Jade's only hope was that whoever worked within the facility wasn't a sexual predator and had a towel to give her.

Dripping wet, Jade snatched Chloe up in her hands and rushed across the bridge to the door. It was so *cold*. She felt like at any second all her limbs would freeze and shatter. The sliding door appeared automatic, but it didn't open when she approached.

"Shit!" She slammed her numb hands against it, her mind immobilized and unable to come up with a solution. But she *needed* one. She needed to get inside. She needed clothes. She needed warmth. "Shit!" she screamed again. Her fingers were blue. She was sure her toes were in a similar condition but didn't bother to look. She was going to die. Not on the field of war, not gloriously, not heroically, but like a fucking loser. She was going to die alone. Tears bit at the edges of her eyes. Jade pounded her fists against the door. It didn't budge. She wasn't going to get in. She was going to freeze to death. Jade pressed her forehead against the metal, her throat tightening as she tried not to cry. Aris was searching for her, and Jade was going to die on some Vix-forsaken ice planet. What a way to go.

"You're just going to give up?" A'doxia chimed, a chuckle in her voice. "You're just going to lie down and take it? My, you've changed, Private."

Jade sucked in a breath of air through her clenched teeth and glared at the door. For a hallucination, A'doxia had a point. Giving up was never Jade's style. She had a home to get back to. She had a friend to see again. And she had so many mistakes she still needed to make up for. She couldn't just stop trying. She was going to fight to the bitter end. Jade knitted her brows together and snarled.

"No. I'm not dying." She stepped back and inhaled, taking a moment to look at the door properly. Sliding door. Metal. Electrical panel to the side. Unlikely to get it open without tools. Vent above, out of reach.

"Oooh, that's not good, dear. Looks like you really *are* going to die here." A'doxia leaned against the wall, a smile on her face. "I can't help but wonder if there's a different way in, hm?" A'doxia's red eyes flickered to Jade's, smile unwavering.

Jade stepped back again, her eyes scanning the floor beneath, then, reluctantly, she looked over the water.

"Shit," she hissed. Just off her platform there was a hole in the wall, leading, assumedly, to the other side of the door. But it was submerged.

"Guess you're going to get cold again. Could kill you." A'doxia peered over the edge, into the water. "What are you going to do?"

Jade grabbed at the roots of her hair with her free hand. "Fuck!" She sprinted to the side of the platform and dived in, the water forcing oxygen to escape from her lungs. She forced her eyes open and swam, each stroke sending more of her nerves into a coma. And, suddenly, she felt warm. Her fingers were blue, her toes numb, but her body told her that the temperature was steadily increasing. She pushed through the opening in the wall and shoved up to the surface on the other side, gasping. She did her best to lift Chloe out of the cold, but with most of Jade's strength fading, it was difficult. A metal, grated floor sat above her, blocking her way to freedom. Not that it looked great—the roof was caved, debris was scattered, and…were those bones?

She reached her left hand and her rigid fingers curled around the gaps in the flooring above her. Jade felt nothing.

"Shit, shit, shit," she muttered to herself. There was no time to worry about dead bodies. She swam further down the hallway. She tried to remember if Salene had said anything about survival in cold conditions. Salene had always been the best one at keeping Jade from getting herself killed in the wilderness. But the corporal's mind was filled with a fog. All she could think about was getting warm.

A few feet away, a large metal support had smashed against the flooring, pushing it into the water. It wasn't a large gap to the level above, but she forced her body through the small space and clawed her way up. The floor behind the fallen pillar was cluttered with blocks of cement and bent metal beams. The doors on either side were arched outwards, full of unseen wreckage. Some doors were pried open with structural supports, others were completely gone, displaying rooms full of crushed bones, overturned desks, and shattered chairs.

As she crawled through the tight space with the sunken ceiling reaching ever closer to her back, Jade's shivering slowly died down as the feeling in her arms began to decline. She cursed, pulling her body across broken shards of glass and damaged sections of flooring, where the chilled water licked at her knees. In the distance, lights flickered, beckoning her further, always just out of reach. She was sure she was bleeding still—or bleeding more—but the pain did not register.

She shuffled forward until she could feel nothing, and then, at last, she pulled herself from the crawlspace and into a facility that expanded before her. The circular room had three other hallways branching from it, all of which were caved in to varying degrees. Couches were in a recessed part of the room, blankets and wrappers strewn over the floor. Lights flickered from above, probably on some sort of separate generator.

"Nice place we got here," A'doxia said, striding past Jade and into the room, crouching by a large wool blanket. "You might want to dry off with something else first."

That sounds vaguely like something Salene might say.

Jade scrambled to her feet, dashing clumsily down the three stairs into the living space, dropping Chloe on a couch as she went. She tore a thin sheet that was sprawled over the skeletal remains of a snipper body, causing the bones to rattle and collapse. Jade dried herself off, ignoring the wounds that cut her flesh. She threw the now-drenched blanket to the floor and snatched the wool one up, wrapping it around her shoulders. She shuffled on numb feet and pulled blankets out from under remains, away from clenched fingers, and shoved bones away from one couch. She lay all the blankets she could over it, then climbed beneath. She curled into a ball, her shivers starting again after several minutes of rubbing her hands together. And, eventually, she even started to feel the stabbing pain from the newly acquired wounds. It wasn't exactly enjoyable, but it was reassuring that she could feel again. After the minutes dragged on, she fell asleep.

ϕϕϕ

Jade was lucky to wake up. At least, that's what A'doxia said when the Green's eyes fluttered open, her body back to a normal temperature. A'doxia sat in the middle of the room, cross-legged, and leaned against a large flag pole. Jade rubbed her eyes, grimacing at the outside chill.

"What do you think this place is?" A'doxia inquired, looking up at the flag attached to the pole. Jade's lips pulled downwards, irritated with herself for conjuring up A'doxia.

"I don't know," Jade hissed back. She sat up in the couch to take a look at herself. Every cut was scabbed over, or otherwise not bleeding. She ran her hands over her legs and feet, wincing as her skin pulled around the tight edges of wounds, but was pleased to find no glass or metal stuck into her flesh. At least that was good news. "Maybe it's water treatment for some city? Fuck if I know." She pulled the blankets up around her, glancing around the room. The skeletons were still wearing clothes—some of them, at least. Some of them…weren't. She'd have to scavenge the dead some more in order to feel comfortable around A'doxia, however hallucinated she was. Jade met A'doxia's eyes.

"Turn around."

A'doxia arched a brow. "What?" A small smile pulled at her lips and she chuckled. "You're not shy, are you?"

"Just do it."

A'doxia raised her hands in surrender, snickering as she turned herself around on the floor.

"It's odd everyone is dead though, isn't it?" she asked. Jade took one of the blankets with her in case A'doxia turned around and walked over to a kodarian's skeletal remains. She pulled a large sweatshirt, pants, and an undershirt from him. From a human female's remains, she stole a bra and underwear, then dressed herself. The sweatshirt was warm enough to keep her temperature at decent levels, so she placed the blanket back on the bed and went about looking around the room for food. The wrappers on the floor indicated there had to be a reserve somewhere, she just needed to find it.

"Are you listening to me?" A'doxia appeared to Jade's left. Jade flinched, then scowled at the smirk that crossed A'doxia's lips. "Still scared?" she purred.

"Leave me alone."

"Oh, you need me, though, don't you?" A'doxia strode past Jade and sat down on a large chest and crossed her legs. Jade frowned. A'doxia giggled, the wind chimes dancing in the small, enclosed space. "What's the matter, Private? Am I upsetting you?"

"You're sitting on the food box. Move."

"No, no, no," A'doxia waggled her finger at Jade. "You need to ask nicely."

Jade grit her teeth. Frustrated, she glared away. Crimson caught her gaze and she shifted her attention to the flag. *What on...?* Slowly, she inched over to it, taking one corner and spreading it out to see the design on the red fabric.

"What is this?" she whispered.

"What a curiosity," A'doxia murmured, placing a hand on Jade's shoulder. She peered at the flag. "Wonder what it means."

The flag stared at them idly. The golden ring with the words "We Do Not Bow" inside its band encircling a bloody handprint reminded her of war and blood and death. It was the Opes flag.

They found the Opes base.

Chapter 33

Jade stared at the flag. Ages passed. The chill washed away as she sat, stock still. A'doxia smiled at her.

"Looks like that dog wasn't lying," she cooed.

"It's really here." Jade tentatively reached out and touched it. The fabric was covered with a layer of dust, but underneath, she could feel its fibers linking together. Somehow she thought touching it would make it more real. It didn't.

She never allowed herself to really consider whether or not the base actually existed on Hallow, never stopped to consider what that would entail for her people—for the war. This flag existing here proved that the Opes had, at one point, been to a planet controlled by Thrax for hundreds of years. She let her hand fall back to her side. It didn't make any sense. How would this not have been reported anywhere? How did the rest of her people not know they were once on Hallow?

A'doxia was gone when she looked to her left, finally pulled from her trance by the realization that she was starving. Perhaps a focused mind was a sane one. She sucked in a lungful of air and got to her feet, finding a tool-box full of protein bars, all of which had expired fifteen years ago. With a frown, she bit into them. These bars weren't known for early expiration dates. Combined with the skeletons and overall wreckage, just how old was this base?

As she chewed on her stale bars, forcing the hunger beast away, a familiar sound made her pause. From the couch where Chloe sat, a beep resonated, indicating her rebooting systems. Jade rushed to her, kneeling on the couch and taking Chloe in her hands.

"Chloe?" She grabbed a blanket and wrapped it around the chilled helmet. "Shit, Chloe? Are you okay?"

"Please n-never go swimming again, mistress." Chloe grumbled, her voice distorted. Jade flashed a smile.

"Deal. How are you feeling? Are there any processor issues I need to know about?"

"Systems are slow, mistress, but they will—will recover with time. Where are—oh?"

Jade's brows furrowed. "What is it?"

"Mistress, it's—it's a distress signal."

"A distress? Here?" Jade frowned. Weren't they under several layers of ice? "Can you play it?"

Chloe responded with a flickering, lagging hologram projection of a man from the shoulders up. His face was square, he had brown eyes and black hair. He stared directly into the camera as he spoke:

"Hello," he said. "My name is Malkov." Jade froze. Tension spilled into her muscles. *Malkov? As in, Thaddeous Malkov?* "I am the guardian of a great weapon, hidden away per my creator's instructions." He smiled. "Yes, I am Artificial Intelligence. At the time I am recording this, I am aware my existence is heavily debated.

"My code dictates that I am to send out a distress should something go awry. And something has." His smile faded. "I worry my ability to guard the weapon is beginning to fail. My lifespan is coming to an end, and I have not yet been relieved from my duty and retired. This is concerning.

"Perhaps you have not heard of this weapon?" He tilted his head. "I am not sure when this message will be heard and the systems keeping track of my age have long since been lost. Perhaps in your time, memory of me has been lost.

"Regardless, the weapon I hold is of great danger and importance. It has the ability to create a great sickness that targets specific types of people—from specific species to specific hair colors. There is nothing else like it in existence. It could be used for tremendous good, and great evil.

"This is why I must have someone to relieve me of this duty. I cannot ensure my own stability for much longer, and there is no telling what I might do alone. I do not hold the functions to fire the weapon myself, but this should not delay your arrival. My coordinates are being transferred to your current communications device.

"Please hurry."

The hologram cut out. Jade didn't move.

A superweapon. A superweapon that could cripple the Exuro Empire.

"Chloe, what direction are those coordinates?" she asked as she processed all the information.

"They are approximately f-four sectors towards the Trade Stream, mistress."

"And which direction did we come from to get to Hallow? Do you know?"

Chloe was silent for a moment. *"Mistress, we came from four sectors t-towards the Trade S-Stream."*

Jade froze. She turned slowly on Chloe. *"What?"*

"Mistress, could the Thrax truly have a weapon like that? Why ha-have they not used it yet?"

"Fuck. *Fuck!*" Jade grabbed a bundle of her hair. *Why haven't they used it? What's stopping them? What's—*

"Thaddeous," she breathed. "Chloe, it's Thaddeous! He must be keeping them from using the weapon. He said I was their only hope. He must be doing something to delay the attack."

"Or it needs a Green to operate, mistress. Thaddeous is not a true Green."

Jade chewed on her lip. "Maybe." Her chest tightened. She didn't want to believe Thaddeous brought her here so she could use a weapon against her own people. Against Aris.

She pressed the palms of her hands against her temples until the pressure made her head spin. *No. I won't think about it. I can get out of here. I can hunt down that weapon. I can get it before it's used.*

Her mind wandered to the Mad Queen. If that woman got her hands on something able to target certain people, she would surely cause a holocaust. Jade could practically see Nevar in flames, and thousands upon thousands of people dead. She had to get to that weapon. She had to keep Aris safe.

"Mistress?"

Jade's eyes flickered over to the helmet. She touched the red skull.

"We need to get out of here," Jade whispered.

"I will l-log the weapon's coordinates for when we get home, mistress. And...mistress, where—where are we?"

"That Opes base, apparently." Jade motioned towards the flag. "If I wasn't pressed for time, I'd see if I could figure out what this is doing here, but we've got go. How are your systems holding up?"

"They will sur-survive, mistress."

She frowned. "Shut down for now. Boot back up when you've fully recovered."

"Mi—"

"If you shut down on me when I need you, you'll be no help. Fix yourself up. I'll try not to die in the meantime." Jade flashed a smile, her heart heavy. Nausea bubbled up through her chest. She didn't know why the Thrax hadn't used the weapon yet, but she wasn't going to wait to find out. She needed to get to it. She needed to destroy it.

She could, potentially, stay with Thaddeous. The thought passed through her mind and she gave herself a few seconds to ponder it while Chloe shut back down. She could stay, figure out why an attack hadn't been launched, why Thaddeous believed she could end the war. She had the coordinates. She could go after it when she was ready. She chewed her lip.

I don't think I should be around Thaddeous more than I have to.

Focusing herself, she turned and gathered as many stale bars as she could, stuffing them into her sweatshirt before donning layers upon layers of jackets and pants. She tied blankets around her extremities and around her core, using one to tie Chloe to her side. It made breathing difficult, but at least she was sure Chloe wouldn't fall off. She lingered at the flag for some time before, at last, she decided to take it with her. She tore it from its post and wrapped it around her neck and face, the way she had learned on Taotar. Desert planets were sort of the same as freezing planets, right? She curled and uncurled her fingers. She had found boots off some dead bones, but no one seemed to have gloves. She grimaced. Well, it was something she would have to deal with.

She picked a hallway at random, and after a few hours of crawling she came to a dead end and had to double back. She tried another hallway that ended in a similar fashion, and ate before she pulled her way under the debris and back to the main room. The last way was her only hope of escape.

She pulled herself over glass and shattered pieces of metal, scowling as she heard fabric rip. At least she didn't feel anything touch her skin. That was a plus. And, after hours of this, she came to a semi-collapsed staircase leading upwards. A way out. It had to be.

Jade was able to stand in this area—if only barely—and gaze at the spiraling staircase that led, hopefully, to the surface. Made out of cement and metal, sections of it had collapsed onto the floor or onto itself. It appeared to have had, at one point, a steel railing on each side of the staircase, but it was now broken, rusted, and jutting out at odd angles as if someone had come by and bent it out of shape. She placed one hand on Chloe.

"All right. You ready to get out of here, Chloe?" After a pause to collect herself, Jade bounded up the first steps, taking long strides to get her to the top as quickly as possible. She scaled debris and leapt over gaps on her way up, occasionally pausing to warm her hands. The air was starting to get cooler.

"Quite a long walk, hm, Private?"

Jade jumped, throwing herself into the nearby railing, eyes frantic, mind blank. A'doxia stood a few feet away, laughing. The wretched sound of wind chimes sent chills down Jade's spine. A'doxia was in her Taotar outfit, however. That was good. That meant she wasn't real. That's what it meant, right? So why couldn't Jade move?

Warmth flooded her right side, and, shortly after, all her nerves were individually stabbed.

"Fuck!" She jerked away, spinning around where a bloody, fragmented metal piece jutted from the rusty railing. She pressed her hands to her side. A large puncture wound spat blood from beneath her layers of clothing. "Fuck, fuck, *fuck!*"

"Quite a mouth on you, isn't there?" A'doxia cooed. Jade shot her a vicious glare, terror rising up in her throat before she pushed it aside with fury. This was all *her* fault. If A'doxia didn't exist, Jade wouldn't be here, wouldn't be bleeding out in some unknown base on some distant planet. *Fuck!*

Blood squeezed past her fingers and Jade unwrapped a blanket from around her left leg and tied it around the wound as tight as she could handle. The crimson started to soak through within moments.

"Fuck!" she snapped, jerking her head upwards. How much further until the surface? She needed out, she needed anywhere but here.

"You're going to freeze to death with an open wound like that in the snow." A'doxia chimed with a knowing smirk. "It would be wisest for you to stay here. With me." She stepped closer. Jade's green eyes locked on hers and, strangely enough, A'doxia seemed to hesitate.

"No," Jade growled. "I'm leaving." She pushed forward, brushed past A'doxia, and leapt up the steps and jumped the gaps until, moments later, she made it to the top. Blood pumped from her wound unceasingly, aggravated by her swift movement. It spilled down her side, covering her pants in crimson. She really managed to fuck herself over this time. She paused a moment, gasping for breath before a massive metal door, the air immensely colder at what she presumed was surface level. She pressed her hand to her side, frowning at the red liquid that coated her fingers. *This is bad. This is so fuckin' bad.*

"Are you leaving or not, hun?" A'doxia said behind her. Jade locked her jaw and yanked the doors open. Wind burst through, picking up snow and throwing it down the staircase and into her face. Ahead of her, everything was blindingly white.

She staggered into the brightness, shielding her face with one arm as the other pressed against her side. Snow danced around her as her eyes adjusted. She took a few deep breaths and lowered her arm, taking stock of where she was.

Stones made up a large circular platform that hugged the base of the mountain she stood on. Massive archways formed window-like breaks that looked out upon Hallow. To her left, the path ended in a wall. To her right, a trail curved around the mountainside and out of sight. She dragged herself to the edge, crimson dotting the path behind her. The ground was a good forty feet down. If she were to jump, she'd undoubtedly break something. Her eyes flickered to her gash. The bleeding was showing no signs of stopping.

"Shit."

"Are you injured, private?" A'doxia's voice rang out. Jade grimaced and glanced towards the sound. Below her, A'doxia stood smiling. She was surrounded by a group of seven soldiers, all dressed in warm clothing. In fact, A'doxia was dressed in a large jacket and scarf. Jade glanced to her left, where another A'doxia stood in the outfit she wore on Taotar. Jade's face paled. The hallucination chuckled.

"Well, this is awkward."

"She's not—she's *real?*" Jade looked down at A'doxia. The Red smirked. She lifted her hand, paused, and flicked her wrist. Her seven soldiers split off, two running to climb the stone beams, the rest dashing ahead, to some unforeseen entrance to the upper levels. Jade backpedaled and sprinted to her right, each thrum of her foot against the ice-covered stone sending more blood spurting from between her fingers. Adrenaline kept the pain at bay but she knew it wouldn't last. She heard A'doxia laugh. She heard it in her chest. She felt it dance around as her feet slammed against the stones. How had they found her? How had they gotten to the exact place she'd be? Her ears rang, her head spun. She blinked several times to clear her blurring vision. The curve of the path didn't seem to be going downhill. As long as they didn't catch her, as long as she had a way out, she'd be okay. She just needed to get home. She needed to warn everyone about Malkov.

Focus, Jade. Focus on Aris. Focus. Her fingers curled around her drenched fabric, hot blood leaving a telling trail. If she didn't stop the bleeding, they'd find her no matter what. Jade spared a glance over her shoulder. The Thrax below dashed after her, their red eyes locked firmly on her silhouette. She was going to need to stop them. She was going to need to fight.

Shit.

Her foot smashed against the rock beneath her, a familiar crunch of ice sending waves of panic through her. A crack formed. She heard the shift of stone a moment before the ground gave way. Together, her and the rocks fell several feet to the ground below. The rocks splintered upon impact, some of the more fragile ones shooting out shards into the air. Pieces cut into her layers and she staggered, barely able to keep herself standing. Her knees ached. Her head rang.

Maybe being captured isn't that bad. I'd get patched up. I'd be warm.

She slammed the butt of her hand against her temple, shook her head, and turned her attention to the Reds that slowly moved to surround her. She glanced towards her right, the only unguarded exit route. If she was going to do this, she had to do it smart. Without a weapon, without armor, without backup, she was going to need to think about this tactically. She was going to need to do this like Aris would.

She fled.

"Don't let her run off, you idiots!" A'doxia howled, her voice echoing against everything—the walls, the floors, Jade's bones. The sound of footsteps rushed after her. The stone path ended in a large archway that opened up to snow. Jade threw herself into the powder, stumbled, but kept going. She could only let one catch up to her at a time.

Her heartbeat stuttered and smashed its daggers into her wound. She swayed, the world doubling. A hand touched her shoulder and instinct consumed her.

Jade grabbed the pursuer's fingers, spun, and swept his feet out from under him. The kodarian eyes widened and Jade smashed her elbow into the space between them. The fragile bone there buckled inward. Blood splattered onto her face from the nostrils above his eyes and he fell onto his back in the snow. The world spun around her and Jade grabbed her skull. Her breath grew labored. Sweat broke out onto her back and vomit swelled up in her throat. Two soldiers tentatively approached her as A'doxia watched from afar, a cruel smile on her lips.

Shit.

The human to her left lunged, her arms swelling with Charge. She kept low, moving to grapple. Jade twisted to face her, let the woman grab her torso, and smashed both her elbows into the back of the woman's cranium as she was forced to the ground. With her attacker dazed, Jade untangled herself and got to her feet just as her third opponent slammed his fist into her side—right where she was injured. The contents of Jade's stomach spilled from her lips and acid filled her throat. The chunky liquid showered the man's arm, and a look of revulsion overtook his human face. Jade gripped his wrist with one hand and punched his throat with the other. He staggered away, coughing.

Jade wiped her mouth and glanced over at where A'doxia stood with two soldiers, the last two climbing down the side of the stone pathways. A'doxia was dressed rather nice. Her scarf matched her jacket, and her large fur boots looked warm. Jade swayed where she stood and put one hand to her side. *I dare say she looks rather pretty, for a homicidal bitch.* Her heart thundered in her ears as more of her life gushed out between her fingers. *Maybe...* A'doxia's look of smugness vanished. *Maybe she isn't so bad.* A'doxia sprinted forward. Jade's eyes rolled into the back of her head and she pitched forwards into the snow.

Chapter 34

The factory warehouse was surrounded by a sharp wire fence, and was situated off the beaten path. Aris had to walk behind buildings, through alleyways, and past drunks simply to reach the edge of the warehouse's vicinity. She stared at the cement building just past the spiked links of wire. The factory behind it spewed out black fumes. She took a deep breath. It was time to be a hero.

Aris walked back a few paces and her Helix swarmed her legs, bolstering the muscles. She sprinted at the fence and leapt into the sky. Aris' shoes skimmed the top. The impact with the ground on the other side sent snakes up her legs. She grimaced and dusted herself off.

The warehouse door faced the factory, something that may have posed a problem had there been any workers watching. All of them, however, kept their eyes averted. A few in the distance spotted her, but looked away quickly and said nothing to their coworkers. Aris frowned. They all knew, then.

She turned her attention to the door in front of her, the large metal frame imposing and cold. Aris wrapped her hand around the handle and a shiver of anticipation rushed through her. She did it all. She planned it. She executed it. Aris didn't need Jade to do anything. She was good enough on her own.

Aris pushed the door open and, when the lock gave her trouble, she filled her arm with Charge. She broke through and quietly closed the door behind her.

The massive space was dark, save for a blood-stained light hanging from the high ceiling. Aris stepped forward, her fingers leaving the door handle, her eyes attempting to adjust.

"Jade?" she murmured. Something crunched underfoot. She glanced down.

A man without a torso lay beside her, her shoe planted firmly on his exposed spine. Aris grimaced at the sight and looked away. *I've seen worse*, she told herself as she ventured further into the dark. *I've seen worse.*

"Jade?" Her voice was louder and it echoed across the walls. She caught glimpses of more mangled bodies thrown about like children's toys. In the distance, something dripped into a puddle and the floor beneath her was slick. She could guess what it was. She didn't have to look.

This isn't right. Something's wrong.

The smell of rancid meat and vomit filled her lungs. It was suffocating. Her stomach churned.

Did she snap? Did she do all this?

"Jade, it's me," Aris pressed, stepping away from the bloodied light's gaze. "Everything's going to be okay, now, all right? I'm here. Aris. Your best friend, remember?"

It has to be Jade. She just…something happened. I'll calm her down.

A form shifted in the distance. Aris squinted. It was bulky and about the right height. A smile tore her features.

It's her! She's okay!

"Jade! Thank Vix. Jade, it's okay. I'm here now. I saved you." She moved towards the figure. It turned towards her as it grew taller. A pair of gleaming, swamp-green eyes stared at Aris as it rose to twelve feet in height, looming over the smaller woman. Aris backpedaled a few steps, staring wide-eyed at the creature that watched, unblinking. Its eyes weren't quite human and its pupils were thin slits. It stepped closer, and rows of teeth glinted in the dim light.

Aris kept backing up. *It's…it's…*

"Hello, Aris," it growled in a voice like a man's if it were laced with metal. His words were labored, his tongue clearly not designed to speak Os. Each constant bled into each other, while the vowels held greater emphasis. His strides carried him closer. The light fell upon him.

Aris froze.

The cloak he wore covered the majority of his body, but his face was black as pitch. White markings spread across his scale-like flesh. His oval head was angled in the back like a shield. Four muscled mandibles sat above his jaw. It was as if someone had taken a dagger to his cheeks and cut three lines in each side. Those fleshy scraps moved as the creature spoke. He lacked lips entirely, and his fangs were visible even when he was not speaking. His sickly, jade-colored tongue flicked behind the rows of ivory.

That's not Jade. That's not—

"My name is Kuroda," his unknown accent was thick. He made an expression on his foreign face that was something akin to a smile. "And I am pleased to meet you."

Chapter 35

"What do you mean she's bleeding to death?" A'doxia cried, her voice cutting through the silence of Jade's mind. "Isn't there anything you can do? Anything you can do to keep her from…from *this!?*" Jade's eyes opened a fraction of an inch, and in the haze she saw A'doxia standing beside her, screaming at a halo doctor. A'doxia grabbed at her own hair. "No, this isn't happening again. Save her, or I'll kill you."

Jade blinked. A'doxia sat in a chair by Jade's bed, her arms crossed over the edge of the mattress with her head resting atop them, fast asleep. Another blink. A'doxia rubbed a bandage on the crook of her arm. Another blink. A'doxia sat, quietly watching Jade. Another blink. Jade's hand was in A'doxia's, while A'doxia stared at the floor, sniffling as if she had the flu.

The room was dark when Jade's eyes opened fully, grimacing at the nausea that rose up in her gut. She pressed her hand to her mouth and yanked herself to the side of the bed, vomiting on the floor. She didn't have much food in her, seeing as she had hardly eaten in the last twenty-four hours, but what little she had spilled across the hard ground until she had nothing left to expel. She wiped her mouth and lay back on the bed, reaching up and rubbing her temples. It felt like she had a hangover. She hadn't had a hangover since she was eighteen.

A door to her right flew open, spilling light into the darkness and momentarily blinding her as someone rushed in.

"You're awake." Thaddeous strode inside, green eyes bloodshot and hair messy. His tuxedo was stripped down to just his undershirt and dress pants. Sweat beaded his brow. He paused momentarily as his nose scrunched up. He looked over his shoulder, hollering for a nurse. He then continued to the side of Jade's bed.

"How are you feeling?" he asked. His eyes were hard. Frustrated. Exhausted. Jade looked away.

"Fine."

"You almost bled out."

Jade's brows knitted together and she glanced back at him. "What?"

Thaddeous gestured to her side, currently covered by a blanket. "You got fourteen stitches. So don't plan on going anywhere for a while." He rubbed his eyes. "If it weren't for A'doxia you would've died out there."

Jade's jaw locked at the memory of a sharp railing jutting through her side. "If it weren't for A'doxia I wouldn't have been bleeding out."

Thaddeous blinked, looking at her with confusion. "She attacked you?"

Jade ground her teeth together and glared up at the ceiling. If A'doxia hadn't taken her sweet time cutting lines into Jade's back years ago, she never would've appeared as a figment of Jade's own imagination on Hallow.

"You can ask her about it. I'm sure she'd love to tell you all the gory details."

"Jade, if she caused this injury—"

Jade closed her eyes and cut him off with a sigh. The blankets around her pressed against her worn-out muscles, threatening to suffocate her. She wondered where Chloe was.

After a few moments of silence, Thaddeous spoke again. "That was really stupid, you know. If it weren't...you could've died."

"Didn't though."

"But you *could've,*" Thaddeous insisted. "Where did you even go? How did you survive that storm? You were clothed in a different fashion than what I gave you. And you had…you had an Opes flag wrapped around your face."

For a moment, Jade contemplated spilling that she found the Opes base and took refuge there. But then the fragmented image of Malkov flickered into her mind. Why hadn't he told her that they had a superweapon? Why hadn't he warned her that everyone she knew was in danger of dying? More than usual? Jade opted for a simple shrug then grimaced at the pulling of skin around her wound. Thaddeous put a hand on her shoulder.

"Stop moving."

Jade snarled at his touch, hating the warmth it brought to her body. Hating that she wanted him nearby. Hating him because the only other person she felt comfortable letting touch her was Aris. She wanted to trust him—she perhaps even had for a moment there—and she hated herself for that most of all. Thaddeous pulled his hand away, shaking his head.

"We can talk about what happened later. Are you hungry?"

Jade looked up at the ceiling again. She felt ready to throw up again. She closed her eyes. *What an idiot I am. I really thought I could escape on a planet filled with Thrax? And covered in ice? I don't know anything about survival.*

Salene was good with environmental bullshit. And where was she? What did I do to her? Guilt gnawed at her ribs.

"I'll bring you some water and crackers, just in case." Thaddeous stood, then hesitated. "What did A'doxia do to you?" he whispered.

Jade didn't respond. After a few minutes, she heard him leave the room.

ϕϕϕ

Jade wasn't sure when she fell asleep exactly, but when she woke up, crackers and water were placed on a side table for her. She scowled. If she wasn't supposed to move, how the hell was she supposed to eat and drink?

"Oh!" A woman's voice, startled. Jade glanced to her right, where a small-framed halo was standing next to her. Her ivory fur and ice-blue feathers seemed to glow in the darkness of the room.

"I didn't know you were awake. How are you feeling today?" Her voice was high-pitched and kind, but her glowing red eyes only made Jade more agitated. If only she hadn't punctured herself on that stupid piece of metal.

If only A'doxia hadn't appeared and messed everything up. Maybe instead of lying in a Thrax bed, she'd be smuggled

336

onto a ship, ready to take control and figure out her way home. She ground her teeth together.

After not responding fast enough, the halo continued to talk. "You were in really rough shape, you know." She held up a wet cloth and reached over, dabbing Jade's forehead with it. Jade flinched and grimaced at the pain in her side. "It's a good thing your friend found you when she did." Jade's green eyes narrowed at the nurse. "And it's lucky she has the same blood type as you, too. You would be in a lot worse shape if it weren't for her."

Jade's face paled. *Blood type? Oh Vix. Oh Vix, please, no.*

"What do you mean?" Jade murmured, looking to the nurse in hopes her fears would be abolished.

"Well," the nurse pulled the wet cloth away and smiled. "She donated some blood so you could still be with us today."

"No," Jade breathed. "No!" She forced herself upright, her stitches pulling tightly against her flesh. "Get it out of me. Get it out of me!" She extended her arms to the nurse, eyes frantic. The halo woman stepped back, shock crossing her canine features. "Please, get it out! I don't want her blood inside me! *Please!*"

"P-please, Green, we cannot do that! We don't have the means to pull out specific blood cells, and even if that were possible, it would put you into critical condition again!"

"I don't care!" Jade threw off her blankets, finding herself only half-clothed with shorts and a bra. Her gruesome stitch wound was red around the edges, clearly agitated.

"What are you doing? Green!" The nurse grabbed Jade's arm as she reached for her stitches, hoping to tear them from her flesh and release every ounce of blood inside. She struggled against the nurse, who called for aid when Jade's efforts started to rip the edges of the wound open. Blood trickled down her side.

"You can't do this to me!" Jade cried, wrestling against the nurse who was beginning to overpower her. "You have to get it out of me, please!" Two more halos entered the room, rushing to pin Jade to the bed. She tore one arm free and reached for her side. A black halo grabbed her wrist and pressed it to the bed.

"Someone get a needle!" he cried. A different halo took the nurse's place, allowing her to rush out of the room. Jade kicked and hollered, trying to break free. She could hear A'doxia now, whispering how they had the same blood. They were the same. They were one. A cold sweat broke out over her body. She didn't need one more thing to keep her awake at night.

Movement caught her eye and she glanced to the right, where the door was wide open. There, standing almost out of sight, A'doxia watched Jade struggle.

The nurse rushed back inside, and Jade screamed, tears falling down her face. It was clear what the doctors were planning. They were going to sedate her. And then what would A'doxia do, when Jade could hardly think, hardly move? She stopped fighting, her tactic switching instantaneously to begging.

"Please, I-I'll stop," she stammered, her pride pushed aside by her growing terror. Her mind played out scenarios of what would happen. What A'doxia would do. *Please, Vix, don't sedate me. Please.*

"This is for your own good, Green," the nurse said with a soft voice. Jade yanked at her arm, trying to get it out of the way, but the nurse hit the mark nonetheless. The needle pressed into Jade's skin, biting her nerves on the way. A warm buzz swam through her body. Jade blinked, trying to clear the blurriness from her vision. The pressure on her arms let up. Jade groaned. She went to rub her eyes, but her arm was sluggish and slow. It moved a few inches before Jade gave up.

"How is she still awake?" someone to her left muttered.

"Maybe it's because she's a Green?" another answered.

"Should we dose her again?"

"No, don't bother." A female voice, sweet like caramel on an apple. "It won't last long, anyway. Leave, I'll watch her."

"As you say." The sound of people leaving and entering filled her ears. Jade blinked and tilted her head towards them. A'doxia stood a few feet away, arms crossed, red eyes on Jade. Jade turned back to staring at the ceiling. *Get on with it, then.*

"You put on quite a show," A'doxia said, glancing back at the open door. She moved to close it, shutting out the light. Jade sluggishly blinked, her eyes having a hard time adjusting.

"This will be easier on your eyes," A'doxia explained, walking to Jade's bedside. "They gave you a normal dose. When you were first captured, it seemed to mostly affect your ability to see in harsh light. You woke up a few times, if you remember." She sat down on the edge of Jade's bed. Jade wanted to roll away, but her body was rather unresponsive. She only managed to lean slightly to the left. A'doxia smirked.

"Do I truly make you that scared? After all this time?" She chuckled, the sound of wind chimes dancing in the room.

Jade closed her eyes. Her body filled with spiders, all dancing beneath her skin. She was exposed. She was barely wearing anything. What was A'doxia going to d—no. No, she wouldn't think about it.

A'doxia's hand brushed Jade's arm. Her touch was warm. "How are you feeling?"

The words were normal, something anyone would ask considering Jade's condition. Jade tried to move her arm away, and it shifted a few meager inches. She groaned against her growing discomfort. Who decided to leave her alone with this woman? Did no one know she was insane?

"Oh, shush, now," A'doxia hummed. Jade felt the side of the bed dip and she spared a look, her head lulling to the side as her eyes opened. A'doxia rested beside her, her hand moving to Jade's and their fingers entwining. "I saved your life, after all." Her crimson eyes flickered to Jade's as her thumb rubbed Jade's hand. "Aren't you indebted to me?"

There it was. The leverage, the additional thing A'doxia had to torment Jade with. Jade turned her head away, staring at the left wall. A'doxia laughed.

"Oh, don't be so upset, love," she cooed. "Besides. I have a present for you. I think you forgot something in the snow when you were running. Do you know what?"

Of course Jade knew. She knew the instant she woke and didn't feel Chloe around her head, or near her, or telling her whether A'doxia was real or not. Jade couldn't find the strength to frown, or even speak. Her eyes fluttered open and closed. A'doxia's fingers walked Jade's sternum while she propped her head up with her other palm.

"Hmm," she murmured. "I'm sure you know what I'm talking about, even as you are now. Your body is pretty good at keeping sedatives and other drugs out of your system. I'm guessing we probably only have about ten more minutes together like this." She scooched closer, her body curling around Jade's side, and rested her head on Jade's shoulder. She kept her flesh away from the large bandage wrapped around Jade's wound.

A sigh escaped A'doxia's lips. "I'll give your precious helmet back, not to worry. But there's just one thing you have to promise me."

Jade didn't move, waiting for A'doxia to make demands.

A'doxia swung herself on top of Jade, hands on either side of Jade's shoulders. She was merciful enough not to rest her weight on Jade's damaged abdomen, but the action was enough to shoot icicle shards into Jade's lungs. For a moment, the Red cherished the sight of Jade beneath her. Her eyes wandered and found the single scar that wrapped towards Jade's belly button from her back. A visible blush sat upon her cheeks.

The Red took hold of Jade's chin and forced her to look at those wretched, smirking lips. Lightning sparked over her gloved hand, small enough not to cause any damage to Jade's face, but enough to cause pinpricks of electricity to shoot through her nerves. A'doxia leaned close, moving her face so that her lips brushed Jade's ear.

"Don't forget why you fear me." She pulled back so Jade could see her smile, kissed Jade's nose, then released her hand on Jade's jaw. She moved so that she was lying next to Jade again, head on her shoulder. Jade closed her eyes, her sluggish mind trying to keep panic at bay. They only had ten minutes, right? That's when the drug would wear off and she could move again. She just needed to hold out until then. Once she got her body back she'd… do something.

A few minutes later, A'doxia yawned, stretching out her arms over Jade's neck and letting them fall, momentarily complicating her breathing. She giggled at the sound of Jade choking, and brushed Jade's freckled cheek before swinging her legs over the bed and standing.

"Come see me when you're better, love. And I'll give you your little helmet back." She winked and sauntered out of the room, closing the door behind her. Jade's nerves started to tingle about five minutes later, and soon she was able to move again. Her heart took that as a cue to catch up on all the events that had transpired, and it thundered against her ribs. She covered her eyes with her forearms, biting back tears and ignoring her agitated wound. Her whole body shook. *Not this again. Please, Vix, I can't do this again.*

It was almost as bad as that night on Taotar. With the song, the knife, the electricity. The feel of A'doxia's body beside hers as she cried out, voice hoarse, blood spilling onto the sand. About an hour in, A'doxia had stopped asking for information. She continued torturing Jade for her own amusement.

Hot tears streaked silently down Jade's cheeks. *I can't do this again.*

Chapter 36

A'doxia didn't come back. Over the course of a few days, Jade regained her strength, eating what she could and drinking as much water as her body would allow. She didn't have any visitors besides the nurse, who came in with food and water whenever Jade requested. Often it was comprised of a delicious soup and crackers.

The nurse commented on Jade's recovery once, praising the strength of the blood 'her friend' donated. Jade threw the bowl of soup at her head and the nurse scampered out of the room. She didn't mention A'doxia again.

Jade insisted the lights remain on at all times, and so the chandelier overhead often glared down at her. The tiled floors led to brick walls, and there were no other pieces of interest in the room besides the side table and the bed she lay on. And, of course, the door out.

She lost track of time rather quickly without being able to see outside. So after waking up the seventh time, she scooted over to the edge of the bed and put her feet to the floor, facing the door. The tile was cold, unwelcoming. Her exposed back tingled, the tangle of scars on display for anyone curious enough to look. Jade inhaled and exhaled, steadying herself.

She was going to need to go eventually.

The nurse walked in and yelped with surprise when she saw Jade sitting up. She put her hand to her heart, laughing nervously. Jade looked at her, unamused.

"I need a shirt," she said. The nurse waved the command out of the air.

"You're still too weak to go anywhere, Green. Just rest for a while longer, okay?"

Jade fixed her with a stare. "I need a shirt and I need to walk around."

"Green, please—"

Jade frowned a little at the title. It felt weird for people to call her 'Green.'

"Please. I'm not going to get any better sitting here and contemplating my fucked-up life," Jade replied.

The nurse stood in the doorway, hesitating, before at last she nodded and walked away. She returned minutes later with a large shirt.

"Sorry, the clothes you were wearing got covered in blood and this is all we have." She offered Jade the large, gray shirt with a green spider wielding a machine gun printed on the front. A smile pulled at Jade's lips.

"You like them, too?" Jade asked, gingerly pulling the shirt over her head. The nurse quickly aided her with an awkward smile.

"Who doesn't? They're great performers." The nurse stepped back and offered Jade a hand. "Let me help you walk around." Jade gave her a look and the nurse continued. "At least until I'm sure you can do it on your own."

With a reluctant nod, Jade took the shorter woman's fur-covered arm and shakily stood. Jade's head swam for a moment, confused by the sudden standing sensation, but after a few seconds it calmed. And the corporal took her first steps forward.

The two didn't talk as Jade walked around the room, testing her strength. And Jade didn't argue when the nurse led her back to bed and told her she'd return later. Just from that short walk, Jade was exhausted. She needed more strength if she wanted to face A'doxia. Much more.

And so it went. The nurse entered, helped Jade stagger around, and put her back to bed. The time Jade spent staring at the ceiling grew shorter. She wondered if she was ever going to get out of here. She wondered if Malkov had already been used on her people. She wondered if she'd ever see Aris again. She closed her eyes. Even if she destroyed the weapon and got home, even if she was a loyal soldier, one day they would find out. They would discover her eyes. She had been lucky thus far, but she doubted her luck would continue much longer. And when they found out, they would kill her and everyone who knew her. Her parents, Salene, Aris. They'd all be butchered for being traitors. How was she supposed to fight for people like that? How was she…?

After a few more sessions of exercise, the nurse gave Jade a satisfied nod and informed her she was able to leave the room. Jade sat on the bed for a while in silence. She had to get Chloe. She needed to destroy Malkov. Aris would survive this. With a sharp inhale, she stood and left.

Outside there was a sitting room, like that of a domestic home, with windows that faced a hot spring surrounded by rock. A couch was shoved underneath the large windows, a coffee table set up in the middle of a rug, and two chairs faced the couch. It looked nice. Jade wasn't here for that.

She turned to her left, where the sitting room narrowed to form an entryway, then widened again into a dining room on the other side. Seeing as there were no other rooms past the sitting area, she figured A'doxia had to be staying somewhere on the other side of the house. She placed one hand on the wall and walked slowly that direction, past the door that led outside, and into the dining room. It split off into a hallway that led past a small kitchen and down to a large window, two doors on either side of the walls beckoning her closer. Jade scowled. She didn't want to do this. But she also didn't want to leave Chloe with a psychopath.

Jade stumbled down the hallway until she reached the first door, the one on her left. She placed her hand against the wood and pushed it open, revealing a dark room with no one inside. She gritted her teeth, heartbeat frantic. A'doxia would've chosen the furthest door down just to torment Jade into prolonging the horrendous experience. She shambled to the door just before the hallway's end and paused beside it. She inhaled, closing her eyes a moment.

This is for Chloe. You can do this. She put her hand on the door, thought better of walking in on A'doxia, and knocked.

"Come in," sung the voice on the other side. Jade had guessed correctly. She chewed the inside of her cheek and opened the door before she leaned against the doorframe. She took a few steadying breaths. She wasn't as bad as she used to be, but her body still wasn't ready to run any marathons.

A'doxia's room was covered with wood floors and brick walls framed it out. A window showed other houses in the small community. She had a single bed beneath the window, a chair, a dresser, and a side table. The floor was littered with clothes—everything from shirts and skirts to bras and underwear. A'doxia herself was getting dressed and was in the middle of wrapping a scarf around her neck. Jade glanced at the low light that came through the window. Either it was quite late, or morning had just arrived.

"Come in, love," A'doxia beckoned, motioning Jade inside with two fingers as she picked up a mirror from her side table and looked at herself. Her long skirt swung against the floor and her half-shirt was tight to her breasts. The black scarf looked to be made out of silk and was tied so it draped down across her sternum. A'doxia fluffed her hair. "And close the door behind you, we don't want to be disturbed."

Jade frowned, hairs standing on the back of her neck. She shouldn't move. She shouldn't step inside. A'doxia shot her a look, a single brow arched as a smirk crossed her lips. Jade scowled. If she didn't step inside, she further proved how terrified she was of A'doxia. If she *did* step inside, she would have to deal with whatever A'doxia was about to do to her.

With an exaggerated sigh, A'doxia rolled her eyes. She set the mirror down and strode up to Jade, grabbing one of her hands and pulling her into the room. Jade stumbled, her mind shocked into fight-or-flight mode, barely registering her wounds' violent bite into her nerves. If she fought back…would she see Chloe again? Would she even win?

She settled for yanking her hand away. A'doxia giggled.

"I'm not going to do anything to you, Private," she hummed. She walked around Jade and closed the door. "I just want to talk." She strode behind Jade and wrapped her arms around Jade's middle, just above her partially healed wound. Jade lifted her arms slightly, out of the way, and stiffened. Her breathing faded into almost nonexistence. A dull pain gnawed at her.

"Talking to me surely doesn't scare someone like you, does it?" A'doxia murmured into the soft of Jade's back, her lips causing the fabric of Jade's shirt to ripple against her scars. Jade swallowed hard, her mind growing hazy with fear. A'doxia embraced Jade tighter. Her stitches burned.

"Mmm," she muttered. "You smell nice."

Jade wanted to collapse. She chewed the inside of her cheek and took a deep breath, trying to relieve the tension in her body. *She's just a human. Just like you. Breathe, Jade. Breathe. You came here for a reason. Remind her.*

"My…my helmet?" Jade croaked, the words coming out shaky and pathetic. *Yes, let's just continue to show fear in front of this woman. Great fucking idea.*

"Oh, of course." A'doxia released her and Jade let her arms fall back to her side. A'doxia strode over to the bed and knelt down, reaching beneath it.

Jade took the moment to steady her breathing and heartbeat. *She's just a woman. She's just a woman. Focus, Jade. I'm here for a reason and once I get Chloe back, I can leave.* Jade's mind reeled. *What if she doesn't let me leave?*

Then I can force my way out. Yeah. I'll just…I'll just fight her, if I need to. In my weakened state. With a giant gut wound. I could…I could totally take her.

Jade grimaced. *Please, Vix, don't let her keep me here.*

"Ah," A'doxia chimed, pulling Chloe out from under the shadows of the bed. She stood, a smile on her lips. She set Chloe down on the mattress. "It made a racket this morning," A'doxia said, looking over at Jade. "It shut up not long after, though. Hasn't made a peep since." She rested her hand on Chloe's crimson skull, tapping it with one finger. Jade didn't move. Fetching Chloe made her stand too close to A'doxia.

No, I can't think like that. I need to get Chloe out of here. That's priority. I've got to suck it up and walk over there.

Before her pep talk took effect, A'doxia picked Chloe up and looked the helmet over with a scrutinizing eye.

"Did you make it?" she inquired, setting Chloe down on her lap as she sat upon the bed. She seemed to relish in the uncomfortable look that crossed Jade's face.

"No," Jade replied.

"Who did?"

"Not sure."

"Mm." A'doxia tapped Chloe with her fingernails, then traced the shoddy paint job Jade had given the helmet. She chuckled. "You painted it though."

"Yeah." Jade cleared her throat. "Can I have her?"

"Her?" A'doxia arched a brow. "It has a gender?"

Stop giving her more reason to talk to you.

"Like how you name a ship, and stuff," Jade grumbled. She knew she'd hear an earful from Chloe at such an inhumane answer, but if it shut down the conversation, Jade was willing to risk it.

"Ah. How cute." A'doxia held Chloe out to Jade. "Well, I suppose you'll want her, then."

Jade hesitated, then walked forward. She cautiously took Chloe from A'doxia's hands and took a few steps back before she allowed herself to look the helmet over.

"I didn't do anything to it—*her,*" A'doxia said. "What sort of friend would I be if I did?"

Jade glanced at the snickering woman before tracing a jagged cut in Chloe's visor.

"You owe me three times, now," A'doxia said with a grin. She stood. Jade stepped back. "I hope you intend to pay me back."

"How do I owe you three?" Jade murmured. A'doxia's grin grew twisted.

"One, for saving your cute butt from dying out in the snow. Two, for giving you some of my blood to keep you alive. And three, saving your precious little helmet." She tilted her head, letting her words sink in. Jade swallowed.

"What do you want?"

"Oh, thanks for asking, sweetheart! First," A'doxia hummed, moving closer. Jade moved back. "You need to shower. You reek of sweat and blood. And as sexy as it is to see you filthy and beat up, well, it can get a little too much to bear. Second," she held up two fingers and kept walking towards Jade. Jade kept taking steps back. "When we return to our little ship in the sky, spar with me. Third," Jade's heel hit the wall. She pulled Chloe to her chest, feebly attempting to keep the helmet out of harm's way. A'doxia stopped before Jade and placed her hands on Jade's arms. She leaned closer. "Call me Dox."

There was a knock at the door. A'doxia smirked at Jade. "Unless, of course, you want to have your debt wiped away in one go." Her voice was soft, seductive. "I can lock the door."

Jade cleared her throat. "I'll think about it."

A'doxia stepped back and put one finger in her mouth, her gaze hungry. "Don't take too long deciding, love. Else I'll decide for you. Come in."

A raven-haired prince opened the door.

"I can't find Jade any—" Thaddeous began, worry rising in his words before he noticed Jade to his right. He blinked, glancing between the two women. "Jade?" His brows knitted together. A'doxia waved her hands, giving Jade permission to leave. Jade ducked her head and slipped out of the room.

Jade kept a quick pace, her mind spinning, her head light. She was aware of how shallow her breathing was, how fast her legs were moving, of the buzz of her disturbed wound, but she wasn't aware of Thaddeous until he touched her arm. She jolted, yanking her arm away and stumbling back. Her green eyes focused on Thaddeous' face. She reached up and ran one hand through her tangled red hair. She looked around. She was standing in the sitting room. Thaddeous' concerned gaze followed her as she sunk into the couch.

"What happened in there, Jade? What's going on?" Thaddeous sat on the couch as well, but kept a respectful distance between them. Jade wrapped both her arms around Chloe and pressed her forehead to the top of the helmet. She focused on slowing her breathing and not thinking about what A'doxia meant by having her debt wiped in one go. She started to shake. She couldn't think about anything else.

"Jade?" Thaddeous hesitantly reached for her, pulled her closer, and wrapped his arms around her. Aris held her the same way.

"Shh, Jade. It's okay. It's okay," he murmured.

It wasn't okay. She wanted out. Out of this place. Out of her debt.

Don't take too long deciding, love. Else I'll decide for you.

She pulled into herself further, shutting her eyes.

"Come on," Thaddeous whispered. "Let's get you to your room."

With a silent nod, the two stood and shuffled into Jade's room. Thaddeous closed the door while Jade moved to her bed.

"Oh, Jade, you're bleeding." Thaddeous rushed over to her while Jade sat on the edge of her mattress. She looked down at her side, where blood was bubbling up from where her stitches were. He turned to call a nurse, but Jade reached up and grabbed his tuxedo's sleeve. She didn't want anyone else here. She wanted a friend. And he was the best she had.

Thaddeous sighed. "All right. But I'm going to need to wrap it, okay? Can you lift your shirt up for me a bit?"

Jade set Chloe down beside her and lifted the right side of her sweatshirt up just enough. Thaddeous opened a drawer in the side table and pulled out gauze, then turned to wrap Jade's middle. He paused a moment when he undoubtedly noticed the scars that consumed her back. He said nothing as he finished his work. He stepped back when it was completed and Jade scooted herself to the headboard, pulling Chloe to her chest and wrapping her arms around her legs. Thaddeous sat at the end of her bed.

"You want to talk about it?" he asked gently.

Jade closed her eyes and shook her head. She felt like a child scared of the boogeyman. She was supposed to be some battle-hardened warrior. Some badass that kept fighting with a broken arm and shattered ribs. Her entire unit looked up to her. Looked to her for strength when the battle was turning sour. She moved her hands to her hair, tangling her fingers in the red strands. Some hero she was. Would she even be able to protect Aris if A'doxia was in the same room? Would she even be able to *move?* Let alone *fight?* She was a fool if she thought she could do this. Her fingers tightened around bundles of hair and she clenched her jaw. A'doxia had her on a leash.

A hand touched her shoulder and she froze, waiting for her nerves to overcome the initial panic to realize the hands were that of a man, not a woman. She looked up. Thaddeous watched her with brows pulled upwards.

"Please, talk to me Jade."

Jade eyed his face. She wanted to trust him, just like she wanted to trust Aris years ago with the secret of her eyes. Her instinct on Aris hadn't been wrong. *Perhaps Thaddeous is safe. Perhaps he is good.* She took a deep breath and sat upright. She put one hand to her side, checking to see if she was still bleeding. Luckily, it didn't feel like it.

"You really don't know?" Jade said. Thaddeous pulled his hand away and shook his head. She exhaled and tilted her head to the ceiling.

"I was about seventeen or eighteen. I don't really remember anymore. I had been ordered to count all the sand on Taotar for being 'unruly.' Had to go out there after dinner every dawn. Basically, I punched a general in the face for grilling Aris too hard." A tight smile pulled at her lips. "He was an ass though." She closed her eyes. "I wandered off a bit. In the distance, I saw a few Thrax soldiers and decided to capture them for intel. Figured that'd shut everyone up. Earn me some respect." She spat out a bitter laugh. "Turns out there were four of them, and I wasn't nearly skilled enough to take them on alone. They knocked me out and dragged me through the sand as I slipped in and out of consciousness. Woke up shortly before we got to the base and I started fighting back, you know? Who wouldn't? They held me pretty tight, cuffed me, and threw me in a tent with A'doxia."

Call me Dox. Jade grimaced.

"What happened then?" Thaddeous quietly prompted. Jade opened her eyes and gazed at the ceiling. It was white.

"She tried to get information out of me." Jade exhaled. "Went on for hours. She sang this…this *lullaby* the whole time, too."

Beautiful art… Jade pressed her hands to her temples, hoping she could keep the hallucinations at bay.

"I must've passed out at some point," Jade growled, "because I woke up without a shirt, in the sand, bleeding out, and the Taotar suns were about to rise." She released her hold on her head and looked at her hands. "She enjoyed herself a lot. I'm surprised she never told you."

Thaddeous was silent for a long while. Quietly, he spoke:

"I'm so sorry. I didn't know. I didn't…Wait." Realization dawned in his voice. Jade glanced at him. His eyes shifted from horror to rage. "Why were you in that room with her?"

Jade patted Chloe in her lap. "I dropped Chloe in the snow. A'doxia got her and said I could have her back when I was better." She didn't look at him. "I needed Chloe back."

"You could've asked—you could've had me—"

"I haven't exactly seen you in the last several days," Jade snapped, harsher than she intended. Thaddeous flinched and looked down.

"I'm sorry about that. I just…You got me drunk then ran off into the storm. I was…I was furious." He exhaled. "You really could've died."

"I had to try. You know that."

"I know. I just…I wish you didn't feel like you had to. I do mean it, you know. I intend to send you back home. I just want you to see that this place isn't as awful as you think it is."

Jade offered him a weak smile. "Not so sure about that."

"Because of A'doxia." Thaddeous shook his head. "I had no idea, Jade. I'm so sorry. She even oversaw you while you were unconscious."

Jade imagined A'doxia looming over her while she was sleeping. She imagined A'doxia's hands…She shivered and pushed the thought away.

"She mentioned it, yeah." Jade opened and closed her fist, finally starting to settle down. "She…she says I owe her now."

Thaddeous closed his eyes. "Because she saved your life."

"Yeah."

"You don't owe her, Jade. You don't have to do anything for her."

"I know." Jade looked at Chloe. "I just…don't really think I have much choice in the matter. She said if I don't decide then she'll decide for me."

Thaddeous scowled and glared at the door. "She always seemed so…so perfectly…*sane* when I spoke to her. I don't get it."

Jade ran one hand through her hair. "Um. Thaddeous. Could…is it possible that…I don't have to see her again?"

"Oh, Vix, of course, Jade." He put his hand on her knee. A shiver of discomfort ran up her leg. "I will do everything in my power to keep her away from you." Thaddeous stood. "Which means we're leaving. Right now. We'll head back to Soldar."

Back? Back to...was I on the Thrax home planet before? Jade blinked with surprise, but it was brushed away a moment later. Thaddeous looked at the door.

"When we get back, I'll call her and have a talk with her. I won't mention that you said anything to me—I'll blame the information on passersby and those who…overheard you two on Taotar." He offered Jade his hand. "I'll give her a direct order: do not come near you for any reason ever again."

Jade felt the weight in her chest lessen and her anxiety slowly start to fade. She would be safe from A'doxia. Even on the Thrax planet. Even on the home of her enemy. A cautious smile crossed her lips. He reminded her so much of Aris.

"Thanks, Thaddeous." She took his hand.

Chapter 37

The two snuck out after Thaddeous called for an escort to be waiting at the edge of the town. Jade wasn't dressed for the cold, so their mad dash had to be just that—with a hint of caution to keep Jade's stitches from ripping. She glanced back at the hut a few times, worried she would see A'doxia standing at the door. Even after a few hours in the carriage, she found herself peering out the window in search of the Thrax woman.

She and Thaddeous were able to climb up the ladder to where the ships were waiting without interruption. He helped her board, shed his tuxedo jacket and gave it to her, then called for the crew—who he had summoned earlier, apparently—to get going. Without question, they pulled up the anchor and exited Hallow's atmosphere. Thaddeous slipped away and returned with several blankets which Jade greedily took. He set her up in a chair, helped her wrap all the blankets around herself, then sat down on the floor, his back against the main mast. Jade smiled at the sight of Hallow vanishing.

"Thanks," she muttered. Thaddeous waved her thanks from the air with one hand.

"Any time, Jade. It's important you feel comfortable."

"So you can more easily steal Opes secrets from me?" Jade flashed him a smile.

Thaddeous chuckled. "You know me."

Jade pulled Chloe out from under the blankets and set the helmet on her lap. She traced the cut in Chloe's visor again before speaking aloud:

"Chloe?"

Thaddeous glanced at her, brow arched. Jade ignored him. She lifted Chloe up and looked inside the padded helmet. A'doxia hadn't done anything to her that Jade could tell, and Chloe was working earlier, so she should've already responded.

"Chloe, c'mon. Speak to me." Chloe did not respond. Jade frowned, crossing her arms over her chest. *Oh, shit. She heard me with A'doxia, didn't she?*

"I'm sorry for dropping you in the snow and saying you were like a mindless ship. Please forgive me."

There was silence for another few moments.

"Are you okay, mistress?" Chloe's coded sentence rang out of her external speakers.

"What do you mean?"

"I'm just wondering if you're sick, mistress. I mean, why else would you drop me in the snow and let me get taken by a Thrax?"

Jade rolled her eyes. "I said I was sorry, Chloe."

"I was rather surprised when I woke up to find myself on someone else's bed, mistress."

"Okay, I was *bleeding out*, Chloe. I couldn't do anything!"

"And then you enter the room looking like a scared animal, mistress! I was so embarrassed to call you 'mistress,' seeing how you acted around that woman. Rather distasteful, mistress."

Jade huffed and glanced at Thaddeous, who smiled at her, then back at Chloe. "That's not my fault either."

"Mistress, I understand you have issues with that woman, but you cannot let her do the things she does to you. You need to push back." Chloe paused. *"Otherwise, mistress, I fear for what might happen to you."*

Jade rubbed her eyes. "I know. That's why I need you around, Chloe. You help sort me out." She smiled. "I'm glad you're okay."

"I fear I will smell of mildew for a while, mistress, but yes. I am glad I am otherwise unharmed."

Jade chuckled. "I'll give you a good cleaning when we get to Soldar. Good to have you back, Chloe."

"It is a pleasure to be back, mistress. I hope you'll catch me up on what I missed?"

Jade began explaining the events that transpired after Chloe blacked out. Thaddeous listened in, watching as Jade explained it all. She switched between Os and code when she mentioned her hallucinations so that Thaddeous, who remained nearby, didn't know more of her weaknesses. He already knew that A'doxia had Jade trained to roll over, but he didn't need to know Jade saw A'doxia when she wasn't really there.

"Then yeah, I came to get you and you know the rest," she concluded.

"I don't," Thaddeous interjected. Jade shifted uncomfortably in her chair.

"I just went in there to get Chloe back," she insisted. Thaddeous frowned.

"But A'doxia did something to you. Why was the door closed?"

"I closed it," Jade muttered.

"You're a terrible liar."

"So what? I don't want to talk about the small details. I went in there then I came out with Chloe. That's what happened."

"But that's not the *entirety* of what happened. Jade, you can't just brush it under the rug. If I don't know what she's trying to do, how am I supposed to h—"

"You said you'd tell her to stay away, didn't you?" Jade spat. "So there shouldn't be a problem!"

Thaddeous' shoulders dropped and a sigh escaped his lips. "If I know what she wants from you, I can better protect you should she disregard my orders."

"I don't need your protection," Jade retorted. Thaddeous arched a brow.

"Oh? Oh really? That's why, when I opened the door, you looked like a child facing the boogeyman?" Jade winced at the metaphor. "That's why you have nightmares of her? That's why you hallucinate her?" Jade's face paled. He had pieced it together.

Of course he pieced it together. He's just like Aris.

"Jade, don't push me out! I'm just trying to help! And talking about these sorts of things will help not only you, but help *me* help *you*."

Jade got to her feet, her side screaming from the movement. "Just leave it, Aris!" She spat. "I'm not your child to protect! I can keep myself safe! I can—"

"What did you call me?" Thaddeous' brows knitted together. Jade opened her mouth to bite back before the words died on her tongue. Aris. She had called him Aris.

"W-what's this about Malkov, anyway?" Jade stammered, changing the subject as quickly as she was able. "You have some superweapon and you didn't even think to tell me about it?"

Thaddeous' eyes narrowed He watched her and slowly responded. "The weapon Malkov is non-functional. It sits in the bottom of a ship and sends out a distress signal constantly. We have not discovered how to access its power, and I figure we never will. Besides," his gaze grew suspicious, "how do you know about it?"

"Mistress, I understand you are beginning to trust this...Thrax, but please be cautious of what you say. While he may be a friend, his companions may not be."

"Is there any harm in telling him?" Jade grumbled down at Chloe, her words consumed by numbers and letters in the form of their code. Thaddeous looked irritated to be left out. Chloe contemplated Jade's words for a moment.

"I am unsure, mistress."

Taking a breath, Jade placed one hand on her side and sat back down. "We received one of its distress signals when we were on Hallow."

The prince frowned. "How is that possible? Malkov is back by Soldar. There's no way its signal can travel that far." He tapped his lips. "Unless it has specified locations that it can transmit to? But even then…" He trailed off, staring intently at the ground. Jade glanced at Chloe, a brow arched. Thaddeous' eyes wandered back up to hers. He smiled.

"You know what? I think it's time for some wine."

Jade chuckled. "It's always time for some wine."

They shared a bottle on the stern of the ship, watching the stars go by. Thaddeous carried up a table and an extra chair so he wouldn't have to sit on the floor. He told her more about the odd jobs he worked and Jade couldn't help but laugh. They were unlikely friends, but friends nonetheless.

Chapter 38

The vast system of distant stars expanded around Jade as she sat in the crow's nest, gazing out, Chloe situated over her face. The Stream's immense wind speed was blocked by the ship's shields, though at this height, a small breeze slipped through and played with the folds of her shirt. She breathed in the cool air, inhaling stardust—or, at least, she liked to think she was.

To her right, a vibrant blue and red nebula collided and warred with itself, stars managing to shine through the colors' fight. Jade rested her chin on her hands and smiled. The urge to travel always sat strong in her, and when she sailed through the stars, she liked to pretend she was a voyager, off to discover new worlds. Not off to murder daughters and sons. Not off to disembowel mothers and fathers. She closed her eyes a moment. No, she liked to imagine that, for once in her life, there was peace.

"Jade, there you are," Thaddeous hollered at her from below. She glanced down at him. He stood at the end of the ratlines, smiling and offering her a slight wave. He grabbed hold of one of the ropes and started climbing. In his tuxedo. It looked absolutely ridiculous. Jade couldn't help but chuckle.

"Are you laughing at me?" he asked as he grew closer, mocking offense. Jade smirked.

"Have you ever climbed up these before? Because you look like a drunk baby."

"We can't all be as skilled as you, Jade," he teased, grabbing hold of the crow's nest and pulling himself in. There wasn't much room left with the two of them sitting in the small space.

"It's nice up here," Thaddeous said, turning his face towards the slight breeze that slipped past the shields. He smiled as he breathed it in.

"Come just to take up space?" Jade asked, crossing her arms over the railing. He chuckled.

"That's not all there is to it, no." He pulled his holo from his jacket pocket and tapped at the screen. His green eyes flickered to hers. "While you were gone, someone showed me a video of you shooting Black Lightning out of your body."

Jade's face fell. "Oh."

"Can…I ask some questions?" Thaddeous ventured. He looked at his screen. Chloe snapped a picture of it, then flipped the image so Jade could see what he was looking at. Her. In that wretched hallway, lightning pouring out of her body and consuming A'doxia.

"Depends on what you're going to ask." Jade turned and continued to analyze the photo. If he was going to ask why she was bested so easily, he should know that already. If he was going to ask what happened, well…she knew nothing.

"I have some theories about it, if you want to hear." He hesitated. "You said a few days ago that you didn't have a Helix."

A momentary wave of panic washed over Jade, as if she had been found out by a Blue, or even a Gold. She looked over at him, watching his eyes fill with understanding and compassion. Unlike her own people, he wasn't going to kill her for being a Green. He was one himself. She relaxed.

"Never got one when I was a kid." Jade looked at her hands. "Dad and I built gloves that could offer small sparks and bouts of electricity, which kept me from being discovered while we waited for my powers to show up." An exhale escaped her lips. "Never did though."

"It's amazing to me that you learned to fight better than anyone else without one of your own," Thaddeous replied. Jade furrowed her brows and scrutinized his face for any indication of sarcasm. He was sincere. He looked at her as if she were a god.

"Just took some extra practice," she said with the hint of nervous laughter.

"Mistress, you are not the best fighter out there."

Jade promptly ignored Chloe's comment and soaked up his praise. "It helped to train with a few of my fellows. I had these special bracelets and it could store and redirect lightning, so it helped when I battled Blue Lightning and Red Lightning users. Invisible Hands would've been tricky, since how can you combat an invisible hand, but I haven't met someone who had an IV strong enough to use against a living creature. Now, Wall was pretty tough. I once fought this Thrax general that could use it on his entire right arm, and he could just block blows left and right with it. We eventually were able to ki—best him, but it took a while."

He gawked at her. "That's incredible. Do you think that sometime you might teach me how to fight?"

"If we get a chance between, you know, not dying in this war, maybe I'll help you out." The two of them laughed, and Jade gestured at his holo. "What were your questions?"

"Oh!" He looked down at his pad and swiped, pulling up a voice recorder. "Do you mind?" She shrugged. He clicked the record button and stuck the holo in his jacket pocket. His eyes fixed on her helmet. "Since I was born with a Helix, I'm not exactly a 'true' Green. I think I've mentioned this to you before." He nodded at her. "But you are, and I think this is a perfect opportunity to get to know exactly what Greens are capable of."

Jade chuckled. "I'm not sure if *I'm* a true Green. I just have the eyes. It's not like I have something incredible or some war-changing ability."

"That's not true," he said. "When you were first brought here, the scientists conducted experiments. It was nothing too invasive—we drew blood, we monitored brain waves, and we introduced Helix essences. Your sensitivity to Helix was understandable, as without a Helix you do not gain the immunity to your own power like Blues do."

"Reds, too."

Thaddeous shook his head. "Reds don't. We've kept that pretty secret, since your war force seems not to have noticed it so far. We do, however, have two Helixes at a time. From our…interviews with your kind, you seem to have only one worth mentioning, with an additional Invisible Hand to use for small things, like moving items or—"

"Or picking up cups. Yeah, they can't use it on anything living for some reason." She shook her head. "But that doesn't make any sense about Reds—you guys don't have an immunity? I thought that was something everyone had."

"We're not entirely sure why we don't and your kind does. Some different strain in our DNA is a possibility, but we can't be sure." He smiled at her. "No using this against us in the war, all right?"

"No promises."

With a chuckle, he looked back at his holo. "But back onto the subject at hand, when we tested your sensitivity, you were *three times* more sensitive to BL."

"All right, but that doesn't make me special. If anything, it makes me weaker." She glanced at her hands. "Hey, who exactly are you going to show these notes to?"

"No one, Jade. This is for my own personal research," he assured her. "No one else will know. Now—you see this sensitivity as a weakness, and perhaps it is. Yet when you were struck with A'doxia's lightning, her own strands turned black and heeded your call. For whatever reason, you were able to change the lightning's color into that which we've never seen, and push it back on your foe.

"The thing is, Jade, we checked your lightning sensitivity. If your power is activated by the introduction of lightning, why didn't it show up then? Perhaps it was how much lightning was involved, perhaps it was a certain pain threshold. Or, perhaps, it was the person who shocked you. Perhaps it was A'doxia."

Jade's face hardened. *Is he going to suggest I meet with her? To confirm his stupid theory? Is he going to ask to watch?*

Thaddeous must have noticed the shift in her posture because he hurried on. "Nothing is certain yet, Jade. That's why I have to ask you: before you met A'doxia, did you ever get hit with lightning? And afterwards—were you ever struck again?"

Jade rubbed her neck, her anxiety growing. "No. I hadn't got struck by it before, but I wasn't really in the war until shortly before I met A'doxia. Scouting missions and the like don't usually see that much action." She looked away from him, settling her eyes on the stars where she found some solace. "The only time I was struck was with her. Afterwards, yeah, I was placed on the front lines and was hit from time to time. I wore armor to redirect the lightning, but sometimes the machinery fizzled out, and I was exposed. It hurt like hell. Worse than breathing with a punctured lung."

"And you didn't throw Black Lightning back at them?"

"No."

"Interesting. And what of other Helixes? Were you ever hit by any of the others?"

The corporal considered this, watching the stars dance in the distance. "I've been hit by Charge, been in Atmo storms, and had someone with a Walled arm punch me in the face. A few of the healers helped me out when I got badly injured and they say that shit isn't supposed to hurt, but it was excruciating." She used her fingers to keep track of the list of Helixes. "Where I was there were only three who could use Telepathy and none of them wasted it on me."

"That leaves Sight," Thaddeous prompted. Jade shook her head.

"Sight users can't really expose anyone to that Helix." Jade glanced at him. "That's all of them, I think."

Thaddeous nodded, silent as he took the information in, putting pieces together that Jade couldn't see. She wondered who was brighter: him or Aris.

"I have a theory," he said at last. "But you won't like it."

Jade arched a brow beneath Chloe's protective helm. *He is. He's going to say it.* Her smile fell. "You probably don't want to suggest it."

"Jade, do you understand how powerful that Black Lightning was?"

"I sort of blacked out afterwards? So no?"

"You knocked A'doxia out and shut off the power for half the floor. Do you realize how massive each floor is, Jade? And you shut down half of it, locking people in rooms, turning off training simulators, bursting lightbulbs. Everything mechanical went haywire and you weren't even *trying*." Jade's eyes narrowed. He continued: "You don't get the Lightning from other interactions. Which only leaves—"

Jade punched him in the chest, where the holo sat in his jacket pocket, silently recording. She felt it crack beneath her knuckles as Thaddeous, surprised, stumbled backwards. She grabbed his tie and pulled him away from the edge. Through Chloe's visor, she glared at him, her boiling anger hardly contained.

"Next time I won't catch you." She released his tie and jumped over the edge, grabbing the ratlines on the way down.

ϕϕϕ

That night he apologized to Jade over a bottle of wine.

"I was consumed by my work," he muttered. She watched him with a vicious gaze and drank her wine.

"Don't suggest it again," she growled.

"I won't." He looked her in the eye. "I shouldn't have in the first place. What you went through with her is not something I should ever push under the rug. You have my respect, Jade Cavvar, and that is not a way I should show it. I truly am sorry."

Conviction flickered in his eyes. He seemed sincere. He had otherwise been kind to her, so she was certain she could give him a pass on this one mistake. Jade gave him a nod.

"Thank you."

Relieved, he smiled. "I hope we can continue being friends." He lifted his glass. Jade allowed herself a smile.

"Sure." Her glass tapped against his.

ϕϕϕ

On the fifth day of travel, Jade saw Soldar, the home of her enemy.

It appeared in the sky, shaped like a snow globe, with a fleet of ships escorting the massive floating base. Its glistening dome was semi-transparent, and she could glimpse the buildings inside towering upwards. Along its lower rim, where the dome met metal, glowing red jets hummed, pushing it steadily along. The blackened metal below was formed into layers, each smaller than the last until it came to a point. The fleet circled it protectively, numbering at about thirty ships, each with sails furled and their own engines, propelling them at the same speed as Soldar. Jade stood at the railing and stared out, surprise cutting lines into her face. *The Thrax people don't live on a planet? They live on some sort of...mobile home?*

She scrunched up her face. It sounded really lame when she thought about it like that.

"Not what you were expecting?" Thaddeous strode up next to her and Jade glanced at him, brows upraised.

"Not at all. We got rumors that you had two moons, not that you were on some sort of mobile...*ship*."

Thaddeous nodded. "It's a feat of engineering for sure. Takes everyone working together to keep it running right. We stay on the move so we're never in the same place twice." He smirked at her. "So you won't be able to figure out where we are when you head back home."

Jade sneered. "Oh drat."

"I will continue recording just in case, mistress," Chloe said from Jade's hip. Jade patted her.

Thaddeous chuckled as their ship sailed towards Soldar. They stayed near the underbelly, finding the harbor in a large opening cut into the side. They dropped anchor and disembarked. The harbor had high ceilings and a slim space for walking between the docked ships. People crowded the floor, shoving past each other with crates in their arms. It smelled of sweat and exotic spices.

"The king wants to meet you," Thaddeous said when they stepped into the elevator situated in a nearby hallway. Jade arched a brow.

"Oh boy, I'm honored. Should I be ready to stab him?"

Thaddeous smirked. "I'd prefer if you didn't kill my father." He crossed his arms behind his back. "We'll have dinner with him later today, if that's acceptable." He looked at her. She nodded.

"Sounds fine with me. Not that I really have a choice in the matter." She put her hands in her pant pockets. Thaddeous chuckled.

"Well, I'd tell them you weren't feeling well if you decided not to show." The elevator shook and Thaddeous cleared his throat. "I've been meaning to tell you. I talked to A'doxia." Jade's nod was stiff as she struggled to keep the woman's song out of her head. Thaddeous took a breath. "She agreed to stay away so long as you don't want her around."

"Why would I want her around?" Jade scoffed.

"She seems to be under the delusion that you like her." Jade opened her mouth to rebut, but he lifted his hands in surrender. "I'm just telling you what she said, don't shoot the messenger." Jade rubbed her jaw, scowling, but allowed him to continue. Thaddeous offered her an apologetic smile. "Regardless, she says she's going to stay away from you the best she can. On top of that, I'm going to give you a flat, so she won't even know where you're staying." The elevator doors opened as Thaddeous beamed. "You'll be safe here."

Jade smiled at him, the tension in her jaw fading. He was good. She stepped out of the elevator.

A city expanded before her, towers reaching up to the glass dome that surrounded Soldar's populace. People mingled on sidewalks, chatting and purchasing things from the market set up around a large fountain. Not a car was in sight, probably due to the lack of space, but it made her wonder how everyone managed to get around. Perhaps people just didn't travel to the other half of the city.

Cooking meat, melting candies, and hot drinks filled the air with a mixture of smells, all mingled with the sound of laughter and bartering. All the Reds here looked happy, and children played in the fountain. People sat on nearby benches or on the ground, chatting and eating at ura, candied popcorn—a delicacy from one of the original human ships—and covered in niyra sauce, which was a purple liquid made out of niyra berries. Jade stood and stared for a moment, taking it all in. The normalcy of her enemies. The joy they all expressed.

Thaddeous walked in front of her and smirked over his shoulder. "Soldar to Jade," he said, waving his hand. "C'mon, your flat is this way."

Jade blinked and walked after him. "How do you guys do all this? Can you make your own food?"

"We have places for that," Thaddeous said with a nod. "They're in the northern half. Plants and animals alike are grown for us, and we do a lot of trading with allied planets." He shrugged. "It's not ideal, but if we house anywhere, we put that entire planet at risk." He glanced at her. "Your people would massacre anyone with red eyes."

Jade frowned. It was true. *And if they got their hands on Malkov...*

They headed towards the heart of the market that sat in the city square, the crowd bustling and the Reds occasionally glancing and muttering about Jade's eyes. People—Reds—walked on either side of Jade. At first, the sight of so many smiling faces and nods in her direction was fascinating. If she walked around like this on Nevar, she'd be stabbed in the neck. But eventually, tension began to rise up in her bones. These were all Reds. Sure, they were smiling, sure, the children were playing, but Jade had no armor on. A knife could come from anyone. Her stitches itched as her anxiety grew. A single slice. A single jerk in her direction. She could already feel the warmth of her intestines in her hands. She could hear them splatter to the ground. A cold sweat started on her spine. Her eyes shifted from one person to the next. She eyed the children.

Is that a weapon? Is that a scream? Why are they smiling—are they going to kill me? Maybe none of them actually like Greens, maybe this is all a façade. Maybe they want me dead. Are they going to attack? Send children to do their dirty work? Are they going to lash out against the Green Demon? Destroy me once and for all? I've killed their family members. I've butchered their husbands and wives. They want revenge. They're going to circle me and cut out my eyes. Her mind spiraled further. Everything blurred together. Sounds filled her skull and made it hard to calm down. A constant static consumed her ears. *Is someone humming? Is that humming? Someone's definitely humming, someone's definitely humming, she's here, she's back, she and everyone else are going to kill me, I'm never getting home, I'm never going to see Aris again. Oh Vix, oh Vix.* She grabbed at her hair and withdrew into a stall, out of the crowd. Thaddeous glanced behind him and stepped in after her.

"Jade, your eyes…What's wrong?"

Jade rubbed her neck. She had no armor. She opened and closed her left fist while her grip tightened on Chloe in her right. Anything could happen. Anything. She wouldn't be able to react. She'd get her guts torn from her abdomen. She's have her eyes ripped from her skull. Her own people would do it. Her own people would. These were Reds. They had more of a reason to murder her and desecrate her corpse. She was injured and at a disadvantage. She had no way to protect herself.

Thaddeous glanced at the throng of people meandering by. "The crowds scare you."

"I'm not scared," Jade snapped back. She rubbed her shoulder with her thumb, trying to release the tension. It took the majority of her will to keep her voice from shaking. She and Aris avoided crowds for the most part. Jade never enjoyed them, but she never panicked like this either. She had never been in a group of Reds who were all...*smiling*. At her. "I just don't have any armor in case something *does* happen."

"They're not going to try to hurt you, Jade. Our people aren't like yours. We *want* Greens around." He stared intently into her eyes. Had they changed? Was she a Red now, because she was frigh—because she was uncomfortable? Was she a traitor, just like the Blues suspected Greens to be?

"How do I know that?" Jade grumbled. "A'doxia doesn't subscribe to your whole idea of 'everyone loves the Greens,' does she? Not...not in the same way..." She trailed off, her face twisting with disgust at the thought. She definitely heard humming. Thaddeous took her hand. The humming faded.

"Jade, do you believe in Vix?"

Jade pulled her hand away and looked at him. "What?"

"You see," he continued without answering. "In our story of Vix, Greens came directly from Vix's own eyes. I'm going to assume Ghawor has green eyes in your myth?" Jade nodded, brows furrowed with confusion. "And that means you have the eyes of the devil among the Exuro." Jade frowned. Thaddeous continued: "Don't you hate that? That you can stand in sermons and listen to the pastor preach about how Greens are the root of all evil, that they were sent by Ghawor himself to destroy all of us?"

Jade gritted her teeth. "What do you know, anyway?"

"I know that you sat in those sermons and took it." His lips pulled at a frown. "I watched you shift in your seat when he talked about Greens, nod when he talked about their demonic nature. Why is that, Jade? Don't you hate them for believing you're a demon?"

Jade shoved him away. "Why the fuck were you following me?"

Thaddeous stumbled back but recovered. "Don't you hate that the same people who believe you to be a war hero would hang you the moment you revealed your eyes? Don't you hate that, no matter what you do, you will always be overshadowed by the fact that your eyes happen to be green?"

"Shut up!" Jade screamed. "You don't know anything!"

"Are you what they think you are?" Thaddeous pressed. "*Are* you a demon?"

"What the fuck do you want from me, Thaddeous? All I said was that I was uncomfortable walking in a crowd of people and all of a sudden now I'm on trial because my eyes are green? What do you want me to say? You want me to admit it?" She shoved him back again, into the crowd who startled and skirted as far away from them as possible. "Because here I go! I fuckin' admit it, Thaddeous, I'm a demon!" She spread out her arms and laughed bitterly. "I've killed people, I've committed traitorous acts, I've done things I myself don't even understand! So yes, I sit there and take it when the pastor talks about how evil I am. Yes, I nod in agreement. Because it's fucking *true*, Thaddeous. I've let children die, I've murdered husbands and wives, and I've had to kill some of my own! I'm a monster, Thaddeous! I'm everything the stories say and more!" Tears burned at the corners of her eyes. "And you know what? I've come to accept that shitty part about myself! That one day, just like the legend says, I'm going to snap and kill everyone I love! So yes, Thaddeous. All of it's true!" She dropped her arms, her face flush with anger and guilt. "All of it."

Thaddeous stared at her hard, then stepped forward and wrapped his arms around her, pulling her close.

"That's where you're wrong, Jade," he whispered. "You're not a demon. You're just a human being with the potential to change things." He rested his chin atop her head. "And that's what everyone here sees you as."

Jade blinked. She stood there, her anger forgotten, her guilt lessened. She breathed in his smell that reminded her of coffee and vanilla. Why was he doing this? Why...? She closed her eyes and wrapped her arms around him.

He was her friend. That was why.

"You're no demon," he muttered, smoothing out her hair. "But you do smell."

Jade pushed him away and laughed, wiping the corners of her eyes. "Way to ruin the moment, asshole."

Thaddeous laughed. "Listen, I'm just saying that maybe we should get you to that flat and let you shower before you contaminate the whole air supply."

Jade smiled. "Bastard."

He offered her his hand. "I'll find us a different way through the crowd. C'mon."

She took it.

ΦΦΦ

They slipped past vendors and stalls until they reached the edge of the market. They skirted around it before eventually being able to escape into one of the many walkways through tall buildings. A few turns left and there they were, in front of a sleek building with windows that looked out over the entire city.

"You're on the top floor," he said as he walked up to the glass sliding doors. Jade blinked. *The top?* Her chest swelled with excitement. There weren't many buildings taller than this one, which meant she was going to be living like royalty. For the first time in her life. She chuckled.

I wish Aris were here to experience this with me.

She followed Thaddeous inside, past the lobby, and took the elevator to the thirtieth floor. There, a red carpet spanned the hallway, with one door on either side of the wall.

"You don't have a neighbor, so you have this entire floor to yourself." Thaddeous moved to the left door and fished into his pocket for the key. "You can see a lot of the city from here." He unlocked the door and held it open. "Hope you like it." Jade stepped inside.

The kitchen was to her left, massive enough to fit a whole party of people. It was equipped with a stove, fridge, freezer, two ovens, marble counters, and a sink she could probably bathe in.

On the opposite wall were floor-to-ceiling windows, staring out over the bustle of the city. A white couch was set up facing it, along with two chairs and a coffee table, all of which sat upon a white rug.

Jade walked over the dark hardwood floors and glanced to her right, where her room branched off of the main living space, separated by a tall curtain. The bed was made with beautiful blue covers and a company of massive pillows.

"The room you need is to the left," Thaddeous said, stepping inside with a smirk, the door closing behind him. Jade arched a brow and looked to her left, where the bathroom door sat open with a massive tub and shower inside. Jade pursed her lips.

"Very funny, asshole." She set Chloe down on the kitchen counter.

"There are fresh clothes in there for you, by the way. Tomorrow we can go shopping to get you a set of armor, too, if you'd like." He leaned against the wall. Jade glanced at him as he began to pull his jacket off. Jade arched a brow at how neatly he folded his jacket, tucking the sleeves and watching each move his hand made intently. When he finished, he met her gaze.

"What?"

"You're such royalty," Jade huffed with a sarcastic tone. He smiled. "I'm going to shower."

"I'll be here when you get out."

Jade threw him a thumbs-up as she grabbed Chloe and strode into the bathroom. She locked the door behind her.

"Mistress."

"I know," Jade muttered as she turned on the water. "I need to focus."

ϕϕϕ

Jade stepped out of the bathroom, dried out her hair with a towel, and dressed in loose fitting jeans, a tank-top, and a thin jacket with the sleeves rolled up to her shoulders. Thaddeous was on the couch in his undershirt, his tie and jacket folded on the kitchen counter. Jade placed Chloe beside Thaddeous' clothes and draped the towel over her shoulders, walked to the fridge, and opened it up.

"We have anything to eat?" she asked.

"Oh, you probably can't tell, but it's almost time for dinner."

Jade glanced over at him as he got up, straightening his shirt out. His eyes flickered to hers and he froze. For a moment, his eyes held a similar glint to A'doxia's. There was hunger there. Jade arched a brow and shifted uncomfortably.

"Yes?"

Thaddeous' eyes were on her arms. "Those are…" He cleared his throat. "Big."

Jade nodded slowly. "I guess?"

Thaddeous rubbed the back of his neck, a flush coming across his cheeks. "Can I, um…"

Jade's brows furrowed as she stared at him. Then, slowly, she realized what he was asking. "You want to touch them?"

Thaddeous rubbed his neck more furiously, the redness on his face growing stronger. Jade stood, confused and uncomfortable. She and Aris had shown off to each other before, felt each other's muscles, compared. It was a sort of friendly competition, and that's what Thaddeous was doing, right? Jade glanced to her right. No, she couldn't even pretend that was what he was doing. She opted for teasing him instead and tugged at her sleeves.

"Muscles? Really?" Jade said. Thaddeous looked away with a nervous grin.

"Strong women are attractive. There's nothing wrong with that."

"Well, I might need to cover them up if they're going to distract you at dinner," she muttered.

Thaddeous rubbed the back of his head, laughing. "They might distract the whole table. But uh, is that a bad thing? You should show them off more."

Jade coughed into her fist. "Do I need to dress fancy to meet the king?" she said as she picked up Chloe. "Maybe I can get a tuxedo and match your everyday wear." She pulled her sleeves down.

Thaddeous smiled. "Sure, Jade."

Chapter 39

Despite Jade's wishes, Thaddeous insisted she leave Chloe in the room.

"We are going to have dinner, after all. You can't eat with her over her head," he said. Without Chloe, however, she was beginning to regret her lack of thick clothing as she strode around in the cool Soldar air. Thaddeous donned his jacket and tie again and lead the way, the two of them walking beside each other.

"So I'm guessing that you don't actually run cold?" he asked, breaking the silence. Jade chuckled.

"No, I just needed to get extra clothes for when I ran off into the sunset."

Thaddeous snickered. "You planned it from the very beginning?"

"I know, I'm surprised, too." Jade stretched her arms over her head, trying to disperse the feeling of vulnerability. She felt like she was being watched. She glanced over her shoulder, but there wasn't anyone there. There was no one there to hurt her, or stare, or anything of the sort. It was the most she had ever been exposed in years. And here she was, walking with the Thrax prince, and feeling generally…good.

"You okay?" Thaddeous asked. Jade shrugged.

"Just feel…weird. I don't know the last time I walked around in jeans and a shirt without layers of armor over my body."

Thaddeous nodded. "We can get you something warmer, if you like."

"It's okay." She exhaled. "If…um. I'll get used to it." She ran a hand through her hair. She didn't remember the last time it was so soft. Fuck, she really didn't take care of herself, did she?

More silence as they walked. The streetlights faded to a low light and Jade looked up at the stars. Somewhere out there, Aris was alone. Guilt gnawed at her gut. What was she doing? Befriending a man while her best friend was in solitude? Jade was losing her mind. She couldn't do this. She needed to focus.

"I've been looking into that base on Hallow," Thaddeous said. Jade looked at him.

"Find anything?"

He shook his head. "Not yet. We followed A'do— instructions to where that entrance was, but we've been having a hard time discovering anything about its existence."

Silence.

"I should mention that my sister will be there," Thaddeous said, his voice suddenly full of venom. Jade looked at him. He motioned to a building to their right, indicating this was the place. It stood three stories tall, with no windows on the first floor, and a few guards by the entrance. They didn't question Jade or Thaddeous as the two approached. "I wouldn't suggest telling her anything about yourself," Thaddeous continued. "She's a little crazy." He shook his head, pulling the door open for Jade.

They entered a tiled room with a single red carpet leading to another set of doors a few paces away. There, Thaddeous let Jade enter first, where the royal family and its advisors waited. Where everyone Jade should be trying to kill sat, vulnerable. Where she was about to dine with the enemy.

I'm being so fucking stupid.

The room was massive, housing a long table with every seat but three filled. Only drinks had been served, but when Jade and Thaddeous stepped inside, everyone turned from their wine and conversations to stare. Murmurs of 'the Green' radiated the room, making Jade's skin crawl. Now she really wished she had armor on. She was a fool for walking in like this. She could feel tension curl into her shoulder blades and wrap around her spine. Thaddeous' hand clutched hers and he led them to the two seats beside each other that were empty, nearest to a large man at the head of the table. His face was bearded and his crimson eyes held a smile as he watched the two approach. To the man's left was a pale, freckled woman with red hair pulled into a bun. A large scar arched from the corner of her right jaw up to the bridge of her nose.

And her eyes were two different colors. One was chalk-white, the other a sunset-orange.

The room shifted beneath Jade and she felt as if her head were spinning. A Plural. *A Plural?*

"But all is not lost!" The preacher spread his hands wide, a bold smile on his lips. Jade watched from the back row, Chloe snug over her head. "There is one and only one who can slay the Green Demon! A Plural! Sent from Vix himself to save us from Ghawor's evil beast, this creature of majesty! A being of great virtue, who is gifted with a Helix no one has ever had before: Slayer. A special ability designed specifically to seek out and kill Greens! A Plural has not been seen in generations, even when a Green has shown its wretched eyes, but this does not mean they are a myth. No, for I believe that the Plural will arrive only when the threat the Green poses is great enough. And when one arrives, not only must we treat the majestic being with reverence, but we must also fear the appearance of

a Green, who will without a doubt try to slay the Plural before the Plural slays it."

"Jade, this is Voshell, my sister," Thaddeous said, gesturing to the Plural. His eyes were watching Jade with caution. "Voshell, this is Corporal Jade Cavvar, the Green everyone has been told about."

"Oh, it's so lovely to meet you," Voshell replied. "Though I'm surprised you haven't managed to escape by now."

Thaddeous frowned. "Sister." His tone was chastising. He pulled out Jade's chair and the corporal sat down, smiling stiffly back at the woman with two different eyes. Thaddeous sat beside her.

"Sorry to disappoint," Jade said. *Why is she antagonizing me?*

Voshell laughed and waved her hand in the air. "Oh, I'm sure you're trying your hardest. I dare say we're pretty alike! Did you know that it's a common belief among my people that Plurals were made to help Greens with their Vix-given tasks?"

Jade's brows furrowed and she glanced at Thaddeous. He was watching his sister with a bored expression.

"In fact!" Voshell continued. "It's said that the two share the same fate! Which probably means if I cut off your foot, eventually my own foot would get cut off!"

What the fuck?

"Okay," Jade replied slowly. Voshell didn't seem to care much what Jade had to say and pressed onward, barely even letting Jade finish her one word.

"We're already pretty alike, aren't we? I mean, neither of us have normal eye colors."

Jade arched a brow. "You, me, *and* Thaddeous."

Voshell's smile grew. "That's true, isn't it?" she chimed. The princess looked to her brother. "The two Greens sitting together. So weird there's two of them in the galaxy at the same time."

Thaddeous scowled and waved for wine.

"Yeah, it's weird, but it's not like much is known about Greens," Jade replied. An attendant appeared and poured Thaddeous a glass of red, which he downed and had refilled. Voshell laughed.

"I see, so it's going to be one of *those* kinds of dinners," Voshell said. Her eyes shifted to Jade. "Would you like something to drink?" She turned and waved down one of the butlers, who approached Jade with a collection of choices. Jade blindly gestured to one, her attention still on Thaddeous.

"Why are you drinking like that?" Jade muttered.

"As it seems my children have opted out of introducing me," the man at the head of the table said. Jade was suddenly aware of how silent the room had been. "I am King Daxgor Malkov, leader of the Thrax and ruler of Soldar." He dipped his head at Jade. "It is an honor to meet you at last, Corporal Cavvar."

Jade offered a tight smile to the king. "Yeah. Thanks."

Daxgor laughed, his heavy chest shaking with the sound. "You are quite welcome, my dear! Now, bring out the first course!" He clapped his hands twice, and a few butlers fled the room through a doorway Jade had not noticed before. They returned laden with dishes of various sizes holding a mass amount of food. Jade glanced down the table, where at least twenty other people sat. No wonder there was so much food at the ready.

"Thaddeous has told us a lot about you," Voshell said as they dished up, keeping Jade from being able to interrogate Thaddeous further. Shoving her curiosity and suspicion down her chest, Jade took a kennock leg, frowning at Voshell. "A soldier in the Exuro army. My, what an interesting experience that must have been." She whistled. "And they never found you out? Not even once? Oh—" she laughed— "Of course they didn't, if they had, you wouldn't be joining us for dinner, would you?"

Jade eyed her. Voshell was smiling, a blissful expression plastered on her face.

"That's right," Jade said. "I'd be dead. So no, they never found me out." She poured gravy over her meal, drowning the vegetables and the kennock meat in it. "But if that's all he told you, then you must be pretty curious about me." She took a sip from her glass. Some sort of alcoholic fruity concoction. There were hints of pear notes mixed with cinnamon. She caught Thaddeous eyeing her, frowning. He had, after all, told her not to speak about herself.

"Oh, I am," Voshell said. Daxgor chuckled.

"She is curious about eye colors just as much as her younger brother." He smiled at Thaddeous, who didn't offer one in return.

"I heard a rumor that you are resilient to most anesthetics. Is that true?" Voshell pressed.

"I guess." Jade felt A'doxia's body against hers, the woman's fingers dancing over Jade's sternum.

"Fascinating!" Voshell replied with a grin. She looked at Thaddeous. "Isn't that the most curious thing?"

"Quite," Thaddeous growled. "Would you stop bombarding her with questions? She's sure to get tired of you."

"Oh, don't be like that, brother. I've only asked one so far," Voshell huffed, placing her elbows on the table. "I mean, it's not like I can ask *you* these questions. It's not like you're a *real* Green."

Thaddeous scowled at her. Voshell laughed, waving the tension from the air.

"Relax, brother! I won't tell her." She put her fingers to her mouth. "Whoops."

Jade frowned but held her tongue. Voshell wanted to get a rise out of her. Jade wouldn't give her the satisfaction.

Voshell's eyes settled on Jade and a giggle erupted from her lips. "So stoic! Well, if that's the way you're both going to be, I have some exciting news to announce to everyone!" She stood. The rest of the table turned to her. "Unlike Thaddeous' failed attempt at ending the war—" her eyes pointedly looked at Jade as Voshell raised her hands dramatically— "and after years of fighting on the front lines against the hapless Blue pawns, I have discovered something that can end the war once and for all. While we have been holding Sobek strong—even managing to push the Blues back over the past few months—the fact is that we're losing the war. It doesn't matter how many of the Exuro I blow up with my bombs."

Ice flooded the corporal's veins. *Wait. She can't mean...*

"It doesn't matter if I throw their body parts into the trees." Those Plural eyes watched Jade intently.

She can't be.

"And it doesn't matter if I procure a reputation for myself among my enemies. 'The Mad Queen,' they call me."

"Vosh, what are you *doing?*" Thaddeous hissed. He glanced over at Jade, an expression of worry washing over his features.

Thaddeous' sister...is the Mad Queen? Jade's ears rang with the sounds of explosions. Her vision blurred.

A third of her unit lay bloodied on the burnt earth, bleeding out, missing limbs, missing heads. Several had large rocks or branches thrust through their chests. A few were holding their dismembered arms and sobbing. Jade picked herself up off the ground. Her armor was half melted, large sections of the metal now smeared several inches downwards or altogether gone. Luckily the suit beneath it kept her skin from being too badly burnt.

"Salene? Aris?" She called out, the screams swallowing her hoarse voice. Her spine ached. She reached up and rubbed the goggles she wore around her eyes, wiping the blood off the cracked glass. Her gaze ran over the crowd, searching the bodies.

Vix, please don't let them have been caught in the immediate blast. Please let them be okay. Please, *Jade thought.*

She spotted Salene dragging an unconscious Aris back a few feet and Jade rushed towards them. Salene looked up when she heard Jade approaching. Jade froze.

The right half of Salene's face was burnt, and the hair on that half of her skull fried off. Pain-filled tears brimmed at the corners of Salene's eyes. Jade jolted forward to help carry Aris.

"Salene—Salene, are you okay?" Jade said as she knelt down and began to pick up Aris. Salene touched her arm.

"Jade, wait," she said, each word pulling at her fresh burn and causing the tears to spill down Salene's face. "Your leg."

Jade followed Salene's gaze, where she found the armor and Rye-mail on her right leg had been torn off from the explosion. Sitting there instead, a massive gash in her flesh bled heavily. Jade scowled.

"I'll be fine." She heaved Aris into her arms, more blood squirting from her leg wound.

"Jade—" Salene started, standing. Screams in a greater volume filled the air around them. Both Jade and Salene glanced towards the source. To the east, Tharx soldiers came from the trees that bordered the burning earth. They tore into the less injured soldiers on the fringes, slowly making their way through the Opes ranks. Jade cursed.

"We have to go," Salene said, grabbing Jade's arm. "We have to go!"

"Our people—" Jade started as the less harmed soldiers began to turn tail and run.

"We've lost, Jade! Let's go!" Salene pulled Jade behind her a few steps before, reluctantly, Jade turned and *limped her way back into the trees, back towards the distant Opes base. She kept Aris close to her chest, happy to save one.*

The screams of her dying comrades followed her.

It wasn't until weeks later that they found out which Thrax general had planned such a flawless trap. The Mad Queen. She was ruthless. She used her own soldiers as bait, drawing the Opes into minefields and letting them all die together, Thrax and Opes alike. Once, the Opes tried to intercept her transport and assassinate her. They had everything planned. It was supposed to be foolproof.

The Mad Queen proved to be a valiant warrior who fought harder than any of her troops. Only three of Jade's comrades survived in a team of over two-hundred. Their eyes were distant. They committed suicide a week later.

"I have found Malkov, a weapon capable of destroying every last Blue!" Voshell proclaimed, grinning at Jade and bringing the corporal back from her memories.

The woman who destroyed Salene's face, who took Salene's legs. The Mad Queen was standing right before her, boasting. *If it weren't for her, Salene could still walk. If it weren't for her, Salene never would have fallen.*

Jade's vision darkened. All she could see was Voshell. All she could hear were the screams of everyone she knew dying. Her mother. Salene. Aris.

If she wasn't sure one woman's death could end the war before, Jade was convinced now. She had to kill Voshell. She had to end this now.

"You activated the *superweapon?*" Thaddeous hissed, standing up and slamming his hands on the table. "And you propose to end the war by eradicating an entire race of people!? Are you *insane?*"

Jade's hand curled around the knife beside her plate. Her mind began playing the odds of success. One good lunge would likely get the job done. And despite her stitches, Jade had recovered a lot of her strength. She could probably take Voshell.

The princess beamed. "Is that a jab at my mental state, brother? You must know how sensitive I am about that." She beamed. "Besides, this weapon will save all of the Thrax without a doubt. We will be able to live our lives without fear of a Blue slaughtering our family." Her last comment was dry.

"A Blue never killed our—the Blues are just following orders!" Thaddeous shouted.

"They were *born* to follow orders!" Voshell countered. The rest of the table watched in silence. Jade rose to her feet. One good hit. She couldn't let Voshell, the Mad Queen, use this weapon. Jade had seen what the Mad Queen could do with regular explosives. She didn't want to know what would happen with a superweapon.

Jade needed one good hit. She wouldn't let Aris die.

"We can't massacre an entire group of people, Voshell! We can't do this! Father," he spun to the king. "Tell her we can't do this! Tell her that the Green will be enough!"

Daxgor frowned. "And what is your Green capable of doing?"

"She has the ability over Black Lightning, a Helix we've not ever seen before. It shut down half a level below deck when she wasn't even trying to. Imagine what she could do with that gift! Not to mention she's a *Green*. She was born to change things!"

The king looked at Jade. "Show us."

Jade's grip on the knife tightened. Thaddeous turned back to her, horrified at what his father asked. His eyes flickered down to the knife.

"Can you?" Daxgor asked.

"I can," Jade said, pushing away from the table. Thaddeous' hand moved towards her discreetly. "But first—" She spun and launched the knife at Voshell. Voshell's eyes widened as she threw herself back. Thaddeous screamed.

The utensil dug itself into the Mad Queen's right eye. The chalk-white one.

Voshell's primal scream rose up to join the terrified howls of the other guests. Many leapt to their feet and backed away, uncertain of what to do. Thaddeous reached for Jade while Daxgor's face grew flush with surprise. Jade evaded Thaddeous' grapple, leapt onto the table, and rushed towards Voshell as the Plural yanked the knife from her eye, spilling blood everywhere.

"Is this the demon you want in charge of ending the *war?*" Voshell cried as Jade tackled her to the ground. Both of them toppled over the chair, the ground throwing them apart on impact. The doors to the room flew open and guards rushed in.

"Jade!" Thaddeous cried, rushing to the other side of the table. Jade shoved herself to her knees. Voshell was lying on the floor, one hand gripping her wound as she propped herself up with her elbow. Her sunset-orange eye settled on Jade's face. It twisted with hatred and triumph.

What on Nevar?

"Jade, sto—"

Daxgor stood, kicking his chair back and cutting Thaddeous off. "That's enough!" He boomed. As Jade caught her breath, she noticed red dots floating on her shirt. A handful of pistols were trained on her. Jade scowled. If she had a half-decent set of armor, lead bullets would do nothing to her. Not unless these guards were somehow sharpshooters and could hit between the gaps. Her dark eyes rested on Voshell and she wiped her mouth. Daxgor helped his daughter to her feet. His eyes met Jade's.

"I've seen enough."

"No, father, please," Thaddeous started. "There are children out there, *babies,* innocent lives that would be murdered by what Voshell is proposing!"

Daxgor held up his hand. "You Green appears powerful and reckless enough to do something as crazy as end the war. But her actions here tonight have convinced me she may not even know how to control herself, let alone that power of hers." His eyes narrowed on Jade. She rolled her shoulders back, unflinchingly staring back. "You may stay on Soldar for now, Green, until I decide what to do with you. Until then," he looked to Voshell, who had a hand pressed tightly against her gushing eye, "show me this weapon."

"Father, she won't—" Thaddeous began.

"My decision as king is final, Thaddeous," Daxgor hissed. "You'd be best to remember that. Am I clear?" Thaddeous scowled. Voshell smiled.

"Yes, father."

ϕϕϕ

Voshell was escorted from the room by several medics, and Thaddeous and Jade were politely asked to leave. A few blocks away, Thaddeous turned to her.

"You ruined it," he hissed. "That was our chance, that was our—"

"She's the Mad Queen! Why didn't you tell me?" Jade spat back, the two of them arguing in the middle of the street and their voices echoing off buildings. Thaddeous scowled.

"You threw a *knife* into my sister's *eye!* How do you think that looks?"

"Like I wanted to kill her? Your sister is insane, Thaddeous!" Jade swept her hand through the air. "She wants to kill everyone I know and love! She has the superweapon, and now it can be unlocked, and she's going to use it to start a fucking epidemic that only affects my people! And they're all

413

going to get sick and die, and who knows how painful that will be? Who knows if there's even a way to stop it? I *wanted* to kill her. I wanted to slit her throat or shove that knife right into your sister's twisted brain." Thaddeous' snarl grew and his shoulders rose with anger. Jade pressed on. "If she died, then I'd have a chance of destroying that weapon. I'd have a chance to throw it back into space where it belongs! And maybe this stupid war would finally end!"

Thaddeous' face twisted with fury. "You think more death will stop it? You think by displaying your profound ability for violence, you will endear my father to you? Now he's going to approve Vosh using that thing on the Exuro Empire!"

"I'm having a hard enough time as it is, Thaddeous!" Jade shot back. "I've grown up learning everything wicked about your people, and I've been taught since the day I was drafted—at *eleven years old*—that your people are lunatics, wanting to kill all of us! Wanting to rape our women and murder our children! I struggle talking to you every day that I'm here, every day that I want to trust you is another day I grapple with what I've been taught. I want to go home, and here I am, hoping that we can, somehow, become friends! And doing that takes away from my efforts to leave, and all of it is so confusing!" She grabbed at her hair, her stitches tugging at her flesh. "I'm reckless and foolish and aggressive! That's who I am, Thaddeous! That's who I've always been! And that won't change!" She exhaled and closed her eyes, her misplaced anger falling from her shoulders. "And now I've fucked up once again. You should've told me what you wanted to get out of that dinner. You should've told me your sister was the Mad Queen. Maybe then I wouldn't have stabbed your crazy sister in the eye." She glanced at him. "Probably not though."

"She *was* sent to an institution when she was a kid." He offered a slight smile. Jade found herself relaxing a little.

"See? Fucked up, man. Can't trust a woman like that with a weapon," she replied.

"I would trust you with one, and you're pretty fucked up."

Jade let her hands fall back to her sides. "How do we stop this?"

Thaddeous glanced behind him, looking for any indication someone was listening. He stepped close to Jade, his voice low.

"I need you to teach me how to fight."

"To fight?" she murmured back, frowning up at him. "Are we…?"

"Maybe. If it comes to that, yes, we'll stop my sister. But I'd rather we refrain from hurting her any further."

"You two aren't that close, are you?"

"She's family, but that's where my love for her ends," Thaddeous replied, his eyes resting on Jade once again. "And her mind isn't all there."

"Well, glad I don't have to apologize for stabbing her then. I don't really feel sorry for that."

Thaddeous smiled. "Yeah. You're pushing your luck. You know, Voshell seems to believe you two are linked in some way. Guess the fact that you can still see out of your eye proves her wrong, huh?"

"Guess so."

Thaddeous appeared distant for a moment before sighing. "You see, the real reason is that there's a way I can take control right out from under her. If I can fight my father and kill him, I will be able to take the crown."

Jade blinked. "Woah, what? You want to kill your dad? Do you have daddy issues, too?"

"I don't want to do this, Jade. But our laws say the king's children can challenge and kill him for the throne. And you're a war hero. If you can teach me how to fight and win, I can stop this whole thing. I can exile my sister. I can make bigger strides to end this war."

Jade frowned. "Why haven't you tried this before? Your sister would be taking the throne otherwise, right? Weren't you concerned what she'd do before all this?"

"Of course I was. But as prince, I can do things to lessen the ruler's power, things that I would be doing against my sister when she took control. I don't want to hurt either of them after losing so much of my family already, Jade. This isn't easy for me. But I really need you to help me with this."

"I don't suppose I can fight him for you?"

He chuckled. "No, you can't."

Jade pulled away, giving them distance and rolling her shoulders back. "Then we can meet tomorrow and get started."

Thaddeous' face filled with relief. "Thank you, Jade. Thank you."

"I'm saving my own ass by doing this, you know."

"Yeah. I know."

Chapter 40

Jade woke up screaming, throwing off her blankets and pushing herself away from them as she tumbled off the edge of the bed. She smacked her tail bone hard against the floor and her head swam. She rubbed her eyes, trying to focus on calming her breathing.

It's just a dream, she could hear Aris say. *Shh, Jade, it's okay. I'm here. I'm here.*

Jade sat up, pulling up her shirt to check that her stitches were all right. She could see where several of them had already dissolved. It was definitely going to scar, but at least it appeared it had mostly healed. She let her shirt drop and rubbed her back, grimacing as she tried to shove the pain away. She was dressed in her clothes from the previous night. She vaguely remembered throwing herself onto her bed without doing anything else.

"Mistress?" Chloe said. *"Mistress, are you okay?"*

"Yeah, just nightmares again." She picked up Chloe and tucked the helmet under her arm, shuffling into the kitchen. "All right," she began, before Chloe could prompt her. "A lot happened last night."

She set her helmet on the counter and moved to get herself some food from the fridge. She pulled out an apple and sat on a barstool as she recalled the events of the dinner. When she finished, Jade set the core of her apple down and wiped her hands off on her jeans.

"Mistress, it seems we are under a time constraint."

"Yeah." Jade placed her knuckles to her mouth in thought. "I'm not sure what to do. The king hates me, Voshell has his ear, and Thaddeous seems to be the underappreciated son. If I can train him up to kill his father before Voshell uses the weapon to murder everyone I know, then wonderful. But training doesn't work like that—it'll take a long time to ensure he's any good. And what if he fails? What if he dies? Will the Thrax throw me out, kill me?"

"It appears you have little choice, mistress. Unless you can find a way to get onto Voshell's ship—wait. Mistress, might you request for their duel to be held there? By the weapon? Perhaps while Thaddeous fights, you can deactivate it, potentially even destroy it."

Jade arched a brow. "That's good thinking. As long as there isn't some sort of traditional sparring place, that might work. Then it won't matter if Thaddeous wins—I can train him to block and evade, and that'll buy me time. Before anything happens, I can step in and sour the duel, or he can call it off." She chuckled and patted Chloe. "You're a genius."

"Mistress, there is one last thing."

"Oh?"

"Voshell seemed to be taunting Thaddeous about his eyes, according to what you told me, mistress. Yours can change—this we know well. And Thaddeous' have changed once before, mistress. Yet his emphasis on not being a true Green, and his sister's actions, make me curious as to what he means."

"I mean, there's a lot about Greens we don't know. I don't see why it's too big of a deal if two Greens exist at the same time."

"Mistress, I am unsure. Something about the whole situation feels…off."

"He's trustworthy, though," Jade insisted. "He's kept me safe and hasn't done anything to wrong me. I'm sure he'd tell me if he was hiding anything."

"He is still your enemy, mistress. And while he is of a friendly sort, and has proven himself to be a decent sentient being, he kidnapped you for a reason. And I suspect this thing

about being authentic has something to do with that motive, mistress."

Jade chewed on the side of her finger. Chloe had a point, as usual. Jade wanted to trust Thaddeous—she did, to some extent—but at what cost? She had to get home. She had to destroy this weapon and find a way back. She couldn't live here. She couldn't be friends. She had to leave. She had to get back to Aris. With a resigned sigh, she nodded.

"I'll be careful."

"No you won't, mistress. But I appreciate the sentiment." There was a hint of a smile in her synthesized voice. Jade chuckled.

"Yeah, yeah."

ϕϕϕ

Thaddeous arrived a few minutes before noon, looking nervous. He wore his suit, madly enough, and his eyes flicked left and right. He smiled when she opened the door. Her green eyes met his.

"Ready to go?" he asked. Jade arched a brow, making a point of looking him over.

"Are you?" she scoffed. "We're not going to a fancy dinner, you know." Jade stepped out of her room, clothed in a loose jacket with the sleeves rolled up to her elbows, a white tank top, and shorts. Chloe was clipped to her belt loop at her hip. Jade closed the door behind her, forcing Thaddeous back a few steps.

"I don't...I don't really wear anything else," Thaddeous murmured, wringing his hands. Jade turned and grabbed them.

"For Vix's sake, Thaddeous. You've got to stop. We're going to figure this out." She looked at him, and there was a pink hue to his cheeks. Jade let go of his hands and moved towards the elevator. "You're going to lose wearing a tuxedo like that, Thaddeous," she shouted back at him. "Now, where are we going to train?"

He led her to a grassy park, their walk filled with Thaddeous' nervous tension and Jade's determined silence. The park took up a few blocks of what appeared to be the mid-city. In the distance, a playset with swings and slides was set up for children. Thaddeous and Jade stood together beneath a series of planted trees. Jade set Chloe down by the trunk.

"Mistress, will you be all right?"

"Record when we start, Chloe." Jade replied, glancing at the helmet. "We need to get him into fighting shape as soon as possible."

"Of course, mistress."

Jade returned to Thaddeous, who stood, fidgeting again. She rubbed her eyes, exasperated already.

"If we're doing this, you have to stop with that hand nonsense. You're making *me* nervous."

"Right." He stuck his hands at his sides. "Okay, how do we do this?"

"First, let's work on your stance." She bent her knees slightly and moved to the balls of her feet. Her left foot moved forward and her shoulders rolled up beside her cheeks. She placed her left fist in front of her while her right knuckles brushed her right cheekbone. She demonstrated how springy he should be by bobbing a little on her feet and shuffling around him, her feet never crossing. She lowered her guard and gestured at him.

"Now you try."

ϕϕϕ

Progress was slow. Thaddeous, despite the muscle he had built up from exercising, was not mentally built to be a fighter. As they trained, Jade found herself watching Thaddeous' eyes often, looking for indication that they might be a different color. But nothing showed. They were green. And nothing about them ever changed.

Around two hours later they took a break and sat down against a tree, sweat beading their brows.

"Well, teach?" he muttered, pulling off his jacket and setting it on the ground. His white undershirt was damp with sweat. "How'd I do?"

Jade spat out a laugh. "Well," she started, "I can't say you're any faster than my last student."

"You've taught someone else to fight before?"

She nodded. "My friend, Aris. She was dreadful at it, but she got better as the war went on." She smiled. "Every now and then she asks me to remind her of certain aspects of fighting."

Thaddeous chuckled. "You must really miss her."

Jade looked up at the tree canopy. "Thanks for reminding me." She rolled her shoulders back. "Thaddeous?"

"Yes?"

"What was that all about last night?" She looked at him. "About your eyes?"

Thaddeous stiffened. "Jade, I—"

"And please don't lie to me." Jade's gaze hardened. "If you want me to trust you, you've got to be honest with me."

"That goes both ways, Jade."

Jade frowned. "What does that mean?"

Thaddeous met her gaze. "I'll tell you what my sister was getting at if you tell me one thing in return."

"You first."

Thaddeous exhaled and looked at his hands. "In some ways, I've been telling you the truth this whole time. I'm not a true Green. I'm not a Green at all."

"How?"

"Jade—"

"How are you not a Green?"

Thaddeous swallowed hard. "Do you remember those droplets I mentioned before? That can change someone's eye color? There's a pill form you can take. It lasts longer but suppresses my Helix. I'm able to appear as someone I'm not." Jade nodded. He watched her. "You don't seem as surprised as I thought you'd be."

"Don't get me wrong, I'm upset you've been lying to me this whole time." She shrugged. "But I don't think I really have time to be angry with you, especially when you've proven over time that you're—" She hesitated. He arched a brow. "Well, you're not half bad."

Thaddeous peered at her, a hint of a curious smile on his lips. "About your—"

"I'm going to need you to request to spar your father in the belly of Voshell's ship, where that weapon is," Jade interrupted, not wanting to tread down an uncertain path.

"I—well, it's a public event," Thaddeous said, frowning at her. "I'm not sure if that's a very public place."

"I think it can be. Make the ring small. I don't know if you noticed, but I've been teaching you defensive techniques more than offensive. Keep you alive while I destroy the weapon."

He blinked. "That's a good idea."

"Thanks."

"It was my idea, mistress."

"I thought of it all myself." She shot a smug look at Chloe. Chloe made a sound like a sigh.

"I don't know when Voshell is going to use the weapon."

"I'll need at least all day today and tomorrow to get you into shape. If you can keep her from using that weapon, then we'll be okay."

Thaddeous nodded, thinking on this. His face grew hard. "I'll request to duel my father in three days' time in the bowels of my sister's ship. He will not allow Voshell to do anything until the outcome is decided." He looked at her. "Do you really think I'll be ready by then?"

"I hope so."

He fell silent, his expression grave. "Oh."

φφφ

The two fetched lunch from a nearby street vendor and downed a few bottles of water before making their way back to the training grounds. There, Jade did her best to teach Thaddeous what she knew while ensuring she didn't agitated her side wound too much. But he just wasn't getting it.

Exasperated, she grabbed two sturdy sticks and tossed one to him.

"All right, maybe you're not getting it without any actual weapons involved." She fell into her stance. He pulled off his shirt and threw it behind him. Black hair laced his tanned chest.

"Stripping again?" Jade's voice lacked humor.

Thaddeous smiled coyly. "Is that too distracting, teach?"

Jade fixed him with an agitated glare. *We're only trying to keep my entire race of people from dying, but yes, let's make jokes.*

"Focus, prince," she said. He laughed. "All right, your key here is to block my attacks as best you can, all right? And don't get off balanced, otherwise I'll push you over."

"Got it."

She pressed forward, swatting at his stick, which he almost dropped after the first few blows. He staggered away and she ducked under his weapon and swept her ankle against his. He pitched backwards, falling onto the grass, blinking. She offered her hand to him. He chuckled.

"You're not nearly as distracted as I hoped you'd be."

ϕϕϕ

They returned to the grassy field throughout the day, pausing now and then to find water or food. When they broke for the evening, Thaddeous squeezed Jade's hand.

"I'm going to go talk to my father now." His voice shook. Jade pulled her hand from his and patted him on the shoulder.

"I'm going to make sure you survive this, Thaddeous. All right?"

He hesitantly smiled. "Right. Maybe after the weapon is destroyed, we can see what else you crazy Greens can do?"

The idea of being a test subject didn't appeal to her all that much, but Thaddeous was sweating profusely. His nervousness radiated off him like a sickness she might catch. She gave him a small nod.

"Sure."

With his forced smile still in place, he stiffly turned and walked away.

ϕϕϕ

Early the next morning he arrived at her flat.

"He accepted. I have until tomorrow afternoon to face him."

They arrived at the park shortly after, and the moment they did, Thaddeous pulled his shirt off. Jade blinked. He flashed her a grin. Wasn't he solemn a moment ago? Wasn't he worried he was going to die tomorrow?

"It's too hot otherwise," he said. Maybe it was because he was about to face his father in a life or death match that he was so chipper. It was his last full day without that sort of weight on his shoulders. She figured she'd humor him as much as she could, as long as it didn't interfere with their training.

Jade rolled her eyes.

They sparred back and forth, most of the time with Thaddeous ending up in the dirt after a handful of minutes. After a few hours of this, Thaddeous launched his stick at the ground and paced away, curses escaping his lips. Jade tossed her own stick to the grass and walked after him.

"C'mon, you're getting it. It's not easy, but you're getting it. It just takes time."

"How much time do we have?" Thaddeous snapped back, stopping by a set of trees. "Voshell could be looking to fire that weapon as soon as I lose! And I'm not able to even make a dent in this training! I've not managed to last longer than a few seconds with you, and my father is strong, Jade! I'll get myself killed, and then what good will I be? I couldn't fight to protect my brothers, and I can't fight now."

"Thaddeous, you can't give up. You have to keep working at this, otherwise you really *will* die tomorrow." She paused. Maybe not the best way to motivate someone. She cleared her throat. "I just need you to last long enough for me to destroy the weapon. A few minutes. And we can get you to be that good if you just keep working with me."

Thaddeous leaned against the trunk of a tree and ran a hand over her face. Tears welled in the corners of his eyes. "I'm just going to die."

"Stop it. You're not going to die. You're going to buy me time, I'm going to destroy that weapon, and we'll have saved the day. All right? Focus on all those innocent people you're going to save by staying alive as long as you can. Okay?" Jade was never good at comforting people, but she did what Aris had always done for her, and set her hand on Thaddeous' arm. "We'll be okay. And after you survive your father and we save the day, we can figure out what Greens can do. Maybe that Black Lightning can be used in other ways, I don't know."

Thaddeous looked at her hand, then at her. "Jade…" He murmured. He reached up and touched her face. "You're so strong."

Alarms rang in the back of her head. He looked at her like A'doxia did. He hungered. He leaned closer. Jade pulled her hand from his shoulder and opened her mouth to tell him to stop.

He pressed his lips against hers.

His mouth was wet and forceful. Vomit swelled into Jade's throat. For a second, he wasn't Thaddeous. He was *her.*

Without missing a beat, Jade slammed her fist into the side of his skull and pulled away. She spat on the ground, her heart in her ears, her body buzzing with violation. She wiped her mouth on her sleeve and swallowed the contents of her stomach a second time. *Why'd he do that? Why'd he have to do that?*

"You…" He started, brows furrowed in confusion. "You like me." He reached up and touched his temple. "I thought…"

"You're my *friend,*" Jade said. "We're *friends.* We're…" She shook her head and let out a bitter laugh. "I can't…I can't give you that. I can't…" She looked at him. His eyes were full of pain. "I need to take five."

Jade collected Chloe and returned to her room. She spent her time in silence, lying on the couch and staring out the window. Chloe asked what happened a few times, but once she realized Jade wasn't ready to talk about it, she let the corporal be. Jade closed her eyes, choking back unwanted tears.

It was too much. All of it was too much.

Chapter 41

The knock at the door indicated it was time to train again. She couldn't mope forever. She had things to do. Jade stood, rolling her shoulders back. She rubbed her eyes. She was going to need to set up boundaries. She was going to need to tell him that she's not here for that, and never was. She took a breath. *It's not going to be awkward. It's not. Just go over there, and answer the door. You have bigger problems to deal with than this.*

She picked up Chloe and tucked the helmet under her arm. She walked to the door and pulled it open.

"Listen, I really like you, but I don't—"

"Mistress! Real!"

Jade's eyes widened and her body froze. A'doxia stood on the other side of the door, a smile on her blood-red lips. She wore exactly what she was in the day they first met: long skirt, a strapless bra-like cloth over her chest, black gloves pulled around her hands.

"I'm loving the red eyes," she said.

"You can't—you don't know where I live," Jade stammered, backpedaling farther into the house. A'doxia strode inside, closing and locking the door behind her. She looked around, her smile never leaving.

"Nice place, love." Her eyes flickered to Jade's horror-stricken face. "Where's the bed?"

Jade spun and dashed towards the bathroom, reaching the door before a hand grabbed her wrist and shot it full of electricity. Jade screamed, her sprint frozen as the currents coursed through her. She collapsed to her knees, dropping Chloe, until, at last, A'doxia released her. Jade gasped for breath, pulling her wrist into her. Her left arm was covered with the curling Lichtenberg design, the same pattern A'doxia had traced into Jade's back. If given time, the marks would fade.

A'doxia knelt down beside Jade, smiling. She revealed a knife. Jade grew rigid.

No, not again. Not again. Please, not again.

"Looks like you showered, hm?" A'doxia giggled, the wind chimes sending terror through Jade in waves. "That just leaves two things left on our list."

"Mistress, fight back!" Chloe cried. *"Mistress, this is not Taotar! You can beat her! You're stronger than she is, mistress!"*

"Oh, sweetheart," A'doxia purred. "Is that wretched little helmet filling your head with lies?" She grabbed Jade's wrist and yanked her closer. Jade, thrown off balance, fell into A'doxia's embrace. The Thrax wrapped her arms around the Green, inhaling the smell of Jade's hair. Jade stared at the folds in A'doxia's skirt, fear rising through her spine.

This can't be happening. I fell asleep on the couch. I'm asleep. This can't be happening. She doesn't know where I've been staying. She doesn't know. She can't know.

"You know," A'doxia murmured into the top of Jade's head. "There is the second option for repaying me." Her hands found their way under Jade's shirt. "And you do smell so nice." Her finger brushed one of the many scars that laced Jade's back. Jade's eyes widened. She pushed A'doxia away and scampered to her feet, retreating until her back hit the living room chair. A'doxia laughed, twirling the knife in her hand.

"A fight it is, hm?" She stood, her smile crazed. "But I warn you, the only pleasure in this path is for me." She giggled at Jade's horrified expression as she strode closer. Jade turned and dashed around the furniture, leaping over the couch and into the kitchen. She pulled open a drawer, hoping to find knives. A blade cut into her left arm, tearing at the flesh and splatting blood onto the floor. She cursed and staggered back, pressing her right hand against the wound. A'doxia grinned, standing only a few paces away. She was fast.

"Sorry, sweetie. Did that hurt?" A'doxia jerked forward, slashing with her knife. Jade sidestepped, swinging with her right arm at A'doxia's head. Her knuckles smashed against A'doxia's skull, only for the Thrax woman to swipe blindly with her knife, cutting a jagged line in Jade's right arm. She hissed through her teeth, ducking under A'doxia's slice for her face. She retreated out of the kitchen, fleeing to the largest amount of space available in the flat: between the living room and the bedroom. Blood drooled down her arms. Her side screamed.

"Use me, Mistress! Use me as a shield!"

"No, Chloe," Jade growled. "She'll fill you with lightning."

"I'll be fine! Please! Let me help you!"

A'doxia sprinted after her and stabbed towards Jade's gut. Jade dodged and grabbed the hand that held the knife. She slammed A'doxia's wrist against her knee, and the knife fell to the ground. But the woman didn't care. Her other hand clutched Jade's neck, and lightning coursed through her throat. Jade gasped. The burning sensation cut off her breathing. Her legs crumpled beneath her. *No. No, Vix, no.*

A'doxia laughed. "What's wrong, sweetheart?" she purred. Jade grabbed at A'doxia's hand, her vision darkening at the edges. She tried for breath. It felt as if layers of skin were being peeled from her body, one at a time. "You asked me to come. Weren't you ready?" She kneeled in front of the corporal, who was struggling to stay conscious with electricity stabbing into her lungs. "Or did you really think you could take me as you are now?" She released Jade. Jade doubled over, coughing out her insides, her ears ringing, her throat aflame, and her stitches tugging at her flesh with each movement. A'doxia brought her hand to Jade's cheek.

"Are you done, love? Have you had enough of me?"

Jade pushed A'doxia's hand away, glaring at her from underneath a tangle of knotted red hair. A'doxia arched a brow, a smile on her lips.

"Oh? You want more, love? My, you are a glutton for punishment." She moved closer, her face within inches of Jade's. "Mmm, but that's what I love about you."

The corporal yanked her head back and smashed her forehead into A'doxia's. The Thrax recoiled, her hands moving to her reddening flesh as a grimace stole the smile from her face. Jade swung her elbow, cracking it against A'doxia's ear, throwing the woman on her side. Jade scrambled for the knife, grabbed it, and got to her feet. She took a few steps back as she looked down at the woman of her nightmares. A'doxia watched her from the floor, her eyes half-open and a playful smile on her lips. Blood splattered on the floor from Jade's wounds. They were deep. She could feel her heartbeat in them.

"Get out," Jade hissed, her voice hoarse. It nearly brought tears to her eyes just to try to speak.

A'doxia arched a brow, propping herself up on her elbows. "Now, why would I do that just when things are getting good?"

"Get out, A'doxia," Jade growled. Each word burned. "I have the knife."

"You think that cute little thing will keep me from you?" She pushed herself to her feet. Jade backed up a few more steps, falling into her fighting stance. A'doxia dusted herself off. Her eyes flickered to her right.

"I see we've found the bedroom." Her eyes returned to Jade. "Oh, love, if you wanted option two, you should have just said so." She looked Jade over and chewed her lower lip. "Unless this is just a warm up."

"Shut up!" Jade screamed, gritting her teeth. "Get out of my room!"

"You can't back out now, sweetie. You asked me to come here, and I expect to be satisfied before I leave."

"I didn't call you here."

"Oh, but you did." A'doxia reached into her shirt and pulled out a handwritten note. "You left it on my doorstep. 'Come to my apartment, block 423, room 560.'" She turned it around and tapped the signature where Jade's name had been written. "Right there, you see?" She smiled and folded the note before putting it in her shirt again. "I came all this way to see you."

Jade shook her head, brows knitted together. "No. No, I didn't call you here. I never would've called you here."

A'doxia chuckled. "Excuses won't help you now, Private. And frankly, they're not all that arousing."

"Stop it! Shut up!" Jade pointed the knife at her. "Get out of my room!"

A'doxia's smile fell and her face darkened. "This is growing tedious, love."

Jade flinched from the new inflection in A'doxia's voice. She glanced over the woman's shoulder. She had to get out. The door was locked, so she would need a moment to unlock it. And the elevator would take Vix-knows how long to close its doors. She'd need a solid five minutes to escape. Could she do that? Could she stun A'doxia long enough?

A'doxia sighed, a hum playing on her lips as both Red and Blue lightning danced on her gloved hands. Jade's face grew white.

Beautiful art….

"Shut up!" Jade screamed, voice desperate. "Shut up, stop singing!"

"You don't look as cute when you're hysterical, sweetie." A'doxia smiled at her. "But I *know* you look good on the floor."

A'doxia lunged, and Jade bent her body out of A'doxia's swipe for her stomach, electricity buzzing from the Thrax's fingers. She brought the blade down on A'doxia's face, digging a harsh line across the woman's cheek and upper lip as A'doxia used her other hand to grab hold of Jade's arm, wrapping her lightning-covered fingers around Jade's flesh. Jade gritted her teeth. This was going to hurt.

Blue Lightning consumed Jade's arm, burning designs into her skin. Jade stepped closer and A'doxia's face flashed with surprise. The Green grabbed A'doxia and pulled her over just enough so Jade could bring her knee into A'doxia's sternum. A sickening crack filled the room.

A'doxia gasped, releasing Jade. All Jade's nerves tingled from the Thrax's touch, and Jade's hand threatened to let go of the blade, but she swung it still. She lacerated the exposed flesh on the Red's chest and blood gushed from the wound, spilling onto the floor. A'doxia pressed her hands to it, hissing a curse from her lips. Jade dashed past her, turned towards the door, and reached for the locked latch.

A hand wrapped around her hair and pulled her to the floor. Her spine smashed against the ground, the impact forcing the blade from her hands. Spots dotted Jade's vision and her head spun. A'doxia swung her leg over Jade and sat on Jade's stomach, both hands pressed against Jade's wrists. Jade blinked furiously, clearing her vision just in time for her heart to clog her throat. A'doxia's weight atop her caused her side injury to buzz with agitation. A'doxia smiled, the cut in her chest dripping crimson on Jade's white shirt. The wound on her face bled down A'doxia's lips and she licked it away, a shiver visibly running down her body.

"You surprised me, love," she purred. "I didn't expect you to be able to fight back so well when I filled you up." Lightning buzzed at her fingers. Jade squirmed, trying to kick A'doxia off, trying to free at least one hand. A'doxia chuckled.

She leaned close to Jade, her breath against Jade's face. Jade turned her head away, desperately trying to free her hand. Just one. She just needed one. *Please, just give me one. Just one. Please!*

"But sadly, I've been fighting much longer than you have," A'doxia continued. "And you simply do not have the experience needed to resist me."

Jade looked at the Thrax, shaking her head. "Don't—"

Lightning coursed through Jade's arms, through her chest, into her skull. A'doxia's twisted grin grew as Jade fought the pain for a moment, biting down on her lip hard enough to draw blood. She closed her eyes. Tears streamed down the sides of her face, and she thrashed beneath A'doxia, using every ounce of her strength not to give the sick woman what she wanted. Not to scream. Not to cry out. Not to—

And like that, Jade's resolve crumbled. She arched her neck back and screamed, yanking fruitlessly at her arms.

"Mmm," A'doxia moaned, closing her eyes as she listened to Jade struggle. "How I've missed this!" Her grip on Jade's wrists tightened as she leaned closer, kissing Jade's neck. Her heat warmed the side of Jade's face. Jade snarled, forcing one eye open. A'doxia's lips pressed against her flesh, again and again. The Red's hair fell around her face, obscuring most of what Jade could see. But she could see one thing, even as she fought and screamed. She could see A'doxia's ear. Jade turned and bit it, blood squirting into her mouth. She tugged it back, hoping to pull A'doxia's lips away.

"Oh Vix," A'doxia breathed, seemingly unperturbed. Her body pressed against Jade's, her hot breath growing quick. She moaned. Jade grimaced. Not what she wanted.

The electricity, however, fizzled out for a moment. A'doxia's back arched and her fingers uncurled from Jade's wrists. Jade jerked her head to the side, tearing a chunk of flesh from A'doxia's ear before flipping the woman onto her back. Jade sat atop her, free from the pain of electricity—though it still buzzed within her nerves—and pressed her hands to A'doxia's throat. A'doxia, in turn, grabbed Jade's arms, her Helix returning to Jade's body.

Jade grimaced, pressing her entire weight onto A'doxia's neck, cutting off the woman's breathing. A'doxia's eyes fluttered and her lips curled in a smile. The pain consuming Jade was growing ever more intense. She couldn't feel anything else. She couldn't hear her own thoughts. Every nerve was simultaneously committing suicide by stabbing themselves with dull knives over and over again. If she could just get A'doxia to pass out. If she could just get her to stop. If she could just—

Jade yanked her hands to her head, grabbing at her face and screaming. She closed her eyes against it. It wouldn't stop. Was there ever a time she was not in so much pain? Her mind buzzed but could not remember. She was always here. Always.

Nothing had changed. After all these years, she was going to lose. She was going to be beaten. It was Taotar all over again. Outrage built up in the back of her mind, growing just as quickly as the pain in her body.

No. I can't fail. I've changed. I'm stronger now.

And then the pain died.

The electricity seemed to subside into a low buzz. A distant reminder of the agony that was, but far enough away to be manageable. She opened her eyes and looked down at her hands. Black Lightning danced over her fingers. A'doxia's fist smashed into Jade's nose and she fell backwards, off the woman.

A'doxia yelped. Jade grabbed her bleeding nose and pushed herself up to her knees. A'doxia swatted at black tendrils of electricity dancing over her fist and making their way up her arm. Jade took her chance. She scrambled to her feet just as A'doxia shoved herself to hers, and Jade dashed forward, driving her leg into A'doxia's torso. A'doxia gasped, the electricity jumping from Jade to the Thrax. She staggered into the wall and the lightning sent her shaking to the floor.

"Sorry," Jade hissed. "Did that sting a little?" She kicked A'doxia's ribs, forcing the woman onto her side. Black Lightning spiraled around her body and she spasmed and screamed.

Hurts, doesn't it? How's it feel when you're the victim? How's it feel when you're the helpless one?

A'doxia shuddered, calming as the lightning dissipated. Her eyes moved to the door. Jade rammed her foot into A'doxia's gut. Spit flew from her mouth and her face contorted into a pain-filled grimace. Jade knelt over her and shoved the woman onto her back. She cracked her knuckles against A'doxia's face.

"This is for Taotar!" Jade screamed, striking the woman again. Electricity caused the Thrax to shake uncontrollably. "This is for everything you did to me!" Jade punched her again. "This is for making every touch *your* touch!" Again. "This is for destroying my dreams!" Again. "This is for—!" Jade stopped mid-swing. Her face went slack for a moment, then twisted with hatred. Tears burned at the corners of her eyes.

Through the blood that covered her face, A'doxia was smiling.

The lightning fled from A'doxia, remaining only on parts of Jade's body where the two women weren't touching. A'doxia readjusted herself underneath Jade, a distinct blush on her cheeks. She chewed her lip as she ran her hands over Jade's legs.

"Why are you doing this?" Jade hissed. A'doxia watched her but didn't respond. Jade dug her nails into her own palms as she clenched her fist tighter. "I can't even hurt you without you *enjoying it?*" She was certain she was going to shatter her own jaw from how tight she clenched it. "You won't even let me have that? You won't let me hurt you without twisting it into pleasure?" She yanked her arm back threateningly, but tears spilled down her cheeks.

"You sick fuck," Jade said. Her shoulders slumped and her arm fell to her side. The Black Lightning fizzled and vanished. Jade looked away. "I hate you."

The door splintered behind them, throwing shards of metal through the air. Thaddeous stood on the other side, his eyes wild. The moment he entered, Jade moved off of A'doxia.

"Sorry, prince," A'doxia said from the floor, looking over at Jade, "but you're interrupting."

"I told you to stay away from her!" Thaddeous growled, grabbing A'doxia's arm and yanking her onto her feet. He pushed her towards the door. She giggled, allowing herself to be moved. Back on her feet, she patted Thaddeous' shoulder.

"Thanks for inviting me, prince."

Jade's ears were ringing, but she heard that. Her green eyes filled with fury.

"*What?*" she hissed.

"It's not what it sounds like," Thaddeous started.

A'doxia laughed. "Oh, tell the poor dear the truth, will you?"

"Get out of here, A'doxia," Thaddeous snapped. "You've done enough."

"Don't act high-and-mighty, prince. You left that letter at my door, didn't you?"

"I don't know what you're talking about," Thaddeous growled. "Now leave!"

"I think you do." A'doxia smiled at him, then turned her eyes to the violated expression Jade wore. "Oh, don't be so upset, cutie. It was obvious, wasn't it? You'd never ask me here, especially being so unprepared. It only made sense the prince would want me to come. Surely you figured that much out on your own?"

"Get *out!*" Thaddeous spun on her, pointing to the decimated door. A'doxia smirked.

"I'll see you later, sweetie." A'doxia blew a kiss at Jade before striding out of the room. Jade's eyes moved to Thaddeous.

"You…*asked* her here?"

"Jade, please try to understand," Thaddeous said, eyes filled with hurt and concern. "I didn't want…I didn't want this. I just…if we could get you using your Black Lightning on camera—"

"There are *cameras* here!?" Jade looked around, eyes wild. "You put cameras in my room? Who else was *watching?*"

"My sister and father, but Jade—"

Jade scowled, tears welling up in the corners of her eyes. "You *watched* that? And you did *nothing?*"

"I had to, Jade. I had to. If I could show them how powerful you were, how you could beat one of the strongest generals we have, if I could show them my theory of how your power works, then my father would not allow my sister to use the weapon, even if I lost to him. Both our people would be safe!"

"Well, congratulations," Jade hissed, spreading out her arms, scabs beginning to form on the wounds. "You must have got what you wanted, huh? Vix, I've been so stupid. Trusting you? Trusting the enemy?"

"You mean…you mean it worked?" Thaddeous asked, his face filling with joy. "I was right? I was right!" He spat out a victorious, one-note laugh. Jade's face twisted into growing hatred. "Now we know how your power works, Jade! Don't you see? I was right! This is wonderful, you can stop the war! You'll have to travel with A'doxia, but that's a small sacrifice to make for the greater good, right?" He moved towards her. "Don't you see? I was right!"

Jade's brows pressed together as she spat out a bitter laugh. "Yeah. And I was right about you."

Thaddeous' face fell. "Jade—"

Jade got to her feet, her whole body shaking. Her throat still burned. "I trusted you. I told you what she did to me, and you still brought her here." Her dark eyes met his. "You brought her here to do exactly what she did to me on Taotar. You brought her here so I could relive that day! I told you what she did and this is how you repay me? Vix, I was even going to pretend the kiss didn't fucking happen! I was going to help you!" She laughed. "By the way, king," she shouted to the room. "Your son is planning on killing you! Not that you have much to worry about, he is a coward and a pathetic piece of shit!" Her eyes narrowed on Thaddeous' face. "I should've killed you."

"Jade, I didn't want to make you relive that day, I just—"

"Shut up!" Jade snapped. "You don't get to speak!" She turned and picked Chloe up from her place on the ground and clasped the helmet to her belt loops. Thaddeous followed and touched her shoulder. She grabbed his hand, holding him in place, and smashed an elbow into his nose. And she demolished it, shattering it into pieces as he fell to his knees, grasping his face. A scream of pain escaped him. Jade turned and spat on his head, her own nose still bleeding.

"I trusted you, Thaddeous. I believed in you. I ate it all up, didn't I?" she scoffed. "Just for you to perform your own little experiment on me. Did you even do it for anything other than to satisfy your own curiosity? You didn't, did you? It was just that. You just wanted to see what happened." She spat out a laugh.

"No," Thaddeous wheezed. "No, Jade. Please. Understand." He looked up at her, blood gushing from his face. Jade didn't hide the disgust that washed over her.

"You let her in here, you let her…you let her touch me *again*. Fuck you, Thaddeous." She turned and strode to the elevator. She heard him calling her name, but didn't stop. When the doors opened again, she sprinted from the building and kept going until her legs burned.

She found herself a bar and drank until she couldn't even remember her own name.

Chapter 42

A'doxia stepped out of an alley, licking her gloved fingers free of blood before striding down the dark street. A hum touched her lips and an orgasmic chill washed through her body. He was the one who said he liked it rough. Considering how sore she was growing from her fight with Jade—with aching ribs, a cut lip, and a bitten ear—she hadn't even gotten *really* into it.

Not my fault if he can't handle me when I'm playing nice.

The man had spilled everything he had heard as a butler during the royal dinner. A super weapon, Jade's panic, Thaddeous' outburst, Voshell losing an eye. She mulled all of it around in her head, considering every angle. Obviously Jade would be searching for a way to find Malkov, and if she played her cards right, A'doxia would be Jade's only hope.

Oh Vix, how absolutely delicious.

Stragglers from the day wandered the streets, gazing at the stars and whispering sweet nothings into each other's ears. A few stared as A'doxia sauntered by, only to be slapped by their partner. A'doxia snickered.

"Fuck off." The words came from down an alley between two business buildings, followed by the crash of glass and a startled shriek. A few moments later a couple rushed past A'doxia, the male hugging the female close, muttering words in hopes of calming her down.

A'doxia arched a brow and looked to her right, heading towards the alley. Shadows stretched long across the space between the buildings, hiding, for a moment, the figure that sat in the dark. But A'doxia would know that voice anywhere. Her heart pumped blood to her ears, her face, and her groin. Jade shifted in the dark, her red hair catching the light. A smile painted itself across A'doxia's lips and she swayed her hips seductively as she strode towards the unaware Green, skirting the condoms and miscellaneous shit that cluttered the ground—including the glass bottle shards that were scattered a few feet away from her. The smell of vomit and alcohol bombarded A'doxia's senses, making her head swim.

Oh, what a perfect place.

Jade sat on the ground with one leg bent and the other stretched out in front of her, her back against the wall. Red strands of hair covered her face, and when she readjusted herself, the blood that was splattered over her white shirt caught A'doxia's eye.

A'doxia knelt down beside Jade, stealth seemingly working in her favor as she wrapped her arms around the unsuspecting soldier. She pressed her face against Jade's hair and, in turn, against Jade's cheek, breathing in the scent of alcohol, sweat, and the sweet smell of her shampoo.

"Hello, Private," A'doxia whispered, her lips pressing against Jade's flesh. She expected Jade to jerk away, to fight back in that way that made A'doxia want her more. To stare at A'doxia with those eyes filled with terror and hatred. *Oh, Vix, please. Please look at me like that.*

"Hey, Dox," Jade grumbled, her words tired and slurred together. A'doxia pulled back, brows furrowed. She brushed Jade's hair away and tucked it behind the woman's ear, revealing not only the black bruise that swelled up around her right eye and the dried blood from their fight earlier, but the bloodshot gaze with undried tears glistening beneath.

A'doxia's smile faltered.

"I thought I could get us some food money," Kathla muttered. Her lower lip was split open, her eye swollen shut, her arms bruised. "But they fought back."

"What happened, love?" A'doxia growled out, her sweet tone tainted with aggression. Jade glanced at her out of the corner of her eye.

"Threw a bottle at a couple." She shrugged and gestured lazily to the shattered glass. "They were kissing. It was gross."

A'doxia arched a brow. "Did they hit you?"

"Them?" Jade spat out a laugh. "They wish." She rubbed her temples. "They didn't realize I was here, I guess."

A'doxia sighed and took Jade's head in her hands. She moved Jade's face so those green eyes were on her red pair, and scrutinized Jade's gaze.

"How drunk are you, love?"

Jade made a face as she mentally tallied. "Um. I had a beer. Then like, thirteen shots? Or was it fifteen…then I had another…beer? Or maybe it was a cocktail." She snapped her fingers, "Cocktail! Definitely a cocktail. I think." She looked at A'doxia. "Please don't tell Aris."

A'doxia released her and chuckled. "I won't, doll. Our little secret."

Jade stiffened at the sound of A'doxia's laugh. A'doxia couldn't help but relish in the sight. She chewed her lip. Jade eyed her.

"Are you going to make this weird? I don't really want it to be weird. I mean, I can't really walk right now. So I can't do much to stop you. But I'd appreciate it not being weird."

"You can't walk?" A'doxia murmured, finding a place next to Jade to sit. Her arm brushed Jade's. Pleasant shivers ran through her nerves. "How did you get here?"

Jade made a face. "I don't really remember." She reached up and rubbed her eyes, the large, scabbed gashes in her arm that A'doxia had given her earlier gleaming with blood. They must have recently been reopened. "Maybe I crawled." She glanced at A'doxia, as if looking for approval. A'doxia arched a brow, a soft smile spreading across her face.

"Sis, look!" Kathla stood in the lopsided doorway, holding up a rat. "I caught us dinner!"

"Very funny," A'doxia purred. Jade grinned.

"I have my moments." She closed her eyes, an exhale escaping her lips.

A'doxia swallowed. She wanted her fingers to be tangled in Jade's hair, her lips pressed against Jade's, their bodies entwined together. She was sure she could have that now. Jade was too drunk to realize what was happening. And

A'doxia's body hungered for it, forced premature adrenaline into her veins.

A'doxia looked to the sky, where the stars could be glimpsed between the tall buildings.

"Stars are pretty cool, aren't they?" Jade murmured. A'doxia nodded.

"Yeah, I suppose they are."

"I wonder who lives there, you know? Maybe there's someone just like me out there."

"No one could replace you, love." A'doxia wove her fingers between Jade's. Jade laughed.

"I wasn't suggesting that. I'm just saying, you know? Just talking nonsense."

A'doxia looked at her, Jade's green eyes glistening as she stared at the sky above. Tears found their way down her cheeks. A'doxia's heart constricted in on itself.

"I don't get it, sis." Kathla sat in what once was a living room, arched under the sunken roof. "Why won't anyone even look at us? They act like we don't even exist." A'doxia put her hand on Kathla's shoulder. "They just want us to die, don't they?" Kathla pressed, looking up at A'doxia. "Die silently,

where they can't see us. Don't they? What are we supposed to do? No one even cares!"

"Jade?" A'doxia murmured, the word on her lips taboo, foreign. She wasn't even sure if she'd spoken it before. Jade sucked in a lungful of air, and forced a smile onto her lips.

"It's just so stupid. I trusted him. And I shouldn't have. At least I know what you want. I didn't know what he wanted until the last minute." She looked at A'doxia, pain written clearly across her face. "I thought he and I…I thought we were kindred spirits, or some mumbo-jumbo shit. I don't know. I guess I just…" She trailed off, her eyes lowering. "I just…"

A'doxia touched Jade's cheek with her free hand. "Shh, it's okay, love. I know he hurt you. But fuck him, right?" A'doxia's voice was in a soft whisper. Jade spat out a bitter laugh.

"Yeah. Fuck him."

A'doxia patted Jade's cheek. "That's my girl. Do you have somewhere to stay?"

"He'll be at my apartment." Jade pulled her hand from A'doxia's and ran her fingers over the faded designs burned into her flesh from their fight earlier that day. A'doxia missed the warmth of Jade's hand the moment it was gone. "I don't want to talk to him."

"I know, sweetheart. How about you stay with me? He won't look for you there."

"Is that safe?" Jade looked at A'doxia, her drunken gaze concerned. A'doxia had to force a smile onto her face. *Is that safe?* The words rang in her ears and stabbed needles into her heart. "I mean…" Jade murmured. "It's not a mystery what option two was."

"Never, love." A'doxia's brows pulled upwards. "I would never force myself like that on you."

"You didn't have a problem doing it earlier."

"That's different." Jade didn't look convinced. A'doxia moved to sit in front of Jade and put her hands on Jade's knees. "Jade Cavvar," she started firmly, "you will be safe in my house. I won't so much as touch you unless you allow me to."

Jade stared at her for a few seconds. She tilted her head, rubbed her shoulder, and frowned. Her face was painted with discomfort.

"You're weird when you're serious. I don't know how to handle it," she said.

A'doxia blinked, then a grin split her face and she laughed. How delightfully unexpected—the woman that feared her was more concerned about her change in attitude than staying the night at her house. Jade watched her, brows furrowed, confused. But apparently she found A'doxia's laugh contagious, despite the stiffness that spread through her body. She laughed, too, and it was the first time A'doxia had ever heard it. It was beautiful. Strong, loud, honest. Jade's eyes almost shut completely, as if the pure joy of the act was too much for her.

"Kathla? Kathla, look at me." A'doxia knelt in front of her sister and grabbed both her hands. She stared into those frightened brown eyes. "I'm going to protect us, okay? They won't find us. We'll move in the morning. Shh, don't cry. We're going to be okay. I won't let them hurt you."

"Come on, you drunken fool," A'doxia murmured, standing and offering her hand to Jade. "Let's get you home."

Jade took her hand and pulled herself up, staggered, and leaned against the wall for support. A'doxia wrapped her arm around Jade's middle and tugged her away from the wall. The Green flinched and, remembering Jade's stitches, A'doxia adjusted her hold on her.

"I won't let you fall," she whispered, looking up at the taller woman. Kathla would've been this tall. Jade leaned against A'doxia, her weight making A'doxia hot. Jade's unsteady steps made going slow, but eventually they made it out of the alley.

"Who hit you?" A'doxia asked. Jade squinted at the horizon, considering this.

"I'm not sure which one landed the punch anymore."

"There was more than one?"

"It may surprise you, but I'm actually really good at fighting." Jade flashed a large smile. "Just not against you."

A'doxia chuckled. "I would think so, since you've survived the war up to this point."

Jade nodded with a sigh, then grimaced. "How far away is your house?"

"A little bit of a distance, sweetheart." A'doxia glanced up at her. "Are you going to make it?"

"Was asking to make sure you'll make it," Jade grumbled. "I know you're probably exhausted from…I don't know…whatever you do at night."

A'doxia giggled, and hints of a smile tugged at the edge of Jade's lips. Why couldn't it always be like this? The two of them, stumbling home, exchanging banter? Jade's fear turned her on, but perhaps they could have something more than just that sort of relationship. Perhaps they could have…depth.

"He kissed me, you know," Jade admitted abruptly, destroying A'doxia's thoughts. She fixed her gaze on the street they were walking down, the emptiness of the path, the dim lights offering some protection from the darkness.

"Oh?" She forced the words from her mouth. She didn't want to know. She didn't care to know. If Jade and Thaddeous were together—no, how could they be? After what happened? There was simply no way. Jade would never forgive him. Right? She swallowed hard. She didn't know. She didn't exactly know Jade.

"It was terrible," Jade said. Relief washed over A'doxia. *Terrible? I bet he did a shitty job. I could…I could show you something better.* She glanced up at Jade. Jade stumbled, tripping over her own feet, and A'doxia pulled her closer, holding her steady. Jade flashed a thankful smile. A'doxia swallowed again.

"I don't know why he did it," Jade continued. "Even if I liked him like that, how stupid can he be? We're on different sides of the war. And he doesn't even see me as a person. Just someone to experiment on."

I'd change sides for you.

"Though, if Aris ever found out I had my first kiss, she's flip a lid," Jade said.

A flash of jealous anger ran through A'doxia—*he took her first kiss? Something she'll remember forever?*—before Jade's laugh bubbled up from her throat. A'doxia couldn't help but smile at the sound, the tension and anger leaving her body.

"Aris is your friend?" A'doxia asked.

"Yeah, she's my bestie. She's really cool."

"I'd love to meet her someday."

"I don't think that's a good idea." Jade rubbed her eyes, a yawn escaping her lips. "She doesn't know about you."

A'doxia's brows furrowed. "What?"

"I never told anyone about what you did," Jade elaborated. "I didn't want her to worry."

"That doesn't sound like a very good friendship practice to me."

"I didn't want her to worry," Jade repeated, her tone sour. "You wouldn't understand."

"Sis! Wow, where'd you get all that money? We can get some serious food with this! Did you steal it, or something?"

The image of the man suffocating on his own blood stained her mind more than her hands. A'doxia smiled.

"Yep! Picked the pocket of some old fool. Wasn't watching where he was going."

"You'd be surprised," A'doxia muttered. Jade shrugged.

"I don't know you at all, so I'm sure I would be."

The silence lingered. A'doxia caught Jade staring at the stars again.

"Do you miss home, love?"

"Not really." Jade looked at her. "Just Aris, if I'm being honest."

Don't be jealous.

"Not your family?" A'doxia asked.

"Nah." Jade smiled. "Mom's a bit of a hard-ass. She's cool, but sort of a dick. Dad's nice, but we don't talk much anymore."

"How come?"

"No reason. Just don't." Jade watched the stars again. "Do you want to travel, Dox?"

A'doxia smiled at the name. "Not really. There's a lot I still have to do here."

"Like what?"

"Well," A'doxia began, before pausing to consider this. She frowned. What *was* left for her here? Besides a title, a home? She had no child, no sister, no parents. Why was she still here?

"I don't...I don't know," A'doxia admitted at last. Jade's eyes moved back to hers. A'doxia flushed with embarrassment. "I don't. I just...I just stayed. For no reason."

Jade chuckled. "That's a shitty reason."

"Well, it's a shitty reason for you to stop talking to your dad."

"Fair." Jade grinned. "You're pretty funny."

A'doxia blinked, staring at her, unable to say anything. Was this what Jade was really like? Jade snickered at her expression.

"You know, you and me should have a drink sometime." Jade swayed. It was only a few more blocks now. "I bet you'd be cool with a few drinks in you."

"I don't really drink much," A'doxia said.

"That's weird. And lame," Jade grunted, her face twisted with disappointment. "You should take it up. Makes you feel fuckin' great."

"You feel great right now?" A'doxia arched a brow at her.

Jade pursed her lips. "Okay, you're not playing fair."

A'doxia laughed, and Jade flashed a grin. *If only I was as drunk as you. Maybe I wouldn't care. Maybe I'd break my promise. Maybe you'd like it.* She pushed the thoughts away. No. She wouldn't pass those memories onto Jade.

A'doxia's two story house was small and humble, with four steps leading up to the front door. Jade had particular trouble walking up them, but with A'doxia's aid, the drunken fool made it up.

"Your house is cute." Jade looked up at the curved roofline that formed a point in the middle, the red accents and black wood used to frame it out. A'doxia beamed.

"I'm glad you like it."

"Do you like it?"

A'doxia hesitated while reaching for the door handle. *Did* she like it? Did she like the emptiness, the idea of owning her first home without Kathla by her side? Did she like the warmth of a bed after watching her baby freeze to death in a cold alley? Did she like the silence of her own mind?

"No." She pushed the door open. "Not really."

Her house opened up into a hallway, the door in front of her leading to her bedroom. To her right was the path to the living room and kitchen, and to her left was a set of stairs that lead to the mostly unused second bedroom. Jade stepped inside with A'doxia's help and looked down at her feet.

"Carpet?" She flopped down to the floor, startling A'doxia into reaching to catch her, only to realize it was a purposeful fall. A'doxia closed the door and she peered at Jade quizzically. Jade pulled off her shoes, smiled broadly, and looked up at A'doxia.

"Feels nice."

A'doxia crossed her arms and smiled, watching the redhead run her toes and fingers over the floor. Jade laid back and yawned, stretching out across the ground. A'doxia blinked.

"Wait, Jade, you can't fall asleep here."

Jade groaned and rolled onto her side. "It's so nice though." She looked up at A'doxia and reached out one hand. "C'mere."

A'doxia glanced to the side and nervously itched the side of her scalp. "What?"

With a sigh, Jade pushed herself into a sitting position and grabbed A'doxia's hand. "Come here, you creep. It's really comfy. I'll show you." She tugged on the Red's hand, looking at her with a half-conscious gaze. Jade wouldn't remember any of this, A'doxia suddenly realized. She was too far gone. She wouldn't remember. A'doxia wasn't sure if that made her happy or sad.

Relenting, she let Jade pull her to the floor and lay down next to her. She was right. The carpet was pretty nice to lie on.

Jade smiled, looking victorious. "See?" She curled up onto her side, facing A'doxia. There was barely a foot between them. "Comfy." She yawned and her eyes fluttered close.

A'doxia watched her. Would this be a domestic life? A life like this, with times like these? A'doxia turned onto her side, facing Jade. She could do this every night. She could lie on the carpet with her drunken girlfriend and watch her fall asleep. A'doxia reached out and touched Jade's arm. She gently ran her thumb across the woman's flesh. Jade's eyes opened a sliver. She looked down at A'doxia's gloved hand. She touched it gently with her fingers.

"Why do you wear gloves?" Jade murmured, her tired eyes peering at A'doxia.

"Take a look."

Jade stared at A'doxia for a few seconds as she processed what was said, then took A'doxia's hand and gingerly pulled the black glove off. Beneath, electrical burns marred the skin, twisting and spiraling down to her wrist. Jade's brows furrowed as she held A'doxia's hand as carefully as she could.

"What are these?" she muttered.

"They're scars, love."

"Why?" Jade brushed the back of A'doxia's hand with two fingers. Shivers ran through her and she had to suppress her desires before she could respond.

"I don't have immunity to my Helix."

"Thad said that." Jade wrapped her arms around A'doxia's and closed her eyes. A'doxia was, once again, surprised by the act. "I could…I could make…" She trailed off.

It didn't take long for her to start snoring. A'doxia smiled. She scooted closer and rested her forehead against Jade's. After a few minutes, she closed her eyes.

Chapter 43

Morning came in the form of harsh knocks at a nearby door. Jade grimaced, a headache forming in the front of her skull. She reached up and touched her head, groaning loudly. She rolled onto her back and—wait, was she on the floor? She opened her eyes and ran one hand over the ground. Carpet. When had she recently been to a carpeted home? The apartment Thad gave her was all hardwood.

She looked around, ignoring the pain and sickness in her gut. There was a door to her right, a few feet away, where the sound had come from. To her left was another door, which was open. A bedroom with the blinds drawn shut. She squinted and shoved herself onto her elbows. Her stomach lurched, and she badly wanted to gag, but she'd have to throw up all over herself another time. Firstly, she needed to figure out where on Nevar her drunken ass had ended up last night. Another series of knocks brought more needles of pain to her cranium and she scowled, moving to stand to her feet.

"Of all the times," someone hissed as they strode around the corner in front of Jade. Jade froze. A'doxia stopped mid-step. They stared at each other. Jade looked at the bedroom, at A'doxia—who wore only her underwear, bra, and gloves—then quickly scampered back, her stomach flipping.

"I didn't—" A'doxia started, reaching for Jade. Jade shoved herself back further before forcing herself to her feet. She held her hand out.

"Don't come any closer," Jade warned. Her other hand moved to her mouth. "What did you do to me?" She wanted to vomit. She wanted to throw her entire stomach onto the floor at the mere thought of why she was lying on the floor in A'doxia's house.

A'doxia's face twisted from concern to annoyance. She put a hand on her hip. She stared at Jade for a few beats before turning and swinging open the door, blocking Jade's view of her.

"Thaddeous." She heard A'doxia say. Jade stiffened.

"I've been searching for Jade all night." He sounded exhausted. Jade gritted her teeth. "I need her."

"Why are you bothering me then?"

"Don't give me that," Thaddeous hissed. "We have cameras all over the city. I know you brought her here. If you did anything—"

"Don't point your finger at me, prince." A'doxia's voice dipped from uninterested to threatening. "She told me she doesn't want to speak to you."

I did? Jade frowned. *What exactly happened last night?*

"She was clearly intoxicated, A'doxia. Whatever she said and did—"

"I'm getting bored, Thaddeous."

There was a moment of tense silence.

"Where is she, A'doxia?" A'doxia didn't respond. The tension grew thicker. "A'doxia, this is *important.*"

"Then why don't you tell me and I'll judge if it's worth talking to her about? If you're here to grovel, then go somewhere else."

"I'm not—what I did was—I did it for her!" Thaddeous shouted. "Now get out of my way! Jade! Jade, where are you? Jade—*hurk!*"

The sound of someone falling on their ass echoed into the house.

"Don't try to force your way into my home, Thaddeous. Remember who you're dealing with. Goodbye." A'doxia closed the door. She crossed her arms and peered at it for a moment before her crimson gaze shifted to Jade. Jade's brows furrowed.

"What…happened last night?"

A'doxia's face held no answers as she stared at Jade without a distinct expression. She reached up and rubbed her eyes, a sigh escaping her lips.

"I'm giving him five minutes before he decides to break this door down." She leaned against the wall. Jade glanced at the door. "Do you want me to let him talk to you?" Jade, even more confused, looked back at A'doxia. Thaddeous started knocking on the door again, demanding to be let in.

"What?" she sputtered. "Why are you—" Her face twisted with revulsion. "What did we *do*—?"

"We slept on the floor." A'doxia answered before Jade was done being horrified. "You wouldn't move and I can't carry you, so you stayed there all night. I was going to make breakfast until our friend here interrupted."

"He's not my friend."

A'doxia's lips twitched upwards. "I know, love."

"Jade!" Thaddeous called from the other side of the door. "Please, let's just talk!"

A'doxia nodded at the door. "So what should we do about him?"

"Why do you even care?" Jade pressed. A'doxia's smile fell and her face took on a disinterested look once again. The knocking became more violent.

"You're so curious, love. I brought you somewhere safe to sleep and somehow I'm on trial."

"You call sleeping near you *safe?*"

A'doxia chuckled. She touched the cut in her face. "I don't consider either of us exactly *safe*, sweetheart. But we made it through the night, didn't we?" Her smile grew coy as she regarded Jade with a familiar, lustful expression. "And what a night it was."

"Stop it," Jade snarled.

"What's wrong? You don't like me when I'm not interested, and you don't like me when I am." A'doxia tapped her lips with her fingertips. "Are you playing hard to get? Because, truly, as alluring as it was before, your flip-flopping is getting a little confusing."

"A'doxia, open this door or I'll break it down!"

"Oh, and there it is," A'doxia chimed, snapping her fingers. "What's your decision, sweetie? Should I help you eject him onto the street, or would you two like some alone time together? We didn't use the bed last night, so it's nice and clean for you. I promise I won't watch." She winked at Jade. Bile rose up in Jade's throat. She clamped her hand over her mouth and turned away, dumping her stomach onto the floor.

"I'm coming in—" Thaddeous shouted, only to be cut off by sirens. A hand pulled Jade's hair out of the way as she vomited. A'doxia stood beside her and rubbed Jade's back, the fabric of her shirt catching against the scars there. Jade hated the feeling, but she was too preoccupied to shove A'doxia away.

"Shh, let it all out," A'doxia murmured. After a few moments, Jade straightened and wiped her mouth against her sleeve. She almost always got rid of hangovers after she threw up, and her headache was all but gone. She glanced at A'doxia, who smirked back. Jade opened her mouth to say something, when she heard a loud voice over the sound of sirens.

"I repeat, this is an emergency broadcast to all citizens. King Daxgor has been bested in combat by his daughter, Voshell. His funeral will be held in a week's time. Voshell Malkov is now the new ruler of Soldar and the Thrax. A message from our new queen."

The speakers crackled and Voshell's voice rang through. "It has been many generations since a new rule has been decided like this, and for that I apologize. I should've done this sooner. My father was weak, and he was going to put his trust in one meaningless person instead of a weapon that could bring the Exuro to their knees. You heard that right—I have a way to end the war today. And that's what I plan on doing. Today, the Thrax will finally be free to settle on a planet.

"There are going to be some among you that will fight this, specifically my brother, Thaddeous, and his toy, the Green. I need them detained until I return. If you see them, please, stop them from destroying our only chance at freedom."

With another bout of static, the original voice resumed. "I repeat, this is an emergency broadcast…"

Jade's eyes widened. "No," she whispered. "Oh Vix, no." She shoved past A'doxia and threw open the front door, where Thaddeous was standing. He looked at her. His eyes were no longer green. They were blood-red.

"She did it," he muttered. "She killed him before we could."

"The weapon," Jade said.

"I know." He glanced over his shoulder. People on the street murmured and shot them both some glances. A hand slipped into Jade's and she was yanked back inside the house.

Thaddeous swiftly followed and closed the door behind them. Jade tore her hand from A'doxia's and scowled. A'doxia chuckled and leaned against the wall.

"You're welcome, cutie," she said.

"What are we going to do?" Thaddeous asked, looking at Jade. Jade arched a brow and rubbed her aching head. "I was going to fight him *today!*" Thaddeous continued, "I was going to—and you were going to—"

"Shut up!" Jade snapped, forcing Thaddeous to stop his hysterics and look at her with surprise. "Shut the fuck up." She took a breath and rested a hand on Chloe, who was still on her hip. They'd talk later about what exactly happened last night. "We're going to get down to Voshell's ship, and we're going to destroy that weapon and anyone who gets in our way. And you're going to shut down that jamming signal so I can warn Aris about this."

"N-no, if I do that, they might be able to trace the signal back here—"

Jade grabbed him by the front of his shirt and glared. His broken nose was black and blue. "You're going to do it because you fucked me over yesterday and you fucking owe me."

A'doxia giggled.

Thaddeous frowned. "If they track it here, everyone I know will be killed and all of this will have been for nothing."

"Who says that weapon won't be turned on those who oppose Voshell's new rule?" Jade said. "Who says the killing will stop here?"

Thaddeous pushed away, his eyes dark with thought.

"Fine," he said after a moment of pause. "I'll do it. And I'll meet you in the docks. Wait for me."

"I will, you're the only one who might talk sense into her."

With a nod, Thaddeous slipped out of the house. Jade turned to A'doxia—she didn't like it, but the woman was all she had right now. The Red seemed to know this, for a smug expression sat upon her face.

"I need a weapon."

A'doxia shoved away from the wall and slipped into the nearby room. She returned fully-clothed and holding two H-blades. She handed one to Jade.

"You're not really going to wait for him, are you?"

Jade donned Chloe and took a steadying breath. She looked at the sheathed weapon in her hand.

"No. Let's go."

φφφ

Charging headlong into a rioting city without any armor was never on Jade's to-do list, yet she found herself sprinting down side-alleys, following A'doxia's silent movements. Protestors to the new queen shouted in busy streets, and those loyal to Voshell smashed beer bottles over dissenters' heads. Screaming filled the air and the smell of vomit and blood coated Jade's nostrils. Chloe did her best to filter it out, but the city stunk of violence.

"We can't murder an entire race of people!" cried some.

"What of the Green? She can still save us all!" cried others.

"This weapon will save us all!"

"This city is going to explode, mistress," muttered Chloe. Jade took a steadying breath. It sure looked like it.

A'doxia came to a stop at the edge of an alley, on the fringes of the city square. Where there were once stalls and vendors, shouting men and women stood. A few of them held pots and pans, gripping them with whitening knuckles. Several kodarians used their size to loom over halos.

"Mistress, there!" Chloe projected a red arrow in Jade's visor which appeared over a woman on the opposite side of the crowd. She was surrounded by four others and clad in a sea-blue suit. The female glanced to the roaring mass to her left, and Jade could see the jagged scar that crossed from the point of her jaw to her nose. A metallic eye was nestled where her right one should have been.

A swell of pride filled Jade's chest and a corrosive smile spread across her lips. *I hope you like it, you crazy bitch.*

"There," Jade said, pointing to Voshell for A'doxia to see.

"She's headed for the elevator." The Red tightened her grip on her weapon, glancing over at Jade. "Her ship is likely waiting at the harbor."

"Right." Jade rolled her shoulders back, pushing the tension out of them. "You ready to fuck up some folks?"

A'doxia giggled. "That's my favorite thing to do, love."

Together, they burst out of the alleyway.

From all the commotion, Voshell didn't notice them at first. Jade managed to get nearly halfway to the rectangular box that sat on the far end of the square, skirting around the throng of arguing forms. An indicator sat over Voshell's head, at first at a calm zero, then leaping to an exclamation mark.

"Mistress, she's reaching for a gun."

"Fuck," Jade hissed. "Keep watch, Chloe."

"In three, two, o—" Chloe stopped short and Jade dropped into a quick roll, her shoulder hitting the ground and throwing her back to her feet without missing a beat.

The crowd panicked from the sound of gunfire and spiraled into violence. Blood splattered across the ground as civilians attacked each other, yelling, crying, smashing their neighbors' heads into the pavement. As the rioters surged forward, Jade ducked between them, avoiding the violence the best she could. A leather-skinned kodarian with tusks that curled outwards swung a pot at her head. Before she could react, A'doxia was at her side, her blade slicing through the meat in the woman's wrist. Crimson drenched Jade's right arm and showered onto Chloe. It painted A'doxia's face with glee. The kodarian screamed and staggered back, grabbing her stump as tears filled her eyes. Her crimson irises moved to Jade's helmet, and her jaw went slack.

"The Green," she muttered. Then, louder: "The Green!"

Several people turned, looking at the helmeted Jade. Murmurs took the place of fighting.

"How do we know that's really her?"

"I saw her yesterday with cuts like those on her arms."

"She's wanted."

"She's better off dead."

"Take off her helmet!"

"Kill her!"

Civilians rushed her. Jade flinched, grappling with the idea of fighting unarmed civilians. She sidestepped someone's wild swing and dodged a broken bottled thrown her direction. She couldn't kill them. She couldn't—she couldn't steal more lives than she already had, and yet, when she glanced in the direction of the elevator, the doors were closed and Voshell was nowhere to be found. She couldn't stay here. She couldn't do nothing. She had to fight. But knocking them all unconscious would take too long.

A hand in hers. The startling touch of electricity swam into her nerves. She spun towards her assailant to see A'doxia's blood-soaked face grinning at her.

"We can't waste time here. You've got regicide to commit."

Lighting burst from A'doxia, covering her gloves and consuming Jade without hesitation. Chloe's screen filled with static before shutting down completely. Darkness filled Jade's vision as cheers began to crowd her skull. Distant shouts of protest were consumed by elation as she tried to yank her hand free. A'doxia held tight, her fingers interlaced with Jade's.

"Get back!" The words died in Jade's throat, choked by pain and molded into an agonized scream. The blood within her veins turned into needles and her mind grew dark. Her knees smashed into the ground as she tried to wave the civilians away. She couldn't do this. She couldn't kill them. She couldn't let herself kill them. Her fingers curled against the hard ground. A bottle broke against her back. She bit her lip and the taste of iron washed over her mouth.

"Dox," she gasped. "You can't. You can't."

A'doxia's grip grew tighter. Jade's teeth tore through her lip as she curled into herself. The cheering. The noise. The pain. She was home. She was on Nevar. Nothing had ever really changed. All of them, they were all just people.

Numbness washed over her, signaling the beginning of Black Lightning. She could distantly feel it on her fingers and heard it buzzing around her just before the screaming began. The pressure of A'doxia's hand vanished and Jade pushed herself to her feet, her body tingling. She pulled Chloe from her head and looked over to A'doxia, who stood untouched by the black tendrils of electricity. Jade tossed the helmet to her. Her eyes moved over the bodies. Everyone within thirty feet of her lay still on the ground. Burst eyeballs oozed liquid into the city square. Those still living sprinted away, screaming profanities laced with terror. Jade closed her eyes.

Am I any better than the Mad Queen?

Chapter 44

Jade picked her way over the bodies as swiftly as she could, and pressed her hands to the elevator doors, allowing her Helix to consume the controls. She didn't think about the dead. She wouldn't think about them. She needed to save Aris.

"That's not going to—" A'doxia started, staying a good distance away. The elevator doors slid open and revealed a dark shaft, the small lights blown out by Jade's lightning.

"—work," A'doxia finished, her word a mutter. "Well, fuck me, I guess."

"What floor is she going to?" Jade swung herself over the edge and onto a slim ladder. She kept her eyes on A'doxia as the woman approached the ledge. Jade ignored the carnage in the square, and stuck her sheathed H-blade into the waistline of her pants.

It wasn't my fault.

"The fourth floor. I'll follow behind you, so long as your lightning doesn't try to lick me." A'doxia smirked. Jade frowned, placed her hands on the sides of the ladder, and began to slide down. She gritted her teeth against the searing heat that coated her fingers, her momentum turning the metal almost unbearably hot. As her flesh grew raw, she looked over her shoulder and noticed a distant elevator box. It was stopped about forty feet below.

Jade's skin peeled off, and blood smeared across the iron ladder. A yelp rang out from above, where A'doxia was slowly sliding down with Chloe precariously balanced under one arm.

"Are you bleeding, love?"

It became difficult holding onto the ladder as more of Jade's nerves were exposed. She chewed her still-bleeding lip and sucked in an unsteady breath. This was probably a terrible idea, but she was going to go for it.

"I'm jumping!"

"You're *what!?*"

Before A'doxia could protest further, Jade shoved herself away from the wall and turned herself around. The roof of the box approached quickly, and she fell into a roll the moment her feet hit the ground. Her recent injuries ached and her mind buzzed with a distant hangover-induced headache. As she rolled onto her knees, she pressed her bloody handprint against the roof and exhaled, the black tendrils of electricity rushing to consume its new target. It spilled over the metal and a few satisfactory screams and yelps in agony put some of

Jade's worries at ease. She pushed herself to her feet and shoved stray hairs from her face, smearing red over her freckled cheeks. A thump behind her signified A'doxia had jumped as well. Jade turned to look and A'doxia slapped her.

"That was dangerous!" Her words were laced with concern.

Jade blinked, her face tingling.

"What?"

"What if you hadn't landed properly? You could've broken your leg!"

Jade furrowed her brows, confusion rooting her for a moment before she recovered.

"Fighting a war is dangerous," she replied. She spun towards the hatch and grabbed the handle, swinging it open. She took hold of her weapon, the wounds in her hand sending several needles into her palm. She did her best to ignore it and focused on the elevator below her.

She could see two bodies from where she stood: a kodarian with large tusks up to her popped eyes, and a snipper with one arm missing. Neither of them moved. She took a steadying breath, praying to Vix that she would find Voshell dead. She curled her left hand into a fist, Black Lightning still dancing over her skin. It was fading, however, its light dimming and its tendrils less pronounced. She likely wouldn't have it for much longer. She jumped into the box.

Before Jade's feet hit the ground, a blade cut through her face, tearing from her jawline to the bridge of her nose. She threw herself back and lifted her weapon to defend herself, unsheathing it as she moved. Iron filled her mouth from the wound, and the wet, crimson substance drooled over her lips. She narrowed her eyes on her opponent, who stood beside two other unmoving bodies. Voshell's single human eye gleamed from above her scar. She grinned.

"Now I just need to take your eye and we could be twins."

"Why aren't you dead like the others?" Jade hissed, trying to find a place to stand.

"Me?" Voshell snickered. "You think a little lightning could kill me? Honestly, were you really the one my brother thought could save this wretched galaxy?"

Jade frowned. "Your brother isn't here to keep you alive, Voshell." She pointed her blade at her opponent. "I can't let you use that weapon."

"But that's the beauty of it, isn't it?" Voshell lowered her blade and placed her free hand on her hip. "You see, it's been sending a distress signal ever since I picked it up. Until just now."

"What?"

Voshell pulled out a flat, circular device from her breast pocket. Its silver design was marked with blue stripes. They glowed.

"It fell silent the moment your lightning came in here. So I think I have you to thank for activating it."

"You're lying."

Voshell pocketed the device again. "If you want to risk that, then go ahead and let me go. See what happens."

Jade spat blood onto the ground. "You'll never get the chance to use it."

"We'll see."

Jade slashed horizontally, only for Voshell to parry and step forward, stabbing for Jade's chest. The corporal instinctively stepped back before her foot hit the body of the snipper and tripped her. Her shoulders hit the wall, and she narrowly shifted her weight to avoid Voshell's blade as it stabbed through metal like it was nothing more than water. Jade got back to her feet and ducked forward, jabbing at Voshell's center while also slamming her left hand onto the ground. What was left of her Helix fled her and clamored towards Voshell as the woman pushed Jade's weapon off target. Electricity clawed its way up the Plural's legs and over her body and—

Nothing. Nothing was happening. Black tendrils spun around Voshell's body and she wore a maddening grin.

"I'm immune."

Metal bent as the elevator doors were smashed inwards by what looked like a fist. A pair of hands slid into the opening and shoved the doors apart as much as they would go. Thaddeous stood on the other side, his right hand a mess of bruising and clearly broken bones, and his eyes alight with worry. Voshell rushed forward, shouldering Thaddeous out of the way and sprinting down the hall.

"Fuck!" Jade dashed after her, but Thaddeous grabbed her wrist with his good hand, halting her in her tracks.

"Jade, don't kill her."

"Are you fucking *kidding me?* She has the weapon!" Jade jerked her hand back, but he did not let go.

"Please, she's my only family left! She's all I have!"

Jade didn't hesitate. She shifted her blade and sliced off his left hand. Then she turned and kept moving. The sound of his hand hitting the ground echoed behind her. His scream, filled with agony, rage, and betrayal followed shortly after.

It's just a small sacrifice for the greater good, right, Thaddeous?

The hallway spread into a large space with a high ceiling and numerous docks for ships to rest. A crowd mulled in a corner but spooked at the sight of Jade chasing Voshell. They fled to their ships or through doors Jade could not see.

Jade was gaining. And before the two of them got halfway to the ship Voshell was dashing towards, Jade swung her blade and tore a line through the back of Voshell's shirt. Voshell spun around with her weapon brandished and squared off against the Green. Her chest heaved and sweat dotted her brow.

"I'm going to end the war, Jade," she growled. "Why won't you just let me save my people?"

"You're fucking mine over to do so," Jade spat back, her breath labored. Her body felt ragged, and she could sense her stance weakening already. She wasn't doing well. Recent events had taken more of a toll than she realized. Her body still hummed with A'doxia's recent electrical violation.

"If it'll end the war, isn't that a sacrifice we should be able to make? I'll destroy the Exuro's fighting force and then we can negotiate a peace!"

"You think people will bow down to you that easily? After you slaughter their friends and family?" Jade slowly started to move to the side. Voshell mimicked her, and the two began a slow, uneasy dance.

"What choice do we have?" Voshell said. "My people are *dying*—"

"This isn't the right way and you know that!" The moment Jade's back was to Voshell's ship, she lunged, swiping her blade diagonally through the air. Voshell scowled and blocked the attack, stepping back to buffer the blow.

"What choice do I have?" Voshell shouted. She shoved Jade off and slashed at her stomach. Jade sidestepped. "I don't want to see these innocent people die because of their eye color! I don't want to see us become slaves to a bunch of blue-eyed freaks!" The edge of Voshell's blade cut into Jade's right shoulder, leaving a large crimson line. Breath escaped through Jade's clenched teeth.

A'doxia appeared at the end of the hallway in the distance, holding Chloe in her hands. Thaddeous staggered into the expansive space a moment later, his shirt tied around his stump and a tourniquet knotted further up. Jade focused on Voshell.

"You think massacring thousands will somehow make things better? You think it'll fix all your problems?" Jade said.

The two exchanged blows, Jade's weapon finding purchase across Voshell's chest. The smell of burning fabric filled the room, and small beads of blood bubbled up beneath the blue uniform she wore. Voshell spat curses.

"It'll eliminate the biggest threat to my people! It won't be easy recovering afterwards and forming relations, but at least we won't be dead!"

Jade ducked under a wild swing for her neck. She smashed her shoulder into Voshell's stomach and sent the woman to the ground, then quickly pressed her knee to the queen's wrist, keeping her from swinging her weapon. Jade held her blade to Voshell's throat, her teeth clenched.

"I can't let you use that weapon, Voshell. We'll find another way without you."

"Jade, don't!" A heavy force smashed into Jade's side, and she went skidding across the ground beneath Thaddeous' larger form. The wound on her face caught against the floor and tore further open. A burning sensation made her eyes water. Jade cursed.

Thaddeous sat atop her, pressing his handless arm against her neck. "You can't kill her! She's the only family I have left!"

"Thaddeous, you fucking idiot! She's going to murder *my* family!"

Thaddeous' eyes filled with tears. "I can talk to her. I can sort something out. I can fix this!"

"Get off me! She's going to get away!"

Thaddeous looked over his shoulder. Voshell moved to her feet as A'doxia dashed towards Jade. Thaddeous put more pressure on Jade's neck, causing her to cough. Sandpaper filled her lungs and she winced against the agony of breathing.

A'doxia kept forward, her face twisting with hatred.

"Get off of her!" A'doxia cried.

"Stay away or I'll kill her!" Thaddeous growled.

More pressure. Jade closed her eyes and moved to swing her blade when Thaddeous' broken hand pressed against her wrist.

"I mean it, A'doxia!" he cried. Tears burned Jade's vision. She couldn't even swallow.

Fuck, I don't have time for this.

Jade jerked her knee upward, smashing it into Thaddeous' groin before using his pain to sweep his legs off to one side. With her lower half free, she kneed him in the ribs hard enough to feel something give. He coughed, his hold on her weakening. She slipped from his grasp and got to her feet, clearing her lungs of sand. Chloe was sitting a few paces away and A'doxia was now engaged with Voshell, buying Jade time. Jade's eyes wandered to Thaddeous before she stepped around him, picked up Chloe, and donned her helmet. The pressure burned at the cut across her face, but she ignored the constant buzz of torment.

"Are you ready to end this, mistress?" Chloe's voice was intermingled with garbled static.

"I couldn't be more ready."

A'doxia held her own against Voshell, but it was clear the Red's mind was distracted. She narrowly dodged a few blows before she spotted Jade back on her feet. She smiled and focused her attention on her opponent, locking blades with her as Jade snuck forward behind Voshell's back.

"I'm your queen, A'doxia!" Voshell shouted. "You are loyal to *me!*"

A'doxia giggled. "I'm loyal to me, love. You were just a passing fling."

Voshell cursed, her muscles rippling as she pressed against A'doxia's blade. "You would kill me? After what we had?"

"Ooh," A'doxia purred, "did you think we had something, sweetie?"

Jade gripped her weapon with both hands, daggers digging into her nerves. Voshell stepped forward, and A'doxia lost a few inches.

"The Green would see us all *killed*," Voshell said.

"Yes, but she'll be a gorgeous, bloody mess before then."

"You sick fu—"

Jade stabbed at the Plural's back. The tip of her heated blade dug into Voshell's shirt before a heavy shove sent Jade flying to the right. Startled, she managed to keep her feet under her for a period of time, until she tripped and rolled on the ground. She cursed, her ribs aching.

"Jade!" A'doxia screamed. Voshell jerked forward as Jade got back to her feet. A'doxia threw herself to the side, dropping her weapon in the process as Voshell's blade swung heavily downwards in the space she had just been. In a swift skittering of feet, A'doxia dashed to Jade's side, her right hand bleeding. She was missing the tips of her three middle fingers. Jade grimaced, placing a tentative hand on her ribs as she wheezed, breathing difficult. Thaddeous stood at Voshell's back, several paces away.

"I won't let you kill her," he said. "She's my only family, Jade."

"Are you all right, love?" A'doxia whispered.

"Mistress, with Thaddeous here, we cannot deal with Voshell."

"I know," Jade muttered.

"Unless you can distract him, you must—"

"I can't kill him, Chloe." Jade gritted her teeth. A'doxia touched her arm.

"Love?"

"I'm fine, A'doxia." Jade touched the cut on her shoulder. "I don't want to do this. I *can't* do this, Chloe."

"You saved my life," Voshell said. The Plural turned to Thaddeous. Her brother nodded, holding his stump close to his chest.

"Of course, sister," Thaddeous said.

"I can't begin to wonder why," Voshell replied. Her expression was empty.

"What?" A look of confusion and pain washed over Thaddeous' face. "You're my family—I can't lose you, too."

Voshell smiled. "You killed mom and our brothers. Suddenly *now* you care?"

Thaddeous stepped back. "What?"

"You didn't do a single thing when we were all there, being massacred by that victer. You hid under your bed and cried. Even when I begged you to run for help, you sat there staring at me, doing *nothing*."

"That—you weren't there," Thaddeous stammered. "You made the whole thing up. You make things up. You weren't there!"

"How do you think I got this scar, Thaddeous? You think I slipped and fell down some Vix-damned stairs?" She grabbed his shirt, scowling. "You're the one who makes things up, Thaddeous. You made up everything about the Green. You made up this idea of peace. You made up an entire relationship with her."

"I—I didn't—you went to a ward!" Thaddeous spat.

Voshell laughed. "Do you think you'll ever realize just how toxic you are?"

Thaddeous' brows pulled upwards. "Please, sister, just listen to me. We can't do this. We can't keep killing each other. We have to—"

Voshell flicked her blade. Thaddeous' head rolled off his shoulders and onto the floor. Vomit filled Jade's mouth.

"Shut up," Voshell whispered.

Chapter 45

Jade couldn't make a sound as she watched Thaddeous' head fall heavily to the ground. Blood spewed from his severed veins. Gore showered Voshell. The prince's body crumpled and collapsed onto the ground.

Jade's ears rang and the world around her tilted, morphed, and was covered in a slight film of red. She swallowed the contents of her stomach down again and stepped away.

Does nothing humor you? Thaddeous' voice was a whisper in Jade's mind. Her rage boiled into a single, sour note. Her breath quickened. She moved one foot towards the Plural, then another, and another. She dashed towards the murderer, brought her H-blade high above her head, and screamed.

Their blades met in a swift exchange of parries and jabs. Jade swept her foot across the ground and moved A'doxia's fallen blade in front of her, ducked beneath Voshell's swing, and picked it up with her aching left hand. Voshell frowned and stepped back, and the two of them smeared Thaddeous' blood across the floor with their shoes. The handle of A'doxia's weapon was covered in it.

You're not a demon. Thaddeous smiled at Jade.

Jade's right blade smashed against Voshell's and as she went to slice down the Plural's middle, Voshell moved to the side and let Jade's blade tear through her right arm. Jade's eyes widened. She met resistance as her weapon cut through bone before reaching the other side. The limb fell to the ground, twitching, staining the floor and the entirety of Voshell's right side in blood. Jade pitched forward, off balanced. Her eyes met Voshell's. They were filled with determined malice. Jade paled.

"Mistress, move!"

Voshell cracked her knee against Jade's sore ribs. All the air in her lungs escaped and Voshell quickly swept Jade's feet out from under her. Jade fell hard onto her back, her weapons falling from her grasp, her head ringing, Thaddeous' broken body to her left. Voshell kicked Jade's side, sending more wheezing breath from her as she struggled to get back to her feet. Her fingers grasped at the wet ground, dragging herself away. Shards of glass cluttered her airways. Each inhale was agony. Thaddeous' blood soaked through her clothes as Voshell pressed her heel to Jade's sternum.

You're just a human being with the potential to change things. He believed in her.

"Mistress, breathe! You can grab Voshell's leg and throw her off of you!"

Voshell lifted her weapon, the tip pointed towards Jade's neck. Her shoulder gushed down on Jade's fallen form, drowning her in red. Jade grabbed at Voshell's leg.

"Mistress, you cannot just lie here! You have to move! You have to move!"

I'm just going to die. His words rang in her ears. Tears spilled from her eyes, drowning her vision.

"Jade, please!"

The blade jerked down.

A'doxia's fist smashed into the side of Voshell's skull and knocked her off, sending her staggering to the side to regain her balance. A'doxia stood protectively over Jade, her chest heaving. Jade grimaced, trying to stand as her lungs fought to collapse. Breathing hurt. Thinking hurt. Everything hurt.

Footsteps rang in her head and A'doxia knelt down beside her, helping her up with soothing words. An engine roared to life. Jade's head snapped towards its source, and Voshell stood on the deck of a ship, staring at the wounded Green. The ship sailed out of port. Jade forced herself to stand

and sprinted after it, her feet unsteady, her body unable to take a deep breath.

"No," she said, the word weak and hoarse. "Vix, please, no. Chloe. Chloe can you—?"

"There is no signal to track, mistress."

More tears fell. "No. Vix, no!" She wobbled on her feet. "Aris. Chloe, where is Aris? Send her a message, ask her where she is." She spun towards A'doxia, who stood, watching with concern. "A ship. We need a ship."

With a slow nod, A'doxia grabbed Jade's hand and led her down the dock. They found a small privateer and A'doxia murdered the captain. The crew fled as she threw the man's body overboard. Jade grabbed her ribs and attempted not to think about it. She leaned against the main mast and tried not to think of anything. Not of Thaddeous. Not of the weapon.

"Where to, love?" A'doxia's voice was a soft whisper.

"Get us out of here. Fly towards Exuro space. I'll let you know."

ϕϕϕ

Jade received a response from Aris a few moments after they left the harbor, before they even entered a Stream. It was typed, silent, without emotion: *Sobek. Meet at these coordinates.*

Jade couldn't help it—she smiled. She hadn't heard from Aris in so long. Even if she didn't hear Aris' voice, even if it was only a text message, at least it was something. She exhaled, doing her best to collect herself. She'd get Aris out of there, then she'd find Voshell and cut out her heart.

ϕϕϕ

The planet Sobek was painted green and blue, and stood out against the black expanse of space. With A'doxia at the controls, they pulled out of the Stream as they grew nearer. The jerk from the sudden lack of momentum sent them both stumbling forward. It hadn't even taken a full day to get there, which explained why the Thrax were so keen on controlling Sobek. It was closest to their floating home. Voshell's ship was nowhere to be seen in the mass of warring Thrax and Opes fleets fighting for control over Sobek airspace.

Slipping through the battle took swift maneuvering on A'doxia's part, but she somehow seemed rather adept at such things. Jade found a Thrax flag under the deck and flew it, keeping one side from firing upon them. They stuck close to the larger frigates before lowering the flag and replacing it with a white one as they moved closer to Sobek's atmosphere. The split surface of the world gave rise to magnetized floating islands, and water covered everything below, constantly maintained by waterfalls that tumbled over the edges of hovering land. The smell of wet grass crowded Jade's cranium.

"Keep low," Jade said. "The magnetic fields will keep us relatively hidden."

With a nod, A'doxia kept them gently skimming over the ocean's surface. When they reached the island designated by Aris' message, the Red pulled the ship up. Jade climbed over the railing and landed on the soft dirt of the island, wanting nothing more than to lie down in it. She glanced back at A'doxia, who gave a gentle smile.

"I'll be around, sweetheart."

Jade walked away.

Chapter 46

Aris paced behind her troops, watching them spar against each other and practice their aim on small, long-distance targets. Her uniform was strapped to her snugly, military boots pressing against the soft earth and creating indents in the land. The Opes base sat behind her, a small outpost for scouting and tactical missions. Her unit of twenty-seven elite soldiers trained and battered each other for her approval. Her blue eyes regarded them all with little emotion.

A small pebble hit the side of her boot and she turned the direction it came from. There, in the shadows, she caught the glimpse of a crimson skull. She had come.

Aris couldn't believe it.

ΦΦΦ

Jade watched Aris slip away from the other troops and enter the line of trees, stepping through the brush without so much as a sound. As soon as Aris stood beneath the shadowed canopy, Jade pulled Chloe from her head, clipped her to her belt, and wrapped Aris in a tight hug. Tears bit at the corners of Jade's eyes. She hadn't embraced Aris in years. Aris made a surprised sound, her arms stiff by her side.

"I'm so happy you're okay," Jade muttered before pulling away and smiling. Aris blinked at her, her brows furrowing. She reached up and touched Jade's cheek. The cut across the corporal's face had sealed, but it burned at Aris' touch.

Jade didn't move away. She could hardly feel any part of her body, her elation consumed every nerve. She had finally made it. She had finally made it home.

"It's really you," Aris whispered. Jade nodded, reaching up and touching Aris' hand. The back of Jade's throat burned as she kept the tears locked away.

"Yeah," she said. "It's me."

And then Aris stabbed her.

Jade staggered away, blood spilling from the wound in her gut, drenching her hand. Her eyes widened. Aris stood still, face shadowed, the dagger-sized H-blade clutched in her hand. Blood sizzled and filled the air with the smell of burning iron.

"Aris—?" Jade started, gritting her teeth against the pain. Aris looked up, her blue eyes filled with hatred.

"What's the matter, Green," Aris spat, stepping towards her. Jade kept backing up. "Didn't expect your dearest *friend* to hurt you?" A sneer twisted her features.

Jade's shoulder hit a tree trunk and, in the second Jade paused to move around it, Aris lunged. Jade threw herself to the side and Aris' blade burned a line through the bark. She scowled and twisted her face towards Jade again.

"What's going on? Aris, it's me! It's your Jade!"

"Mistress, what's happen to the madame?" Chloe's voice shook. Aris laughed. Her sour notes filled Jade's skull.

"I know who you are, Green. I know *now* at least." She grinned a frustrated, furious grin. "I didn't before! I didn't see it once—not even *once*. And I should've! I fucking should've." She grabbed at her face with her free hand, her blue eyes focused on the ground. "I don't know why I ever trusted you."

Jade stiffened. Her throat closed up before she could speak. She reached out towards Aris. *It's me. It's your Jade.* Aris looked at her and Jade hesitated.

"Can't even say anything?" Aris snapped. "I spent all these years looking up to you, and you can't even say one fucking word to me?" Her hand gripped her hair, tugged at it, then released as she let out a sigh.

"I spent every night awake with you, calming you down. And you did it all on purpose, didn't you? You stripped me of my sleep so when the battle came, you shone the brightest. That's what you did, didn't you? I've got to admit, that's pretty clever. Befriend the only person gullible enough to protect and love a Green. Vix, how did I ever trust you?"

Jade stepped back as if she had been struck. "Aris," she stammered, swallowing hard. The loss of blood was making her head fuzzy. Her feet were unsteady as the ground lapped up every drop that spilled from her. "I would never do that to you. You're my best friend, Aris. You've always been my best friend."

"Is that what you said to Salene before you stole her legs from her?" Aris' eyes narrowed.

Jade blanched. "That—that was an accident. You know that was an accident."

"Just like blowing up the Thrax base with our general inside? The one that questioned your eye color? Was *that* an accident, Jade? Was it an accident when you let Tyrn die? What about when you smashed my head into a rock?" She stepped forward.

The Green backed up, gripping her gut as more of her life squeezed past her fingers. She was going to throw up. She had fought so hard to get here. She had fought so hard to find her home again.

"Aris, please," Jade said through clenched teeth. "Voshell has the weapon and she's going to use it. She's going to wipe out all Blues. I have to get you out of here."

Aris scowled. "That's all you care about, isn't it? You. How *you're* perceived, how others see *you*, how *you'll* go down in the history books!"

Her words grew louder as she spoke, her arms flaring with each angry word, ever stalking towards Jade. Jade continued retreating, back and back, stumbling past trees, through bushes, over roots. Jade couldn't hear the sound of Opes soldiers sparring anymore.

"You never once considered that *I* might want to be in there with you! That I might want to be as good as you, and not just a footnote!" Aris shook her head. "But you wouldn't, would you? You're a Green. You've always been this way. You can't help it, can you? You just want to tear our whole system apart. You want to tear everything we've worked for away!" She pointed her dagger at Jade's chest. "But you know what?" She flashed her teeth. "I *am* going down in the history books. I'm going down as the Blue who stopped the Green. I'm going down as the new general who slayed a timeless demon."

Jade's face fell. "I'm not a de—"

Aris dashed forward, forcing Jade to duck and dodge, her movements slowed from her recent battle and the gut wound that wouldn't stop bleeding. Aris' attacks were filled with hatred and anger, making them wild and hard to avoid. Her blade nicked Jade's shoulder, carving a jagged line through her skin. Aris swung towards Jade's center and Jade sidestepped before pulling her bloodied hand from her gut and grabbing Aris' arm. She yanked the Blue's wrist against her knee, and with a yelp, Aris released her weapon and fled a few steps back. Jade kicked the blade away. She raised her hands, her head swimming. The trees doubled and tripled, dancing around before her. She kept her eyes focused on Aris.

"I'm not a demon, Aris," she breathed. "I'm your friend. I've always been your friend."

Aris pulled a sheathed, full-length H-blade from her belt. The weapon extended, its searing red tip gleaming horribly bright in Jade's unfocused gaze.

"I believed that lie, once," Aris hissed. She held the hilt of her weapon in both hands. "I believed it with every part of my being." She stepped forward. Jade's brows pulled upwards.

"It's true," Jade insisted. Tears welled up in her eyes. "Aris, it's true! Can't you see it's true? Can't you see everything we've done together?"

Aris screamed and dashed towards Jade with weapon in hand. Tears spilled over Jade's cheeks and onto her shirt. She didn't want to retreat any further. She didn't want to move from Aris' path. They were best friends, weren't they? They had saved each other's lives on the battlefield, hadn't they? They had fought together, fought *each other*, had argued and fumed, but ultimately became closer than family. Aris was Jade's reason for living. Aris was Jade's home.

She stared into Aris' eyes, searching for the woman she knew, the woman she loved and who loved her. And Aris wasn't there.

She wasn't there.